ELora Dax

A.M. McCoy

CONTENTS

CHAPTER 1 – ELORA – 7 years ago

"**T**ell me again what she said."

"Dad." I droned on in exasperation and looked over at him.

He watched me out of the corner of his eye with a grin on his face as he drove.

"Once more." he said, "Please."

Hearing such a strong dominant man ask so politely made me soften a bit. It was how he always got to me, and he knew it. He never spoke softly to anyone else in the world but me.

I huffed, blowing my bangs out of my eyes, and recounted what the Chancellor at Calstock Grove Academy said to me this afternoon. "She said, that by looking at my grades and remarks from all of my teachers this year, I was on track to get into my pick of any Ivy League school."

"That's my girl!" My dad said enthusiastically and slapped the steering wheel. I couldn't help the smile that pulled at my lips, even if I was trying to play it cool.

I was a freshman at one of the most prestigious private schools on the West Coast and the Chancellor had pulled me aside today to congratulate me on my hard work the last few years under her guidance.

I looked over at my dad as he kept smiling like I'd just won an Olympic medal and rubbed his jaw. His suit jacket was off, and his shirtsleeves were rolled up, showing the tattoos on his arms that I loved to see, as he relaxed back into the leather seat. His dark hair was cut short to his scalp on the sides, but messy on top from his hands going through it constantly, and his five o'clock shadow was thick, and I knew when he kissed me goodnight tonight, it was going to tickle my face.

It'd been three days since I'd seen him last, and I had missed him.

I hated when he and mom were fighting because she would go on a kick and find a way to keep me from him and force me to stay at her house.

I hated staying at her house. She was mean and always treated me like I had the plague, making me stay in my room while she *entertained* friends. My dad was a workaholic, but I was always welcome at his place so when she didn't let me go, I felt confined and suffocated.

"Can we order pizza tonight?" I asked, hoping my good news would help my cause.

He looked at me out of the corner of his eye and laughed. "I guess we can get pizza."

"Awesome!" I yelled and fist bumped the air.

His laughter echoed, and with a tender touch on my neck, he pulled me against him. The kiss on my hair smelled faintly of his cologne and felt comforting.

I wrapped both arms around his stomach and breathed him in. I loved the scent of his aftershave; I remember laying in his arms late at night when I was really little and letting the spicy scent lull me into sleep. He worked even more now than he did back then, but he juggled his responsibilities better and he was home most nights so I could come over. He was the boss of so many other people, but he always made time for me when I needed him.

"I missed you." He said softly, the mirth leaving his voice as a more serious tone took its place.

"Can I just live with you all the time?" I asked. "I hate staying with her."

He sighed and put his hand back on the steering wheel, letting me sit back up.

"Someday." He said and winked at me.

"That's what you always say." I whined and looked out my window and sulked. The hem of my uniform skirt, stiff and unforgiving, felt like a weight in my hands as I braced myself for his rejection; a silence hung heavy in the air.

"I know baby. But I mean it. Someday, when things slow down a bit, you can come live with me full time."

"Can Ry come over for pizza tonight?" I asked, trying to move the conversation on to happier topics.

"I think he's got plans tonight." Dad said.

"What kind of plans?" I asked, trying to keep my curiosity low in my tone.

"Work."

"What kind of work?"

"Elora." Dad warned and looked at me again.

"What? I didn't know if it was the kind of work he could take care of before or after pizza or if it was the kind of work that was going to leave him covered in someone else's blood and guts and render him unsuitable for the dinner table." I said flippantly.

"Jesus Christ." Dad cursed and muttered under his breath but stayed quiet for a moment.

"So—" I pressed on, "Was it option A or option B?" I asked.

"You're exhausting when you want to be, you know that?" He asked.

"I was shooting more for tenacious, but I guess exhausting is better than some other words I've been called." I quipped.

"Called what by whom exactly?" Dad asked, curiosity piqued as he steered us towards his neighborhood.

Crap.

I shrugged my shoulders and grabbed my backpack off the floor by my feet. "So was that a yes or no to Ryker coming over for pizza?"

"Answer my question." He deadpanned and looked at me as he drove down the street. "Who has called you worse?"

"Just people." I shrugged again.

"What people Elora?"

I raised my shoulders to my ears and widened my eyes in exasperation. "Just people, Dad. They walk on two legs and eat and sleep and do practically nothing else to contribute to society. You know, people."

We came to a red light, and he slammed the brakes, sending me sliding forward in my seat without ever taking his eyes off of me. "Cut the shit and tell me exactly who and what they said. Now."

Gone was the happy, easy going doting daddy I loved so much, and in his place was the terrifying, dominating, alpha crime boss that the world knew Gavin Dax to be.

"Mom's friends." I said quietly. I hated it when he yelled at me, especially when he managed to do it without even raising his voice. "They just say things like how she never even wanted me and the only reason she didn't abort me with a coat hanger was because I'm her paycheck." I replied. Trying to keep a flippant tone to my voice to mask the hurt that stupidly hadn't gone away since the other night.

He turned my head towards him with his finger under my chin, and I looked at him. "They're fucking wrong, you know. I've never wanted anything else in the world more than how much I want you. Every single second of every single day, baby girl. You're the only reason I'm alive; that's how wanted you are." Fire burned behind his eyes as he stared into mine intently. "I've never regretted you for a second."

"Okay." I whispered into the quiet silence of the car.

Dad kept my stare, even after the light turned green and I could see him trying to force me to believe him through pure brain waves alone.

He leaned over again and kissed my forehead. "I mean it Ellie, without you, I don't exist. I love you."

"I love you to daddy." With conviction, I replied. "I don't exist without you, either."

He smiled down at me and then let off the brakes and continued on to our destination. "You'll never have to, because you're stuck with me forever." He slid his phone from his pants pocket and hooked the aux cord into the end and dialed a number.

Through the speaker of the car, I heard the line ring and then the deep baritone voice of my second favorite person in the world answered. "Hey man, I'm almost done here with—"

"Ellie wants you to come have pizza with us tonight." Dad said in place of a greeting, cutting him off from whatever scandalous information he was about to divulge to my ears.

"Hey Ryker." I said, scowling at dad. "Dad means to say, would you like to come eat pizza with us tonight?"

Ryker, my dad's best friend since they were in diapers, laughed into the phone and then softened his gruff voice. "Hey Ellie girl, you know me, I'm always down for pizza night at the Dax house."

"Yay!" I bounced in my seat. "I was thinking Tony's, but I know you and dad like that crappy place down on Front street." Dad scowled good heartedly and Ry grunted in offense. "So I was thinking maybe we could compromise and get Tony's?"

Dad started to say something witty in response but was cut off by a deafening crack as the back window of the SUV exploded, sending shards of glass into the back seat.

I screamed in shock and covered my face with my arms. Within seconds, the other windows in the car started exploding and shattering.

"Get down, Elora!" My dad yelled and put his hand on top of my head and forced me down until my face was at my knees.

"Dad!" I screamed as I realized what was happening. We were being shot at.

Bullets ripped through the car and windows as my dad gunned it and accelerated through the dark streets of his kingdom.

"Where are you?" Ryker screamed through the phone, and I could hear commotion over the line as he barked out orders to men.

Dad told him and continued swerving through cars and somehow at the same time drew one of the guns from his shoulder holster and fired out his shot-out window at the black sedan that pulled up alongside of us. The car rammed into the side of our SUV, and we bounced off the curb on my side.

I was terrified but I was trying desperately to remain calm, and not scream or draw any of my dad's attention to me at all. He needed to focus on what he was doing if we stood any chance of getting out of this.

Who would attack him a couple of miles from his own home? These streets were crawling with his men and surely, it was a suicide mission.

More bullets peppered the sides of the car as I clung to the seat in fear, keeping my head down.

Pain ripped through my leg, and I screamed in agony as burning misery exploded down my thigh.

"Fuck, El!" Dad screamed and put his hand on top of my thigh where red blood started pouring from my skin.

"Talk to me Gavin!" Ryker yelled through the phone, "We're almost there. We're a few blocks away that's it. Hold on man!"

Dad grunted in pain, "Elora's been shot, and so have I." I looked over at him and saw that red blood seeped down the blue dress shirt over his chest.

"No, Dad!" I screamed. The car next to us crashed into a light pole as Dad rammed it back with ours but another one took its place a moment later and started the assault anew.

Dad fought back as best as he could while trying to hold pressure on my leg, drive, and fire back.

"I got it." I said and pushed his hand away from my leg and I put my own shaking hands on the warm blood pumping out of my body.

He aimed his gun out the window and fired off more shots as they rammed into our truck again. The impact sent us swerving and spinning on the damp road and next thing I knew, the truck flipped and started rolling violently. The sound was deafening as our brand-new Tahoe was crumpled more into a twisted ball of steel with each rotation against the pavement. When it came to a stop, we were upside down and I hung in my seat by my seatbelt.

Pain exploded in my body, a deafening ringing filled my ears, and I could only look around in shocked agony. Dad was slumped over against the door, free of his seatbelt but not moving.

I looked out the broken window to see who was near us and saw the car that had been chasing us speed off into the darkness as a flame grew under the hood of our car.

"Dad." I whispered, trying to fight through the fog in my head. He didn't respond so I tried again, louder, "Dad!" I fought with the seatbelt and screamed again. "Dad, wake up!"

I looked at the orange fire growing on the other side of the dash and started to choke from the smoke that was filling the cab.

I wrenched the seatbelt buckle free and fell two feet to the roof of the truck and landed in a heap amongst the glass and debris.

My bare legs scraped across the sharp edges, and I crawled over to my dad frantically. "Daddy, wake up! Daddy!" I shook him and tried to get his door open, but it wouldn't budge.

He stirred a bit, and his eyes opened as I crawled back over and fought with the door on my side and screamed in agony as I tried to force it open.

"Baby!" He said, grunting and crawling across the cab. He shoved it open and crawled out, hauling my body over his to protect me from the glass. When we got to the pavement outside we both took deep breaths and coughed trying to clear smoke from our lungs.

The streets were shrouded in darkness, a heavy silence pressing down, and a chilling wave of fear swept over me as multiple sets of eyes, gleaming with an eerie light, advanced from the surrounding structures.

A wave of recognition washed over me as I saw my dad's men—their faces grim, eyes blazing—racing down the street, weapons raised, the sight of their fallen, bleeding king fueling their frantic rush.

The high-pitched squeal of tires, like a banshee's wail, ripped through the air as they rounded the corner, and my heart pounded – they were back. A scream ripped from my throat as I watched my dad collapse onto the hot, cracked pavement; his legs buckling beneath him in slow motion.

"Daddy, no!" I sobbed and crawled over to him frantically. His entire shirt was covered in blood, and it poured from his mouth and nose as he lay there struggling to breath. "Please, God no! Please no, no, no." I begged as I ripped my blazer off and pushed it against his chest, trying to stop the bleeding.

Men circled us and watched in horror as they formed a ring of protection around us from any other threat, but none of them could help my dad from the threat that had already struck.

"Baby, don't cry." He whispered as he slid his hand against the side of my face.

I was sobbing on my knees, my head buried in his chest, the rough fabric of his shirt scratching my cheek as I frantically tried to stem the bleeding. "Please, you're going to be okay. You have to be okay. I need you!" I screamed as another sob ripped from my chest.

More tires screeched to a halt behind us, the sound echoing like thunder, and I threw myself across my dad's chest, to shield him from more bullets, but when I looked over my shoulder at the pounding feet, I saw only allies.

And Ryker.

He and the rest of their men came barreling towards us as I clung to my hero's chest.

Dad turned my face towards his again and I cried from the pain and sadness in his eyes as he looked up at me. He coughed and tried to talk, but choked on the blood in his mouth. He finally managed to whisper, "I love you. You are my whole entire world Elora, I'm so sorry I let you down tonight."

He fell into a fit of coughing again as Ryker kneeled on the other side of him and took his hand. Tears fell down Ryker's face as he looked at his best friend laying there between us struggling to breathe.

My dad turned to him and grunted, "Promise me—" He swallowed back on blood and emotions as he stared into Ryker's eyes, "Take care of her."

Ry nodded and gripped his hand white knuckle tight in his, "On my life Gav, you have my word. I'll take care of her for the rest of my life." His shoulders shook as he fought to remain poised. Dread filled his usual strong, giant frame, reducing him to pain on the pavement next to me.

My dad nodded and looked back at me.

I shook my head, hating the sorrow I saw in his eyes as he accepted his fate. "Please Daddy. You have to get up. I can't live without you. Please, you have to get up." I begged endlessly as his grip on my hand loosened.

On the cold, wet pavement of his hometown, I held my father as his breath hitched and then ceased, his body slumping against mine; the chilling silence ringing like a scream in my ears. I couldn't bring myself to look away or move or breathe, long after his own breaths stopped leaving his body.

This wasn't real. The only person in the entire universe to love me was dead, and he took my very heart with him.

CHAPTER 2 – ELORA – PRESENT DAY

I walked into the swanky apartment of my best friend, Carly, and yelled out for her.

"In here!" She yelled back from the bathroom.

When I pushed the door open, she was standing at the mirror with a curling iron in her hair and a joint hanging from her lips.

"What are you getting all dolled up for?" I asked, leaning on the doorjamb.

She turned and looked at me and rolled her eyes. "You're impossible when you want to be." she said and huffed. "Shower if you want, your outfit is laid out on the bed and the guys will be here in a half an hour to pick us up."

I raised my eyebrows at her, "I'm not going out anywhere."

"You're not staying in tonight, either."

"Carly." I warned.

She waved me off and dismissed me. "It's your twenty-first birthday, El. You're not staying in tonight."

"I don't care what day it is; I worked three of my four jobs today. I'm beat and I don't want to go out. Besides, I have to work tomorrow morning, so I need to sleep."

"You have tomorrow off until three." She said as she fluffed her hair and handed me the joint.

I looked at it for a minute and then said fuck it, I could use some help to relax right now.

I took a drag off it, "Do I want to know how you know my schedule?"

"Because I made sure you didn't get scheduled for the morning shift the day after your coming of legal age birthday, duh." She said and shooed me back out of the bathroom as she walked towards her bedroom. I followed her and watched as she dropped her towel and grabbed a shiny dress off the bed. She didn't care about nudity, given her profession, and I had stopped being scandalized by it a long time ago, so I just watched as she slid the silky dress over her tiny body.

Carly was a stripper at the sexiest club in Shadeport, and she loved every single second of her lifestyle. She was beautiful in a classic way that every person could recognize as beauty with just one glance. With sun-kissed skin and an athletic surfer's body, she had long blonde hair and bright blue eyes to match. She was the complete opposite of me and when we hung out, we got more than a few stares at our stark differences, but she was the one best friend I had made since my life turned to shit, so I wasn't letting her go anytime soon just because we were so different.

Carly finished zipping up her gold dress and then picked up the outfit she had picked out for me and threw it at me. "Seriously, you can either get dressed in that, or I'll make you go out on the town dressed as a waitress. Your choice, but you're going. And if I were you, I'd change because I'm sure there will be some weirdo that gets off on the thought of banging a chick over a fryer out tonight."

"You're a pain in my ass, Carly." I said, throwing the dress back onto the bed. "I don't want to go out. It's my birthday, shouldn't I get to choose what I do or don't do for it?"

"No, because if you got to choose, you'd never leave your shit ass apartment and you'd end up dying of old age before you had any fun."

"People like me aren't allowed to get old, Carly. We die before we reach our golden years. I just don't see any point in celebrating one year closer to the end."

I took another drag off the joint before handing it back to her and welcomed the smoky warmth that started to relax my muscles.

"Get in the shower now!" She yelled and pushed me towards the bathroom. "We are going out!"

I huffed at her but did as she said, since she was getting all worked up about it. I clipped my hair up and quickly showered and washed the smell of French fry grease from my skin and then got out. Carly stood at the sink when I was done and did my makeup for me and then added some waves to my long dark hair.

When she was done, she winked at me and handed me the dress again and shut the bathroom door so I could get dressed.

I held up the scrap of green lace that she deemed a dress and groaned.

I yelled through the door, "You do realize I'm like 4 sizes bigger than you, right?"

"Shut up and put it on!" She yelled back as someone rang her doorbell.

"Ugh." I groaned and looked in the mirror, I had no choice but to put it on or walk out into her living room in my towel and now that there were people here, probably the guys, I wasn't walking out there naked.

I put the dress on and looked in the mirror at the final product. My dark brown hair fell in waves around my shoulders and the black and emerald eye makeup Carly had put on for me matched the dress perfectly and made my hazel eyes glow.

The emerald, green lace dress was gorgeous, but I felt so out of my element in it. It had small straps and a deep v cut that ended below my breasts, which I had to admit, looked pretty damn good tonight. The fabric was thick and gave good support, making them look perky and firm. The rest of the dress clung to my wide hips and ass and ended right at mid-thigh with a scalloped lace edge.

It was beautiful and while I felt beautiful in it, I was so worried about a boob popping out or my panties showing if I forgot to cross my legs when I sat down or something, it was hard to relax enough to walk out in it.

The door opened slowly, and Carly popped her head in to look at me before opening it fully, giving me an up down look. "Holy shit, El." She said wistfully and handed me a pair of black lace heels. "You look fucking delicious."

"Delicious?" I asked as I stepped into the strappy heels and snorted at her.

"Yes, delicious. Everyone at the club is going to drool the second they see you."

"Where are we going?" I asked.

She turned and walked out of the bathroom, turning the light out as she went and shrugged her shoulders. "Somewhere to get you to loosen up and have fun." She yelled as she sashayed her way back into the kitchen, where I could hear male voices.

Now or never, I suppose.

I took a deep breath and smoothed my hands down the fabric of the dress and put my brave face on and walked out into the common room. I had gotten really good over the years at perfecting a damn good poker face around others and used it to protect myself.

When I walked into the kitchen, I saw our friends Jay, Mason, and Frankie standing around with drinks in their hands as Carly grabbed her clutch and things to leave.

Jay saw me first and nudged the others as his jaw dropped. "Damn El." He said and stood up right, he leaned over and kissed my cheek and put his arm around my shoulders and pulled me into him in a way that used to make me feel weird, but now I was comfortable with it. "Happy Birthday." He said softly to me as I let him pull me against his side and looked at the others as their eyes wandered over my exposed body. I crossed my arms over my chest to shield myself, but it just pushed my breasts together and up even more, showing their hungry eyes much more, and I quickly dropped them back to my sides with a huff.

Jay was hot as sin. His long dark hair, styled in a man bun with faded sides, and dark chocolate brown eyes, warmed me from just looking at him. He was tall and broad in the shoulders but not in the way a real man was. He was only twenty-two, and he had some growing left to do in that area, but he was strong and fun to look at and touch on occasion.

"C'mon guys, let's go or we're going to be late." Carly called and opened the front door. I followed her out towards Frankie's car parked on the curb. She slid in the front seat next to him and Mason held the back door open for me to slide into the center between him and Jay.

The familiar laughter and easy banter of our usual get-togethers surrounded me, but the unfamiliar fabric of the dress instead of my usual jeans and sweater—made me feel acutely self-conscious.

Frankie started driving and headed east, deeper into the city and the hair on the back of my neck stood up as I shivered.

"Are you cold?" Mason asked, leaning over, and wrapping his arm around my shoulders. He smelled good tonight, a new cologne maybe, but it was a little overpowering. He was a surfer boy, rocking the bright blonde hair and blue eyes like Carly, which made him so much easier to befriend than his dark and broody friends.

"Just a bit." I said but sat back up and nudged his ribs with my elbow. "But I'm fine."

He held his hands up in surrender and laughed at me, "Whatever you say, birthday girl. We're going to have so much fun tonight." He grabbed a joint from behind his ear and lit it up, taking a drag and handing it to me. My buzz from before was beginning to fade so I accepted it and he smiled brightly as I wrapped my lips around the end and took a big inhale.

He watched me closely as I let it out and raised an eyebrow at him. "You're getting good at that." He said and took it back but let his eyes linger on my lips.

I didn't smoke often, and I had made an ass of myself more than once trying to fit in with them by choking on the weed, but I had gotten better over time.

"You guys are a bad influence on me." I said and looked back out the windshield. "Where are we going?" I asked again. Carly looked over her shoulder at me and winked.

"It's a surprise."

"Why?" I scooted forward to lean between the front seats.

"Because birthday girls get surprises." Frankie looked at me in the rearview before turning to look over his shoulder at me and letting his eyes drop to my chest. "Who knew you had such nice tits, Eloise." He licked his lips and gave me a hungry smile. He always called me Eloise to mess with me. When I first started hanging out with Carly, he said I was too prim and proper to be from around here, so he took to calling me Eloise instead of El or Ellie, like everyone else.

Carly swatted him, and I leaned back into my seat. "Knock it off, Frankie, you're making her uncomfortable."

He laughed and went back to driving. Jay laid his hand on my leg and squeezed. His fingers brushed the scar on my thigh that he always asked about and I watched out of the corner of my eye as he looked at it as he ran his fingers along it.

"Are you sure you got this jumping a fence?" He asked suddenly.

"Why do you ask?" I said, keeping my voice flat.

"Because our buddy Tate has one like it on his arm, looks almost identical, but he didn't get it from a fence."

"What did he get it from?"

"A bullet."

I swallowed and took a deep breath. Mason looked over at my leg and nodded in agreement. "That's definitely a bullet wound." He said as he took another drag from his joint.

I took it from his fingers and took a deep drag, "Do I really look like the kind of girl that would be shot at?" I asked, trying to make the idea sound bizarre.

They didn't answer right away as they contemplated it for a moment.

"No baby. No, you don't." Jay finally said and smoothed his palm over the scar and took the joint from me.

Out of all of them, I was most comfortable with him because he reminded me of someone from my past that had always protected me and made me feel safe.

I knew it wasn't the same thing as having that person around anymore, but it was easy to let my body pretend for a moment at a time that I was taken care of. He had tried to make a move on me more times than I could count. Most of the time, I would brush him off and tell him I wasn't interested in anything with anyone, and he'd grumble but let me be.

However, a few times, I'd let myself fall into his strong arms and let him kiss me and even fewer times, I let him put his hands on me in places I shouldn't have. But I'd never slept with him, though he had sure tried.

I didn't have the heart to tell him that when I was in his arms, I closed my eyes and thought of someone else. Because I didn't want to hurt him, and I knew I'd never be in the other man's arms in real life, so I just pretended and felt guilty afterwards every single time.

The thing was, I shouldn't have even wanted to be in the other man's arms. It was forbidden and unrealistic and taboo, but when I was alone, late at night in my tiny studio apartment, I'd let my hands and my mind wander as I imagined what it would be like to be taken by the man that I'd compared every other guy since to. But as soon as the orgasm would fade from my system, I'd feel shame and embarrassment for even thinking such things and I'd focus on who I was now in this life instead of dreaming about my past life.

None of my friends knew who I really was, or where I'd come from. One day, I'd just appeared on the outskirts of town, sixteen, broken, jaded and outcast. The perfect kind of girl for this town and I had blended in perfectly.

And every single day since then, I lived my pathetic pseudo life, barely surviving, wasting away, and trying desperately not to get sucked back into the life that had destroyed me once already.

Nothing good happened to a girl like me in Shadeport, California. Which was exactly why I tried not to venture into the city limits ever, but as Frankie drove his car deeper into the darkness, I felt the cold fingers of fear sliding around my throat as I started to recognize the skyline.

Well karma, here's to hoping I survive *this* car ride.

CHAPTER 3 – ELORA

I groaned inwardly when we walked into Erotiq. We reached the hottest club in Northern California, a sweaty, pulsating mass of bodies, with a line that stretched around the block. The guys, however, had connections and they did their handshake thing at the ropes, before we were just let right in.

Perks of the job I suppose. The three amigos we hung out with worked for the most notorious crime boss in modern history. He was like Voldemort from Harry Potter, people feared even saying his name out loud if it was in a less than favorable context because his people were everywhere, and they were almost as ruthless as he was.

He ran this entire city with no mercy and neighboring rivals never even dared to cross him, for it would take a national army to infiltrate his walls.

He was feared by all, respected by most, lusted after by every woman, and envied by every man. He was an enigma that I once had wanted to consume.

He was also the man who had vowed to take care of me for the rest of my life.

He was Ryker Lawson.

And he was the bastard who dropped me like a ton of bricks and left me to the wolves to be devoured without a backwards glance.

A wave of noise and bodies washed over me as we entered the club, the music a physical force, and my usual carefree expression solidified into its carefully constructed replacement. I wore a mask in public because I'd seen what happened to people when they knew your true softness.

Women and men danced high into the sky in cages and on silk ropes. Some of them were in beautiful lingerie or bright colored outfits, while some of them were completely naked.

I felt a blush creep up my neck when a naked man stood on the ledge of a window between two areas and stroked himself as he danced for everyone.

I looked away and Jay leaned into my ear, placing his hand on the top swell of my ass as he weaved us around the bodies, "You look scandalized El." He chuckled and let his hand slide down onto my ass fully. "It's sexy as fuck."

I looked at him out of the corner of my eye and bit my lip as I let him lead me through the crowd, shielding my body with his. Carly walked over to a large U-shaped booth along the edge of the dance floor that had a reserved sign on it and slid down onto the leather seat and scooted in.

Settling into the plush booth, I cast a cautious glance around. I tried to keep my stare from landing on all of the naked bodies around the room and instead, made myself focus on the men in various different levels of crime business.

Some were easy for me to spot, whether they were wearing suits, joggers, or regular thug clothes, it was something I hadn't forgotten in my years away from the scene. Some though, I knew I missed as I looked around the space, and those were the ones that worried me.

I didn't recognize many faces as I spotted the men that worked for Ryker, a few of them sent flickers of recognition down my spine, but I couldn't remember who they were exactly.

They had used to work for my dad and Ry before Ryker stepped forward as sole leader of the city. The two men used to stand, side by side and control the darkness of the streets while protecting those who wanted to stand only in the sunlight, like me.

But after my dad had been murdered, the darkness pulled Ryker under and now he was the leader of all things bad and scary that happened here.

Or so I had heard through the rumor mill. I hadn't actually laid eyes on him in almost five years. Right after my dad died, he had essentially stepped into the role my dad had left empty and he took care of me, just like he said he would.

But I wasn't surprised when he started becoming more and more unapproachable and our contact lessened. He was young, and the new leader of the city and I understood why taking care of his late best friend's kid wasn't high on his priority list.

But I'd be lying if I said his disappearance from my life hadn't hurt almost as badly as it did to have my dad die in my arms.

My dad and Ry were the same age, they had only been fifteen when my mom got pregnant with me, and my dad had stepped up instantly and accepted responsibility for his actions from the second she told him she was pregnant. But he was twenty-nine years old when he was killed, and Ryker was only twenty-nine years old when he became a king, and being a parent wasn't something that came naturally to him like it had for my dad. So, he had dropped me from his list of responsibilities, and I had barely survived it.

It wasn't just the emotional pain of being abandoned; he left me with absolutely nothing, and I had been fighting for survival every day since in ways I never imagined.

I worked hard to distance myself from the Dax name and the dangers it brought with it from rival gangs over the years. Without Ryker's protection, my father's last name felt like a bullseye on my back, so I had gone by my mom's last name in the shitty south LA school I had transferred to when we moved away from Shadeport.

I needed to tell Jay that I was the daughter of the fallen King of Shadeport, seeing as how I was sitting in his crew's club, but I just couldn't bring myself to say the words out loud. I hadn't spoken the Dax name in years, and I didn't want to start again tonight. I didn't even want to be here. So, I kept my mouth shut and prayed that none of the men from years ago recognized me while we were here tonight.

Besides, I'd grown up a lot over the years, so I didn't expect any of them to be able to pick me out in a group of scantily clad women in the dark.

A waitress in a bra and thong walked up to our table and acknowledged the guys and then asked what we wanted to drink. I shrugged and let Carly take the lead and a couple of minutes later there were bottles upon bottles sitting on our table with five glasses to share. Each bottle had a custom cocktail in it and a sexy name written on a label around the neck of them.

"Did you order enough for the next three tables?" I asked in horror as Jay handed me a glass filled with an electric orange bubbly drink in it. I took a sniff from the lip of the glass and was surprised to smell mint alongside the sweet orange scent.

It slid across my tongue, a delightful explosion of flavor with the faintest whisper of alcohol. I drank pretty regularly with my friends, but I didn't like getting drunk or high enough to lose my senses. This world wasn't safe enough for someone to let their defenses down, even amongst friends.

"Just sit back and enjoy!" Carly smiled then yelled at the top of her lungs, "Happy Birthday Ellie!" No one besides our table heard her because of the volume in the space but my cheeks reddened, and I looked down as everyone at the table laughed at my awkwardness.

As I drank more of my drink, I felt the relaxation calming my tense muscles a bit and before long I slouched back into the booth watching the scene of the club without so much embarrassment.

"Have you ever been here before?" Mason asked, leaning over into my ear to talk over the crowd.

I shook my head no and smiled at his shocked face.

"I don't have much free time for clubbing." I said.

"You could quit your millions of crappy jobs and go work with Carly, and then you'd have all kinds of time for it." He said, letting his eyes drop to my tits. I didn't shrink back or cover myself up as he looked, and I blamed it on the alcohol in my head. But a part of me liked it.

"Can you imagine me on a stripper pole?" I asked doubtfully, "I'd fall off and break my neck." I added.

"I can imagine you on a stripper pole just fine." Mason said as he leaned back and put his hand on my thigh, "And my imagination doesn't have you looking silly at all."

Jay leaned over and talked past me, "What are you two talking about?" He asked, looking from me to Mason and back.

"Nothing." I said and shook my head.

"I'm telling El how much better her life would be if she worked with Carly instead of at her shitty jobs."

That grabbed the attention of Carly and Frankie, and they leaned forward to join in the conversation.

"I agree!" Carly gushed winking at me, "The guys would eat you up like catnip." She added. "They love the shy but erotic look that you've got going. You could make a killing doing it."

"I don't know the first thing about stripping. I can't even dance on both my feet let alone a pole." I rebuked. We'd had this conversation a million times.

"No time like the present to learn." Mason said and pulled me from the booth.

"What?" I asked, digging my heels in as I stood up and wobbled a bit.

He turned and grinned, grabbed my drink off the table and pushed it into my hands. "Drink it. All of it." He said and waited until I tipped the glass up to my lips and did what he told me too. When I set it on the table, he pulled me out onto the dance floor.

Carly cheered and clapped as she followed after us with Frankie and Jay in tow.

Mason was tall with shaggy blonde hair to match his surfer vibe, and he wore jeans and a short sleeve t shirt that showed off the tanned muscles in his arms. He was very attractive and there were times that I found myself wondering what it would be like to kiss him or feel his body on mine, but I couldn't let myself take that chance.

He spun around in the center of the dance floor and pulled me close to his chest, I caught myself leaning into him for more reasons than just the crowd of people pushing us together.

I laughed as he snaked his hands around my waist and shimmied his hips against mine obnoxiously and then started moving us together to the music.

His hands were big on my waist and hips, but he was able to lead me easily with them and I let him.

We danced for a couple of songs, and I was enjoying myself as I bounced back and forth between Jay and Mason's arms and ended up in Carly's where I decided I was going to stay now that my blood was pumping with more than just weed and alcohol.

Arousal, a more dangerous companion than either of the other two, simmered alongside them.

CHAPTER 4 – RYKER

I closed my eyes and leaned my head back against the headrest of my chair and stretched my legs out wide. "Fuck." I groaned and let my hands tangle in the hair of the blond that was kneeling between my legs, bobbing her mouth up and down on my cock.

I couldn't remember her name; she was new here and was apparently on the fast track to climb the ladder—perhaps she would do it quicker with my come on her face.

Who the fuck was I to tell her she was wrong?

She was doing a decent job at sucking me off, but every time the head of my cock pressed against the back of her throat, she gagged and pulled off quickly.

She tried to make up for it by using her hands to chase her lips as she sucked on the head of me, but it wasn't what I wanted.

"How bad do you want this?" I asked, pulling her hair, and snapping her head up until she looked at me through her watery eyes.

"I want it bad." She gasped as she fisted my cock up and down in the absence of her mouth.

"Then put your hands behind your back and open your mouth." I said as I pushed her face back down until my cock thrust into her mouth.

She put her hands at the small of her back and looked up at me questioningly as I stood up with her still wrapped around my cock.

I held her face where I wanted and started thrusting into her mouth, going all the way in until her teeth rubbed the base of my cock and then pulled out long enough for her to gasp and pushed back in.

She reached out and pressed her hands against my thighs and pushed back the next time my cock went down her throat, but I yanked her hair harder and pushed down all the way into her and held still. As I controlled her air supply, I caught her panicked gaze and raised an eyebrow, noticing her hands on my dress slacks.

The challenge was there, and she understood it.

She dropped her hands and put them back behind her back when I pulled out, letting her take a deep breath.

But I didn't wait for her to take two. I shoved my cock back down her throat and thrusted my hips savagely, fucking her mouth like it was a pussy as she gagged and gasped.

She obediently left her hands off my legs as I fucked her mouth like a beast, pretending to be a good girl for me.

"That's it." I said as I felt my spine start to tingle and my balls tighten. "That's a good fucking slut." I groaned and pulled from her mouth completely.

I jerked my cock and sprayed her face and tits with my come, covering her dress in the process, and roared through my orgasm.

When I looked down at her, shock covered her face as much as my mess did and I chuckled evilly. "Only *really* good girls get to swallow." I pushed my dick back into my pants, zipped up and walked away.

I grabbed a towel off the bar and tossed it to her and watched as she tried to clean herself up. It was useless though. She was wreck and if I was a better man, I might have felt sorry for ruining her work clothes and make-up, leaving her unable to return to the floor for the rest of the night.

But I was far from even a decent man, and I didn't care in the least. She wanted to suck my cock to get further in life, these were the consequences.

My office door opened, and I turned to watch Zeke walk in with a pensive look on his face. He glanced at the blond on the floor and the corner of his mouth turned up as he shook his head.

"Maybe you should head on down to see if any of the boys want to add to the stains on your dress tonight. Might get you a few more favors seeing as your outfit is already ruined." I said dismissively and she gawked at me in shock. I turned to her as I picked up my tumbler of whiskey and took a shot. "Suck a few cocks, please a few men, make a few friends and make the most of the evening babe. This is a dog-eat-dog world, and it's always good to have a few pit bulls in your pockets."

I watched as realization dawned and then a small smile crossed her bruised lips. She stood up and walked out the door, no doubt on her way to the room downstairs that some of my men brought girls into, looking for a cock to suck for a buck or a favor.

She was new to the scene, and I had no doubt she hadn't seen this side of the lifestyle yet, but if she played her cards right, she'd win herself the attention and protection of someone useful.

"You just couldn't help yourself, could you?" Zeke asked as he watched her walk away and shut the door behind her.

I shrugged my shoulders and brushed it off. "What do you want?" I asked.

His eyes darkened as the smile fell from his mouth, and he walked over to the large two-way mirrored windows along the edge of my office that looked out over the entire club.

Erotiq was one of my best money makers because it offered services to a variety of different types of people. It was a great place to conduct dirty business and pleasure, and I was getting ridiculously richer every single weekend from it.

"We have a problem." Zeke said as he looked down at the floor below.

I set my glass down and walked over to him, sliding my hands into my pants pockets as we went. My fingers brushed the worn piece of metal in my pocket and the texture calmed me as my body started to react to his words.

"What is it?" I hated problems, especially when I was actively trying to enjoy my evening post ball blasting.

He turned to me and held my stare, "Elora Dax is here."

Pain rocked the chest cavity where my heart used to be.

Elora Dax was the only person in the world that held the ability to destroy me in her dainty little hands, and she didn't even know it.

"Where?" I asked, my voice thick with emotion as I clenched my fist in my pocket.

Zeke, pointed over to a booth along the wall and I leaned forward to look through the darkness where he pointed.

"Green dress." He said, but I didn't need him to point her out once I knew where to look.

"Dear God." I cursed as my eyes landed on my dead best friend's little girl for the first time in over five years.

Only, his little girl was gone, and in her place was a beautiful, elegant, and mature woman in her place.

"I know." Zeke said from next to me and shook his head. He had been our second in command when Gavin and I ran things years ago and he had been around Elora almost as much as I had, so I knew this was taking him back in time as much as it was me. But it wasn't paining him like it was me, because he hadn't abandoned her like I had.

Elora sat in a booth with another girl and a couple of guys and a whole lot of booze. She tipped her head back to laugh at something one of the guys said into her ear as he ran his fingers down her neck and dangerously close to her plunging neckline. I watched as her slender neck stretched when she laughed. I swallowed hard when I realized who was whispering into her ear and hanging all over her. And it wasn't only one man.

"Is that Jay and Mason?" I asked, through clenched teeth.

"Yes, Sir." Zeke replied.

"I want men watching her and her girlfriend like hawks. They don't leave and no one gets near them. And I want Jay, Mason, and Frankie up here now." I said, ordering Zeke off on the task as I stood riveted in place, unable to take my eyes away from the beautiful woman that Elora Dax had grown into.

Within moments two of my men stepped forward to order the guys upstairs and then posted at the end of the booth, instructing the girls to stay put. I watched as Elora's smile dropped and she looked around the room quickly, and then watched where the guys walked up the stairs to my office.

Her eyes quickly scanned the mirrors and stopped at a spot, very near to where I actually stood. I knew for a fact she couldn't see me, but a part of me wanted to know what she thought as she looked for me.

She had to know I was King here still. She had to know this was my club and this was my turf and that the guys were my crew.

What I couldn't figure out though, was why, if she knew I was in charge here, hadn't she come to me the second she stepped foot inside my city again? How long had she been back within reach, and I hadn't even known?

I was going to find out the answers, and heads would roll when I figured out who dropped the ball and didn't inform me of her return to Shadeport.

The door to my office opened and in walked the three pawns that had been sharing space with Elora and the blonde friend of hers and I forced my face to stone as I took a drink of whiskey.

"Hey boss." Frankie said with a toothpick between his teeth. He was the leader of the trio and the one who moved orders down their chain. I enjoyed the uncertainty in the eyes of the other two as they looked around my office for the first time, surrounded by myself, Zeke, and three others that I trusted.

"You three did a good job last week getting those files I asked for." I started, taking another sip of my whiskey, and walking towards the windows again. I didn't want to show my hand so early, but I needed to lay my eyes on her again; to make sure she was still here.

"Thanks for trusting us with it." Frankie answered.

I looked down at Elora where she sat in the booth still and could feel her anger radiating off of her from here. I needed to make this quick, and then get her up here before she bolted.

I looked over my shoulder at the other two, trying to figure out which one of them was going to give me the most information on her.

"I assume you want more jobs like that one coming your way, right?" I asked, looking at Jay specifically. His lips had been on her neck a moment ago and my blood boiled as I remembered. He cleared his throat and stepped forward slightly.

"Of course. We're ready for more responsibility. We can get anything you need done."

I held his stare and let my scowl darken slightly.

"And you Mason?" I turned to the pretty boy of the group. "You think you can step up and take on more? Because with more responsibility, comes more money and more perks."

Mason nodded eagerly and smiled. He was the only one out of the three that was usually always smiling. And it pissed me off right now. "Yeah, I'm game boss."

"Good. I need to make sure you three are dedicated though. And focused on what I need from you, and not letting outside influences distract you."

They stayed silent, waiting for me to fill them in on what I meant. "Women." I said and looked back out the window at the paradox that held me captivated. "Women are a great distraction when we want them to be, and even more so when we don't."

"Women aren't a problem for us, Sir. We don't get tied down or wrapped up in them when it comes to work." Jay offered.

"Yet you came with two of them tonight."

Jay looked from me to Frankie, unsure of what to say before he stood taller, straightening his spine under my stare.

"Friends of ours. Nothing crazy." He said.

"Who are they?" I snapped, quicker than I wanted too.

Frankie answered. "Carly and Ellie. Carly works at Lux, I'm sure you've seen her there before."

Lux was the strip club I owned a few blocks over. When he said that, I did get the sense that I'd seen her there before.

So help me God, if Elora stepped foot in there to work—.

"And Ellie?" I asked, as my teeth cracked from the tension in my jaw.

Jay looked around at the other two and then kind of shrugged his shoulders. "She's a friend of Carly's."

"Sure looked like she was a friend to both you and Mason." I told him plainly.

"She's a hot chick we mess around with." He said flippantly. "But she's no one important."

I recognized he was trying to downplay stuff, to show me he was dedicated to me, but he didn't realize that he was skirting dangerously close to peril with every disrespectful word he said about her.

I looked over at Zeke and noticed the way the muscles in his neck bulged above his suit jacket. He looked at me and I nodded towards the door. "Bring her here."

He exited the room as a flash of fear lit the three sets of eyes staring back at me.

"Is there a problem boss?" Frankie asked. "Carly and I go back almost ten years, and her girl Ellie is newer to town, so we bring her with us sometimes. But honestly, we don't hang out with her too much."

"Why?" My palms were sweating as I realized how soon I'd be standing face to face with Elora Dax again. Would she be happy to see me? Probably not. The last I knew of her, she was so much like Gavin, she held her cards close to her chest in all things and rarely ever gave anything away that she didn't want to. She'd been off living her dreams in the halls of Princeton and flourishing in life. So, what was she doing here with a stripper and three thugs?

"She doesn't come to this part of the city often. She actually avoids it if she can, to be honest." Mason said.

I looked from one to the next and back as I let that statement settle in my brain. I shook my head and scoffed at them as I could no longer contain the menace inside of me. "Do you three fucks really plan to stand here in front of me and tell me you have no fucking idea who you've been spending time with? Are you all really that fucking stupid?" I yelled.

They looked at each other again, but they were saved from coming up with an explanation because the door to the office opened up and in walked the blonde with my Elora right behind her.

The blonde was scared, her shoulders were bowed and her eyes shaky as she looked from the guys and then to me.

But not Elora. Her spine was straight and her shoulders square and her eyes—her eyes were glowing as she locked them onto mine.

Up close, she was magnificent, every single inch of her body was grown and elegant. Her hazel eyes burned as they looked at me and her cupids bow lips parted as she let her gaze travel from my head to my feet and back and my entire body ached to touch her, to prove to myself that she was real. She had been in my life almost every single day for fifteen years and then—poof.

Nothing.

But now she stood in front of me in a tiny scrap of green lace and fire.

And I was ready to feel her burn again after so long without it.

CHAPTER 5 – ELORA

"What do you think is going on?" I asked Carly as the guys disappeared through a doorway at the top of the stairs.

She shrugged her shoulders and took another slammer of vodka, "Probably work stuff."

"Then why the guards?" I asked, nodding to the backs of two giant men posted at the end of our booth, keeping anyone from approaching us, while also keeping us from getting out.

That made her pause as she set her drink down and looked around. "I don't know." She said and looked at me. I hated seeing the sense of worry fall upon her face as she started paying attention to what was going on around her, because she should have been aware from the start.

"I want to go home." I said and reached for my clutch on the seat.

"How? Frankie drove and he's busy right now." she asked, pulling my arm to make me stop sliding towards the end.

"I don't know, I'll call an Uber or something."

"Uber's don't run in this part of town baby." She said and I whipped back to her.

"I don't care, Carly." I widened my eyes to show her how serious I was being. "I will worry about the how later, but right now, I need to leave this club."

I brushed her hand off my arm and scooted to the end of the seat, meathead one was standing in my way, so I set my foot to the back of his knee and kicked, causing his leg to give out and he fell forward before quickly turning back to me with a scowl the color of death on his face.

"Sorry, you must not have heard me over all the muscle wrapped around your shoulders," I said and stood up. "But I need to leave."

As I got my feet under me, he put his hand up and blocked my path. "Boss said you stay."

"Ellie, sit down." Carly said from behind me, as she looked from one meathead to the other.

I ignored her and rolled my eyes at the dude in my way. "Tell your boss—," I threw air quotes up around the title, "that he can go choke on a bag of dicks. I'm leaving."

I pushed at his shoulder to move him, but he put his hand flat on my chest and pushed me backwards causing me to fall backwards into the booth. I wacked my elbow on the corner of the table on my way down and jolts of electricity shot through my arm.

"Fuck." I cursed and held my arm to my side. I pulled my hand away to look at my elbow and saw a deep cut into the flesh.

"Oh my god." Carly gasped and grabbed a towel off a bottle of booze and pressed it to my arm to stop me from bleeding everywhere.

"What the fuck is going on down here?" A commanding voice boomed from behind the meathead that just manhandled me, and chills ran down my spine.

I snapped my head up and looked into the eyes of a man that I'd known nearly as long as Ryker.

"Zeke." I muttered, my mouth betraying my brain as it told me to feign indifference.

He was a terrifying man to look at. He was tall and had a bald head and a brown beard that was trimmed short, and the darkness of the facial hair made his light blue eyes glow.

Tattoos covered every single inch of exposed skin except his face and head. His hands and neck were covered with them, and my memory was trying to tell me most of his body was too.

He looked down at my arm and his eyebrows scrunched together, "What happened?" He asked again, this time aimed directly at the meathead still standing between my ankles leaning over me.

"She fell." He grunted and shrugged his shoulder.

"He pushed me." I bit back, letting my eyes burn into his.

"Ellie, please." Carly begged as she held the towel to my arm. She lived and worked in this world and to her best knowledge, I was a total newbie to this life, and I was sassing the men directly under the boss of the streets here. The weight of her fear pressed down on me—a heavy silence punctuated only by the racing of her pulse pressed against my skin—I recognized how my actions jeopardized her, but the bitter reality was, I couldn't guarantee her safety, not when my own was so precarious.

But I did know I wasn't going to be a little bitch in the face of Ryker's men.

Zeke looked at the ass hole again and shook his head, "We're all going upstairs. You're going to have to answer to that." He said and nodded towards me.

Finally, the assholes' face started to slip a bit as he contemplated what Zeke meant.

Yeah, you're fucked buddy.

Zeke held his hand out for me to stand up, but I eyed it suspiciously. "And if I say no thanks?" I asked him straight.

"Then I'll carry you over my shoulder, kicking and screaming if I must." He said and then a smile turned up his lips in a way that I knew he didn't do often. "We both know it wouldn't be the first time I've done that to you, Princess."

Carly gasped and squeezed my arm tighter. "What's going on?" She asked.

I just shook my head and took my arm from her, holding the bloody towel myself and stood up, ignoring Zeke's hand, and then eyed him skeptically as I stepped out far enough for Carly to stand behind me.

"Let her stay." I said to Zeke, but he just shook his head and nodded for all of us to follow him.

Carly clung to my side as we walked up the stairs. "How do you know Zeke Evans?" She hissed. "He's the second in command over the entire Shadeport crew."

"Believe me, you don't want to know." I said back and then forced myself to stand tall and put on my best fuck you face as Zeke opened the door that the guys disappeared through ten minutes ago.

Carly walked in first and headed straight for Frankie on the side of the room, but I just looked straight ahead at the man that had haunted my dreams for years as he leaned against his desk with a tumbler of liquor in his fingers like he was a fucking God.

And in a way, he was.

And I hated that.

As the door shut behind us and the two meatheads filed in against the wall, I let my eyes travel over Ryker's body for the first time in years.

Fuck he was one hell of a man now.

His dark black hair was faded on the sides and styled on top, he had a dark five o'clock shadow on his jaw and tattoos on the backs of both hands. Those weren't there five years ago, and I couldn't stop my traitorous body from wondering what the rest of his skin looked like now.

I shouldn't wonder such things, this man was my dead dad's best friend, and he had destroyed me. Dad would be rolling in his grave if he knew I was slightly attracted to his devilish counterpart.

Ryker had grown up and grown out in ways I didn't know was possible. He had been big before, but perhaps that was only in the eyes of a fourteen-year-old girl who idolized him for being her best friend and protector, but now, he was massive.

And he was angry.

His eyes dropped to my arm where I held the towel and then shot over to Zeke.

"What the fuck happened?"

Zeke nodded to the asshole in the corner, "Skills pushed her."

I watched in fascination as Ryker turned to the man who at least had the decency to look a bit remorseful as he started to make excuses, "She tried to leave boss, you said to keep them there."

But he didn't get another word out because in those two seconds, Ryker had crossed the room and punched him in the face so hard he was knocked unconscious, falling against the wall and then to the floor as his breathing took on an odd rattle.

Carly gasped and Frankie pulled her behind him a bit as he looked at me with question in his eyes. Jay reached for me and slid his arm around my hips and pulled me towards him, but Ryker turned on him from across the room and bit out angrily, "Touch her one more fucking time tonight kid, and I'll cut off whatever part of you that you dare to put near her. Do you understand?" His voice was lethal, and his face made me wither a bit.

I'd never seen him in this element before, my dad had protected me from this side of things as best he could.

But I had known, that out of the two of them, Ryker was the one to fear physically. Even I couldn't help the small part of me that did. And I fucking hated it.

Jay pulled back and I shot him an apologetic glance, "I'm fine."

I turned back to Ryker and watched him take off his suit jacket and toss it on the chair behind the desk as he began rolling up the sleeves of his shirt and stalked towards me. Ink swirled up both arms and I pressed my stupid thighs together to quell the ache that just seeing the ink on his skin had put there. His eyes bore into mine so powerfully I felt unsteady on my feet and regretted all the booze and weed I'd consumed tonight.

Ryker pointed his finger at me like he was going to say something but clenched his jaw and shook his head. He instead turned to the guys we'd come with tonight.

"I'm going to assume that you three numbskulls have no idea who the fuck you've been spending your time with. Or how did you put it, Jay?" He asked, scratching his jaw as he pondered dramatically, "She's just a hot chick you guys' mess around with."

I bit my lip to fight the urge to throw something at Jay for the bold-faced lie, but instead turned to Ryker, "Don't." I commanded. My voice was low and powerful in a way I'd never heard it sound before and the fact that I had just ordered Ryker Lawson to do something with it, sent chills down my spine.

"Don't what?" He asked, "Tell your friends who you really are? Perhaps find out how you were able to keep your return to Shadeport from me to begin with?"

I could feel the eyes of everyone in the room on me, but I couldn't drag mine away from Ry as he snickered at me with no actual humor. He turned back to the guys and continued on, "Your hot little friend Ellie here is actually, Elora Dax." He said, letting his eyes drop down my body again. "Daughter of the late and great king, Gavin Dax."

Frankie cursed and Carly gasped but I still couldn't let my eyes leave Ryker's. My dad's reputation was still one to be honored, even after seven years, because he had been loved by nearly everyone.

I sneered at him, "Is there a reason you're putting on a show like a peacock? That was never your style before, and the change doesn't suit you."

His nostrils flared and his fists clenched before he shoved them into his pants pockets. He looked at the heap of the man on the floor by the door and then to my friends and I saw the moment he'd decided to change tactics.

He spoke to the room, "Make word spread quickly, that any person in this city that dares to touch Elora Dax will not be spared for any reason at all. I don't care who the fuck you are. No. One. Touches. Her." He bit out each word to make his point. "And every single person in my employ is expected to protect and worship her every wish. Now get everyone out of my sight." He said to Zeke and everyone in the room turned to leave, including me.

I was a half a step closer to the door than I had been, when a hot calloused hand wrapped around my upper arm and held me still.

I could feel his body heat radiating off of him as he stood behind me and watched everyone else leave. Carly turned at the door to say something to me, but Frankie pushed her through the frame and the door clicked shut behind Zeke, leaving me alone in the room with Ryker.

My eyes fluttered closed, and I took a deep breath through my nose as I accepted my fate. He still stood at my back, with his giant hand wrapped around my arm, but didn't say anything.

I turned and faced him, but that was a mistake because he was nearly a foot and a half taller than me, and even with the lace heels on I had to tip my head back all the way to look up at him.

"Elora." He said and swallowed. "It's been too long."

My brows creased and I forcefully pulled my arm from his hand, "See, here I thought it hadn't been *nearly* fucking long enough."

Now it was his turn to scowl at me. "Let me see your arm." He demanded as he reached for it, but I backed up again and kept my body out of his reach as he tried grabbing me again.

"Don't touch me. Stop acting like you have a right to put your hands on me, because you don't." I spit out.

He clenched his teeth and sighed. "But you give Jay and Mason the right to touch your body?"

"Who I fuck is none of your business!" I snapped back and his body coiled tight like a snake ready to strike. I stabbed my finger at him and then shook my head in disdain.

"They aren't worthy of that gift, Ellie!"

"You don't know anything about me anymore, Ryker." My body shook with anger.

"I know why you're mad." He said and stepped forward faster than I was ready for and latched onto my arm and all but dragged me over to a plush velvet chair in front of his desk and pushed me backwards until my knees bent over the seat and I fell into it. "I know I should have tried harder to keep contact with you over the years—"

I scoffed at him and rolled my eyes, but he kept going.

"It sounded like you were thriving, and I didn't want to be a constant reminder of all you lost."

"Thriving?" I asked, shocked. "You have a warped sense of success if you think what I was doing was thriving."

He eyed me for a second, letting his stare penetrate deep into my eyes, looking for a lie.

"She said—," He froze.

"Who?" I snapped.

"Your mom."

"You mean the crack whore that gave birth to me?" I snorted out and hissed as he took the towel from my arm and ripped the wound back open that had started to clot.

He knelt on the ground in front of me and any words I'd been about to throw at him died on my tongue. My mouth went dry as he lowered himself to my level and pulled my arm into his hands.

"How did you cut it?" He asked.

I dropped my attitude when his voice went soft and sweet, it reminded me so much of how he used to talk to me when I was a kid. "I fell against the corner of the table."

He looked into my eyes, "You fell when Skills pushed you?"

I shrugged my shoulder and couldn't help the tiny smirk that pulled my lips back, "I may have pushed him first."

A predatory smile formed on his face and a chuckle bubbled up as he looked back down at my arm, "That sounds like the Ellie I knew once upon a time."

I didn't say anything back, because sparing with him was hard when he was mean, and it was downright impossible when he was nice.

He got up and grabbed a first aid kit from the bathroom connected to his office and came back to me. I sat there in awe as he crouched to the ground again and worked on my arm, cleaning and bandaging the wound with gentle fingers.

I watched each movement he made and tried to memorize every single thing about him in the short time I was going to have with him. "What do your fingers say?" I was unable to figure out what the letters said across his knuckles when he was moving them so quickly. Pausing briefly, he looked at me before closing his fists, putting them next to each other on my lap so I could read them.

"Honor Him." I whispered, and I couldn't help but let the tip of my pointer finger trace the m on his pinky for a second before I ripped my fingers back.

"Everything I do, I try to honor Gavin through it." he said, letting his eyes hold mine again in an intense stare. This close to him I could see the gold flakes in his green eyes and remembered so many times growing up that I would notice the different colors in his stare based on his mood.

"Clearly not everything." I replied, trying to force the brick wall I'd carried around myself for so long to rise back up and protect me, but it was slow to land between Ryker and me, like it knew it wasn't supposed to be there.

"Tell me what happened to you, if you weren't thriving like your mother said you were, then tell me what happened."

I dropped my eyes and shook my head as the sadness I'd felt the last seven years slid back up my spine and took away every ounce of arousal or happiness I'd been feeling from being in his presence again.

"It doesn't matter. It's done. And I am who I am today because of it."

"Tell me." He said strongly, trying to force his way with me, and I knew he was used to doing it with everyone. But I wasn't like everyone else he interacted with.

"No." I said and stood up, forcing him to lean back to let me go.

"Where do you live? Mason said you didn't come into the city often, so where do you live then?"

I turned and looked at him over my shoulder as I walked to the windows and looked out over the club. "It doesn't matter, Ry."

"It fucking matters, Ellie." My eyes fell shut when he said the nickname he had given me, and I ached to feel like the little girl who was protected by two strong alpha men again. But that had been a fairytale, and this was my reality.

"I need to go find my friends; they're my ride home." I said in response.

"I'll drive you home."

"No, you won't Ryker."

"Don't tell me what I'll fucking do damnit." He exploded and stalked towards me again.

"Then don't you dare stand there and tell me what to do either. You have no right!"

"I have every right! I told your dad I would look after you for the rest of my life—"

"Then where the fuck have you been?" I screamed into his face and then dropped back in shock. His eyes widened as he processed the fact that I'd just screamed in his face. Not once in my entire life had I raised my voice at Ryker. I turned away again and begged the tears pooling in my eyes to go away.

His voice softened in a way that felt like warm honey sliding down my skin, "Your mom told me you moved away to start fresh. And then she said you'd gotten into Princeton. I thought I was doing what was best by letting you be. With you away from the threats of this city, you were safe and didn't need my protection, Ellie. I thought you were safe."

I laughed humorlessly and swiped at the single tear the dropped from my lashes. He stood at my side, and I knew he could see it and I hated that. "Princeton huh?" I shook my head bitterly. "Those dreams died the same day my dad did."

"I don't understand. I sent her—" He stopped, and I turned my head to look up at him as I watched some sort of realization dawn on his face.

"You what? You sent her money?" He didn't say anything, and I had my answer. "You sent her money to send me to school and instead she sent me to the streets. I wish I could say I'm surprised."

"That fucking cunt." He whispered in anger and his eyes closed as he fought to force his anger down.

"At least that, we can agree upon."

He opened his eyes and put his hands on my arms and turned me towards him. "I didn't know Elora; I swear to you I thought you were growing and thriving. If I'd known she was lying—fuck!" He yelled and then contained it, "I should have known she was lying, that's what she does. I'm so sorry."

Our moment of admissions was broken when a knock sounded on the door and Zeke stepped in. "Boss."

"Not now, Zeke!" Ry snapped but I stepped back out of his arms and wrapped my own over my chest. My high was gone, my buzz had faded and the sixteen hours I worked before going out were starting to weigh heavily on me as fatigue weighed me down.

"Sir, it's Charlamagne." Zeke said and it was enough to get Ryker's attention.

"Shit." He cursed and looked at me and then back to Zeke who stood impatiently at the door. "I'll be right back. And we will finish this conversation." He said, not giving me a chance to agree or not, but he did pause long enough to press his lips to my forehead in a way that he used to, but it felt completely different now.

He left the room, and I looked around his massive posh office. It was my chance to get out of there and get away from him before he sucked me back into this life. I got lucky last time and walked away with my life.

But something told me that I wouldn't get so lucky a second time around.

I opened the door to the office and as I expected, there was a guard.

However, it was meathead number two from downstairs, and I figured I could use Ryker's anger towards his friend to my benefit.

He turned to look at me as I stepped out into the hallway.

"I need to go to the bathroom."

He nodded back into the room, "There's a bathroom in there."

"I need a female bathroom." I said and took a step towards the steps.

"Why?" He asked, following me.

"I have my period. I need a tampon or a pad or both. It's like a blood bath down there and I need some things to stop the mess." I said dramatically looking down at my legs as I walked away down the hallway. "Is it running down my leg? Shit. My friend has my tampons, so I need to find her."

His face paled at my gross description, but he at least stayed quiet as he followed me.

When we hit the main floor, the crowd was insane, bodies were everywhere and there was hardly any space to walk.

I looked over at the booth my friends and I had been sitting in and saw a different group of people sitting there now, and my friends were nowhere to be seen.

I turned and headed towards the front door and saw my opportunity when a couple of guys started to get into a fight a few feet away. I walked closer to the fight and managed to duck between the two idiots as they started swinging. Meathead was too big and got busy trying to pull them apart with a few others in the crew and I made my break for it.

I kept my head down and blended in with a group of girls who were leaving and grabbed one's arm. She looked alarmed but I leaned over and said, "There's a guy following me, can I just blend in with you guys for a second to lose him?"

Her face softened and she nodded quickly, pulling me closer and into the center of their group.

We walked out the front door and I nearly squealed with joy when I saw the group of taxi's waiting at the curb.

Thanking my cohort with a grateful smile, I walked to the idling cab and climbed in, the leather seats cool beneath my heated skin. I gave the man my address and turned to watch Erotiq fall away into the distance as he drove me away.

I leaned back into my seat and took a deep breath as I got further away from the city that had caused me such pain once upon a time.

I pulled my phone out and saw a bunch of texts from Carly and Jay.

> *Carly: Frankie is making us leave, where are you?*

> *Carly: We're at the car, he's going to leave.*

> *Carly: I'm so sorry, he wouldn't wait. Where are you? I'll Venmo you cab money.*

Well at least she was nice enough to realize I was too broke to afford this cab ride home before I did.

The ones from Jay were a little less nice.

> *Jay: How could you not tell me who you were? You could have messed things up big time for me.*

> *Jay: Where are you? Are you okay?*

> *Jay: Fucking Christ El, talk to me!*

> *Jay: I'm coming over in the morning and you can explain everything to me then.*

I sent a text to Carly to tell her I was on my way home and that I would call her in the morning and try to explain the best I could.

I didn't reply to Jay though, I didn't feel like I owed him anything and didn't like his tone in his texts, so I tabled that conversation for now.

When I finally got home, I stripped out of the dress that had made me feel beautiful and traded it for an oversized t shirt and crawled into bed while I processed everything that had happened tonight.

I had seen Ryker for the first time in years, and as expected I'd felt anger towards him. And below the anger, also like I'd known would come, was the hurt.

But what I hadn't been expecting was the attraction and arousal he pulled from my body by just being near me.

When I was younger, I'd always thought he was hot, I would have had to be blind not too. But he was fifteen years older than me and my dad's friend, so it was in a weird familial way.

But now, fifteen years didn't seem so bad when I was twenty-one and he was thirty-six.

And my body didn't care about the age; all it cared about was that his physique and his scent and power made me weak in the knees and called to something deep inside of my soul.

It called for me to submit to him, to let him take care of me and guide me like he had promised to do before.

But I wasn't naïve enough to think he would actually stick with it this time if I let him.

So, as sleep pulled me under when the sun started to crest the skyline, I vowed to stay far, far away from Shadeport and everything that involved him.

I'd survived this long on my own, I could keep doing it without him if I wanted to.

I just hated how badly I didn't want to.

CHAPTER 6 – RYKER

Fourteen minutes.

I had been gone, dealing with an issue for fourteen minutes and Elora had managed to give my men the slip and disappear.

I was irate when I walked back into my office and found her gone and instantly pulled up the security footage to see where she had went.

Watching her slide into the back of a cab and disappear had sent me into a panic that I hadn't been able to control.

I had been fucking stupid to leave her alone for even a second when I'd just gotten her back, but I was a stupid man for a lot of reasons when it came to her. My chest ached while I worked to track her down, and my thumb was raw from running it over the edge of the trinket in my pocket as I tried to calm down.

I was embarrassed to say it had taken nearly five hours to find her address, even Frankie hadn't known it when I demanded it from him, which pissed me off further.

There was something in my soul that wouldn't settle now that I'd seen her again after so long. It was more than just the sense of duty to her father or the amount of guilt I'd felt for believing her mother when she'd told me Elora was away at college and loving life.

It was deeper in my core and felt a lot like need and that made me sick to my stomach.

I had hated myself every time my eyes traveled down her body to admire her lush curves and beauty when she was in my office, and I had hated myself even more for how her body seemed to react the same way to me.

I had seen the way her thighs pressed together when I was near her, and how her lips parted before she would pull her plump bottom lip into her mouth and bite it to keep from saying something she would regret.

It was wrong to want her. It was wrong to crave her in a carnal way that left me rock hard and imagining all of the noises I could make fall from her sexy mouth when she was Gav's little girl.

I had helped her learn to ride a bike and study her words for her spelling tests when she was a kid. It didn't matter that I was just a kid myself when she was born, I was fifteen years older than her and she had looked up to me, so wanting to lay her on her back now that she was grown and bury myself inside of her until she no longer existed apart from me, was fucked in the head.

But I still wanted all of those things.

I still craved all of those things and more.

And as I got out of my car outside a shitty rundown apartment building in a part of town that even I didn't like to go to, that craving to possess her and take her far away from there, got even fucking stronger.

Zeke looked around the outside of the building with me and grimaced. "This is no place for a princess." He spoke.

He had always referred to her as a princess because she was the daughter of a king, and she was sweet and innocent all of those years ago.

But he was right about this. I agreed and then shook my head in frustration.

I couldn't understand why she lived in a place like this willingly. She had money and connections from her dad and anyone in the city would have given her a place to live rent free if she had asked.

I would have opened my own home to her if I'd known she was living in such conditions.

Images of her in my home flashed through my mind and I slid my thumb over the smooth cool metal in my pocket to keep focused and not dwell on how appealing it was to think of her sleeping under my roof at night, where I knew she would be safe and taken care of.

I forced the thoughts and images from my head and walked in the front door, leaving Zeke at the car. The lobby was dirty and desolate with flickering fluorescent lights flashing on and off at will.

I didn't even bother walking towards the elevators, I knew they wouldn't be operational and took the stairs to the fifth floor.

The hallway was dark, devoid of light except for what came in from under the doors of each apartment.

"Jesus Christ." I muttered and walked down the hall.

I was probably the most feared man in the city, and even I was uneasy about walking down this corridor, I couldn't imagine what Elora felt every single day living here.

I got to the door that I was told was hers and took a deep breath.

I was still in my suit from last night and desperately needed a shower, but I'd spent every minute since she had run away working to find her and didn't take the time to freshen up before I came to her, though now I wish I had.

Fuck it.

I laid my fist against the door loudly and watched as the whole thing moved on the hinges under my knock.

I listened as I waited for her to answer but heard nothing. I knocked again and cursed once more as the door looked like it was going to fall open at any second simply from being knocked on.

I listened again and still heard nothing. Was she not home? It wasn't even seven am on a Saturday morning. Where the fuck could she be?

"Elora!" I bellowed out and pounded on the door again. This time I grabbed the handle and turned it. It was locked, but it jiggled enough to be useless. "Elora open the door."

I twisted the handle, hearing the mechanisms in it break and give way under almost no pressure and then shoved the door open. "Unbelievable." I muttered and stepped inside, shutting the door behind me, though I knew it wouldn't lock now.

I looked around the tiny space and my blood boiled under the tightness of my skin. It was the smallest apartment I'd ever seen before, and I'd seen some shitty places. Even though it was small and outdated, it was clean and tidy. I caught her scent in the air and took a deep breath, letting her perfume calm me.

It was a studio apartment; the front door had opened into the kitchen and the living room had a small couch and coffee table in it but nothing else.

There was a screen divider behind the couch, and I walked towards it and stepped around the end.

And I froze in my tracks, barely biting back a groan in time.

Elora lay asleep in the center of a small full-sized bed with the blankets wrapped around her feet and rolled between her long bare legs as she hugged them to her chest. She wore only a light pink t shirt that rode up and revealed a pair of black cotton panties that struggled to contain her juicy ass. It made my hands ache to grab ahold of it and shake it, to watch it ripple with movement.

Her brown hair lay in a mess on her pillow and her eyes were covered with a sleep mask and she had earbuds in.

She couldn't see or hear anything, and she lay so vulnerably in an apartment with a door I'd just pushed open with no trouble.

She was not living here a second longer now that I knew about how unsafe it was.

No way.

I let my eyes rove her new body and felt like a pervert as my cock hardened painfully. More images of her naked on her back, begging me to fuck her assaulted me and this time, I could hear her sexy sultry voice beg for my cock.

I fisted my hard on, telling myself I was just going to adjust myself and then wake her up, but the second I wrapped my hand around myself, the groan I had bit back before came out and my hand squeezed tighter.

I stroked myself looking at this beautiful woman in front of me that I couldn't have and knew I was wrong. If I wasn't sure I'd already bought a one-way ticket to Hell, I might have been concerned for my soul.

But I was a goner long before Elora Dax ever walked back into my life.

I forced my feet to walk away and looked around her space. Her fridge was empty except for a bottle of coffee creamer and a jar of jelly. Her cupboards were just as bare.

She had no TV in her living room and a single book lay on the coffee table. I picked it up and rubbed my thumb over the worn cover.

It wasn't as if I'd recognize the title, but I flipped it open anyway and stopped when the pages opened to the bookmark. It was a faded and cracked photo of Gavin, Elora, and me when she was about seven.

It was the day Gavin had bought his first house for him and Ellie, and we had moved them in. She was tickled pink to have a house with a yard after living in crappy rundown apartment buildings like this one for years with her mom while Gavin worked his ass off to provide better for her.

It was one of my favorite memories and apparently, it was for her too.

I thumbed the photo for a minute and then pushed myself to put it back in the book and walk away.

I couldn't think about that time of my life if I was going to do what I'd come here to do.

There were clothes hanging on a line by the bathroom and I walked over to them to see what she wore normally.

There was a full array of clothes, and I looked over my shoulder to where she still laid asleep before letting myself pluck a swatch of red lace from the line. My fingers slid over the satiny fabric of her panties and my mouth watered. I pushed the panties into my pocket and wrapped them around the metal trinket in there that I'd taken from her years ago. It seemed fitting to add to my collection of things from her, for as much as she consumed my thoughts.

God, I was such a pervert.

My cock was throbbing, and I needed to turn my attention to something else before I climbed into bed with her and woke her up with an orgasm.

Next to her bras was a black ribbed corset with a logo on the left breast that I recognized instantly, and my blood once more turned to lava and rage boiled barely contained under the surface.

Lady Luck's was a bar on this side of the city that housed gambling and burlesque shows. It was no place for Elora to work, and she was never going to step foot in there again if I had anything to say about it. Images of Elora in a corset and fishnet stockings, walking through the bar serving drinks or dancing on the stage assaulted my brain and I groaned.

I snapped a picture of the corset and sent it to Zeke, instructing him to terminate her employment with their owner immediately.

I took the knife from my pocket and slit the corset into shreds, letting my body alleviate some of the pent-up frustration on the article of clothing before hanging it back up.

I walked over to the closet and grabbed a duffle bag that was folded up on the floor and started throwing clothes into it from her dresser and clothesline.

Her life experiment ended here. She was coming home with me, and I was finally going to do what I'd promised years ago. I was going to take care of her and treat her like the fucking princess she was.

A sigh sounded from the bed, and I turned to watch as she rolled over onto her back and stretched her arms up over her head. Her t shirt rose and exposed the curve of her feminine stomach, and the fabric stretched tight across her full breasts.

I watched with fevered need as her nipples hardened and pressed against the fabric and then growled out loud when I could make out the distinct outline of metal poking out of each side of them.

Her nipples were pierced. And I was a fucking goner.

Instantly my mouth watered with wonder of what her nipples looked like under that shirt and what kind of rings she had through them. I wanted to know what they felt like in my mouth and what different noises she would make if I played with them.

"Fuck."

I tore off my jacket and undid the top three buttons of my shirt, desperate for some relief from the tension building again in my body. I had to end this torture now, before I did something crazy like strip naked and bury myself inside of her before even waking her up.

I sat down on the edge of her bed and placed my hand on her leg and shook her gently.

"Elora." I spoke.

She jerked awake and kicked and screamed as she fought with the mask and ear buds that were blocking her senses.

I jumped forward and put my hand over her mouth to keep her from screaming loud enough to alarm her neighbors and turned her face towards me as her eyes snapped open and then blinked against the harsh light.

Her breaths were crazed under my hand and her own tiny hand covered mine with her nails dug into my skin. Her eyes widened when she realized it was me in her apartment, silencing her briefly. But I should have known better because I was treated to the sharp slice of her teeth on the inside of my hand as she bit me.

I pulled my hand away from her face quickly and cursed, looking at the bloodied skin as she scrambled to get away from me.

"Get back here." I said, grabbing her ankle and pulling her back on the bed as her one foot landed on the floor. I flipped her onto her back and grabbed both of her arms as she started swinging at me wildly. "Stop it."

"Get off of me!" She screamed and I covered her mouth again, careful not to allow her to open it as I held her while she continued thrashing under me. Little did she know what her curvy body was doing to mine with each wiggle and rub.

"Stop fighting me and calm the fuck down." I ordered and for half a second her body stilled, but then she started fighting anew. She got her feet up and pressed one to my chest and kicked, sliding herself across the bed and away from me but I was three times the size of her at least and twice as quick.

I grabbed her and pulled her on top of me, so her back was to my chest, and sat up with her in my lap. I crossed her arms over her chest and held her tight.

"Are you done yet?" I asked in her ear. She stopped squirming and part of me was thankful, because my rock-hard cock was sandwiched under her hot ass and every time she moved, she rubbed herself on it, driving me nuts. But I was also sad that she stopped because it felt incredible at the same time.

She twisted her head back and forth and tried talking under my hand and I gently pulled it away from her lips far enough for her to breathe and speak but close enough to clamp back down if I needed too.

"What the fuck are you doing here, Ryker?" she asked, panting with rage.

"You took off last night before we could finish our conversation, so I brought it to you instead."

"And you what? Broke into my apartment?" She accused, looking towards the front door like she expected it to be splintered leaning against the wall.

I slid my fingers into her wild hair and fisted it to turn her head to look at me over her shoulder. "I turned the handle and the whole damn thing broke in my hand. You're lucky that it was only me that came in here. What the fuck were you thinking living in a shit hole like this with zero thoughts for your own safety?"

She reached forward with her teeth to bite me again, but I used the hold I had on her hair and ripped her head to the side, narrowly avoiding her teeth connecting with my arm.

"Try it again and I'll fucking take you over my knee and spank you like the child you're currently acting like." I swore and her body froze, like she finally realized she was in my lap, wearing basically nothing, squirming around. I could feel the metal in her nipples under my arm and dropped my forehead to her shoulder and took a deep breath. "I just came here to talk Ellie."

"Then why is your cock hard underneath of me?" She asked and I groaned, still not looking up at her.

"You can't say words like that to me." I sighed, running my nose up the side of her neck, tasting her scent on my soul.

She softly moaned. "Why?"

"Because I'm only a man. And a bad one at that." I answered with my lips touching the exposed skin at her neck.

She shivered and adjusted herself, rocking onto my cock again and she gasped as I groaned. "Let go of me Ry."

"Stop fighting me and I never would have grabbed you in the first place."

"Okay."

I loosened my hold on her and let my hands fall to my sides as she put hers on my thighs and then stood up, pulling her shirt down to her thighs and turning around, eyeing me like I was a rabid animal.

And in a way, that's exactly what I was.

"Go put some fucking pants and a bra on so I can think clearly." I said and nodded towards the bathroom.

She had a decency to listen to what I said and all but ran away from me and locked herself in the bathroom.

I scrubbed both hands down my face and scratched my stubble as I listened to her moving around in the bathroom, but I stayed seated on her bed and only after she stepped back out into the room did, I look up at her.

She had a pair of thick sweatpants and a hoodie on and held her arms around her waist as she eyed me. "How did you find me?" She asked.

Her bare toes peeked from under the hem of her pants, and she curled them under her feet as I let my eyes fall to them, like she could hide them in the fabric from me.

I shook my head and felt the smile tug my lips even though I didn't want it too.

"This is my world; I can find anyone." I said.

"What do you want?"

I stood up and turned towards her as she eyed me carefully. "To do what I thought I'd been doing all along. But I want to do it right."

"What are you talking about?"

"Taking care of you."

She laughed with bitterness and walked towards the kitchen and poured herself a glass of water from the tap. "I've been on my own on the streets since I was sixteen yeats old Ry. I don't need you now."

"Yes, you do. Look around you Ellie, you can't even lock your fucking door. You have no food! You can't stay here." I yelled.

It was then that she noticed the duffle bag sitting on the floor by her clothesline and then her eyes caught the tattered corset on the line.

"Did you destroy my uniform?" she asked angrily, pushing past me to look at it.

"You don't work there anymore."

"You don't get to decide where I work, Ryker!" She yelled back. "I have four jobs to keep these four walls up around me and because of tips from that job I can sometimes swing a meal or two, but I can't afford another corset to replace that one and eat, you fucker!"

"You don't need to replace it because you aren't working there anymore! How else do I need to say it, so you understand?"

"Fuck you!" She bit out.

"Don't tempt me." I growled back and she froze. "I'm not the same man I was when you were a kid Elora. Fuck, I was just a kid then myself. So, you need to be well aware of what kind of animal you're poking every single time you try to defy me. I won't just stand by and let you do it like I would have before. I'm not that kind of man anymore."

"What kind of man are you then?" she asked, her eyes widened with fear as I took a step towards her though her spine stiffened in defiance.

"The kind of man that consumes those who are weak. The kind of man that takes what he wants and doesn't ask for permission or forgiveness. The kind of man that you should have been spared from, yet here you are, years later and in desperate need of my help. So you're going to get it, whether you want it or not." I said and took the final step towards her as her back hit the wall.

"Ryker." She panted and her eyes fell to my lips for a fraction of a second before snapping back up to my eyes.

"Grab whatever else you think you will want from here and let's go. I'm exhausted and in dire need of a shower and I have an ache in my soul the size of Texas to get you under my roof once and for all. So, let's go."

I turned and walked over to her couch and threw myself down on it as she stared at me.

It took her a couple of minutes of staring angrily at me, but she finally started moving around her apartment, grabbing various items and adding them to the bag. Before too long she stood before me, changed into a pair of jeans and a tank top, with a bra this time, thank God, and was ready to go.

"You're not coming back here." I said firmly. "My guys will have it emptied out and whatever else you want we can bring to my house, but this is no longer your apartment, do you understand?"

"I don't want anything else from here. Leave it for the next person." She replied, her eyes were downcast and her voice soft.

I was upsetting her by relocating her, I knew that. But it was for her own good, I would make sure she saw that soon enough.

We walked down the hallway to the stairs, and I could distinctly hear a woman being fucked, and another one arguing with her man through their thin doors. I glared at Ellie, but she just shrugged her shoulders.

"It was what I could afford." she said plainly. I needed to know just how bad her life had been these last few years because the unknown was eating away at me.

When we got down to my car, Zeke stood next to the back door with his arms crossed over his chest as he waited for us. He was a bit surprised to see Ellie walking down next to me and he raised his eyebrows at me quickly before dropping them down. I guess he assumed I'd have to drag her kicking and screaming from here, but he hid it well enough.

I slid my hand over the small of her back as I handed her bag to Zeke and opened the door. She jumped up into the seat and slid over as I got in next to her without any fight.

She looked out the window as we drove away, but there wasn't exactly sadness on her face as she watched the landscape of the city change.

"Where do you live?" Her voice was soft still.

"In East Valley."

She snickered and looked over at me with a small smile pulling her lips. "You live in East Valley?" she asked, shocked.

"What's so hard to believe about that?"

"Your neighbors must be scandalized with your riff raff coming and going into their gated community."

"Believe it or not Ellie, my home is my get away. I don't conduct an overly large amount of business there. It's where I go to relax and find peace."

"Then why would you take me there? It seems as though I bring you anything but peace."

I laughed this time, though it didn't hold much humor. "Something tells me you're the only thing in the world that will ever bring me true peace."

Her mouth fell lax, and her eyes narrowed in disbelief as I continued. "You just have to allow me to give you peace in return El. That's how this is going to work."

She closed her mouth and looked back out her window. "I don't see how that's possible when for the last five years, all you've given me is heartache."

Zeke looked at me in the mirror with a pensive glance but then looked ahead at the road.

I didn't say anything else on the rest of the trip and before too long we were pulling through the gates at the end of my driveway and rolling up to my home.

I watched Ellie's face as she took in the property and loved the way her lips parted in wonder as she saw it for the first time. I was proud of my home; I'd worked hard to buy it and upgrade it how I wanted over the last three years. But bringing her home to it with the purpose of having her live here with me, made me feel something so much more than pride.

We walked in the front door and my housekeeper Margaret came out of the kitchen, wiping her hands on a towel and stopped short when she saw the beautiful brunette walk in behind me.

"Oh, hello Mr. Lawson." She said.

"Margaret." I nodded, I held my hand out for Ellie, and she stepped forward and let me put my hand on her back as she fit into my side. "This is Elora Dax, Gavin's daughter." My housekeepers' eyes widened as she looked at Ellie as if she was some mythical creature. "She'll be living here with me. She is welcome to anything in the home and should be made comfortable any way possible."

"Yes! Of course." Margaret said, reaching forward to take Ellie's outstretched hand.

"Please call me Ellie." She said sweetly and smiled at the older woman.

"As you wish dear." Margaret said. She was in her fifties and was just one of those women who exuded mothering to anyone she came in contact with and as I saw the warm exchange between the two, I couldn't help but hope that perhaps Margaret could help ease some wounds on Ellie's heart from not having a real mother in her life.

"Come with me, I'll show you around." I said into Ellie's ear. I kept my arm around her side and slid my hand over her hip, pulling her closer to my side as I walked through the foyer towards the living area.

She didn't fight me on it, but I looked down and saw how she chewed on her lip as she looked around.

I showed her the kitchen, living room, dining room, my office, and the den before taking her out back to show her the inground pool and hot tub on the back patio. And then I took her upstairs to show her where she would be sleeping.

I opened the door to the guest room that I knew would be perfect for her and stepped aside so she could look around. Zeke had already put her bag up on the bench at the end of the bed and she walked around.

It was a large room, the biggest guest suite in the house. There was a large white four post bed with white and gold bedding, all of the furniture was white with gold accents and there were windows on two of the walls, letting bright natural light in.

She let her hand glide over the bed as she walked by and then went into the attached bathroom.

I followed after her, even though I knew what fantasies my brain would conjure up seeing her in the room.

She looked around the space, eyeing the double vanity, large walk-in glass shower with two showering stations in it and then the giant soaker tub under a window. And as soon as I saw her in the room, I envisioned her laying back in the tub, with her dark hair piled on top of her head and her tiny toes up on the ledge as bubbles covered every other inch of her body while she relaxed with me sitting behind her, holding her in my arms. Or better yet, I saw her sexy curvy body pressed against the glass of the shower while I fucked her deep.

My cock hardened for the millionth time since she walked into my club last night and she turned to look at me in the same moment.

"Thank you." she said softly and walked towards me cautiously.

"You don't owe me any thanks."

"I'm not sure what you expect from me now that I'm here though."

"What do you mean?" I asked, confused as more blood pumped to my lower head and left my actual brain lacking.

"What am I supposed to do with my day? Work for you in one of your clubs? Clean your home? Be at your beckoned call? What do you want in return for this?" She asked as her eyes dropped down my body to my hard on that strained against my slacks. Her eyes widened and she licked her lips quickly.

I should have turned and left the room.

I should have told her she wasn't expected to do anything but enjoy life now that she was here.

But I was a shit ass man and having her here, in my home, looking at me with innocent question in her eyes as she licked her lush lips made me answer her in a way I shouldn't have.

I closed the last foot of distance between us and slid my fingers under her jaw to make her look up at me. My skin sizzled where it touched hers and her nostrils flared as she tore her eyes from my belt to meet my eyes.

"If you're asking if I'm expecting you to spread your legs for me in payment for letting you live here, you seriously underestimate me as not only someone who cares for you, but also as a man." She swallowed quickly, the muscles tensing under my fingers, I slid my hand from her jaw around to the side of her face and tucked her hair behind her ear. "If I wanted you only for your body, I would have taken you on my desk last night when you were pressing your thighs together, trying to ease the ache I put there."

She sucked in a shaky breath and licked her lips again, holding my stare boldly regardless of the conversation. I continued on, "I won't lie to you and tell you that I'm not hard as a rock for you or that your body, all grown up and mature, doesn't drive me wild with need," I growled out and wrapped my hand around the back of her head and pulled her flush to the front of my body as I let my other hand slide down to her hip. She put both of her hands on my stomach and twisted her fingers into the fabric of my shirt. My cock twitched against her stomach and her eyelids fluttered closed and then reopened. "When I give you nice things, I don't expect some sort of payment of skin in return from you. I may be a monster to every other person in the world

Elora, but not with you. If I take you, it will be because you want me as badly as I want you and you'll have to beg me to do it."

"And If I never beg you?" She whispered.

"Then I never take you." I answered easily. Though I hated saying those words out loud. "If your dad was alive, he'd put a bullet between my eyes for what I'm thinking about you right now Elora, but I can't help it. I won't touch you again after this unless you beg me too. You're welcome here for the rest of your life regardless, but I wanted to at least put words to the electricity between us, because I know you feel it just as much as I do. In the end the decision is yours."

I pulled back and took one last longing look at her and then walked out of the bathroom and then out of the room and straight down the hallway into my own.

I stripped on the way to my shower and stepped inside with the water on ice cold.

"Jesus fuck." I cursed as the icy water cleared my brain and softened my dick.

What the fuck had I just done?

CHAPTER 7 – ELORA

H e wanted me.

Holy shit, Ryker Lawson wanted – me.

I threw myself into the center of the giant plush king size bed and tried to suppress the girly giggle that wanted to bubble up at how good it felt to be here.

I needed to keep my head about me because while it was nice to be welcomed in a home with food in the cupboards, that welcome could expire at any given time.

And this warm home also came with something I was scared of.

The predator in Ryker.

I'd seen it years ago when he didn't know I was looking. I'd seen the way he was around women and back then the idea of being treated like a game of cat and mouse repulsed me. But now, as a grown woman who was suddenly finding myself in the role of mouse, I wanted to play.

But I'd be lying if I said I wanted to be just another notch on Ryker's bedpost. I wasn't that kind of girl, I'd never allowed anyone to treat me that way before, and I wouldn't let him. But I wasn't naive enough to think for even one moment that he wanted anything other than a warm body to play with.

If I gave him the chance, he'd play with me, hell I don't think the word play was even strong enough for what he'd do to me. Nonetheless he'd have his fun, and he'd be on to the next one before I even realized how twisted he got me.

He'd twist me up in his bed and in my head and I'd be the one paying the consequences for our actions in the long run.

And I wasn't sure if I'd survive it when he got bored and cast me off again as it was, let alone if I gave him my body to become bored with too.

My phone rang and I pulled it from my pocket.

Jay. Shit.

"Hello." I said quietly into the phone.

"Where the fuck are you?" Jay's voice was loud and powerful through the phone, and I could hear the buzz of traffic around him.

"Uh- where are you? I can hardly hear you?" I avoided the question; I wasn't sure how to discuss this with him yet.

"I'm at your apartment and its fucking empty El, like the door is broken, wide open and every single thing is gone. What the fuck is going on?"

Shit.

"I moved." I tried to sound nonchalant.

"Where?" He was anything but.

"Into Ryker's."

There was a long pause and then he sighed. "What's going on between you two?"

I looked up at the ceiling and weighed my options here. Ryker was his boss, but Jay had been my friend the last few years and I felt like I owed him some sort of reasoning. "He was my dad's best friend before he died. He was a giant part of my life growing up and he promised my dad he would take care of me. Stuff happened that I don't really understand completely right now but–," I sighed and fought to find the words to explain it the best way I could, "it wasn't like I was living the good life on my own."

"So, you just moved in with him, just like that?"

"Well have you met him? He didn't really give me another option."

"Ellie, I don't like this. Ryker is—I mean, frankly he's a bad dude. He's the most feared man in the whole northern half of the state for fuck sakes. I don't think you should be there."

"I appreciate your concern Jay, really, I do. But at this point I don't have another option."

"He's not just doing this because he owed it to your dad. Frankie and Mason agreed when we got kicked out and he made you stay last night. He wants you Ellie and frankly you're in way over your head. He's a predatory man babe, and you're, well you're innocent and trusting and sweet."

"That's just who I wanted you three to see me as Jay, I'm really far more than that." The sunlight glowing in the room suddenly seemed less vibrant.

"Why don't you stay with Carly? Or me? Come and stay with me. I can protect you like he can, and I can provide for you Ellie. It'd be safer to be with me than him."

"It's not that simple, there's past that runs deep here. But don't worry about him, he already said he wouldn't touch me without my consent. So don't worry about me being held against my will up here in his tower or something." I tried laughing but it sounded weak.

"Do you want him to touch you?" He asked, and his voice sounded jealous.

"Jay." I warned.

"Tell me, I've spent the last two years hitting on you and hooking up with you and now you're just what? Just moving in with the king and being his mistress?"

I didn't answer him, his tone was upsetting me and there was a knock on my door, silencing any snide remark I was planning on making to him.

I slid off the bed and walked to my door and opened it, keeping the phone to my ear. Jay continued on his tirade, saying things he'd never be able to take back, but I wasn't listening because a shirtless and wet Ryker stood in the hallway outside of my room and looked sinfully delicious. He was fresh out of the shower, his skin smelled spicy with his soap, and I was snapped back into every fantasy I'd had of him over the years from the sight and scent of him alone. He wore a pair of black athletic shorts and nothing else.

His face was relaxed, more so than when he'd left, but apparently Jay was loud enough that Ryker could hear him because his face darkened, and his eyes burned as he reached up and gently took the phone from my ear before placing it against his. He listened for a moment as his employee said only God knows what, before he cut him off.

"This is your one warning Jay. If you ever say anything so heinous to Elora again, I'll slice every inch of skin off your body slowly and methodically, keeping you alive until the last piece is gone and then I'll shove it all down your fucking throat before I slit it. Better yet, don't let me catch you near her or calling her again. I've killed better men for less, and none of them had tried fucking with what's mine."

Ry hung the phone up and took a deep breath, never letting his eyes leave mine as I leaned on the door for support.

How did this man make controlling me so damn sexy, in a way that I didn't mind it one bit? Where had the strong independent woman gone that had survived on her own for years, enduring unimaginable hardships. Because the woman I'd become, was melting into the door as my body became a puddle.

"You're doing it again Ellie." Ryker said, handing me my phone back.

"Doing what?" My voice was a whisper with a hint of mystique as I tried to calm my racing heart. I went to take my phone from his hand, but he held it firm in his grip and my fingers landed on his. Everything in me wanted to rip my hand back at the electricity that burned my skin, but I forced myself to hold still and endure, accepting the challenge in his eyes.

"You're pressing your thighs together, trying to pleasure yourself. Right here in front of me like I somehow can't tell what I do to you."

I stood up off the door, spreading my legs wide from where they had been pressed together and took a deep breath pulling my phone from his hand firmly. "How do you know I'm not feeling the sexual tension from my phone conversation with Jay?" I knew I'd regret pitting them against each other, and from Ry's threat a moment ago, it could be potentially dangerous to Jay's health to even pretend.

Ryker's nostrils flared and his lips pressed into a flat line as he took a step towards me, I forced my feet to stay rooted in the carpet as he did and the very front of my shirt covering my breasts slid against his bare abdomen as I tilted my head back to look up at him.

He didn't touch me anywhere else other than the soft brush of skin at his chest, but I felt like his entire body caressed mine as he looked at me.

"Don't ever say anything so insulting to me again doll." He purred as his jaw clenched, his eyes dropped to my lips and then he slowly brought his hand up to the side of my face, giving me ample time to tell him not to or move out of his reach but I didn't.

I wanted his skin to touch mine so badly that my face burned where his fingers hovered a fraction of an inch from it.

He was waiting for me to beg. But I couldn't beg for something I didn't understand, and I couldn't comprehend what it would mean to give myself to him. So instead, I kept my lips shut and let my eye lids flutter closed as I tipped my head and rubbed my neck against the calloused tips of his fingers.

And it was enough to tempt him.

He slid his fingers softly along the skin there before cupping my cheek with his large warm palm and tangling his fingers in the hair at my nape.

"Tell me you want me." He whispered, leaning down until his lips hovered over my other ear, but he didn't touch me anywhere else other than where his hand held my face. "Beg me."

I opened my eyes and let my fear of him take over the need for him that I felt coursing through my veins and calmed my racing heart.

But I didn't want to reject him either. Not completely. I just didn't know how to tell him I was so much more inexperienced than he was, and I was scared of being consumed by him. So instead I tilted my head just enough to let my teeth grasp his ear lobe and sucked it into my mouth quickly before scraping my teeth across it as I let it pop from my lips.

"No." I whispered. He groaned and leaned into my touch, and I heard the wood of the door creak above my head where his other hand landed and squeezed. "Not yet." I added and took a shaky step back as my chest rose with a trembling breath.

He turned his head to look at me and his eyes were the darkest I'd ever seen, they were nearly black, and his body vibrated with what I was hoping was need, like mine was.

He held my stare for a long moment as he fought to control his reaction to me and then stood up to his full height, towering over me once more.

"I came here to invite you downstairs for lunch and a long overdue conversation about what has happened over the last five years, but I can't even think straight right now."

"Join the club." I smiled softly at him, trying to lighten the mood between us.

"The only thing stopping me from going back on my word and dragging you into my bed right now is my vow to your father, and my need for food. So consider yourself lucky Ellie." He said, and then took a few steps back and watched me closely.

"I'll be down in a minute."

"Why not just come down right now?" He stopped walking backwards and looked up and down my body, still wearing my jeans and a hoodie.

I wanted him to look at me as a woman, and not a teenager like I'd dressed as, so I decided to poke his bear again. "This conversation has left me with a need to take care of something so I can focus in your presence for the next conversation."

His eyes flashed again and the muscles in his chest and abs tightened as he took a step towards me again, but I had expected that. I quickly stepped into my room and closed the door as I told him, "Be down in a few."

I locked the door and heard his hand land on the wood in frustration and bit my lip to hide my smile.

I ran to the bathroom and locked that door too for good measure as I stripped out of my clothes and jumped into the shower. My intent had been to take a quick cold shower to freshen up, but then I eyed the handheld wand as I washed my body and felt a wicked idea burn into my brain.

I grabbed the handle and slid through the spray settings and found one that I knew would do just the trick.

Placing my foot onto the bench in between the two shower stations I opened myself up as I slid the spray from the wand down my body and gasped when it landed on the sensitive nub of nerves between my legs.

"Holy shit." I moaned and put my free hand on my breast and slid my nails over the tight flesh of my puckered nipple. I let my nails flick at the ring through my nipple and moaned as the dual sensation was exactly what I needed to light a fire in my soul.

I thought about how sexy Ry looked with no shirt on wearing only low-slung shorts, with his hair wet and messy as he stood outside my door. I thought about his possessive words to Jay, claiming me as his and how it had made my insides turn soft. Then I thought about how good he smelt and the way his skin lit an inferno against mine when he had cupped my face.

I imagined what his hands would feel like if they were on my breasts in place of mine, if he was using his strong large fingers to flick and pinch my nipples.

I threw my head back as the spray pulsed on my clit perfectly and pinched my nipple painfully as an orgasm ripped through my body, making my back arch and my toes fall numb as it wrecked me. Dropping the handheld, I grasped the bench as I fell onto it, completely destroyed by the biggest orgasm of my life.

"Oh my god." I whispered into the steaming shower as tingles and jolts of electricity continued to pulse into my clit long after the shock waves had stopped sliding down the rest of my body.

I was in so much trouble with this alpha man.

And I was pretty sure I was going to love every single second of it, if it felt as good as this did.

CHAPTER 8 – RYKER

She was upstairs playing with her pussy, and it was driving me fucking insane.

I sat at the kitchen counter, trying desperately to focus on the hundreds of emails I had to answer but all I could see was Elora spread out in that giant white bed with her smooth thighs spread wide and her hands playing with her little pink pussy.

"Here you go, sir." Margaret said, laying down a delicious looking club sandwich in front of me and setting a soda next to it. She laid an identical one down next to me and looked at me questioningly.

I grunted and said, "She should be down in a moment." She smiled and walked away.

I heard soft feet padding across the marble floor behind me and turned to look over my shoulder.

Fucking hell, the girl was going to kill me.

Elora strode towards me with a face the color of a sunset as she looked at her feet. Which were bare and sexy as fuck. Her hair was wet and pulled up into a messy bun on top of her head and she wore a yellow sundress with small red flowers on it; it was short sleeve and fell to just the tops of her thighs and I was hooked.

Elora Dax was my new favorite drug, and I hadn't even had a taste yet.

"Hi." Her voice was breathless as she slid onto the stool next to me. I looked at her out of the side of my eye and let my gaze rove over her face and cleavage as she arranged herself and then looked over at me with challenge in her eyes. "It's rude to stare." she said boldly.

She picked up her soda and took a small drink as I quarreled back, "It's also rude to play with your pussy in someone else's home and not even invite them to watch."

She choked on her drink and coughed as her face flared to an even brighter color of red. She looked around the room to see if anyone else was near to hear but we were alone, I wouldn't have exposed her in front of one of my men. In fact, the idea of any of them even thinking about her body made me red with rage.

"Tell me about it." I said, turning on my stool to stare directly at her, my long legs caged her in from the front and the back.

She licked her lips as she regained the ability to breathe and turned in her seat to face me head on. Her ability to challenge me kept me so aroused it was painful.

"Tell me what my mom said to you."

My libido plummeted to the basement, and I pursed my lips at her, but she didn't waver.

I turned back to the counter and took another bite of my sandwich, and she did the same. They were too damn good to leave untouched for long. After a few bites and some minutes to get my head focused on the task at hand I answered her.

"It was a year or so after your dad died, I'd been sending money each month for your school tuition and every other expense related to you and she came into my office to ask for more. Said she was moving you to the East Coast to be closer to Princeton for your last two years of high school and that she needed more money for your upcoming school expenses."

"And you believed her and gave her more."

"Of course, I wanted to support your dreams anyway I could. Even if that meant you were leaving me." I hated the emotion that laced the words, it had hurt to let her go, even when she was sixteen.

"You'd left me long before that." Her voice was soft, and I could hear the pain in it but there was no anger that I had expected.

"I didn't know shit about being a good influence in your life Elora. You were a teenage girl who had just lost her father, and I was knee fucking deep in the shit following the fallout of all that."

She put her sandwich down and wiped her hands on a napkin before turning to face me, her brows were pinched and her eyes sad as she looked at my face, like she was trying to find the lie. "I was a teenage girl who had lost the only man who had ever loved me, and in the same year I lost my very best friend, and the only man that could come close to making me feel safe like my dad had. You walked out without a backwards glance, and it hurt almost as much as dad dying in my arms that night."

Her voice broke and she looked down at the floor. I slid my finger under her jaw and made her look back up at me. I hated to see the tears pooling in her lashes as she fought to keep them from falling. "I didn't do it lightly Ellie, I fought the urge to come after you, every single day for years, but I truly thought what I was doing was best for you. Even if it was the hardest thing I'd ever done short of lowering Gavin's body into the ground the day of his funeral."

She chewed on her lip as she contemplated what I'd said. "We never left California, though it had felt like a foreign country when we moved."

"Where did you go?"

"South LA."

My blood boiled, "Son of a bitch." South LA was almost as bad as Shadeport in terms of crime and gang violence, and even her name couldn't protect her there. "What happened there? You said you've been on your own since you were sixteen. That was right about the time you moved."

She sighed and looked away again. She played with the hem of her dress, no longer interested in her sandwich and I turned on my seat again to face her. I put a hand on her lower back and rubbed it in small circles, trying to sooth her as much as I could as she fought through dark memories. I could tell by watching her that it wasn't good, and I knew I had to control my reaction to whatever she told me, or she would clam up and I wouldn't get any more information from her.

"I don't know what mom did with your money, but I assure you I never saw a dime of it, either directly or indirectly through things like rent or groceries."

I stayed silent and let her continue at her own pace.

"She moved us into a shit apartment that made my last one look like a palace. She was never there; she was out getting high or just being a degenerate to society which was fine with me for the most part, but her not being there left me vulnerable."

"Vulnerable how?" I asked, my voice like ice. I knew the answer, but I needed to know.

"The gang that occupied most of the apartments there wouldn't leave me alone. There was a grandmother in the apartment across from ours that most of them respected and she would chase off who she could when she could, but it wasn't any real security. I didn't sleep for months; I was terrified that if I fell asleep there I wouldn't hear when they tried to break in or something. I started sleeping through my classes and began flunking out and spending all of my time at the library for some peace and quiet."

I was going to find her mother and make her pay for leaving her unprotected.

"It all came to a head though, because a few months after my sixteenth birthday, mom pissed away all the money she had, and the landlord was at the door to evict us."

She stopped talking as her eyes got a faraway look in them like she was looking but not seeing anything.

"She was dating a man at the time, or I should say she belonged to a man at that time, who was a pimp. They forced me into his car and took me to a seedy motel down the street and threw me in the room. I knew I was in trouble, and I tried to get away the whole time, but they outnumbered and easily outweighed me."

My fists curled and my body coiled tightly, I was going to snap with anger if I didn't do something. I wrapped my arms around her waist and picked her up and set her down on my lap. Her eyes went wide in shock, but she slid her arms around my shoulders and held on as I took a deep breath at her temple to calm myself.

"They locked me inside the room, and I watched in horror as a line of men started forming outside the window, waiting for their turn to come in and—." Her voice cut out and a tear slid down her cheek. "They were paying my mom twenty bucks each to come in and rape her sixteen-year-old daughter, and my mom laughed and joked with them all, like some skin salesman. The first man, paid two hundred dollars, because he was getting the honor of taking my virginity when he raped me."

Scratch that, I was going to torture Paula Granger for months to make her pay for what she did.

"The bathroom window was nailed shut, and I clawed at it until my fingers bled and ended up getting it open. The thing was hardly one foot wide, but she'd been starving me for so long I managed to get through it before the first man came in. I ran for my life, and I never looked back. I was homeless by myself for years from that moment on."

"You're so incredibly strong Elora, you get that from Gav." I whispered into her hair as she slashed at the tears falling down her cheeks.

Zeke walked into the kitchen, silently catching my eye but stopped when he saw Elora crying on my lap. I nodded to him, and he turned on his heels and left, leaving her to bare her soul to me in privacy.

"It was terrible for that year and a half that I was with her after dad died. She starved me, beat me, and drugged me endlessly with whatever she could get her hands on to control me with. I'd tried to commit suicide three times but failed because I didn't have a clue what I was doing. But being homeless at sixteen in South LA was no walk in the park either. I survived by eating out of dumpsters and panhandling on the freeway and living in shelters one night at a time. I've worked my ass off every single day since then to survive. I have four jobs right now to stay afloat because I refuse to go out and get a job like Carly has. I just can't bring myself to sell my body to survive, it hits too close to what I almost suffered for me to willingly choose it now. So I bartend, and clean houses, and waitress and anything else legal that I can find to make rent."

"It's all my fault." I said, as intense guilt and grief weighed down my black heart. I squeezed her to me and felt regret over every single second that I'd left her alone. "I'm never letting you go again Elora." I pushed her hair back with my hand and she looked at me, but I could see the fear in her eyes that I could be lying to her. "I promise you."

"You don't owe me anything, your vow to my dad, it doesn't—" She tried but I silenced her.

"This vow isn't one I'm trying to fulfil to your dad anymore; it's one I should have made to you. So, I'm making it now, from this moment on Elora, you have my protection from anything in this world that plagues you. I want you to live here with me and let me take care of you the way you deserve, you're a Queen and you deserve to be treated as such. You're never going to worry about where your next meal will come from or who to trust, because you can trust me."

She looked at me pensively but nodded slowly and sighed. "I suppose only time will prove it to me."

That made me sad for her, but I understood it. "Then just give me time."

Turning away, she broke our eye contact, the lingering demand of my gaze finally relinquished as she returned to her half-eaten sandwich; I remembered that overwhelming need to finish a meal when you didn't know where your next one would come from. It was how I'd spent most of my childhood.

Instead of letting her go to her own stool again, I pulled her plate over next to mine and picked my sandwich up and took a bite, signaling to her how I wanted her to proceed.

She scoffed at me and rolled her eyes but picked her sandwich up and took a bite. I watched her fanatically as she chewed and swallowed, oblivious of what she was doing to me.

It was hard to hide though, given that her lush ass was pressed against my crotch, and I was rapidly hardening under her as she enthusiastically ate her meal.

She leaned over to grab her soda, and my cock twitched and she froze, sitting back up right with a straight spine.

I chuckled at her and let my hand fall to the swell of her ass under her hip but didn't say anything and she didn't make any move to remove herself from my lap.

Instead, she swung both legs up and over my other leg and crossed her ankles, settling in more, rubbing her warm center right on top of my erection. Her dress had ridden up and the only thing pressing against my shorts were her panties.

With her in my lap, I couldn't resist the urge to tease her playfully.

"So, tell me about your alone time upstairs." I said huskily.

She stilled and set her empty plate down on the counter as she finished eating, before taking a sip of her drink to wash it all down.

"What do you want to know?" Her voice was breathy and soft as she tried to act dismissive.

But I knew her deeply and I recognized her body reacting to my words.

"I want to know exactly how you played with yourself, and I want to know what you thought about when you did."

"How do you know I actually did and didn't just make it all up to razz you?" She challenged, looking up at me as she absentmindedly played with her dress hem again.

"Tell me the truth, I'm dying to know." I purred into her ear as she rolled her shoulders and let her head fall to the side a bit. "I know you can feel my cock under you, I know you can feel how hard I am. That's all for you Elora, it's all because of you. Throw a starving man a bone here, would you?"

She moaned, the sweet sound swarmed into my senses, and I cataloged it away into my memory bank forever. "Hmm, one of many moans for my ears to hear." I mused and she gasped and opened her eyes to glare at me. I chuckled and let my nose run up the side of her throat to behind her ear and whispered deeply, "It's the sexiest thing I've ever heard before."

"Liar." She challenged. But moved back to the beforehand topic. "You really want to know?" Her voice was still soft, and I could hear the doubt and embarrassment in it.

"Close your eyes." I said, and she balked at me, but I laughed and slid my hand over her long black lashes. Finally, she obliged and closed her eyes, leaving them closed even after I dropped my hand. "Where did you do it?"

She swallowed, the column of her throat worked with the motion, and I imagined it doing that with something of mine in her mouth. I forced myself to focus on the present, breathing deeply to center myself in the now.

"Your giant shower."

I growled and she popped one eye open to look at me and then snapped it shut again when I scowled at her. I laid my hand on her leg, right above her knee and let my thumb slide under the hem of her dress an inch. "You played with your sexy little pussy in my shower?"

"Yes."

"Tell me how."

She bit her lip, and her breathing got deeper as she thought about it. A small smile pulled up one side of her mouth and I knew she was going to make this hard on me like I was for her. "I used the handheld shower head and sprayed my clit with it."

I felt my nostrils flare and buried my nose in her hair. "Fuck, that's hot."

"Yes, it was." She laughed erotically and replied.

"Give me every detail. I need more. I'm desperate with need." I slid my hand up higher on her leg and let my thumb dip between her milky thighs and she surprised me by adjusting herself on my lap and opening her legs a bit wider to me.

"Good girl." I whispered.

That spurred her on for more, "I put one foot up on the bench and used the sprayer on my pussy and played with my tits with my other hand." She started and licked her lips, keeping her eyes closed like I'd told her too and then continued, "I pinched and pulled my nipples while I pulsed the water on and off of my clit, and I had the biggest orgasm of my life."

"Your pierced nipples?" I asked, squeezing her thigh. I wanted desperately to kiss her neck and lips and let my hand travel higher between her open thighs. But I fervently wanted to hear her beg first.

She snapped her eyes open and turned to look at me head on with shock on her face. "How did you—" She gasped and shook her head back and forth in confusion.

"I watched you sleep for a while this morning at your apartment." A smile pulled my lips up as I remembered the beautiful sight she had been. "You rolled over and stretched at one point and your lush, beautiful tits pulled against the shirt you were wearing and now I can't think about anything else but feeling them in my mouth and between my fingers." My hand on her ass squeezed and she rolled her hips, pressing her thighs together, squeezing my thumb between them. "Careful baby, you're rubbing your hot pussy on my lap every single time you wiggle. And I'm only a man with so much restraint."

"You mean you'd do something about it without me begging you to?" She asked, looking at my lips and not my eyes.

"Maybe." I licked my lips and then smirked at the way hers popped open on a sigh. "Tell me more about you in the shower. What were you thinking about while you played with your clit and pierced tits?"

She groaned again and then almost hid her smirk before rolling her hips once more. My hand squeezed tightly on her hip to still her as I dropped my forehead to hers.

"I thought about you. I thought about how much you've changed these last few years, and how powerful you looked last night in your office, commanding men around me. I thought about how hot you look right now with no shirt on, and how sexy your tattoos are and then I fantasized about what it would feel like to have your hands on my body instead of my own. I came so hard I fell to the floor."

"Fuck this." I snapped and stood up quickly with her in my arms. She shrieked and clung to my neck as I sat her on the counter and pulled her thighs apart far enough for me to step between and pressed myself against her. She moaned and her nails dug into my biceps as I rocked my hips against her. "Beg me. Tell me you want me as much as I want you." I demanded.

A pained moan fell from her lips, but she quickly bit them to stop anything else from coming out.

"Anything you want Elora, as little or as much as you want, you're in control."

"Do you promise?" She asked, her breath light on my lips only an inch off of hers. I pressed my forehead to hers again and grasped both of her hips in my hands. I could almost touch my fingers together; her waist was so small beneath my hands.

"I promise, I'm crazed with the need to taste you Elora, but wherever you draw the line I will respect it."

"Kiss me, Ryker." She whispered, and licked her lips, her tongue was tiny and soft pink against the dusty rose of her lush lips, and I groaned. "Please Ry, please kiss me and give me what I've wanted since I was hardly even a teenager."

I couldn't hold back anymore; I pressed forward and eliminated the distance between us and pressed my lips to hers. It was such a surreal array of emotions, feeling her lips on mine. I never imagined her in a sexual way until she walked into my office last night, looking like sin wrapped in a scrap of lace, and now I was obsessed with her. It was like years of being her friend, made it so easy to morph into something deeper now that we were both adults. I coaxed her lips open and pressed my tongue into her mouth and my tastebuds exploded with her flavor.

"Yes." She moaned and slid her hands up my arms and neck and into the hair at the back of my head, scraping her nails over my skin until goose bumps broke out over my flesh. When was the last time someone gave me such a visceral reaction, with just their lips and fingertips before?

She tilted her head and deepened the kiss, and I hungrily drank from her, taking every single thing she was willing to give me. She was hesitant with her kisses when I pulled back and let her take the lead, almost like she wasn't used to being kissed like this. The thought both pained me and excited me. She deserved to be kissed like this every single day, but if no one had been doing it over the years, I wasn't going to complain that she had let me fill that role right now.

I pulled my lips from hers and slid them around to her ear and sucked on her lobe like she had done to me earlier and then scraped my teeth down her neck. She threw her head back giving me better access and a gift I didn't deserve. Fuck if I wasn't going to take it from her though.

I sucked on the skin and bit it, marking her as she moaned and begged me for more. She grabbed my hand from her waist and slid it around her side and to her breast and pressed her chest forward, filling my hand.

"You're so sexy." I panted and dropped my mouth to the top of her cleavage and sucked on the skin as I worked down to the neckline of her dress.

"I need more." She panted and I eagerly pulled the fabric down, revealing one sinfully voluptuous breast to the cold air and my dark stare as I leaned forward to take a taste. Fucking hell, her nipple was so pretty with a piercing in it. Perfection.

"Ryker darling! Where are you?" A shrill voice pierced the silence of the foyer, making Elora gasp as she snapped her eyes open, locking onto mine. She yanked the fabric of her dress from my grasp, the rough texture a stark contrast to her smooth skin, pulling it up to shield herself. She shoved me backwards and jumped from the counter.

Her feet had just landed on the marble floor when I heard the click of heels coming towards us and groaned at the intrusion.

Her eyes, wide and frantic, darted from me to the kitchen doorway; a silent scream held captive behind her lips, and I almost hoped she'd run, sparing us both this difficult exchange. The air crackled with tension and I knew before it was done, she was going to be hurt.

CHAPTER 9 – ELORA

I sought Ryker's help, but his scowl was sharp as he looked away from my rapidly rising and falling chest, to the doorway, the silence amplifying the frantic rhythm of my breaths.

Within seconds a woman appeared and stopped mid step when she saw us standing there. She was blonde and skinny as a rail in an elegant knee length dress the color of her turquois eyes and white pumps.

Her hair was pulled up into a twist at her nape and her makeup was heavy but somehow still elegant. She was probably Ryker's age and standing in the same room as her, barefoot in a cotton summer dress with my skin flushed and my lips swollen, I felt so childish and naive compared to her.

And I hated the way she looked at Ryker's bare chest openly like she had a right too.

Did she have a right too?

"I'm sorry, I didn't realize you were entertaining, baby." She purred and started walking into the kitchen again.

I couldn't tear my eyes away from the car crash in front of me as she walked into Ryker's space and stood up on tip toes to kiss him on the lips, and the son of a bitch leaned down the last two inches and kissed her back, letting his hands fall to her nonexistent hips as he did.

She fell back to her heels and turned in my direction and smirked at me, before sliding on a fake smile and holding out her hand in greeting. "I'm Monica Wellington, and who might you be?"

The hair on the back of my neck stood up as I forced my breathing to slow down and look neutral and unaffected. Walls of hardened emotion, erected long ago, rebuilt themselves around my heart, a cold, heavy feeling settling over me; I stared blankly at her hand, then up to her face, my expression unreadable. For years I played a part, hiding my self and my feelings behind that wall where it was safe, unable to be used against me. And as she stared at me, waiting for me to do what she expected, I slid back into that role. Raising one eyebrow at her, I ignored her hand and turned my attention to the bastard standing behind her, shirtless with my taste still on his lips.

His face was cool and to the untrained eye, someone would think he was unaffected by everything. But I knew better; I saw the barely perceptible squint in his eyes, fixed on my face, conveying unspoken things, his hands clenched at his sides, and the almost imperceptible ticking in his jaw as his teeth ground together.

He wasn't unaffected, and neither was I. But I was going to outdo him and make him pay for this entire situation.

"Elora." I said coolly, "Dax." I offered no title since she didn't, but I enjoyed the way her eyes widened when she recognized my name and who I was.

"Elora." She said softly and turned to look at Ryker and then back to me. "Are you visiting?" she asked me as Ryker continued his silence and his brooding.

"I was." I said and pushed my hair off my shoulder, "But my friend offered to let me come stay with him, so I'll be leaving later today."

"Elora." Ryker warned, finally breaking his silence and Monica turned to him, waiting for more. But he was a coward and offered nothing to either of us.

"Right." I said and nodded my head. "It was nice meeting you Melissa. If you'll please excuse me, I have some packing to do."

I didn't wait for an answer from either of them and turned and walked out of the kitchen with a straight spine and unfaltering steps until I got to the bottom of the stairs and then ran up them as fast as I could.

I knew it was too good to be true.

Tears stupidly burnt the back of my eyes as I grabbed my bag and loaded up the few items I'd been dumb enough to unpack. I slid open the ride sharing app on my phone and ordered a car; relieved to see that it was only a five-minute wait.

Thank fuck for a nice neighborhood.

I took one last longing look at the room I'd wanted so badly to sleep in tonight and then walked out, without looking back as the door shut behind me.

I walked down the stairs quietly and could hear Ryker and Monica talking in the kitchen and I could tell I was the topic of discussion. Ryker was pissed, and her voice was even more shrill than it had been before as she accused him of fucking me on the kitchen counter when she walked in.

I didn't stick around to hear anymore, knowing it was my out. I made it to the front door when Zeke came down the hallway from the right and made eye contact with me as I opened the front door. His brows creased and he opened his mouth to say something, when a loud screech and more yelling ensued from the kitchen. I rolled my eyes and shut the door behind me.

I all but ran down the steps but groaned inwardly when the door opened behind me.

"Ellie." Zeke said as he came down the steps and fell into step next to me.

"What?" I snapped at him as I started the walk down the long driveway.

"Where are you going?" I wasn't stupid enough to tell him that, so I kept quiet. He kept walking next to me for a moment before continuing his inquisition. "Does Ryker know you're leaving."

"Are you planning on stopping me if he doesn't?" I challenged and looked up at him out of the corner of my eye.

"Yes."

Fucker.

"He knows. I told them *both* I was leaving. He stayed in the kitchen with her as you heard."

Silence again as I picked up my pace.

"She's not a threat to you, if that's what you're worried about."

I laughed out loud with no humor and more tears burned behind my eyes.

"I know that Zeke. Because I've met my fair share of people who are threats to me, and pretty little blondes like her, are never the ones I have to worry about."

"So, who do you worry about then?"

I stopped walking and he took a few steps ahead of me and turned back with an eyebrow raised. I shook my head, pursing my lips and started walking again as anger burned in my belly.

"Ryker. Men like Ryker are who I worry about. They're the ones who hurt me."

He stayed silent again, but his jaw clenched.

We were nearing the front gate when a sedan pulled up and parked along the road, matching the car I'd ordered.

"Let me drive you where you want to go." He tried.

"So you can turn around and tell him where I went the second I get there? No thanks."

"So you *are* running from him." He accused and put his hand on my arm, stopping me before I got to the button on the wall to open the gate.

"What does it matter?" I snapped.

"It's my job to protect his interests, and you happen to be one of his biggest interests at this point Elora. I can't just sit by and let you cause problems."

"Cause problems?" I yelled at him, ripping my arm out of his hand. "You protect his interests, but who in this world protects mine?"

I stood nose to nose with the second most physically intimidating man I'd ever met and didn't falter as I challenged him.

His eyes squinted as his brow fell over them while he contemplated his answer.

I nodded sadly and looked away. "Exactly Zeke. No one in this world gives two flying fucks about me, but me. I have no choice here." I paused and took a deep breath as I looked to the car with longing and then back to him, "He'll destroy whatever good I have left in me that other's haven't ripped out of my soul already. And you know it."

"He's trying to do right by you."

"Right. So that's why he was in the process of spreading me out on his kitchen counter like a thanksgiving feast when that woman walked in?" His eyebrows shot up briefly before a flash of anger lit his eyes. "And that's also why he kissed her and stood by while she hung all over him while I stood there burning with shame? To do right by me?"

He didn't say anything back to that, and I didn't need him too.

I nodded and turned to hit the button on the wall and the gate started sliding open as I stood there.

"I think you should stay. He's just going to come looking for you, and this time, he'll drag you back kicking and screaming if he has to Princess." He used the old nickname he'd given me years ago affectionately and for a moment I was a kid again in his presence.

"What would my dad want you to tell me to do right now if he could talk to you?" I raised my shoulders to my ears in exasperation and watched as pain clouded his eyes. He was stuck between a rock and a hard place here, and for a man who didn't show much emotion, he was doing his best to act with a softer side than he normally would, I was sure.

"Precisely. So, I have to go." I walked to the car and threw myself in the back, refusing to look back as the driver pulled away and drove down the road.

As we got further down the street, I thought perhaps I heard a deep baritone voice yelling my name through the open window in the car, but I knew better than to think someone cared that much about me to even bother.

Hours later I laid on Carly's couch and held my swimming head as I tried to focus. To be honest, I knew I was fucked, thanks to all the weed and alcohol I'd consumed in the last three hours, but I couldn't force myself to worry about how bad my hang over would be tomorrow because I was disassociating from my mental turmoil.

"Earth to Ellie!" Carly yelled at me, and I pried my eyes open with my fingers and looked at her.

"What?"

"Did you hear what I just said? Frankie and the guys are on their way here."

"What? Why?" I asked, sitting up quickly and then fighting the wave of nausea that rolled through my stomach.

"To hang out, I guess! I have to go to work later and I'm sure they have a job to do but Frankie just texted me and told me they'd be here in a few."

"Well tell him you're napping or something! They can't come here, or they'll tell Ryker I'm here."

"I should tell Ryker that you're here Ellie! He's not just my boss, he's my boss's boss's boss. And he's scary as fuck!"

"Please Carly—" My plea was cut short when her front door opened and in strode the three musketeers of Ryker's crew.

Jay looked at me and his jaw dropped, I flopped backwards on the couch again and then cursed and groaned, holding my head as everything started spinning.

Frankie crossed the room toward me, yelling, "Do you have any fucking idea how many men he has looking for you right now?" I flipped him the bird and closed my eyes again.

"Frankie, leave her alone. You don't understand what happened." Carly said, huffing from her spot in the armchair but even I could hear her frustration in her voice.

I was causing them drama and potential danger by being here.

I groaned and sat up again. Jay stared at me from across the room but didn't say anything to me. No doubt, Ryker's warning of gutting him was still fresh in his mind.

"I'm sorry I came here." I said and looked around the room for my bag.

I grabbed my phone and tried to order a car, but my screen blurred and then there were two of them to try to look at and I groaned. I'd order a car when I'd walked off my high a bit.

"Where are you going?" Carly asked, standing to follow me as I grabbed my bag.

"I was never here. I'm sorry I darkened your doorstep—"

"El, stop it." She snapped at me, but I was already pulling at the doorknob, fumbling with the locks as I tried to get it open. Why the fuck was the door locked when five seconds ago, the guys had walked right in?

I finally got them free and swung it open to leave and nearly walked into a large, tattooed hand as it rose up to bang on the door.

"Fuck." I hissed as the world tilted, and I fell backwards into Carly.

Ryker's eyes were murderous as he looked at me, struggling to even stand up and then past me to the apartment full of my friends and his employees.

"I thought I made it clear that anyone who saw her was to notify me immediately." He barked out.

"Shut up Ryker." I snapped back and shoved him backwards. I think that shocked everyone, and I probably would have regretted it had I been able to form a coherent thought for more than five seconds at a time. "They all just got here, and I was just leaving, so leave them alone."

"Don't tell me what to do when my employees are involved."

"They're my friends, or at least they were before you made it impossible for me to even keep them in my life because you make everyone think you're so fucking scary."

"People only think I'm scary?" he asked, ignoring my other comment about him.

I shrugged my shoulders and walked down the hall away from him, "I wouldn't know, I try not to think about you at all, let alone talk about you."

He growled after me and slammed Carly's door shut, after saying something to them in a low voice, and then walked behind me as I made my way down the hallway.

It was a much nicer apartment building than mine, thanks to her illicit profession, but the hallway was still small and narrow, and I put a hand on each wall to steady myself as I walked towards the elevators.

"Are you drunk?" Ryker snapped, taking my hand, and sliding his arm around my waist.

I fought against him and tried to shove him off, but he was so much bigger than me.

"Drunk, high, stupid, over trusting, painfully in love with a man that doesn't want me—" I droned on embarrassingly, but I was too inebriated to care in the moment. "The list of negative qualities about myself is at least a mile long at this point in my life, but yes, those are just a few."

"Son of a bitch." He cursed and caught me as I tripped over the lip of the elevator and kept me from falling face first into the wall in the back of the metal death trap. The doors closed behind him, but I wasn't aware of much else, because he had me pinned between the cold metal wall and his hot body. I fought to focus as he pressed his knee between my legs, his eyes heavy-lidded as his arms pinned me against the wall, a warm, musky scent filling the air. "I'm sorry." His voice was soft, and even though I couldn't sense any insincerity in it, I didn't trust my gut given my inebriated state.

Which pissed me off even more, because my gut was the only thing that kept me alive the last few years.

"You have to let me go." I said softly and then let my head fall forward to his chest as I tried and failed to stand up to put space between us.

"Never." He said and dropped his lips to my hair. "I can't. Not now that I've had a taste of you. I'll never let you go, not ever."

I scoffed at him and pushed him back, but he didn't budge. "What does Monique think about that?" I purposely messed up her name again to spite him.

"That's not her name and you know it. And it's not what you think with her."

"Do you fuck her?" I asked, pulling my head back to look at him. His eyes dropped to my lips and his jaw clenched but he didn't say anything. "I'll take that as a yes. And that means there will never be anything more between us because that's not a game I want to play."

"Don't say that." He demanded and finally stepped back, I realized the elevator had stopped moving and we were in the lobby.

I moved around him to leave but smashed my shoulder off of the control panel, trying to make it through the four-foot-wide door.

"For fuck sakes Elora, you're a hazard to your own health." He spun me quickly, making the world tilt completely and I started falling headfirst towards the lobby floor, but he effortlessly picked me up and threw me over his shoulder before striding across the space.

The lobby was packed and there were people openly staring at us as he carried me out in a fireman's carry, and I was incredibly happy that I had changed into yoga pants and a zip up when I'd gotten to Carly's, or the entire lobby would be getting a view of my ass under the hem of my dress.

Ryker's large hand landed on my ass as he stepped through the door, held open by the doorman and my cheeks flushed with a blush.

"Good evening Mr. Lawson." The doorman said and tipped his hat. The man had not once ever acknowledged me when I came over the last few years, like he could sense I was beneath his social standards. But for Ryker, he was the perfect little good boy.

"Prick." I muttered at him and flipped him the bird from my upside-down point of view.

The closer Ryker got to the black SUV, the more I felt the sickening tilt of the vehicle and the increasing pressure of his shoulder against my stomach. A wave of nausea started to rise.

"Put me down." I said, covering my mouth.

"Not until you're in my car." He spoke.

"No seriously put me down!" I yelled, as I kicked and wiggled, trying to get down.

"Elora stop it, you're acting like a child."

"I'm going to puke." I gasped and he cursed again and lowered me to the ground.

I took off at a run to the flowered bushes at the side of the building and hardly made it before I started puking up copious amounts of margaritas and edibles.

A searing shame washed over me as I wretched, the heat amplified by Ryker's touch; his hand gently stroked my spine, offering a strange comfort as I finally emptied my stomach.

"Shh, it's okay." He said as I tried to shoo him away and untangle my hair from his fist, but he held fast to it. "Stop, let me help you." he demanded, tightening his hand in my hair.

I groaned and wiped my mouth on the back of my hand. "You see how well that's worked out for me so far." I complained sarcastically and then slowly stood up.

A man appeared at Ryker's side, in a plain black suit and handed him a bottle of water and then returned to the car door, waiting for us. He was giant. Like I had thought Ryker and Zeke were imposing, but this man was–wow. Close to seven feet tall and as wide as he was tall with impossibly dark eyes.

Ryker broke the seal on the lid and handed the open bottle to me. I took it without meeting his eye and guzzled water, feeling the cold iciness of it slide down my throat and quelch the burn from the acid.

"Slow down, or you'll puke again." He grabbed the bottle from my lips and wiped away the tears from underneath my lashes from puking.

"Stop touching me like you have a right!" I snapped and stepped away from him. "Thanks for the water, but I'll be on my way."

"You can pretend you're daft all you want Elora; but you're not going anywhere other than my house."

"Fuck you." I said over my shoulder and walked away.

Instantly, he wrapped his hands around me and picked me up until my toes no longer touched the ground and carried me kicking and cursing to his waiting car. I tried fighting, clinging to the open-door frame like a cat in a bathtub, but he just folded me to his will and threw me in and then climbed in behind me.

"You are so fucking infuriating!" I screamed at him and hit him over and over again in the arms and chest as the car drove away. "I don't want to go with you!"

He took the beating for a few moments, unfazed by it really, but then grabbed my wrists and pulled me over until I sat in his lap with my hands restrained against my chest, just like he did on my bed that morning.

Jesus, how were we still in the same damn day?

Air ripped from my lungs as I let the fury of events finally roll through my system. He just watched me with a sad scowl on his face, so I turned away and hid my face from him.

"Do you really think I'd do you wrong like that with her?" he asked after silence fell between us for over ten minutes.

I was calmer now, but I was still on the sloppy side of drunk.

"I don't know what you'd do Ryker, because I don't know you anymore. I never really have."

He scoffed at me and leaned back into the seat further, pulling me with him, "You're the only person left on this earth that knows me at all Ellie."

"My dad knew you; I just pretended the small part of your life that you two let me see was enough to know who you were. But it wasn't."

"Bullshit." He cursed and forced my face towards his with a handful of my hair. When I finally looked into his eyes for the first time since I opened Carly's door, I saw that they were tired and sad. "She doesn't mean anything to me Elora."

I tried to look away, I didn't have the capacity to have this conversation right now. "Please stop, I'm too drunk for this right now."

"No, you need to know this. Her father controls something I want, and she's a pawn in my game to get it. That's it."

I felt my forehead crease into a frown as I processed that. "That might be worse than me thinking you were cheating on her with me today."

"No, it's not, because it means my feelings for you aren't tainted by her."

"Feelings." I mused, letting the word roll over my tongue.

"Yeah, like the feelings you said you had for me."

I reared back, "I never—"

He laughed and shook his head. "You did, you were running down a list of things you thought were negative characteristics about yourself and you said that you were madly in love with a man who didn't want you back. And you were wrong, because I do want you back Elora. I thought I'd made that clear to you today between your place and mine, but apparently, I need to step up my game."

"I wasn't talking about you." I whispered and tried to recount what I'd said earlier in my tirade. I had been thinking so much more than I'd intended to say.

"Liar." He said, but I could see the anger in his eyes at that statement. "You were talking about me."

I chewed on my lip and thought about it, "Fine I was talking about you, but it doesn't matter. You want something completely different from me than I want from you. So, it doesn't matter."

"How do you know what I want from you? I haven't even told you."

"You want the challenge, or a taste as you keep calling it. But I'm not that kind of girl and I'd never willingly give myself to you for just a romp in the sheets."

"You insult me Elora, I want you for far more than just to take to my bed, but I understand how you're less than trusting of me right now. So, I suppose I'll just have to prove it to you over time."

I scrunched my face up in incredulity. "Time?"

"Yes, time. We have nothing but time together now that you're back in my life."

"Hmm." I hummed, unsure of what to say to that. "And Maureen?"

He chuckled, "Maureen is unfortunately something we will have to deal with again in the future. It's business that I've already dedicated months too, but I will change my tactics and handle it differently now."

"So, you won't sleep with her?" I hated how hopeful I sounded.

"No, Elora. I won't sleep with her or anyone else that isn't you." I felt the stirrings of arousal in my core as we talked about sex.

"And if I don't want to sleep with you anytime soon?"

He groaned and then laid his forehead against mine, "Then I suppose I will be walking around with the biggest pair of blue balls in the world, and the sexiest girlfriend on my arm who caused them."

Butterflies.

"Girlfriend huh?" I asked, my voice breaking and squeaking embarrassingly.

His eyes crinkled with his laugh, and he leaned in and kissed my nose, "I'm pretty sure after the last two days of me chasing you down, the entire city knows you're mine. There isn't much room for question when I have every man in my employ looking for you twice in twelve hours. It sends a pretty clear picture, but we can take this at whatever pace you want."

"Hmm." I pondered that for a while. "It shows you're terrible at keeping track of me."

He grunted in annoyance and then softened. "Just promise me one thing." He said leaning down to breathe in deeply at the base of my neck.

"What?" My voice was breathy and soft from the arousal he was burning into my body.

"No more running." I groaned but he cut me off, "You stay, and we talk things through like adults. Got it?"

I thought about it and resigned to agree, frankly I didn't have the means to run all the time, even if it had been my MO for years. "Fine."

"And no more booze or drugs."

"No deal." I answered quickly and bit my lip to hide my smirk, "But ask me again tomorrow morning when my hang over is raging full force and I'll probably agree more easily."

"Yesterday was your twenty first birthday, wasn't it?" He asked and his tone was sad as he looked at me. "I fucked up your birthday celebration by coming on too strong and chasing you and your friends out the door."

"I won't tell you that you didn't do all of those things. But I didn't even want to go out last night, so I'm not mad."

"Well regardless, I plan to make it up to you. I knew yesterday was your birthday, I just forgot about it when I saw you for the first time in so long." His hand slid down my back and landed on my hip, "It was like seeing the sunshine for the first time in years when you walked through my door."

I smiled and leaned into his touch and then laid my head on his shoulder. "I'm still mad at you, but when you say things like that, I get a little less mad for the moment."

He squeezed me tighter, and I felt both of our bodies relax into the seat as darkness fell around the city. "I'll have to remember that."

"You do that."

I was dozing in his arms when he gently woke me up, "Honey, we're home." He joked and picked me up and carried me from the car and upstairs.

He stood at the top of the stairs and stopped walking, looking from the left hallway that held his rooms, and to the right hallway that held the guest rooms, and the room I'd been given.

He waited with question in his eyes and I nodded towards the right and looked at him with annoyance.

His white teeth flashed in the darkness, "Can't blame a man for trying." Walking back into the beautiful white bedroom helped ease the nerves in my system from being back inside of his home.

He sat me down on the bench at the end of the bed and then looked around, like he was unsure about what to do with himself.

I asked, hoping I didn't sound pathetic by wondering, "I'm going to shower and go to bed. Will you be here tomorrow?"

"Yes. I should be here all day tomorrow."

"Okay."

Silence hung between us, but I needed time to adjust to this new situation I'd found myself in. I smiled at him as I walked backwards towards the bathroom, "Goodnight, Ry."

"Goodnight, Ellie."

CHAPTER 10 – RYKER

I had thought having Ellie here in my home would make me relax and feel less on edge. But knowing how sinful her sexy body was and how badly we both wanted each other, only made me more uptight and unable to focus.

I'd left her in the guest room like she'd asked, and it physically pained me to walk away from her. But I forced myself to do it because it was what she wanted, and I owed her a few favors after how I'd fucked things up over and over the last few days.

The quiet hum of the office greeted me as I walked in; I went straight to my bar, the smooth wood cool under my hand as I poured a drink. I heard footsteps behind me and poured another glass as I turned around and held it out for my friend.

Zeke stepped forward and took it as we sat down at my desk and silently took a drink before we dived into the shit storm of Elora Dax's life.

"Paula Granger." I said bitterly. "I want her found." Zeke knew she was Elora's mother, and he nodded easily. Silence fell on us again as I worked over everything in my head. Telling him some of her story, was essential, yet I didn't want to expose her that way. Zeke was the only man I trusted with her pain though. "She moved her to South LA, starved her, beat her, drugged her, and then tried to pimp her out. She was six-fucking-teen years old when she finally got away from her, and she's been on her own since then." My voice was angry, and I tossed back the rest of my drink as I tried to calm down.

Zeke's hand tightened around his drink as I relayed the sordid tale to him, and he finished off his own drink. "Gavin would have gutted her if he was alive."

"Which is exactly why I'm going to do it for him. So, I want her found, sooner rather than later."

"Understood. I'll get the crews on it right away."

I got up and poured us some more liquor. "Speaking of crews." I sat back down and handed him his glass. "I don't trust Jay. Frankie and Mason are on my shit list too currently. So, I want them demoted. Make them work twice as hard on double shitty jobs as a message."

Zeke chuckled and nodded, "I've got some shit I can throw their way."

"Good. I don't want them to misunderstand for one second who is the biggest dog in this fight." I sat back in my chair and relaxed a bit, having two pressing issues out of the way. "And Monica needs to be handled."

"Handled?"

"For one, she's not allowed back inside this house, for any reason. We need to finish it up, and I need to do it without pissing Elora off."

"How do you expect to do that when Monica wants only one thing? To be on your arm and in your bed."

I grunted and looked down into the amber colored drink in my glass. "You could always fuck her for me."

"Elora? Consider it done." He said quickly and then laughed at the murderous glare I shot his way. "Oh, you mean the vapid bitch that you said sucked dick like a goat. Yeah, no thanks, I'll pass boss."

"Shit." I rubbed my forehead in exasperation as I tried to come up with something to do.

"So is the princess staying then?"

"She's hardly a princess anymore." He looked doubtful. "But yes, she's mine and she's here to stay. Let word travel quickly that she's the Queen of this kingdom."

He nodded again and stood up, "Anything else?"

I threw back the rest of my drink and stood up with him. "No, get out of here and let me be."

He laughed at me, and I walked him out.

When he was gone, I headed upstairs. I paused at the top of the stairs, looking down towards Elora's room and then back to mine.

"Fuck." I groaned at how badly I wanted to go to her room and crawl into bed with her. But she'd asked me for time, and I was going to give it to her. Even if it fucking killed me.

I went to my room and crawled into my own cold bed and laid there, staring at the ceiling for hours.

Elora Dax was in my home. She was under my roof, in a bed that belonged to me and was allowing me to provide for her.

How warped was it that this was something I should have had for years now, but was only just allowing myself the luxury of enjoying?

No one was ever going to hurt her again.

No one.

And I was going to enjoy hurting the vicious bitch that had destroyed her life while taking my money in the process.

A sinister smile crossed my lips as I thought of all the ways I'd make Paula Granger cry and scream for all the pain she'd put her daughter through.

I'd have the revenge Elora deserved, and I'd protect her soul from being darkened by it all along the way too.

When I woke up, it was barely dawn and I was dragging ass. I'd been up all-night lying in bed awake and aching to be near Ellie. I grumbled my way through my morning routine, including my five-mile run. Getting back home as the sun shined through the windows brightly, I headed to the kitchen and a protein shake to fuel up.

As I rounded the corner, Elora sat at the kitchen Island, looking like death was clawing at her feet.

"Good morning." I said loudly, slightly enjoying the way it made her cringe and burrow into her hoodie further. She had a pair of shorts on, and a hoodie pulled down far over her eyes as she held her head in both hands.

"Shh!" She snapped at me and groaned, unable to even open her eyes in the bright sunlight of the kitchen.

"So, is now an appropriate time to get you to swear off drinking for the rest of your life?" I asked, grabbing water for both of us and sliding onto the stool next to her.

"I wish I remembered exactly what happened, so I knew never to do it again."

"How much do you remember?" I rubbed my hand up her back softly and she mewled softly, leaning into it.

"Uh, well." She started, cracking one eye to look at me before closing it and laying her head down. "I remember you fucking a blonde on the kitchen counter in front of me to start."

"Lies." I grunted, cutting her off.

Her lips turned up slightly into almost a smile. "Then I went and partied in a brothel with very sexy, very hung men in loin cloths that shook their shlongs like elephant trunks."

"Fucking hell." I groaned and pulled her off her stool and onto my lap. She shrieked and then groaned, covering her face as her hood slid down. She gave up on the hood and settled with her face buried in my neck for darkness. Her breath was warm on my skin, and I ached to taste hers, but I forced myself to keep my hands around her waist and my lips to myself. "What else do you remember?"

"Hmm." She mused. I felt her lips turn up into a smile before she began again. "Then I have black out moments and flashes of memories of an ape, banging on the door, demanding I come away with him to his nest in the jungle. It was all very Tarzan fetish-like."

I snorted, "Do you have a Tarzan fetish, Doll?"

"A sexy ripped man in a loin cloth who has never seen any other woman in his life and thinks I'm the crème de la crème, abso-fuck-ing-lutely."

"Oh, but you are the crème de la crème, baby." My hands started wandering over the exposed skin of her legs as the conversation made me burn.

My fingers played with the smooth skin of her upper thigh before touching on raised and bumpy flesh. She froze in my arms as I let my fingertips trace the scars on her leg from the worst day of our lives.

"Does it hurt?" I asked.

"Not physically. Not anymore."

We were quiet, the fun bantering from before now done, overshadowed by the dark memories of that night.

"I should have been there." I said quietly. "I should have protected you and him both."

She pulled her face from my neck and drew back to look at me, it was the first glance I was getting of her full face all morning and I was awe struck at how beautiful she was, even hung over and miserable.

"You couldn't have known it was going to happen, and chances are, even if you were there, it still would have been terrible."

"Then it should have been me instead of him."

"Stop it." she said forcefully. Her small hand slid from my shoulder and to the side of my face, turning it to face hers. "I don't want to think about the possibility of losing you both that night. It's too painful to imagine."

I looked into her light hazel eyes and saw her sincerity in them. It soothed a bit of the burn in my chest from the painful topic. "I would have given up completely if I'd lost you both." She leaned in and pressed her soft, supple lips to mine tentatively, hesitant, and insecure. I suppressed the growl that wanted to rip from my lungs at the decadent taste of her, but I remained poised as she explored. She pulled back slightly until her lips just barely detached from mine and paused. "Is this okay?" Her voice was soft and hesitant.

"It's more than okay Doll. You can kiss me whenever you want to." I answered, running my hands under the hem of her sweater, and groaned as my fingers touched bare skin underneath. "Tell me you have something on under this hoodie."

Her lips pulled up into a smile against mine, "Only of the jeweled variety."

I took her lips in a punishing kiss, consuming her through it as my hands gripped her waist tightly.

She moaned and opened her mouth when I coaxed and then nibbled on my lip, sucking it into her mouth.

"I need to see them."

"You saw one yesterday."

"For a half of a second, it wasn't nearly enough."

She wiggled in my lap, and I could feel her hot center through the thin fabric of our shorts. "I thought I was going to be the one begging." She let her words and her hands toy with me, as she placed her hand on top of mine where it laid on the bare skin of her waist.

My fingers reached out, tracing up her stomach in search of the luscious breast that had captured my attention the day before. When the heavy weight of it fell into my palm, I pinched my fingers together around the hard bud of her nipple, pulling on it and rejoicing in it hardening even further, puckering up towards my hands and seeking attention.

"Let me see." I ordered.

Her eyes snapped open to match the O that her beautiful lips were making before they snapped shut and she swallowed. "Not here. I don't want to be walked in on like yesterday."

She had a point.

Getting to my feet, I let my hands rest on her luscious ass, feeling her legs encircle my waist as we walked together from the kitchen to the den. I desperately wanted to take her to my bed, but I knew I wouldn't stop if I had her laid out in it. And something told me she wasn't going to just offer me her pussy already.

I grabbed the remote off the table and clicked the button to lower the shades, casting the room in shadows and muted light. I then sat down on the couch and kept Ellie on my lap, so she straddled me. "Better?" I asked her.

She tilted her hips forward and rubbed herself on my cock, gripping the fabric of my shirt in her hands where they squeezed my shoulders. "Better."

"Good. Now take your shirt off and let me see your fucking tits. My mouth has been watering to taste them since I saw them in that green scrap of lace the other night."

Her eyes flared with something, and she quickly reached down and grabbed the hem of the sweater and lifted it off over her head.

My jaw fucking dropped when she sat on my lap in only a pair of tight booty shorts and jewels. "You're the most gorgeous woman I've ever seen."

"Touch me Ryker. Please, I need to feel your hands on me." She begged.

And my fucking God, that sweet voice of hers, begging me to ruin her nearly broke me in turn.

My hands slid up her sides and cupped both of her tits in sync, the rings through her nipples were tiny little 'D' hoops, with white diamonds on the lower half of the ring.

I pinched her nipples and watched as her eyes fluttered closed while her lips parted and her white teeth bit into her bottom lip.

"You like that, don't you?" I asked, pulling on them with more pressure and pinching them, rolling them between my fingers. Her hips jerked and she rubbed herself on me again.

"When did you get these pierced?"

"My nineteenth birthday. It was a gift from Carly because she was getting something pierced and she didn't want to go alone."

"So, you chose your nipples instead of your ears or your belly button or something?"

"Well, I could have gotten my pussy done instead. The piercer all but begged me to change my mind for him." She said with a cheeky smile.

"Ellie." I groaned. "Tell me his name, I'll break both of his fucking hands."

She giggled and rocked her hips, ignoring me.

"You like them being played with don't you, Doll?" My cock throbbed under my shorts, against her pussy. She didn't answer me again; she kept her teeth clamped down on her lip as she held on to my arms while I played with her pretty nipples.

"Tell me you like what I'm doing to you Ellie. Or I'm going to stop."

"No!" She panted, "Please don't stop."

"Then tell me what I want to hear."

"I like it!" She rocked her hips again and moaned. "God, I fucking like it."

"That's my good girl." I mused and then leaned in and flicked my tongue over one tight nipple, causing her to moan and slide her fingers into my hair, pulling my head into her chest further.

I bit down on one nipple and sucked it into my mouth, flicking it with my tongue while I sucked it.

"Fuck, Ryker."

I sat back, using her now slick nipple to play with I watched her. Her head was thrown back in pleasure as I toyed with her.

"Rub your pussy on my cock. I want to watch you come." Her eyes snapped open, and she groaned, leaning in, and laying her forehead against mine. "I want to see what you look like when I make you come, Doll."

"I can't." She panted. "It's too much, I—"

"Yes, you can." I grabbed her hips and forced them to rock back and forth in my lap, rubbing her clit against my hard cock. "Can you feel me?" I asked her, pushing up into her with my hard on. "Can you feel how hard you make me?"

"Yes. You're so big Ry."

"That's right. I'm going to ruin you for any other man when I push inside of you for the first time. You'll never want another man for as long as you live." She was working me up as she rubbed herself on me as much as she was herself. "No man will stack up, especially someone like Jay or Mason."

"Jesus." She groaned; she leaned back and grabbed both of her breasts in her hands as she rocked on me. I watched in rapture as she pinched and pulled her nipples, memorizing every single touch she used so I could do it to her myself, just how she liked it.

"Have you given yourself to them? Have you fucked them? Have you let them fuck you together?" I was crazed with need.

Her eyes snapped back open, and fire lit into them. "Did you fuck Monique?" She challenged. "Oh wait, we already know the answer to that."

"Minx." I groaned and flipped her over, slamming her down into the couch and following her with my body. I pressed her hips wide and tore my shirt off over my head and humped her like a fucking teenager.

"Ryker!" She gasped, clawing at my shoulders as I sucked her nipple into my mouth and rolled my hips. "Just like that."

"You let those fuckers into your body, didn't you? Did you ride them like you were me just now? Or did you lay back and let them rut into you like this?" I was fucking irate, clinging to a strand of restraint as I fucked her into the couch through our clothes. I was so fucking close to blowing a load in my pants like some schoolboy it was ridiculous. "Beg me to fuck you. Beg me to tear you open with my cock."

"Is this how you always fuck her?" She asked defiantly, her eyes burned with desire and arousal, but there was anger there too. We were a match made in jealous misery. "Do you control her like you're controlling me? Or do you let her top you?"

"Fuck that. It's never been like this with anyone else for me."

She paused as she looked deep into my eyes, my words taking her by surprise. I didn't stop rocking against her though, I couldn't. The world could have been falling down around us and I would have continued to give her pleasure without a care in the world. I leaned down and bit her ear and then whispered, "I'm not even inside of you yet and it already feels a million times better than any other sexual encounter I've ever had."

"Oh my god." She moaned and then her body locked up tight underneath me as she gasped and clawed at me. "I'm coming Ry. Oh my god, I'm-." I silenced her with a feral kiss and felt her orgasm roll through her body underneath of me and it pushed me over the edge. I filled my shorts like a virgin, as the most beautiful woman in the world shattered underneath me.

She gasped and then opened her hazel eyes; they were so full of wonder and question as she looked up at me. I laid my forehead on hers and fought to catch my breath.

"That was incredible." She said against my lips as her hands slid up and down my back. "You're so sexy."

"Am I?" I asked, leaning back, and sliding off of her body to lay next to her. She followed me and curled in against my chest as I wrapped my arms around her back, holding her close.

"Top ten for sure."

"Top ten of what?" I didn't think I was going to like her answer.

"Of guys I've been with." My hand sliced through the air and spanked her lush ass so fast. She crawled up my body to get away from the painful sensation and bit down on my peck to stop her scream, but it didn't hide her moan that laced the edges of it.

"I'm kidding!" She said quickly, crawling over my body completely and laying with her ass tucked into the back of the couch, hiding it from me.

"Take it back." I growled. I reached over and tugged one of her sexy nipple rings and she moaned and dug her nails into my abs right above my shorts.

"I take it back." She purred and leaned up to kiss me. "I've never been with anyone that even comes close to how sexy you are. Your tattoos –" She bit her lip and ran her fingertips over my chest and abs that were covered in dark ink. "They make me so wet."

I grunted in response, still skeptical. She let her fingers play with the elastic of my shorts and my brain started to short circuit.

"Hey Boss."

Elora shrieked and buried herself in my arms as I leaned up to look over the back of the couch. "Get out!" I roared, pointing at the door.

My man Dante looked questioningly at me. It wasn't unusual for me to fuck a woman anywhere I wanted, at home or in my office or elsewhere, but I never tried to hide any of them from my men's eyes before either. "Get the fuck out while you can still walk!" I bellowed and he turned on his heel and retreated quickly.

I looked down and Elora's cheeks were bright red as she held her fingers over her mouth in shock. "Is there no privacy here?" She whispered.

"I apparently need to make some new rules now that you're mine." I said grumpily. "I've never cared for a woman's modesty before you." I flopped back down on my back and pulled her back to my chest and kissed her hair. "But the idea of any of them seeing you in any sort of undress, makes me irate."

She chuckled and kissed my chest. "How chivalrous of you." She snorted the end and fell into a peel of girly giggles as I tickled her sides in rebuttal.

"Boss."

"Motherfucker!" I yelled. This time it was Zeke, and he stood at the doorway with his back turned to the den and waited for me.

"It's urgent."

"What is it?" I demanded.

"Monica is at the gate."

"Son of bitch." I grunted.

Elora groaned and peeked over the back of the couch at Zeke's back and then looked up at me.

"I'm sorry. I have to go deal with that."

"Hmm." She hummed and I stood up; my body ached with every inch of space I put between our bodies. I grabbed her sweater off the ground and held it open for her to put her arms into, and she did. Yanking her up off the couch and into my arms, I pushed her hair back from her eyes as she looked at me with so many questions on the tip of her tongue, yet her lips stayed clamped between her teeth.

"I'm never going to touch her again." I told her. "I promise."

She held my gaze for a moment longer than normal and then nodded her head in understanding. "I trust you." Her voice was soft but strong.

"You don't know what that means to me Ellie."

"And you don't know what it costs me to say it either." Her body was rigid and unyielding, and I knew she didn't allow herself to trust anyone often.

"I'll make it up to you." I said and kissed her softly.

"Hmm." She hummed once again and stepped back, eyeing me.

I shook my head at her and grabbed my t-shirt, walking out of the den.

"I need a minute." I said to Zeke, he nodded back.

Dante stood to the side by the front door and cut in, "Sir, she's pretty irate, threatening to break the gate down with her car."

"Well, I've got a load full of come in my shorts Dante, so I need to clean up." I snapped back at him, causing his eyes to bug out of his big dumb head.

Ellie's melodic laugh sounded from behind me and Zeke bit back a snort at my outburst.

"I'm glad everyone is enjoying my soggy shorts." I added, throwing my arms up in the air as I got to the bottom of the stairs. Ellie's laugh was rolling, and Zeke stopped trying to hide his own.

It was quite a change to hear laughter in my home.

I kind of liked it.

CHAPTER 11 – ELORA

Ryker had left the house to deal with the insipid cunt that I despised hours ago, and still wasn't back.

Zeke had come in to tell me they had business to attend to at his office and that he'd be back later. I'd walked around the house, unsure of what to do with myself since my orgasm had cleared my hangover and now, I was utterly bored.

I passed by the kitchen on one of my many laps of the house and noticed a room between the kitchen and the garage. Three men sat around a large table in the center playing cards, tv monitors littered one wall of the room, showing security camera footage from around the exterior of the home.

I recognized one of the men as the driver from the car last night when Ryker had kidnapped me from Carly's. He was probably in his thirties, and had those dark eyes that looked bottomless, and he was giant. He just had an air about him that said don't fuck with me.

"Uh, excuse me." I said awkwardly from the doorway. The three heads turned to me, and they all stood up instantly, the man I recognized stepped forward.

"Yes, Ma'am?"

"Uh Ellie." I said, pointing to my chest in introduction.

"Yes, I'm aware of your name Ma'am." He said coyly.

"You don't need to call me Ma'am, just Ellie is fine." I tried.

"We've been given our instructions in how to address you Ma'am. It's that or Ms. Dax."

"Eh." I said quickly, hating the way that sounded worse than Ma'am, he smiled at my distaste. "Uh—if I wanted to go somewhere," I started, dropping my gaze in shame. This was so fucking awkward. I felt like a prisoner. "Is there a car I can borrow or something?"

"I've been assigned as your driver and bodyguard, so you just let me know where you want to go, and we go."

"Oh, I don't really need a—" I started to refuse.

"It's not up for negotiation Ma'am. I'm sorry but I've been instructed clearly. You're free to come and go, but I'm to go with you. And if I'm not available, Zeke or Mr. Lawson go with you, no exceptions."

"Oh." The two guys behind him looked back and forth between themselves and I didn't like being so off kilter in front of others. "I need to go get changed. And then I'd like to go to my friends' house. You picked me up there last night."

"No problem. I'll have the car at the front door when you're ready Ma'am."

"Thank you." I said and backed out of the room and ran to my own.

I quickly changed into shorts and a top and slid my feet into a pair of heeled sandals. I fixed my hair from my shower an hour ago, letting it cascade down over my shoulders and added a light layer of make up.

I was pretty sure Carly was already at work, but I was hoping I'd catch her at home, so I didn't have to go to Lux to apologize to her.

When I got downstairs, the man was standing at the front door waiting for me. As I got closer, he opened it and followed me down the steps to the waiting car. It was a flashy SUV, and it was completely blacked out, the windows, lights and interior were all black and it was impossible to see anything at all from outside. At the car door, I paused and turned to the man, "What should I call you?" I asked.

A corner of his mouth turned up, "My name is Jed."

"Jed." I said, nodding my head and slid into the cool car, "Thank you."

It was quite the change from the city bus I was riding two days ago next to a man slumped over in his seat. I wasn't sure if he was alive or dead and I didn't dare to get close enough to check.

This was quite the improvement for sure.

When we got to Carly's apartment, I let the man open my door because frankly I was scared if I didn't, that he'd yell at me, and I'd probably cry. He was that intimidating.

"I don't know if she's home or not, but I shouldn't be too long either way."

He nodded but followed me when I turned towards the door. "Are you coming in?""Where you go, I go." He answered, taking the door from the doorman that I despised and stepping in front of him to stand between us. The doorman's eye crinkled as he was snubbed, and I simply raised my eyebrow at both him and Jed.

Well, that was a perk I might get used to.

When I got to Carly's door, I knew instantly that she wasn't home. There was no music coming from the apartment and if she was home, getting ready for work, the tunes would be blaring. I used my key anyway and stepped inside to check.

Jed stood at the doorway and watched me look around.

"Shit." I mused. "Can you drive me to Lux?" I asked.

"Lux?" His eyebrows rose to his dark hair. "Boss won't like me taking you there."

"I'm not going there to indulge. I just need to talk to my friend quickly. She works there."

His face stayed stoic as he looked at me. "Fine."

"Thank you." I gave him a small smile and bit my lip to fight the full grin at my triumph. I felt like I was thirteen again, asking my dad to drive me everywhere. But I didn't have money for a cab and besides, I didn't think bigfoot would let me get into one if I did.

I ran to Carly's closet and changed my top, stealing one of hers so I didn't look so out of place in my black jean shorts and flowy top. I traded the flowy top for a low-cut rose gold sequined halter top. It matched my gold sandals perfectly and I clipped my hair up and returned to the living room.

Jed eyed me with something like pain in his eyes as he opened the door and led me back down to the car. I wasn't doing anything wrong though. I was twenty-one, going to a club that Ryker owned with his bodyguard in tow. How much trouble could I get into?

The ride to Lux was short and when we pulled up outside, Jed parked at the front door and helped me out once again. The bouncers at the door addressed Jed, and then let their eyes travel over me as I stepped inside the entrance they held open. The line was wrapped around the front of the building, and I didn't miss the catty glares thrown my way by other men and women as they waited to get inside.

I tried to act like I belonged, but to be honest, I was way out of my element here. One time before I'd braved the club, for Carly's birthday. The noise, lights, and heavy sexual tension around had been almost too much to bare before I faked a headache twenty minutes in and left.

As men and women parted in the busy club for me and Jed to walk through, I felt more exposed than the naked women on stage. I felt like I had a giant sign on my chest that blinked with flashing lights 'imposter'.

I didn't belong here.

I didn't see Carly anywhere around and didn't know where to start looking for her either.

Finally, a girl I recognized walked by, her name was Sammy, but she went by Willow here at the club. She'd hung out with Carly and I a few times at night, doing movies and pedicures at Carly's place so I approached her.

"Hey." I said, over the music. "Is Carly around?"

She looked me up and down and then at Jed and a bold smile crossed her face. "Yeah she's in the back, getting dressed." She nodded towards a door in the wall, with two burly bouncers on each side of it.

"Can I go back there?" I asked, trying to get her attention from my bodyguards' muscles.

She finally looked at me with a ridiculous look on her face. "From what I hear, you can go anywhere you want to now, Ellie." She said with a smirk on her face. "Should I start calling you *boss*?" She asked and winked at me.

I rolled my eyes at her and brushed it off.

It wasn't like that.

I turned to Jed and narrowed my eyes at him. "You stay out here." I turned to Willow and nodded to Jed. "Keep him company for me?"

"Ms. Dax." Jed warned but Willow had already slid between us and pressed her plump breasts into his chest and his attention was torn between us.

"I'm fine, I'm just going in the dressing room, and I'll be right back." I said, stepping away.

When I got to the door, the two bouncers looked at me but didn't move.

"Excuse me." I said to the one who looked less lethal.

"Are you new here?" He asked letting his eyes travel down my body, and honestly looked unimpressed.

Exactly why I never got into the sex industry.

I laughed, because the idea of me dancing was ludicrous, but stopped short when he continued to look unphased. I squared my shoulders and looked at him head on.

Bravely, I decided to see just how far my newfound reach went.

"No, I'm Elora Dax." I said, not offering anything else.

His eyes widened and his mouth fell open.

His cohort pushed him aside and opened the door wide, nodding his head to me and motioning for me to enter. "Ms. Dax."

"Thank you." I said and walked through like I belonged here.

Alone in the dimly lit hallway, the heavy silence that followed the door's closing allowed me to finally let go of my forced bravado, taking a deep, shuddering breath.

What a fucking mind trip it all was.

I got to the dancers' dressing room and saw Carly at a vanity in front of a wall of mirrors surrounded by other girls, mostly naked as they all got dressed and did their hair and makeup.

Carly's eyes found mine in the mirror as I walked up behind her, and she whipped her head around to look at me. I held my hands up in surrender, "I have permission to be here, I promise."

She eyed me for a second and then stood up and pulled me tight into a hug. "I'm sorry." She rushed on and then pulled back, noticing my shirt. "Is that mine?"

I laughed and sat down next to her and pulled her down with me. "Yes, I went to your place first, but you weren't there. I wasn't dressed to come here so I borrowed this. Hope you don't mind."

"Of course I don't mind! What are you doing here though? I can't believe he let you come here."

"Why? He owns the place, and I have a bodyguard the size of bigfoot attached to my hip 24/7 now." I hooked my thumb over my shoulder toward the exit with a shrug.

"Yeah, but you're like his—" She paused and chewed her plump red lip. "prized possession. I'm just surprised he let you come here where men are leaches, without him."

I brushed it off and took her hand in mine, "I don't want to distract you or get you in trouble for me being here, but I wanted to apologize for the last two days. I know I've put you in a shitty spot and I'm sorry." She tried to brush me off and act like it was no big deal, but I knew better. "How mad are the guys?" That made her grimace. "That bad huh?"

"Did Ryker threaten to kill Jay? For talking to you?" Her eyes widened, shining with a naive belief that Ry would actually do it, and honestly, it wasn't entirely unbelievable. His reputation spoke for itself.

I just couldn't conjure up true fear when I thought of him. He'd been too gentle with me over the years and over the last few days for me to believe it.

"To be fair, Jay was saying some really crude things to me about Ryker and Ry took my phone and heard them." I shrugged my shoulders, "And it wasn't the first time he warned people that I wasn't to be messed with."

"Jesus." She said and leaned back in her chair. I noticed more than a few pairs of eyes on me as the other girls leaned in to hear more about their fearless leader. "So, you're his now then huh? What about the blonde chick from yesterday?"

I'd shown up at her place, roaring pissed about Monica and had told her the dramatic tale of what happened. Now I regretted it though, because I hated feeling like I had to recant the story, even though it was true. It was just complicated.

"I can't go into detail about her, but it wasn't what I thought it was." I said, not wanting to expose his ploy to someone in the room that could use the information against him. "And I don't know what I am to him right now. So, I can't answer that."

She looked around the room and leaned back in close. "Word is traveling fast El. And word says you belong to the King."

"If I'm his, then he's mine. And I don't exactly think he's ready for that. Therefore only time will tell." I said, trying to act strong.

"Damn." She mused and laughed a little as she turned back to her mirror and adjusted her bralette top. "I'm friends with the Queen of the underworld."

"And you should reap every single benefit from that title that you can." I said boldly. Carly was the only reason I'd survived the last few years. She'd fed me more times than I cared to admit to. One time I had gone three days without a meal and ended up on her doorstep, desperate for a break from life and she took me in and gave me everything I needed to keep going. "It's my turn to pay you back for your generosity over the years."

She laughed again and stood up, pulling me with her. "How about a movie night in the castle?" She wagged her eyebrows and leaned in close to my side. "Is his house incredible? Tell me it's incredible."

We laughed again as we walked out of the loud room and down the hallway towards the club. "It's incredible. And I'd love to have you over for movies whenever you want. There's a pool and all sorts of things I've yet to indulge in."

"How about him? Have you indulged in him?" she asked with a sinister smile to her pretty lips.

"Gah!" I groaned and threw my head back but couldn't wipe the smile off my face.

"What!" She shrieked, "You gave him your—"

"No!" I cut her off, looking around wildly to make sure no one heard our conversation. "Jesus. No, we messed around this morning though, and it was," I paused trying to articulate how it felt to be in Ryker's arms. "It was phenomenal. And I want more, but I'm scared to give him every part of myself. I've got shit buried deep in my baggage from that man and I'm afraid he'll take off again, fucking me up for good."

She hugged me, pulling me to a stop at the door to the club. "Just take it one day at a time. And don't let him make you feel like you have nowhere else to go now that your apartment is gone. You are always welcome at my place, for as long as you need. I just have to get used to you being so close to such a powerful man."

"He is powerful, isn't he." I mused in wonder. "Thank you for being my friend. Even now."

"Don't mention it. Now, get lost, I have to go make some money." She laughed and opened the door, stepping out into the thumping music. I stood back and watched as men and women alike turned to watch her walk into the room.

She was so beautiful; it was unnerving how easily she commanded the room and how confident she was as she did it.

She walked around, letting her hands brush the shoulders of men and women who were seated, chatting with them as she passed and headed towards the main stage.

I turned and found Jed standing by the doorway, waiting for me. For some reason, I wasn't in a hurry to leave though, I was fascinated with the club for the first time. Maybe it was knowing I wasn't just a nobody anymore and that there was a level of protection to that.

"Can we stay?" I asked him, biting my lip.

"You want to hang out at a strip club?" he asked, crossing his arms over his chest.

I shrugged my shoulders and figured honesty was my best option here. "Can I be honest with you for a second?"

"I didn't realize you'd been lying to me this far?"

"Ha, ha." I said dryly. "I've never felt comfortable in places like this because they make me feel vulnerable. But now, with you looming over me like the angel of death," I deadpanned, and he smirked at me, "I don't feel so weak. I kind of want to explore that."

He watched me for a moment and then looked around. "Come with me." He spoke.

Walking out towards the main stage, I followed after him silently as he stopped and spoke to a man in an expensive flashy suit who looked like he ran the place. The man turned to look at me and then nodded eagerly to Jed and ran towards the bar.

Jed walked deeper into the crowd and then pulled open the velvet rope of a private booth in the darkness along the wall.

"This is Mr. Lawson's private booth."

"Ryker has a booth here?"

"For business purposes." Jed answered quickly. He motioned for me to sit down in one of the expensive leather chairs and I gave in, falling into it.

The man in the flashy suit returned with a thick envelope and a bottle girl. He handed the envelope to Jed and then elaborately bowed to me. "Ms. Dax, what a pleasure it is to have you here tonight. This is Jazmin, she'll be your personal bottle girl for the evening, whatever drinks, or food you'd like to indulge in, is yours. And whatever girls you'd like to entertain you are yours as well. Whatever I can do to make this evening enjoyable for you, all you have to do is ask."

With that he bowed extravagantly again and backed out of the alcove.

I gave Jed a wide eye look, and he sat down in a chair next to me and leaned over to talk to me. "It's rude to watch any of the girls, even from afar, without money to pay them for their time." He said and opened the envelope, pulling out bundles of hundreds, fifties, and twenties.

He handed me a bundle of each and then motioned for Jazmin to come forward. "What do you want to drink Ma'am?

"Uh." I said, at a loss. Ryker had told me no drinking, but I didn't want to ruin the feel of the evening by drinking water. "Can I have a vodka cranberry, weak?"

Jazmin smiled down sweetly at me and nodded and then Jed took a twenty from a bundle and slid it in the strap of her fishnets.

"I thought people delt in one-dollar bills at strip clubs?" I asked when we were alone, thumbing through the money in my lap, trying to add it up in my head. "Whose money is this anyway?"

"It's Mr. Lawson's and as his girlfriend, you're expected to pay the women well for your entertainment."

"Huh." I mused to myself. Jazmin appeared with my drink and set a glass of amber colored liquor next to Jed on the table between us.

Flashy suit man reappeared and grinned openly. "Have you seen anyone that tickles your fancy?"

I looked over at Jed and raised my eyebrows at him, but he just sat back in the chair with a grin on his face as he ran his finger over his lips, letting me take the lead.

"Sunny please." I told the man, using Carly's stage name. "And Willow for my friend here."

"Ah, excellent choices." He clasped his hands together. "Give me one moment."

He practically skipped away towards the main stage. "Is he always so–showy?" I asked Jed.

He laughed, "Yes. He got his job as host because he makes everyone feel important when they come in."

"Oh, so it's not just me?" I fake pouted at him, and he laughed. I picked up my drink and held it up to him to cheers. He shook his head but picked up his drink and clanked it against mine.

"To your first lap dance." He said and shook his head. "Mr. Lawson is going to kill me. But at least I'll have had a bit of fun first."

Two women walked up to our booth with sexy smiles on their faces and I couldn't help the giggle that bubbled up when Carly stalked towards me in a white lace number that didn't hide anything. She leaned down and purred in my ear seductively, "Why Ms. Dax, I was told I tickled your fancy." I laughed out loud and so did she as she eyed Jed next to me and shook her head and added, "Ryker is going to lose his shit."

"I know!" I giggled but held up the money in my lap, "Does that mean you don't want his money first though?"

She slid her white lace kimono off her shoulders and knelt between my legs, pushing my thighs wide and crawled up my body. "Oh baby, I'm going to make you feel so good." She purred exaggeratedly.

I leaned back in my chair and let her do her worst on me. It wasn't the first lap dance I'd gotten from Carly. More than once, she had practiced a new move on me at her apartment and it felt just like it did right now. It was hot and silly at the same time.

I slid a couple hundred dollar bills from the bundle at my side and tucked them into her g string and patted her ass. "Good girl."

She laughed and continued grinding on me. "You're my new favorite customer."

"Ooh I better be!" I snapped back in mock offense and slid a couple fifties in the other side of her panties.

I looked over at Jed and admired the way Willow moved over his body as he sat back in the chair with his long legs spread wide. She faced away from him and rubbed her ass in his lap as she ran her hands up and down his inner thighs. But he wasn't watching her.

He was looking at Carly.

Or Sunny I should say, for her blonde hair and smiley disposition.

She took my hands and ran them up her body as she rocked her hips back and forth in my lap. "We usually don't let newbies touch us, but I'm willing to make an exception for you darling." She crooned, placing my hands on her tits and used my fingers to pull her top to the sides, baring her breasts to my face.

I closed my eyes and laughed in pure embarrassment, while she reached over to slide her hand up Jed's arm, pushing her breasts towards him. "She doesn't like my tits; can you believe that?" She said to him seductively. His eyes widened and Willow laughed as she leaned down and bit his ear. Carly took his hand and put it on her left breast, and he squeezed it. "Do you like my tits?" She asked him.

"Very much so." he said, clearing his throat and staring at them.

She leaned back over to me and whispered in my ear. "He's so fucking sexy. I'm totally jealous of you for having a hot bodyguard."

"Feel free to try him on for size whenever you want." I whispered back.

She snapped back in mock shock, like what I'd said was the most scandalizing thing in the world. "No ma'am. I've got more than a handful right here." She joked, putting her hands on my breasts, and squeezing them, and we both giggled like schoolgirls.

"This dance is going to keep me so busy the rest of the night."

"How so?"

"Every man in here will want the girl that rubbed all over Ryker Lawson's girlfriend, and they'll pay handsomely for it too. You're catapulting me into fame baby."

I laughed and then sobered up. "Don't do anything you don't want to do Carly. Not because of me. You don't need this job."

She chuckled and leaned down to press her lush lips to mine for a chaste kiss. "I love you, Ellie. I love how you never let this life cheapen me in your eyes."

"I love you too." I said, then pinched her ass. "Now draw the attention of every man in this room. Every man except Jed because he hasn't been able to take his eyes off of you."

Carly looked over to my bodyguard, who sure enough, was still watching her closely and she bit her lip and winked at him.

She turned in my lap and sat with her back to me and laid back, pushing me down and back in the chair. She rested her head on my shoulder and took my hands and rubbed them all over her body as she used her ass to grind against my crotch.

I could totally see why men enjoyed this. I grabbed a fist full of hundreds and pushed them into the front of her panties as she fake moaned.

"What the fuck is going on here?"

I tore my eyes away from Carly and looked up to see Ryker standing at her feet, looking down at her practically naked body rubbing against mine, with my hand in the front of her panties.

"Oh shit." I cursed.

CHAPTER 12 – RYKER

J ed had texted me that Elora was at Lux, enjoying the services they offered. I'd been in the middle of a meeting with a man I'd wanted to do business with, but I couldn't think of anything other than Elora. She was surrounded by naked women and predatory men, and I ached to know what she thought as she witnessed all that Lux had to offer.

Finally, I'd broken the meeting off short, feigning an emergency and scowled at a chuckling Zeke as we got in the car and drove directly here.

When I walked in, my eyes instantly searched for Ellie in the crowd, and I found her in my private booth.

At least Jed had taken care of her that way.

But then my blood boiled in my veins as I watched Jed's hungry stare locked on Elora and her friend Carly. Carly reached down and grabbed Ellie's lush tits and then turned around on her lap and sprawled out on her with her tits bare. Ellie had a sinful smile on her lips as I walked through the crowd towards her.

Multiple men and women attempted to stop me on the way to talk, but I flat our ignored them all as I zeroed in on my girl.

I stopped at her feet and stood for a moment. Neither her nor Jed had taken notice of me, both were too busy with their laps full of naked women.

"What the fuck is going on here?" I snapped.

Ellie's eyes snapped to mine, and her lips parted, "Oh shit." She cursed. Jed stood up so quickly he dropped the stripper that had been jerking him off through his slacks flat on her ass and then cursed, helping her stand. He shoved a wad of cash into her hand and sent her on her way.

"Boss." he said, nodding to me and straightening out his jacket.

"Enjoying yourself you two?" I asked, with a raised eyebrow. I had my hands in my pants pockets and tried to feign anger, but I was coming up short.

Ellie's aroused grin broke down all of my best defenses.

Carly had covered her breasts back up with her top but still sat straddling my girl, rubbing her pussy over Ellie's crotch as they both watched me.

I kept my eyes locked on them and swung my head towards the club. "Get lost, Jed."

"Yes Sir." He said, walking out of the booth.

Carly leaned down to whisper something in Ellie's ear and a blush broke out over her perfect cheeks. She grabbed money and slowly slid it into the back of her friend's thong.

I turned to face the club and noticed how a dozen or more sets of eyes were locked hard on my girl and her friend. We couldn't have that. With a tug, I pulled the heavy velvet curtain, a deep golden hue, across the rounded booth, muffling the sounds of the club and creating a private haven.

I took the chair that Jed had vacated and turned it to face El's and sat down, letting my long legs stretch out in front of me. I ran my fingers over my lips as I watched the two's eyes widen and then look at each other in question.

"Don't stop on my account." I said.

Carly nodded her head to me with a sly smile on her lips and took Ellie's hands and placed them on her ass as she rocked it back and forth in time with the music as she looked away from me.

"What are you thinking about, Doll?" I asked, unable to act like this wasn't affecting me. I reached down and palmed my hard on, loving the way her eyes fell to my crotch to watch.

"I'm thinking that I would have expected much more anger out of you finding me here."

"I normally would. And I probably should have, but you caught me at a good time I suppose."

She was flustered, trying to pay attention to Carly and me at the same time. "Carly." I said, drawing the stripper's attention to me. "Give me and my girl a minute, would you?"

"Take two." Carly said, sliding off her lap and pulling her to her feet. Ellie looked good enough to fucking eat in a shimmery halter top that showed off her lush tits and tight black shorts that hugged her ass. Her heels made her legs look a mile long and my cock twitched.

I grabbed the bundles of cash left on the table and handed it all to Carly as she walked out. She looked at me for a second and then nodded her head. "Thank you."

"No, thank you." I said, letting my eyes devour Ellie where she stood in front of me. Carly shut the curtain when she left and we were completely alone, with people just feet on the other side.

"Dance for me." I said.

"I can't dance, Ryker." She said nervously.

"Just do what Carly did to you." I commanded.

Hesitation flashed in her eyes and then she licked her lips and stepped forward. She sank to her knees between my feet and then ran her hands slowly up my inner thighs and leaned forward, pressing her tits into my lap. "Like this?" She asked.

"Exactly like that." I twirled a piece of her hair around my finger as she let her hands glide over my legs and then up my stomach. "Did she touch you like this?"

"Yes." She slid up my body and sexily straddled my hips, slowly lowering herself into my lap but right before her pussy touched my cock, she rolled her hips to the music and brushed her tits across my chest.

"Tell me something love." I said as she leaned down and sucked on my ear.

"Hmm?"

"Are your panties wet?"

She sighed and sagged into me, pressing her body flush to mine, and ground herself against my erection.

"Soaked." She purred and then lowered her lips to mine.

I buried my fingers in her hair and grabbed big handfuls on each side of her head, using them to angle her mouth underneath mine. She moaned and sucked on my tongue, making my entire body hard and rigid under her soft body.

"Let me see."

She paused, confused. "See what?"

"Your wet panties. Take your shorts off and let me see."

"Ryker." She purred. "We're in the middle of a strip club, what if someone comes in?"

"They won't."

"That's what you said about this morning in the den."

"Jed!" I yelled, frightening her briefly. A moment later the curtain moved aside far enough for Jed to look in. He kept his eyes on me, knowing better than to embarrass Ellie where she sat straddling me.

"Yes Sir?"

"No one disturbs us. Understood."

"Got it." He shut the curtain again behind him.

"No one will interrupt us love."

She chewed on her lip and contemplated it for a moment before sliding off my lap and turning around to sit with her ass on my cock. I thrust my hips up, rubbing my cock against her ass and she moaned and twirled her hips, rubbing my cock.

I pulled her back to lay on my chest with her head on my shoulder and watched as her dainty little fingers opened her shorts and pulled the zipper down. I hooked my thumbs in the denim and pushed them down as she lifted her ass. As she discarded her shorts, she kicked them away, leaving her in my lap, clad in a black silk thong.

"Take them off." My voice was deep and husky as I fought to remain in control of my lust for her.

She moaned and brought her hand up next to her head and ran her nails over my scalp.

"You said shorts off. Nothing about my panties off."

"I'm changing the rules. Take them off or I'll rip them off of you."

She moaned and shimmied over my cock again.

"Help me." She purred.

"Fuck yes." I hooked my fingers over the fabric on her hips and pushed them down as she lifted her ass again. When they were wrapped around her knees I sat up and pushed them down to her feet and then slid the fabric teasingly over one leg to her center, leaning back down and pulling her down with me.

She turned her head and watched in enchantment as I brought the silk to my nose and breathed her scent deep into my lungs. "Fuck." I sighed and ran my thumb over the triangle of fabric that covered her pussy. It was soaked, just like she said. "Your pussy is so wet."

"You have no idea." She mewed and ran her hands over her thighs.

"Show me."

"How?" She asked.

"Spread your legs and play with yourself."

"Oh my god."

I took her hand from where it laid on her stomach and lowered it down her body and then pulled my hand off as she slid her fingers through her pussy lips. She hooked one leg over each of my knees, opening her thighs and rubbing her fingertips over her clit in small slow circles.

"Tell me how it feels."

"Like liquid heaven, coursing through my blood straight to my clit."

"Fuck." I groaned. "Show me your fingers."

She pulled her hand up from between her thighs and showed me the glistening wetness covering them. I grabbed her wrist and brought her fingers to my lips and sucked them into my mouth, cleaning them with my tongue and then nibbling on them.

"That was so hot." She whispered.

"You taste delicious, Ellie. I can't wait to taste your orgasm on my tongue. I'm going to have you ride my face until you come so hard."

She took her hand from me and buried it back between her spread thighs and rubbed her clit as she moaned. "Unclasp my top." She lifted her head and exposed the back of her neck to me. "I need to feel your hands on my nipples."

I opened the clasp and roughly pulled down her top, revealing her full breasts to my hungry eyes and needy hands. I grabbed both in my hands and pinched and pulled her nipples as she played with her pussy.

I could hear how wet she was and still tasted her on my tongue. "I want to taste you again." I said and moved her hand from between her thighs and slowly pushed my own fingers on each side of her clit, sliding them down to her bare smooth pussy and dipping them into her and then rubbing her clit again.

"Just like that!" She moaned. "More of that."

"Whatever you want my Queen." I wrapped my hand around her throat as her hips bucked up against my hand. She laid out so prettily on top of me with her legs spread wide and her magnificent tits on display as she rode my hand.

My cock was so hard under her, and it felt so good every time she rocked her hips over it.

"You're the sexiest woman I've ever met. You were made to be worshiped like this. You were made to be worshiped by me."

"Yes! Yes! Yes!" She moaned and her legs snapped shut around my hand as I kept rubbing my fingers over her clit and held her still with my hand wrapped tight around her throat.

"Good girl. Come on my fingers like a good little girl. Fuck, that's so sexy."

She moaned and mewled, clawing at my arm as I dragged her orgasm on and on until she was limp and melted into my lap.

Her legs fell open again as she relaxed, and I brought my fingers to her own lips and held out my pointer finger. "Taste what I do to you." I commanded.

She groaned and then opened her lips and stuck her tongue out. I slid my finger over the entire length of her tongue and moaned into her ear when her lips closed around it and sucked me deep into her mouth. "Good girl baby. Such a good fucking girl."

When I pulled my finger from her lips, I pushed my other one into my mouth and sucked her flavor from my skin again.

I helped her sit up and then kneeled before and put her feet back into her shorts. "I don't get my panties back?" She asked as she stood up and shimmied into the tight fabric.

"No. I'm adding them to my collection."

"Collection?" she asked puzzled, and then realization dawned. "You have more of my panties somewhere?" Her eyes were wide, and her lips were pulled up into a shocked smile.

"Yes. I do. I wrapped the other pair around my cock and stroked it with them last night when you left me wanting and hard."

"You're lying." She gasped, pulling her top up to cover her tits.

"You're right. I jacked off with them again this morning too. This freshly wet pair will add to the collection nicely." I deadpanned to her and then grabbed her drink off of table and took a sip.

Her mouth snapped shut as she watched me drink from her glass and she swallowed hard when I zeroed in on her. "Is this vodka?" I asked, stepping towards her slowly.

"Maybe." She tried.

"I thought we agreed you were done drinking." I said as I stopped in front of her and ran my thumb over her lush bottom lip, plucking it from her teeth.

"In my defense I ordered it weak."

"Elora." I warned.

"You don't get to tell me I can't drink at all. I just turned twenty-one. I agree to enjoy it only in moderation from now on instead of using it to numb the world. Fair?" She said, standing up on tip toes and offering her lips to me and I tried to keep a clear head about it, but

I was struggling. "You can only be my *daddy* in the bedroom Ryker. Not in the rest of my life, or this won't work."

I groaned at the mental warfare coursing through my body. Part of me loved the word daddy falling from her lips sexually. The other part of me loved her dad with every last bit of myself like a brother and it made it touchy.

"Fine." I said, pounding the rest of the drink in one swallow, leaving her none. "But doesn't mean I'm going to like it." I leaned down and took her offered lips roughly and then took a calming breath, relaxing with her in my arms. "Let's go the fuck home."

"Now that sounds wonderful." She agreed.

CHAPTER 13 – ELORA

"**I** need to find Carly before we go, and them I'm good." I took a deep breath as my orgasm settled deep into my bones, leaving me relaxed and sated for the time being. I didn't doubt that I'd be ready for more in no time at all the second Ryker started flirting with me again. He was just too damn sexy to resist.

"Okay, I have some business to handle too. Stay with Jed and I'll meet you when you're done." Ryker said, leaning down to kiss me gently.

"Okay."

He opened the curtain and looked out over his club with me by his side. It was crazy busy, bodies pressed together in every seat and walkway. "Jed." He turned and walked closer to us from his post. "She wants to find Carly, and I have to talk with Theo. Find me when she's done."

"Yes Sir." He nodded and stepped back to let me walk out in front of him.

When we were clear of the alcove I turned to him. "Have you seen her lately?" I asked.

"I think she's in the VIP room. I can find her for you if you want."

"No, that's fine, I'll go check the dressing room, and go from there." When we got to the door to the hallway I turned to him again and held my hand up for him. "Stay here."

"Ma'am." He said, tilting his head at me. "It's much busier in here now, I think it best if I came with you."

"No, the dancers deserve some privacy from men in their own space. I'll be fine." I nodded towards the bar where Willow was hanging out. "She's no Sunny, but she's sexy. Go entertain yourself and I'll be right back."

He huffed at me but then nodded to the bouncers at the door and they opened the door for me. "Make sure she's safe in there." He barked out to them as I ducked inside.

When I walked down the long hallway, I felt a giddy happiness tingling through my body. Tonight, had turned out to be quite enjoyable between my carefree lap dance with Carly and Jed and then my orgasm with Ryker. I owed him one when we got home or in the car on the way home though. He'd been hard as steel under me but hadn't asked for anything from me as I recovered from my own bliss.

I was distracted as I turned and walked into the dressing room, so it took a couple of seconds for my brain to comprehend what I was seeing. Three dancers were huddled around the vanity that Carly had been sitting at earlier, whispering in hushed tones as they looked at something on the counter.

There were other dancers in the room, but they wouldn't meet my eyes in a way that screamed, "Mind your own business."

But that wasn't my style.

I walked forward and could see in the mirror above them that they were rifling through bundles of cash that they were pulling out of a familiar gold tote bag.

The bundles had the club stamp on them that matched the ones I'd used to pay Carly and Willow for their dances.

"Does any of that belong to you?" I asked, clearing my throat behind them. They all turned around quickly and pushed the money behind them as they sized me up.

"Who are you?" One of them sneered. She was bottle blonde with dark ugly roots and a months' worth of old caked on makeup on her face. She was probably in her twenties, but she looked at least forty. And I recognized the signs of hard drug use on her arms and body. I recognized that look because she looked like my mother had the last time I saw her. Shivers of apprehension ran down my spine, but I lifted my chin and held my ground.

"I asked you a question first." I said, looking at the other two girls with her. They were less bold, looking guilty as they glanced around the room at the other dancers.

"I don't answer to you, so fuck off and mind your own business. You shouldn't even be back here. Customers are to stay up front."

She had no idea who I was, and by the looks of it, neither did her friends.

"That bag belongs to Sunny and so does that money. And you're going to put back every single dollar that you decided you'd help yourself too."

"Fuck off." She turned around, giving me her back, and started grabbing more bills from the bundles.

"So that was your only chance at me not involving your bosses in this. Which was a mistake, let me assure you." I turned to look at the other girls sitting around the room. There was one that looked like she was straight off the bus from Toledo, pretty girl next door looks and had a bit of fear in her eyes as she watched the scene unfold. "Will you go grab one of the bouncers from the door please?" I asked her nicely. She eyed me and then the other girls but didn't move. "I assure you sweetheart that you want to be on my side of things when this shit hits the fan in a moment."

Something about my calm demeanor must have spoken to her because she stood up and walked out the door down the hallway.

"Who the fuck do you think you are?" The druggy asked, stepping forward towards me. "Sunny owes us our cut of that money. We helped her earn it. That's how this job works."

"You helped her earn it?" I asked, crossing my arms over my chest. "All of you?" I looked at the other girls, and they looked away but nodded their heads yes when the ringleader nudged them. "Interesting, because that money came out of Ryker Lawson's wallet, and I don't remember you being there when I gave it to her."

The druggy's mouth fell open and one of her cohorts backed away in fear, like I was going to reach out and strike her.

Toledo and one of the bouncers from the door came into the room and looked between us all. The bouncer stepped up next to me. "Ms. Dax, what can I help you with?"

The three shriveled into the counter when I never let my stare fall from them as I answered him. "I walked in on these three stealing money from Sunny's bag. Money that still has the club brand on it that she earned from me and Mr. Lawson."

The bouncer eyed them and saw the evidence behind them.

"Wait a second," The druggy started holding her hands up and plastering a fake smile on her caked face. "There's just been a misunderstanding."

The bouncer talked into his radio, asking for Sunny and Theo to come to the dressing room with another bouncer before turning to them. "Put every dollar you have on you back on that table." He ordered, walking over to watch as the two less bold girls quickly pulled folded bills from their tops and threw them onto the counter.

"What's going on?" Carly asked as she walked in with Jed hot on her heels and Theo, who was flamboyant Mr. Flashy Suit himself.

"They were stealing from you when I walked in." I said, nodding towards the trio.

Carly blew up, rushing forward and grabbing all of the money from their hands and shoving them away from her stuff. "What the fuck, Shay!" She yelled.

The druggy, Shay still tried to placate things, eyeing me up with anger in her eyes. Jed stepped forward and placed himself at my side.

Theo stepped forward and went off on the girls in rapid angry words I had a hard time keeping up with, and helped Carly count her money before turning to me.

I nodded to him, still standing tall, even though I was out of depth here. "That money was straight out of Ryker's wallet for Sunny and Willow and every dollar will be returned to them or I'll involve him myself. Understood?"

"Of course, we don't tolerate stealing here. Not from my girls." He said, standing even taller as I threatened his territory.

"Good. And that one," I said, nodding my nose at Shay, "Is off the floor until she stops looking like a walking case of hepatitis. Get her into rehab or get her out the door. I don't care which." I turned and addressed her directly next. "That's the only warning you'll ever receive from me. I'll be checking in regularly and if any of you," I looked at the other two, "step out of line again, I'll not only kick you out of this club, but I'll blacklist you from any club within a hundred miles from here."

I turned to Carly and tried to not let her shit eating grin affect my tough facade. "When you get a second, I need to speak with you. I'll be in the hallway."

I turned and walked out of the dressing room, leaving stunned silent girls in my wake. The room was much more packed as I left than when I'd gotten there, no doubt drawn to drama, and I left with my head high and the message clear. Don't fuck with me or my friends.

Jed followed me out to the hallway and chuckled quietly at me when I took a deep breath and sagged into the wall a bit. "Holy shit." I whispered to him.

"Well, well, well. I finally see the Queen everyone keeps talking about." he said, eyeing me up appreciatively as he crossed his arms over his chest.

"Yeah, maybe. But I have no idea if I just crossed a giant line with Ryker, stepping into his business like that. Like I had a right."

"Oh, you had a right. And that kind of support is exactly what he needs in a partner. I don't think he'll be mad at all. Though he might be mad you gave them a second chance at all. He's a one and done kind of employer."

"Well, that's just going to have to do for now."

Carly came running out and slammed herself into me, hugging me tight. "Holy fuck El, I've never seen you so stern and serious! I got serious boss babe vibes, and I have to say, it's a fucking turn on." I tipped my head back and laughed loudly at her as she stepped back and shook her head. "Seriously! I need to stop trying to find powerful men to fuck and start fucking powerful women!"

"Oh my god, Carly!" I gasped and shoved her lightly in jest.

Jed perked up next to us, "That's a hell of a plan, except I think a girl like you would miss one thing in particular if you went to chicks."

She turned to him and crossed her arms over her ample chest and stood toe to toe with him. "Oh yeah? And what exactly do you think I'd miss about men?" She challenged.

"On that note I'm going to get a drink at the bar." I said, walking backwards toward the door. Jed started coming with me, but I put my hand up stopping him, "Oh hell no buddy, you don't want to miss out on that conversation, I assure you." I said, nodding to Carly and winking at him. "Carly, I'll call you tomorrow!" I called out as I walked through the door and out into the club.

I turned and walked around the edge of the room towards the back, using the darkness to duck between tables and hide away from the flashing lights of the main stage as I made my way towards the bar.

"Hey, are you new?" A man's hand reached out and wrapped around my wrist, pulling me to a stop as I walked by his table.

I looked down and there were six or seven men in business suits sitting at a large table and it was littered with empty bottles and glasses. They all looked disheveled and sloppy as they looked up at me lewdly.

A dancer had been grinding on one of the guys but when they turned their attention to me, she quickly grabbed her cash off the table and ducked out.

Shit. Even the strippers didn't want to be near these guys.

I pulled my wrist from his hand forcefully and tried to be polite, but firm. "No. I don't work here. Sorry."

"Damn!" He yelled and laughed with his friends. "I'd pay some fucking big bucks to get you in the VIP room."

His buddies laughed and eyed me up obscenely. A couple of them had cigars in their mouths and the smoke made my eyes burn. I tried to walk away, deciding it wasn't worth wasting my energy to tell them off, but he reached out and put his hands on my hips and pulled me down into his lap.

"Let go of me." I snapped, slapping his hands off of me where he held onto me.

"Oh, come on baby. I'm sure I could blow my load in record time on your pretty tits. It'd be the easiest fifty bucks you make all night."

I was going to vomit.

I shoved at him again, elbowing him in the throat and I finally got him to let go of me. But that had enraged him, and he jumped up and stepped into my space with anger dripping from his eyes now instead of drunk stupor.

"You fucking cunt." He said as he swiped his hand through the air lightning fast and suddenly pain radiated through the side of my face as the back of his hand connected with my cheek bone.

"You're a dead man!" I heard a man roar from behind me and suddenly I was pulled backwards as bouncers descended on the table and a full out brawl broke out.

"Ellie!" Carly screamed and grabbed me, pulling me further from the mayhem and putting my back against the wall. Jed picked up the man that had hit me and literally threw him across the room where he landed in a heap at the feet of the most feared man in the world.

"Ryker." I whispered as he looked at the scene with wild eyes. The entire club fell silent as everyone watched the scene unfold. He looked from the man at his feet and up to Jed who looked downright murderous, before swinging his eyes around the room violently. Zeke stood at his side and motioned for two men to pick my attacker up off the ground where he sniveled and begged for mercy, not even aware of the severity of what he'd just done.

"Where is she?" Ryker roared and turned back to Jed, who was now looking over at me where I cowered in pain and shock. Ryker followed his stare, and his eyes landed on me like a heavy weight around my neck.

I held my hand to my burning cheek as tears blinded my vision, threatening to fall. Carly held me to her chest with her body between me and the crowd, willing to protect me if needed.

Ryker crossed the room in seconds and pulled me from her arms and into his. "Ellie." He bit out between clenched teeth and pushed my hair back, pulling my hand down to look at my cheek. A tear spilled over my lashes as I looked up at him and his eyes glassed over completely. Gone was the gentle man I'd laid in the arms of this morning on the couch.

And in his place was the ruthless King that everyone feared.

CHAPTER 14 – RYKER

R age like I'd never known before burned every single nerve in my body as I watched a man backhand Elora across the face.

I'd been across the club, meeting with my manager, when my eyes landed on her beautiful face as she walked across the room towards me. But then a sleazeball attacked her, pulling her into his lap, and I'd seen red.

By the time I'd gotten halfway across the club, he'd hit her, and Jed and two other men had erupted into a mess of violence on him and his friends.

Losing her in the chaos, I nearly tore every man in the place limb from limb to find her. When Jed tossed the man at my feet, I cared for nothing else but getting her into my arms so I could make sure she was alright.

When I finally found her, she was cowering in the corner with Carly's arms wrapped around her as she held her face.

Elora collapsed into my arms, her small body trembling, the moment I reached her; my own body vibrated with barely contained rage as I saw the blossoming welt on her cheek and the tears welling in her beautiful eyes.

The club was silent other than the music as everyone watched me, waiting to see what I did. For two days, whispers and rumors had spread through the city like wildfire—a woman had consumed my every thought and move, they said—and now, here we stood, my people watching with bated breath, their faces a mixture of fear and anticipation.

To leave no room for ambiguity, I needed to publicly declare my claim to Elora Dax; it was long overdue.

Holding Ellie tight against my side, I offered Carly a quick nod, confirming I had her friend, and then turned to face my men, their faces grim in the dim light. They were waiting for their instructions on what to do with the men responsible for disrespecting Elora.

"Make the message clear to all of them and make it fucking hurt." I said, nodding towards the pathetic pieces of shit pissing their pants on the floor that had been with the main asshole. "Where is the one that hit my girlfriend?"

Zeke caught my eye, "Your office."

"I'll meet you there. Let's go."

I kept Elora tucked against my side as I ducked into the doorway leading to the dressing room and then swept her up into my arms as soon as we were in the dark hallway.

She took a shaky breath as she buried her face in my neck. "I'm sorry." She whispered.

I kept walking, not trusting myself to be calm enough to have a conversation with her just yet. Women stared at us as I passed through the hallway and into a small office in the back where our house accountant worked and shut the door behind us.

Setting her down on the desk, I switched on the lamp beside her, and the room filled with a warm, inviting glow.

Her brows were furrowed over her eyes, and her cheek was already a hue of purple. She wouldn't meet my eyes as she sat there, waiting for me to say something, but I couldn't.

She thought I was angry with her, I could tell. But that was so far from the truth.

"I've never been so terrified in my life." I finally grounded out. She quickly looked up at me with confusion in her eyes. "Scratch that, the only other time I've been so scared was the night I listened to your screams through the phone when you were shot."

"Scared?" She shook her head back and forth and then touched her fingertips to her cheek again, grimacing in pain. "I'm so confused."

I laid my forehead against hers and breathed her in for a moment. "I couldn't get to you baby. Watching him grab you, I saw you fight back, and I was pushing my way through the crowd, but before I could get there, he hit you. And, my God, I didn't take another breath until I touched your skin with mine after that."

"I'm sorry!" She gasped and then hiccupped as she fought to control her breathing. "I left the dressing room without Jed; I didn't think it'd be a big deal to walk across the fucking room alone!"

"Shh, I'm not mad at you." I said and leaned down to kiss her lips. She quickly deepened the kiss, using the lapels of my jacket to pull me in closer.

And I was happy to oblige.

I tangled my fingers in her hair and tilted her head to the side and teased her tongue with mine as she moaned and took everything I had to give her. I was a man possessed, and I ached to claim her, needing her to be a part of my soul now more than ever before.

Her hands went to my belt, and she pulled the leather out of the buckle, and then her nimble fingers were pulling at the button and zipper of my slacks.

"El." I said, "Stop."

She paused, pulling back as rejection flashed in her eyes quickly before she slid a mask over it. "You don't want me?"

I groaned and buried my face in her neck, breathing her in. "The opposite. I want you so bad, I want to bury myself inside of you and never pull out for the rest of my life."

"Then why stop me now?" Her voice trembled.

"Because I don't want the first time I'm inside of you to be in a dusty strip club office."

She chuckled and kissed my neck. "For the record, I wasn't going to give you my pussy in this dusty strip club office. I was, however, going to get on my knees and suck your cock to relieve some of the phenomenal anger coursing through your veins right now. And to even the score for the orgasm you gave me half an hour ago."

I groaned and my hips jerked forward, rubbing myself against her hot core. She hissed and slid her fingers into the open fly of my pants, slowly drawing lines of torture down my groin until they touched the base of my cock where it lay, hardening, and growing down the leg of my pants.

"Let me make you feel good, like you did for me." She whispered, biting my neck, and then pressing her supple lips to it and kissing it sensually.

I grabbed her wrist and pulled her hand from my pants and kissed each of her fingertips as disappointment coursed through my veins and flashed in her eyes. "Not here, love. Not like this."

"Fine." She said softly, and I stepped back and did up my pants, tucking my shirt back in as she watched with fascination.

"Are you okay?" I asked, gently kissing her cheek.

"I'll be fine. It just scared me."

"Twice now, you've been hurt in my clubs in the last few days. You're taking years off my life every time you fall injured because of me."

"This wasn't your fault Ry. Don't take the blame off that man and shoulder it for him. It was his fault."

"Why were you not with Jed?" I'd been irate when I saw Jed crossing the room ahead of me to get to Elora when she was in peril.

"I left him in the hallway with Carly; I'd just gotten hip deep in shit in the dressing room—" She groaned, "Maybe I am the problem."

"What do you mean?" I asked, my hackles raising.

"I caught a couple of girls stealing the money I'd paid Carly earlier from her bag. I kind of–I don't know, threatened to fire them, and I guess overstepped my place a bit."

"No, you didn't. I would have thrown them from this club the second they were caught, so you were more generous with them than I would have been."

"Jed said the same thing." She said with a small smile on her lips.

"From now on, Jed goes with you wherever you go, do you understand? I don't care if it's into the dressing room or not."

"No!" She gasped and leaned back. "That's not fair to them, don't cheapen them even more than they do themselves, just because you worry about me. That's not fair. Carly is my best friend and the only reason I've survived being back in Shadeport. Without her, I would have starved to death years ago. So, I'm not about to subject her to more prying eyes where she's supposed to have a bit of privacy."

I paused, taking in the flush in her cheeks and the huffing of her breath as she got worked up about it. "You care about her, don't you?"

"Not just her." She breathed, sliding off the desk and into my arms fully. "They deserve some respect, regardless of their profession. I was on a high from the power trip and wanted to take a deep breath alone for a second, so I left him there to make sure she got her money back. I should have just asked one of the bouncers at the dressing room door to walk me, but I honestly didn't think I was in any danger. Everyone had already been treating me differently since I walked in the door."

"Different how?"

She looked up at me, and the lack of confidence in her eyes broke me more than I thought possible. "Like I mattered." She said.

"You're the only person in this entire world that matters, Ellie."

A gentle smile touched her lips as she stood up on her toes and offered them to me. I leaned down and kissed her sensuously, letting my tongue glide over the plump smoothness of her lips.

"Now what?"

I sighed and pulled back, loosening the button at my throat. "Now I go take care of the asshole that hit you."

"Take care of him, how?" she asked meekly.

I raised my eyebrow at her and tried to choose the right direction here. "Do you really want to know?"

"Should I?" She asked.

"No."

"Then probably not, but a part of me wants to know what that side of you is like."

"There is only one side of me, Ellie. You get what you see."

She laughed lightly and shook her head. "You're so wrong, baby." It was the first time she called me that and hearing it on her lips did things to me. "You have many different sides; you just choose to only let certain people see them."

"You think I let you see them?" I asked.

"Yes, you have. You always have with me. And I want to see this side of you now."

I watched her pensively, trying to decide if it was a mistake to show her exactly how I conducted business or not, but finally decided to let her in.

"You can watch, you can also leave at any point. I'll make sure Zeke and Jed are with you if you leave, so you'll be safe. Okay?"

She nodded and then took a deep breath. With her hand tightly squeezed in mine, we walked up the back staircase to my office. Two of my men stood at the door and opened it for us when we neared and closed it behind us. My office here at Lux was set up like the one at Erotiq, it was above the main floor, and mirrored windows looked down onto the floor below so I could watch everything going on.

Zeke, Jed, and others stood around the room in various moods as I walked around them and pulled Elora in behind me. She took in a quick breath when she saw the man lying on the floor in the center of the office with his face already bloodied and cut up.

"Started without me?" I asked, looking over at Zeke.

"He's got a mouth on him."

"Meaning what?"

Zeke cut a glance at Ellie and then back to me. "About her."

My jaw clicked, and my fists clenched.

I led Ellie over to my desk and sat her down in my chair, leaning down to kiss her hair. "Stay seated over here unless you need to go. Got it?"

She nodded and looked me in the eye, showing she was with me. Regal authority laid beneath her bright eyes and I fought to control the pride that burned in my gut. She was perfect as my Queen.

Taking off my suit jacket, I laid it over a chair next to my desk and rolled up my sleeves as I started playing with my entertainment. "So you came into my club tonight, and disrespected me by touching what belongs to me, huh?" I asked the son of a bitch as he looked up at me with fear in his eyes. He was probably in his forties and was a nobody judging by the ill fit of his suit, though I'd recognized one guy he was with as a mid-level player in the game of drugs around here.

He looked past me to Elora, and that enraged me. "Don't look at her, fucker!" I yelled, kicking him in the side.

He grunted and groaned, rolling over, holding his side.

When the wheezing stopped, he started laughing, and that set off something inside of my head.

"You think this is funny? Do you have any idea how near death you are? A verdict is to be made in the next few minutes, and it will decide if you live a long painful life, or a short mild one."

His eyes flashed in fear before he started chuckling again. "I know exactly how much of a dead man I am, Mr. Lawson." He choked on his spit and then cleared his throat as he sat up and leaned his back against the wall. "The question is, does she?"

Jed and Zeke both took a step towards him, and he laughed some more. He looked back over at where my whole world sat, and he got a serious look in his eye. "I had no idea who she was until you reacted the way you did. And now—God." He gasped, looking at her with wonder in his eyes. "Years ago, the rumor had it that the princess was dead, and the debt was paid." He turned his attention back to me, "But there she sits, beautiful and healthy as ever, and now a *Queen*." His eyes glowed with mirth. "That means the scales are tipped back again, and the hit reopened."

"What the fuck are you talking about?" I snapped, grabbing him, and lifting his pathetic body off the floor and held him against the wall, with his feet dangling helplessly.

"The assassination order that killed the King, was for two body bags, not one. Word will spread quickly that she's still alive, now that you've claimed her openly, and it will be only a matter of time before another hit is called."

"By whom?" I demanded, bouncing his head off the wall.

He laughed again. "What will you give me if I tell you?"

I threw him to the ground and turned my back on him. "Nothing." I spit out, instructing Zeke as I walked away. "Remove every inch of skin from his body, then remove his limbs, and then fucking kill him."

"Wait!" He yelled, holding his hand out as Jed and Zeke walked forward towards him. "Wait, I'll tell you!"

I looked over my shoulder at him and raised an unimpressed eyebrow at him as he started rambling. "Only Kings have anything to gain from the death of other kings. And only princesses have anything to gain from the death of other princesses."

"Stop talking in mysteries fucker!" I demanded.

"The only other princess in the land is Monica Wellington."

The air left my lungs as I looked down at the piece of shit on the floor.

"You're telling me that Nicolas Wellington ordered the hit on Gavin Dax and his daughter?"

"That's exactly what I'm telling you. He hired it out to a crew from Southside and they confirmed the death of both Dax's. Clearly, they lied. And you knew only that the Southsider's were the ones that attacked that night and you wiped them off the face of this earth, but it wasn't their plan originally."

"What does he or Monica have to gain from their death? I took over operations after Gavin's death, not Nicolas."

The piece of shit started chuckling again and looked at me with disbelief in his eyes. "You really don't see what they want, do you?"

I didn't. I couldn't understand it for a second.

"You." A quiet voice whispered from behind me. I looked over my shoulder to where Elora sat, white as a ghost, looking up at me. She licked her lips and stood up, "They want you. And what you can offer them as King. I got in the way of her getting to Dad when he was alive, he never dated anyone serious because of me. And now I'm in the way again, and *you* proved that to her the other day."

I turned back to the man sitting on the floor and saw the confirmation in his eyes. His body relaxed as he smiled up at me. "I think that has earned me a quick death, at least."

I looked over at Elora once again and she was staring at me with such agony in her eyes. "Close your eyes." I told her.

She just shook her head, not understanding why. Zeke stepped over and wrapped his arm around her shoulders, turning her until she looked at him and held her close to his chest with his hands over her ears.

I drew a pistol from my shoulder holster and turned, shooting one bullet off into the asshole's head and tried not to let Elora's shriek gut me anymore than I already was.

Over my dead body was anything going to happen to Elora Dax at the hands of Nicolas and Monica Wellington. I gave instructions to my men and pulled Elora's shaking body from Zeke's arms and picked her up, carrying her out the back door of the club and into my waiting car.

Three other cars joined ours in the quick drive across the city to my home, and Elora stayed silent the entire time.

I held her on my lap, unable to let her get even an inch away from me right now, even if I couldn't offer her any comfort with words.

When we got home, she slid from my arms and walked in on her own, and as bad as my hands ached to carry her, I let her go.

If she wanted space from me, then I needed to give it to her. She walked up the staircase silently with the weight of the world on her shoulders and when she got to the top of the stairs; she turned and looked at me.

"I just need a minute; then I'm going to go to bed." She said softly, not meeting my eyes directly.

"I need to make some plans." I answered back.

She nodded and turned towards her bedroom without another word, taking my heart with her.

I loved her.

Fuck.

I'd always loved Elora Dax, since the moment I met her as a tiny baby.

But my feelings evolved over the years as our relationship did, and now that she was an adult, here and relying on me, I realized I didn't just love her; I was in love with her.

And I wasn't going to let anyone touch her. Especially not someone like Nicolas Wellington.

"Fuck!" I yelled, feeling the frustration pouring from my body as I walked to my office.

I headed straight for the bar and poured myself a glass.

As the minutes passed, more and more of my men entered the room and joined me.

Top generals from my crew, shot callers and even runners all stood around my office and waited for their orders.

Zeke and Jed sat in the chairs opposite of me at the desk and the others milled around the room as I settled my nerves with liquor.

Finally, I sat down and addressed everyone. "The message is clear here. Protect Elora Dax at all costs. We failed her once, the night her father was murdered in front of her in our own streets, and I won't let that happen again." I pounded back my drink.

"A lot has changed since Gavin was killed." Zeke said, rubbing his hand over his bald head. "We could easily wipe the Wellington's and their crew off the face of this earth; don't they realize that?"

"I don't think they ever expected us to know they were a threat at all. We've been allies with them for years, long before Gavin and I even started leading. But I won't start a war based off one fucker's word. I want all ears to the ground. I want proof that they were behind the hit originally and, regardless if they still see her as a threat or not, they'll pay for their sins. Until then, we lock Elora down. She doesn't leave this house without me or Zeke. Jed is still on point for all of her travel, but we add me or Zeke to the mix. If we are at any of my clubs and you see her alone, you take up post on her immediately. She isn't to be alone until we know if there is a threat to her for sure."

My men nodded and added their input on ways to find out information, and we spent almost two hours strategizing. This threat to Elora hit hard in the hearts of my men. Most of my high-ranking members were in the crew when Gavin and I led it together, and they still held guilt from losing him.

After I couldn't think about strategy or plans for a moment longer, I kicked most everyone out, keeping a few extra for security detail, and went upstairs. My feet paused on the landing as I looked longingly down the hallway to her guest room, and before I could make the conscious thought to do it, my feet were carrying me down the hallway towards her.

No light peeked from under her door, so I silently opened it, invading her space. I didn't know if she was asleep or not, but I needed to lay eyes on her to settle the monster in my chest. He called for bloodshed, demanded it, and the only hope I had of calming it down was with her peace. Walking into the dark bedroom, I looked over at the bed where she should have been lying, but it was empty.

"Ellie?" I called out, walking to the bathroom and then the closet, finding them both empty. "Elora, where are you?" I yelled again. Frustration burned in my spine as I searched for her. So, help me god if she took off again!

"Ellie!" I yelled, turning, and running out into the hallway. Zeke was running up the stairs when I got to them, alarm on his face.

"She's gone?" He asked.

"She's not in her room." Just then my bedroom door opened down the hall opposite of her room and she stepped out into the hallway, wearing only a short-sleeve shirt of mine and some sleepy eyes.

"What's wrong?" Walking toward me, she asked, pushing her hair from her face. She squinted at us in the light from the foyer chandelier, and my heart fell into my stomach.

She was so fucking beautiful, and more importantly, she was *safe*.

I groaned, pushing Zeke away back towards the stairs so he wouldn't see her in so little clothing, and then walked forward to meet her. I wrapped my arms around her and molded my lips to hers aggressively.

Zeke sighed and then laughed as he went back down the stairs, but I didn't care.

"You weren't in your room." I said, pushing my hands into her hair and pulling her head back to look at me.

Her eyes were still clouded with sleep, and a soft smile pulled her lips. "I wanted to sleep next to you." She froze and bit her lip. "Unless you don't want me too."

She looked past me to where Zeke retreated to. I didn't give her another second to worry about it.

I slid my hands down under her ass and picked her up, she instantly wrapped her legs around my waist, and I walked us back into my bedroom, slamming the door shut behind us and locking it.

My hands were spread wide, holding onto her lush ass and I was losing all ability to think straight because her ass was bare in my hands, and I could feel her hot center against my stomach.

"Are you wearing panties?" I asked against her lips as I stood at the end of my bed. I looked past her and noticed that there was an Elora sized empty spot in the center under the covers where she had been laying before I found her.

She sighed and just shook her head back and forth slowly, letting her nose touch the end of mine each time. "You stole them from me earlier, remember?"

"Fuck." I growled, leaning forward and laid her flat on her back in the center of the bed and pressed my hard on into her bare pussy. She moaned and dug her nails into my neck. "I want to see."

I may not have poised it as a question, but she could say no if she wanted. I slid my hand to her hip and buried my fingers in the soft flesh between her leg and her stomach and took a deep breath. Waiting for her answer.

"I took them off in hopes that you would look." She said, biting her lip. "Under one condition, though."

"Anything. Literally anything." I was frantic to see her pussy spread open in my bed. I'd tasted her secondhand and felt her earlier, but I needed more.

"I get to see all of you. And I get to taste you."

My nostrils flared and my vision went black as I fought to control myself. "You want to suck my cock?"

"Yes!" She moaned, arching her back and pushing her pussy against my cock again. "I wanted to suck you off at the club, but you wouldn't let me."

"I don't deserve you, Doll." I said before drinking from her lips again. She clung to me as I kissed her with everything I had, like it would be the last time I ever tasted her again.

I slid my hand under the hem of her shirt and raised it, taking the shirt with me and then pushed it off over her head.

She lay there, completely naked and bare in the center of my bed, and I groaned. "You are my biggest fantasy come to life."

She giggled and leaned up to bite my ear lobe. "If you had any idea how many times I played with myself thinking of you over the years, you'd run for the hills."

Any restraint I had snapped, and I lowered myself to her perfect tits and sucked on her nipples as she whined and writhed under me. I slid down her body, kissing her flat stomach and over to each wide hip until I was a breath away from her exquisite pussy. She was bare and silky smooth, and I pushed her legs wide as I lowered my lips to her sensitive skin.

She gasped and arched her back when I kissed the inside of her hip and moved down until my lips landed directly on her clit.

"Oh." She moaned, tangling her fingers in my hair as I pressed the flat of my tongue over her clit and licked upwards.

"Fuck, you taste so fucking good. So much better straight from the source." I growled. Both of my hands went to the inside of her thighs and pushed wider, desperate to spread her open for me to taste the deepest parts of her. I pushed my tongue into her body and groaned at how fucking tight she was. I fucked her with my tongue while she rode my face and fisted the bed sheets.

"Oh, my god Ry." Her voice was airy and light as she tried to control herself. She had the back of her hand against her lips, muffling her moans and pleas.

I reached up and grabbed her arm, removing her hand and wove my fingers through hers, holding her hand at her side in a death grip as I slowly edged the tip of a finger into her pussy.

She had the tightest pussy I'd ever felt in my entire life. My finger was squeezed fucking tight, and I knew I'd rip her open with my cock the first time I fucked her.

How had no one else stretched her further than this, the other times she had sex? This poor girl had been screwing shrimp-dick fools when she deserved to be fucked by a man.

Like me.

My cock ached underneath me as I rocked my hips, pushing it into the softness of the mattress as I brought her to the edge of her orgasm. "I want you to come on my face, doll. Fucking shatter on my tongue."

"Ry!" She begged, and she brought her hand up to her tits and pulled at her pretty nipples and then seconds later her pussy clamped down even tighter on my finger as her orgasm ripped through her. I used her distraction to add another finger and bottomed out inside of her as she screamed my name.

I fucked her hard with my fingers while I continued to suck on her clit, drawing her orgasm out while her legs shook on each side of my head. When she finally stilled, her body went limp, and she laid there, looking at the ceiling in wonder.

I kissed my way back up her body and laid next to her, running my hands up and down her stomach and hips.

"I've never," She started and then swallowed and looked over at me. "I've never come so hard in my life."

A sinister smile crossed my lips, and I leaned in to kiss her lips. "That was just the first of many baby. I promise you that."

"Hmm, that sounds wonderful." She rolled over and slung her leg over mine as she straddled me. "You're way overdressed."

"Oh yeah?" I asked, laying back on the pillow as she sat on me, naked and flushed from her orgasm. She started unbuttoning my shirt, and when she was done with that, she undid the cuffs. I sat up and helped her get my holster and shirt off. She was timid and reserved when she first started, but with each inch of skin that she revealed she got bolder. She wasn't ashamed of her body in any way and she had no reason to be, but it was refreshing that even though I knew she was less experienced then me, she wasn't shy.

She kissed my chest, the same way I had down hers, and I groaned when her teeth nipped at my own nipple. "El." I warned, and she smiled against my chest, lowering her lips to my abs.

"Your body is magnificent." She praised.

Each ab was kissed by her on the way down to my belt, before she quickly undid it and the button of my pants and then slid off the bed.

She meticulously undid the laces of my shoes and took my socks off and then pulled my pants down and tossed them onto the growing pile. I let her go at her own pace, even though I desperately wanted to roll her over underneath of me and force my cock into her body.

She kneeled on the bed and let her fingers slide under the band of my boxer briefs, and she locked her eyes onto mine as she slowly slid them down my legs and off completely.

Biting her lip, she finally let her pretty hazel eyes fall to my waist where my cock laid against my stomach, hard and dripping for her.

She moaned, working her lip between her teeth more and then pushed her pink tongue out over the dented flesh, like she was salivating for a taste.

Her eyes glowed in the dark room as she crawled back up the bed, letting her hips sway and her tits bob under her body as she came up to press her lips to mine.

"I want to taste you so bad." She whispered against my lips. "Tell me how you like it."

I groaned. "You could blow on it and I'd fucking come eventually, I'm that worked up right now."

"I want to make you feel good."

"So do it."

"Beg me." She demanded, and I would have gotten on my knees if she'd actually asked me to.

Her tits barely brushed against my chest as she held still, challenging me, and she touched me nowhere else, and I was desperate for contact.

But I wasn't going to tip my hand to her so easily. I slid my hand up the slim column of her throat until my fingers wrapped all the way around it and squeezed. The alabaster skin of her slim neck looked sexy with my tattooed hand wrapped around it. I didn't restrict her breath, but I did lessen the blood flow to her brain, and soon her face started reddening, and her eyes flashed with desire.

"I won't beg you for something you already told me you wanted desperately. I will however, command you to do it." Her nostrils flared, and her hips swung like she was trying to quell the ache between her thighs. "Get on your knees and suck my cock, Elora. Take me all the way down your fucking throat like a good girl and show me that you need me as badly as I need you."

Her eyes rolled and fluttered shut as she palmed her heavy breast between us and then slid down my body until her face was even with my cock.

I kept my hand wrapped around her throat as she wrapped her tiny hand around my cock and licked her lips. She kept her eyes on mine as she slid her tongue over the underside of the head before swirling it around the entire top and pulled a groan out of my chest.

I let go of her throat and slid my arm under my head to watch the sexiest show I'd ever seen before.

She dropped down to her elbows and left her sexy ass in the air as she wrapped her mouth around my cock and slid it up and down, letting her saliva coat my skin. Her hands started chasing her mouth as she worked me over.

I was surprised how far down she could go on me before she gagged and came back off. She worked me deeper into her throat each pass, pushing past her reflex until her lips kissed the top of my balls and I groaned madly, fisting her hair in my hand, and holding her there for a moment. She hummed, and she ran her nails over the tight skin of my balls and stared deep into my soul.

And that was all the restraint I had. I pulled her mouth off of my cock and she dove back down as soon as she took another breath, and I started coming. Her eyes widened as I filled her pretty mouth with my come. She fought to swallow it all, and some spilled out onto her lips as she continued to suck me deep.

I roared, my hips jerked violently as I felt the last rope of come erupt out of my cock and deep into her throat.

"Holy fuck." I groaned as she let the head of my cock pop out of her mouth. Her pink tongue licked what had spilled on her lips and chin and she swallowed that down too. "You're incredible."

I pulled her up my body and attacked her mouth with mine, tasting my own release on her tongue while she tasted hers on mine. She landed in my lap with my still semi erect cock pinned against the wet lips of her pussy.

I arched my hips up and slid my cock through her wetness and she moaned, dropping her forehead to mine.

"Did I do good?" She asked. "Did you like it?"

"Fuck." I griped. "Terrible. You should probably never try to do that to me ever again."

She smiled at me and bit her lip as she rocked her hips on my cock. "You swear?"

"Hell no, that was the best blowjob I've ever gotten before. And I've gotten a lot of blowjobs in my life."

Her brow creased, and her lip turned up in a silent snarl. "Don't talk about all the other head you've gotten."

I rolled her over and pinned her beneath me. "Does it make you jealous?"

"Positively green with envy."

"Good."

"Careful, or I'll tell you all about my past." She challenged.

My hand instinctively wrapped around her throat, and I turned her head, so my lips were at her ear. I pushed my cock through her wet lips again from root to tip and loved the way her throat vibrated with a moan. "I wish you would tell me the name of every single man who's ever touched your body. Then I can go find them and kill them all. Every single last one of them. It tortures me to think of other men walking around knowing what you look like." I kissed her neck, "What you taste like." I kissed her lips. "What you feel like." I thrust my hips again.

She sighed and looked at me with something in her eyes that I couldn't quite read. It wasn't unusual for me not to read Elora's thoughts clearly, since she had gotten Gavin's famed poker face, but it was beginning to unnerve me.

I needed to possess her every want, every desire, every last thought and need. And I couldn't do that if she had secrets.

"I need you." She purred, rocking her hips under me.

"Need me how?" I asked, wanting her to say the words.

She bit her lip and hesitated, though, and that was answer enough for me. She wanted more, but she wasn't ready for it all.

"I'll give you whatever you want, Doll. You just have to tell me. Tell me what it is you need from me, and I'll give it to you." I sucked on her neck, pulling the skin between my teeth, and leaving a welt that satisfied something inside of me when I pulled back and saw my mark on her.

"I need another orgasm." She said firmly, before finishing softer with, "Please."

"Hmm. Please, sounds so good falling from your lips, baby." I grabbed both of her wrists in my hand and pinned her arms above her head, and started rocking my hips back and forth, rubbing her clit with the underside of my cock. "Almost as good as my come looked on your lips."

"Ah." She groaned, meeting me thrust for thrust. "Want to know a secret?" She asked.

"Of course."

"I've never swallowed before. That was my first time."

"Fuck. That's so sexy." My balls were tight again already as she rode me from underneath, begging and pleading for another orgasm.

"Did you like taking that first?" She panted.

"I wish I had every single one of your firsts. I wish your only memories were of me and my cock."

She moaned, and I knew she was close; her body was tight, and her hips jerked wildly beneath me.

"Ryker, I'm so close."

"I know, baby, so am I. You feel so fucking good under me, pinned beneath me like this. I can't see straight from how good you feel."

"Oh, my god!" She shouted, and her body went tight and snapped like a rubber band as she came. Her legs shook and her eyes rolled, and incoherent words fell from her lips.

I thrust two more times and joined her in bliss as my spine lit on fire and every muscle in my body cramped as I poured myself out onto her belly between us.

She opened her eyes and watched between our bodies as I coated her skin with my release, and she groaned and smiled sexily as she watched. "Why is that so hot?" She asked, laying her head back on the pillow.

"Because it's me, marking you as mine." I answered truthfully. "I can't seem to stop claiming you at every turn."

Releasing her arms, she dropped her hands onto my shoulders, softly running them through my hair. "Don't ever stop." She whispered.

"I won't."

"Hmm." She hummed sleepily.

CHAPTER 15 – ELORA

I woke up to the sensation of lips on my forehead, but when I opened my eyes, I was alone. I lay naked in Ryker's bed in the middle of his grand bedroom, but the man himself was gone.

The expensive sheets felt cool and smooth against my skin as I wearily stretched and rolled over, a sigh escaping my lips. A week ago, I'd been lying in my ratty Walmart special sheets on a mattress on the floor of my teeny apartment, and today I was here.

And I was also in danger because of it.

I knew coming back into this world would be bad for my health. But lying here, still able to smell Ryker on my skin, I almost wasn't scared of it. He would protect me; I knew he would.

And things were different now than they were seven years ago, his kingdom was so much bigger and more powerful now. I had to have faith that he would find a way to eliminate the threat against me from that awful woman and her father.

When I'd sat in his office while he interrogated that man, I'd gotten flashbacks of my childhood. Memories I hadn't realized I'd forgotten until I remembered them, times with my dad when a younger blonde woman had come around, and I remembered vividly, my dad making excuses for his inability to dedicate time to her as she complained and whined on and on about priorities.

And that woman had been Monica Wellington. She had chased after my dad for a while, but the harder I looked back on it, I realized my dad had never brought her around me much. And I couldn't remember why I had a few vivid memories of her, but nothing more.

Shaking the thoughts away, I crawled out of bed and used the ensuite to freshen up, groaning at my bed head in the mirror. We had showered together after he covered me with his orgasm and it had been so sexy, until I'd gone to bed and passed out with damp hair, and now I looked like I got into a fight with a rabid squirrel.

I grabbed the shirt of his I was wearing last night and put it on and quietly opened the bedroom door, listening for voices.

I could hear some downstairs but none near, so I quickly ran down the hall to my own bedroom where I could get dressed and try to tame my appearance.

I put on a pair of black skinny jeans and a v neck white blouse that Carly had given to me when it didn't fit her last year. My closet was full of clothes that Carly had mysteriously bought but then didn't like and tossed my way instead of returning them. I'd fought her to begin with, but to be honest, it was so nice to have nice clothes for once, so I eventually just started accepting them.

The shirt was sheer, so I put on a black lace bralette under it and donned a layered black necklace to match.

I looked in the mirror and tied my hair up in a topknot and pulled wisps from my bangs and my ears to make it look messy.

Something caught my eye in the mirror, and I groaned when I looked closer and saw the mark that Ryker had left on my neck last night with his mouth. Even covering it with concealer only muted the red and purple mark, which I was sure was why he did it. I put on a light layer of mascara and eye liner and sprayed a spritz of perfume and called it good.

From the kitchen, I heard voices as I walked barefoot down the stairs. I didn't know what to do, whether I should avoid the kitchen and stay out of their business or assume that because they were in a common area, it was safe to join.

I hated not knowing where I stood in terms of freedoms in his home.

So instead of stressing it I just held my head high and walked into the kitchen in search of some coffee.

My step faltered though when I crossed the threshold and saw nearly twenty large, imposing men littered around the space in conversation and enjoying a hearty breakfast that laid out on the giant island.

I paused, unsure of what to do.

"Good morning, Doll." I heard from my right and turned to see Ryker sitting at the table with a plate full of food and a sexy smile.

The room paused; conversation ceased as everyone turned to look at me. "I'm sorry to interrupt—" I started.

"Nonsense." Ry said, standing up and walking over to the coffeepot. "This is your home Elora, if we didn't want to be interrupted, we would have been in my office with the door shut."

"Okay." I whispered as he walked towards me with an ease in his step that made him look like a big cat stalking its prey. And I was happy to be his next meal.

He handed me the cup of coffee and leaned down to kiss me, pressing his lips gently to mine. I was eager to take what he was giving, and when he tilted his head and deepened the kiss, I used my free hand to cling to his dress shirt for stability as I was quickly submerged in desire.

"Come eat. You need to replenish your energy." He said against my lips and took my hand, pulling me towards the large table set in a nook of windows. There were no empty seats, and both Jed and Zeke stood to give me their seats, but I held my hand up.

"Thank you, but please keep your seats."

Ryker sat down at the head of the table and pulled me down onto his lap, setting his hand on my hip and pulling me close. "This is a much better way to eat my breakfast." He said into my ear, sending shivers down my spine.

Margaret walked over with a warm smile and a plate full of eggs, hash browns and avocado toast.

"Thank you so much." I said and dug in as conversation resumed around me.

"What have you gotten in the last twelve hours?" Ry asked.

Zeke leaned forward, wiping his mouth. "The hit was surely executed by the Southside crew. We were right about that."

"Well, considering we slaughtered them for it, I'm glad." Ry responded dryly, taking a sip of his coffee, and leaned back in the chair. He slid his hand up my back and let his fingers slide under the hem of my shirt, touching the skin of my lower back. It was innocent enough, but it was sending jolts of electricity through my body, especially in front of his men.

I don't know why, but him being affectionate in front of men he respected, meant something more to me than just his affections in private. It made me feel like he wasn't ashamed of me or anything.

"Apparently lips have gotten loose over the last couple of years too, because we did get enough chatter that the Wellingtons were behind the initial order, to believe it."

"Why did *we* not pick up on that chatter before now? Why did it wait until we went looking for it to hear it?" Ry asked, his body was getting coiled tight as the topic intensified.

I put my fork down and leaned back into his arms, no longer really hungry for the food on my plate. He wrapped his arms around me completely and rested his chin on my shoulder as I leaned into him for comfort.

Zeke looked at me and sighed, "I guess because we stopped looking for information. We wiped out the crew that did it, thinking they had been the ones to order it as well, given that they would have gained the most territory had the Shadeport crew crumbled with the death of Gavin. It just made sense. I guess we were all preoccupied with the shift in power, and we let our defenses down on the topic. We didn't dig any further after that."

I slid my hand over Ryker's arm to relax him when he dug his fingers into my sides as his frustration mounted.

"So how do we hit the Wellingtons without giving ourselves away? We could just wipe them out, but there would be fallout from that afterward that I'd like to avoid. I've already tipped my hand to them unknowingly when I told Monica that I wasn't interested in a relationship with her after she interrupted me and Elora the other morning. Had I known they were threatened by her, I wouldn't have given them more fuel to add to the fire."

Zeke brainstormed with me, "What if we bait them into making their move and hit then? We could take them off the throne without destroying their entire crew and move men up that we trust and co-run their turf. It would add to the overall size of this crew without you having to physically run the entire thing."

"Making their move on Elora?" Ry bit out, anger in his tone. "No. We're not fucking using her as bait to get this job done. There has to be another way that makes sense."

Everyone else stayed quiet after Ryker's outburst, but I had to admit, Zeke's plan had merit.

"What if he's right?" I asked quietly. All of the eyes in the room turned to me and I stiffened my spine to stand tall and strong as I spoke. I thought back to watching my dad command his crew with smarts and refinement and wanted to emulate that.

"No." Ryker said, finality to his tone as he took another sip of his coffee.

"Don't think with anything other than your head here Ry. You've never done business like that before, so don't start on my behalf."

"Stop talking like I'm going to dangle you out on a fucking line for them to shoot at! I'm not fucking around with your safety Ellie, so stop fucking suggesting it."

"So instead of dangling me in front of them, let's come up with something more strategic. Something that we can be three steps ahead of them in."

His body vibrated under me, and he stood swiftly, setting me down in his chair as he started pacing. I hated the physical space he put between us, but I understood it. I crossed my legs at the knee and rested my elbows on the table, looking down the gleaming wood surface to Zeke at the other end.

I knew Zeke was easier to strategize with and gave it a try. "Ten years ago, this crew made moves using two techniques. Physical brutality and strategy. I think more times than not lately, it's relied on one of those techniques to get the job done, and it's worked well for you all thus far. Until now." I steepled my fingers together at my chest as I leaned forward. I watched Ryker out of the corner of my eye as I addressed his generals and tried to speak in a way that would make him proud, without making him irate. "If my dad were at this table today, what would he recommend you do?" I asked Zeke.

He dropped his eyebrows as he leaned forward staring me straight on. "He'd want to outsmart them at their own game."

"Exactly. We need to find the weak link in their chain of command and utilize it to our advantage. If we can find out their plans, we can step ahead of them and outsmart them. The takeover would be less bloody and more civilized, which would lead to more members of their crew falling in line with your own leaders, versus them going into an all-out war with you. And like you said," I turned to Ryker where he stood with his back pressed to the wall and his arms crossed over his chest, "You want to avoid the fallout that follows the emptiness of power that inspires lesser men to suddenly fight to obtain it. That can be messy, I'm sure."

"Very." He grunted.

"Then we find that weak link and get two things by using it. One, we find out if they even still wish for my death, and two, we find out how they plan to achieve it. In the process, you'll be able to get whatever it was that you were originally trying to seduce out of Monica's old shriveled cunt along the way." I smiled sweetly at him.

Snorts and coughs sounded from the table and room, but Ryker's eyes darkened.

I'd poked the beast.

He remained silent, but I heard his voice clear as day in my head. *"Don't play games, Doll. You'll lose."*

"How do you propose we find that weak link exactly?" Zeke asked, drawing my attention back to him.

"Do you remember my father's favorite saying when it came to business?"

He shook his head; a flash of sadness crossing his eyes momentarily.

"My enemies' enemy is a friend of mine."

I sat back in my chair and waited for that to sink into the strategizing brains of the men around me. A small smile pulled at Zeke's lips as he thought about it.

"We find their biggest enemy as of late, we prod and probe them to do what they're going to do anyway, which is strike or attack the Wellington's in some way or another, and we stand in the darkness behind them while they do it. We offer our support and superficial help without ever dirtying our own hands and then we gain our in when we turn and offer our support and superficial help to the Wellington's in their retaliation. Secrets tend to leave lips when they're focused on something else."

Heads nodded and smiles crossed gruff faces as my words sunk in. Zeke looked from me to Ryker, where he still had yet to move from and shook his head in disbelief before Zeke finally broke the silence, "It's as if Gavin himself is sitting at the table again."

Ryker wasn't looking at him though, because he was staring at me, his eyes burned holes into my skin where they held onto me.

"Well?" I asked, raising my eyebrows at him, and pursing my lips at his silence. "What does the King think?"

He leaned up off the wall and uncrossed his arms as he walked across the room towards me. He glanced over at Zeke and barked out orders. "Find out what you can about their enemies, put out feelers on jobs we have going with them already, maybe their lower ranked men will talk more freely. I want to know who their rivals are by sunrise."

"Yes, boss." Zeke replied, the corner of his mouth pulling up at me as I glanced at him in question.

I was caught off guard when Ryker reached my chair and lifted me effortlessly, throwing me over his shoulder roughly and striding out of the room.

"Now get out." He bellowed as he placed distance between us and all of them. Muttering and burly laughs followed us down the hall.

"Ryker!" I gasped as he started climbing the stairs, two at a time. The air was pushed from my lungs with each jolt, and I grabbed onto the back of his belt to hold myself upright. "What are you doing?"

He wouldn't answer me though, instead he just walked us straight into his room and slammed the door shut behind us, locking it like he had the night before.

Instead of laying me down on his bed like he had last night though, he turned and slid me over his shoulder and pressed me into the door with his body to my front.

"Are you—" I started, but was cut off when his mouth covered mine and he kissed me. It was far from a pretty kiss; it was raw and animalistic, and I wrapped my arms around his shoulders and my legs around his waist and hung on for dear life.

"Do you have any idea how fucking sexy you are when you step into your role as Queen? Any clue at all what it fucking does to me?" He growled against my lips and rolled his hips, pressing his erection into my clit for emphasis.

"I thought you were mad." I gasped and pressed my head back into the door as he dove and latched onto my neck. This morning, I managed to cover one mark with makeup, but this one, I knew, was beyond concealing. He was unhinged and wild, his hands frantically tearing at my clothes.

"Madly in love with you is more like it." He said, and I froze solid.

"Love?" I asked, my breath only a whisper. I'd said it to him indirectly when I was drunk, but neither of us had discussed it since then.

"Madly." He chuckled, slowing his hands and lips down and pulled back to look at me. "Does that surprise you?"

"Yes." I shook my head back and forth as my eyes rounded wide. "I figured—"

"What?" He asked.

"I figured you were immune to love; you always acted so untouchable."

He took my hand in his and placed it on his heart. "I'm untouchable to every other person in the world, except you, Doll. I feel nothing for anyone else but you. And for you, I feel the entire world."

"Oh, God." I moaned and devoured his lips as passion coursed through both of us. He was such an enigma, and to have him declare his love for me, in such a poetic and renowned way, drove me wild with desire for him.

He pulled me off the door and walked us over to his bed. My shirt was already torn off by him, and at some point he'd lost his own. He lay on top of me and kissed down the center of my chest, between my breasts and then down my stomach. My muscles quivered under his lips as he lowered himself to my jeans. Making quick work of those, he tore them off, throwing my panties along with them.

Sitting up on my elbows, I watched as he stood at the end of the bed, the muscles of his chest and stomach rose and fell with each deep breath as he simply stared at me. His body was cut from stone, and the ink across his chest and stomach made my mouth water.

"You're so sexy, Ryker."

He grinned at me with a predatory flare. "Spread your legs for me."

Oh fuck.

I listened instantly, opening my legs, and letting my heels bury into the blankets as he looked at my entire body, from eyes to toes.

He slowly undid his belt and the closure on his pants. I was mesmerized watching his tattooed hands move over the black fabric. When he pushed down his pants and briefs in one move, I gasped and bit my lip to keep from outright moaning.

I leaned up on my elbows and looked down between my spread thighs as he fisted his cock and stroked himself.

"I'm going to fuck you so good." His voice was low and smooth, like honey.

Fear raced through my veins, but I tamped it down, forcing my arousal to take the lead to keep my body relaxed and loose. It was going to fucking hurt.

But I wanted it so badly.

He crawled up the bed and grabbed my foot in his hand and brought it to his mouth. He kissed the inner arch of my foot and then ran his tongue over the skin before turning his head and letting his teeth scrape over the ticklish skin.

I gasped and clutched the bedsheets to keep from crawling off the bed away from the sensation. "Oh, my god." I moaned.

He kissed his way up my ankle and calf, licking, sucking, and biting along the way.

"Yes Doll, I'm your God." He leaned down on his forearms and continued his assent until his warm breath was on my open pussy. "You're going to scream my name. Any man on this block will know who you belong to."

I worked to keep my breathing regular and calm. It was on the tip of my tongue to stop him and tell him I'd never—.

"Fuck, you taste so good." His tongue dipped into my pussy, and my back bowed off the bed painfully. He sucked my clit into his mouth and wrapped his hands around my thighs and pulled me into his mouth further, savagely feasting on me.

Within minutes I was coming on his face, riding it, rocking my hips up and down as he held me in a punishing grip. Incoherent rants fell from my lips as my body seized tight and snapped, and he wasted no time in climbing up my body and devouring my cries with his lips.

"I've never met anyone as perfect for me as you, Elora. Never once have I felt so completed from simply being in the presence of a woman before."

"I love you." I gasped as he rocked his hips forward and pressed against my pussy.

He lifted my leg up over his arm, opening me even more for him, and then buried himself inside of me with one punishing thrust.

Pain blinded me as I screamed and tried to scramble away from it, but he held onto me in a death grip as his entire body stilled, frozen in place.

He didn't even breathe as he held still, balls deep inside of me.

"Elora—" He said, but I shook my head back and forth, silencing him as I tried to force air into my lungs.

Holy fuck, that hurt far more than I thought it would.

"What the fuck was that?" he asked, and I finally opened my eyes to see anger radiating out of his.

I swallowed, relaxing my spine to lower my body back down onto the bed. "Nothing. I'm fine."

"Bullshit!" He yelled and then pulled out of me quickly, rolling over and off of me.

I closed my legs and reached for him, trying to keep him from putting space between us.

"What the fuck!" He said, looking down at his cock, where there was blood smeared onto the shaft.

I stared at it and then pulled the blanket up to my chin, shame and embarrassment flooded my body. I could feel the flush lighting my body on fire as he stared at me with scrutiny.

"You're a virgin?" His voice was lethal as he rolled over to me and buried his hand in my hair to turn my face towards him. "Why didn't you tell me?"

I stuttered, starting and stopping multiple times, but nothing would come out. Stupid tears burned the back of my eyes as I fought to control my emotions. "I didn't want you to–. I thought–. You said you wanted my firsts; I didn't think you'd be mad about it."

"Fuck, Elora!" He yelled but then pressed his forehead to mine and took a deep breath. "I never would have fucked my way into you like a heathen if I'd have known you were a virgin. You should have told me!"

"I'm sorry!" I pulled back and covered my face with my hands as an errant tear slid from my lashes. "I'm sorry."

He pulled the blanket off of me and covered my body with his, forcing my legs open to lay between them. "Shh. Please don't cry." He kissed my forehead and my hands and arms before pulling them open to reveal my face to him. "I can't believe you've given me this gift, and I fucked it up."

"You didn't fuck it up, I did." I groaned. "I was going to tell you; I didn't think we'd be having sex this morning until you carried me upstairs like a man possessed and then, I froze."

He kissed me, slowly, dragging arousal from my lips, and rocked his cock against my clit. "Do you feel how fucking hard I am? Your pussy has never been fucked before and you're letting *me* have it. That has me ready to blow my fucking load in an instant. I can't describe to you how badly I want you right now, I didn't think it was possible to want you more than I did two minutes ago, but yet here I am, like a wild animal desperate to fuck you."

With a moan, I leaned up to kiss his neck. "I want you so bad, Ryker. I didn't want this to come between us. I didn't think you'd be able to tell, but you're so big."

"And your pussy is the tightest I've ever felt before, I can't wait to bury myself in it again."

"Then don't wait." I begged. "Please fuck me Ry. I need you."

He pulled back and pressed the head of his cock against me again and slowly pushed the head inside of me. "Eyes open and on me, Doll. I want to watch your eyes when I fuck you for your first time."

"Yes."

He pushed further inside and pulled back out until the tip was barely inside of me still.

I watched his face transform with each thrust, pure, unadulterated need kissed his features as he worked his giant cock into my body. My god, he was so fucking thick and long.

Finally, he rolled his hips, and his pubic bone rubbed my clit as his cock filled me to the brim. I moaned as he rocked inside me. "Yes, that feels so good."

"Does it hurt?" he asked as he slowly pulled all the way out and then pushed back in.

"Yes. But in the best way possible." As he moved within me, I clawed at his shoulders, while he quickened the pace. "I need you to fuck me, Ry. I need it to hurt and feel good; I need all of you. Don't hold back."

"Fuck, you're so tight wrapped around my cock, strangling it. It feels fucking magnificent." He pulled out and slammed back into me, forcing a loud moan from my lips. "You take my cock perfectly. You're so perfect."

He hooked my leg over his arm again and I watched the restraint fall away from his eyes as he started fucking me hard. Each thrust was long and deep and each time he bottomed out, I was thrown further into the abyss towards an earth shattering orgasm. It was building, threatening to consume me.

"You want to come so bad, don't you?" he asked, leaning down to bite my nipple and flick the ring with his tongue.

"Yes. I'm so close, I feel like my entire soul is on fire."

"That's it, baby. That's me burning you, branding you as mine for the rest of your life. Claiming your pussy as mine forever. No one will ever have this gift again. It's mine. You're mine. Your future is mine."

"Ryker! I'm coming! Holy fucking God, I'm–" I spewed off, crazed with need as my orgasm broke over me and pulled my soul from my body. He fucked me like a man possessed, pounding me into the mattress with each thrust. He grunted and groaned curses as my pussy clenched down hard on his enormous cock.

Before I was done coming, I felt his cock jerk and start pumping his orgasm into me, filling me up with each jolt. It was incredible to feel him come inside of me, feeling his warmth coat my insides as I watched his face while he officially claimed me as his.

He was panting heavily and rolled us, so I was on top of him, straddling him without ever pulling out of me while we caught our breath.

I laid my ear on his chest, listening to his heart slow as he ran his fingers up and down my spine.

"I love you, Elora."

I smiled against his chest, feeling the coarse hair on his chest tickle my cheek. "I love you, Ryker."

"I can't believe I just took your virginity. I can't believe I just filled your body with my come for the first time. Are you alright?"

"I'm perfect."

He wrapped his arms around me and held me tight. "Thank you."

I rolled my eyes at him, thanking me for my virginity felt weird, but he kept going. "Seriously, whether you waited for me specifically or not, I don't care. But thank you for giving that to me."

I lifted my head and looked at him, "To be honest, I could never envision being with anyone else because when I closed my eyes, I always saw you and they never stacked up. But never in a million years would I have thought I'd actually get this chance."

"Well, you'll never feel another man's touch again because I'm never letting you go."

"Good." I sighed, resting my head back on his large chest.

It may not have been exactly how I'd envisioned it to be, but I was no longer a virgin, and Ryker Lawson, the King of Shadeport, now owned me. My body and soul. I just hoped we could beat the Wellington's at their own game, so I could live to grow old with him.

CHAPTER 16 – RYKER

I didn't deserve Elora.

I'd been a brute and forced myself inside of her body without a second thought to her comfort or protection because of my lust crazed brain. It'd been a decade or more since I'd been so overcome with desire that I'd lost all sense like that.

Yet, this morning I'd pushed her legs apart and fucked her bare, ripping through her virginity and causing her pain because of how turned on I'd gotten from watching her address my men and lead them with such incredible smarts and grace.

Of course, she had been more than willing to let me in, but she had been afraid. When I looked back on our encounter now, with a clear head, I could recognize the fear in her eyes as I told her how I planned to fuck her. I should have seen it then and stopped or slowed down.

But it was done now, and she was mine.

If there was ever a question about who she belonged to before, there was none left now. I'd been the first and only man to ever feel the inside of her body like that, and I wasn't going to ever let her get within ten feet of another man ever again.

I sat in my office, with the door shut and my computer off, letting all of my thoughts make enough noise to infuriate me.

Elora was in danger, because of me. Because I'd publicly claimed her in my club and had dangled her in front of Monica when she found us in the kitchen. I should have been smarter than that, I shouldn't have allowed my desire for Elora to cloud my judgment where my business was concerned. But I didn't know how I could have kept things going with Monica when Elora deserved so much more than that.

I couldn't two-time her, and I couldn't maintain any relationship with Monica without sleeping with her; It was what she had wanted most from me.

So, the other day when she'd shown up at the house, irate when she was locked out of the gate, I'd told her I was no longer interested in her romantically. And I'd added fuel to the fire that burned in her belly for Elora's death.

And that burned an inferno in my soul, drawing out the monster inside of me.

I got up, needing to feed the fire in my soul.

"Zeke!" I yelled as I opened my office door. My second walked out of his office down the hall and met me as I neared towards him. "I need to destroy something. Or preferably someone."

He raised his eyebrows, and his lip turned up. "We have something small going on that you could get your hands dirty in if you feel like reducing yourself to small-time shit."

"The bloodier the better." I answered. "I need to see Ellie first, then meet you at the car."

"She was out by the pool last I knew." he said with a mischievous glint in his eye.

I walked away, not wasting any more time on him, and went in search of my Queen. I passed by the kitchen on my way to the back patio but stopped dead in my tracks as something caught my eye.

The security room was busting at the seams with men as they all stared at the screens on the wall. I walked over to the doorway and looked at the screens above their heads.

"Do any of you value your fucking lives?" I roared, startling every single burly dumb fuck in the room.

They turned and threw themselves into pretending to do anything other than what I'd caught them doing. Which was ogling my beautiful Ellie on the security screen from where she lay next to the pool.

"If I ever catch any of you staring after her like that again, I'll tear your fucking throats out and shove them up your own asses. Understood?" I bellowed as I turned and walked away towards the patio door.

My blood was rushing through my system, leaving my brain, and pooling in my hardening cock as I saw her through the giant windows. She laid out on a lounge chair on her stomach with her hair tied on top of her head and a satisfied smile on her lips as the sun warmed her skin.

She wore a black bikini bottom that covered absolutely nothing, and all of her exposed skin made my mouth water. Her top was untied, and the straps laid out on her lounger, leaving her back bare.

Opening the door, I stepped out into the California heat and stalked towards her. She had earbuds in, and her eyes were closed behind her sunglasses, so she had no idea I was near. I fought flashbacks to the time in her apartment when she was asleep and there for my taking, so much like she was now.

Her lush ass laid open and bare, and my hands ached to grab hold of it like it had that morning as well. But this time, I didn't resist the urge, and I straddled her lounger and slid my large hands over her juicy ass and gripped it, rippling it back and forth with a good shake.

She gasped and lifted her head to look over her shoulder and then smiled when she saw it was me. She took her ear buds out and laid her head back down, moaning and arching her back, pushing her flesh into my hands.

"God, you are so fucking sexy." I groaned, letting my hands slide up her back to her warm shoulders and massaged them as I kneeled over her legs

"I missed you." She mused and rolled over, causing her bikini top to slide to the side and expose her lush breasts to my eyes.

"Fucking hell Ellie." I yelled and dropped my hands onto her tits and looked over my shoulder at the camera on the wall. "They're watching you."

"Who?" She asked, pushing her sunglasses up off her eyes and covering my hands with her own.

"My men."

"Oh." Her lips formed a perfect O as she thought about it.

"Yeah, oh."

"I'm sorry." She said, letting go of her breasts, leaving my hands on them and stretching her arms up and over her head. "Hmm, maybe you should spank me for being so thoughtless." She mused and smiled seductively at me.

I pushed her lounger around with my knee until it faced away from the pool and in turn, away from the camera and lifted the head of it to shield her completely from any prying eyes through the windows either. I dropped my hands from her tits and wrapped one around her throat and leaned down to press my lips against her ear. "Do you want to be spanked, Doll?"

I pinched one of her pert nipples and then dropped my mouth to it and sucked it into my mouth. She clawed at my hand holding her throat as she squirmed under my lips and teeth. "Oh my god." She moaned, lifting her hips, trying to find friction.

I slid my hand from her breast to one of the tiny ties holding her bottoms on and pulled it and then pulled the other one and tore it down her legs.

She instantly spread her legs for me, and I pushed my fingers through her lower lips and found her clit and rubbed it, making her purr. "Yes. Fuck, that feels good."

"Answer my question."

Her eyes opened and stared into mine as I pushed two fingers into her pussy, using my come from earlier for lubrication. "Yes. Please, I need you, Ryker."

"Not until you answer me how I want you to. Do you want me to spank you?"

"I don't know." She answered, biting her lip. "I've never been spanked before. But I've also never been choked before and yet it makes me soaking wet every time you do it, so."

"Fucking hell." I groaned, her pussy was so tight on my fingers, and she was playing with her nipples while she rode my hand. "Roll over. Keep your head below the top of the chair." She froze and started to question me, but I stopped her. "Now, Elora."

Her tits heaved as she took a deep breath and then quickly rolled over, pulling my fingers from her pussy but doing what I commanded. She kneeled on the lounger and held on to the top of the headrest but kept her chest behind the fabric.

"Spread your legs and arch your back, push that fucking ass up into the air for me, Doll." I was a hair trigger away from losing all control, and I was supposed to be meeting Zeke in the car, but I couldn't control my need when I was near her.

She did exactly as I instructed, opening her pussy to me and her back was so fucking sexy arched deep for me. I stood up and let my hand run over the plush curve of her ass as she watched me over her shoulder. "Do you have any idea how fucking sexy you are spread wide open for me, listening to my every command like such a fucking good girl?"

She moaned and swung her hips. "Ryker, please."

"Beg me to spank you."

"Fuck." She groaned and dropped her forehead to the chair. "Please spank me, baby. Please, I need it so badly."

I brought my hand down on her ass hard before she'd even stopped begging. She shrieked and moaned. I panted as I watched her milky skin flush to a beautiful pink.

"Again." I spoke. "Beg for more." My voice was strained, and my control was hardly contained, and she could feel it.

"Please do it again. Please. Please. Please."

The sound of my palm hitting her ass cracked through the air and I pulled back and did it again, dropping it lower on her ass, closer to her clit.

She moaned and pushed back. "Holy fuck, I'm so wet."

I pushed two fingers deep into her pussy and sure enough, she was soaked. I peppered her ass with my hand, over and over on both cheeks as she moaned and begged me for more. I landed the last two hits directly onto her clit and she screamed, biting her knuckles to muffle it.

I unzipped my pants and pulled my cock out and impaled her before she'd even taken another breath, surprising her.

I fucked her hard, and unforgiving, as she pushed back into each thrust. She started coming on my cock almost instantly and I grabbed her sexy hair all tied up and neat, and pulled on it, angling her head backwards as I fucked her through it.

"You're so tight on my cock right now, Ellie. You're such a good girl begging me for more. Mine Ellie, this pussy is mine." I moaned into her ear as she screamed and came again, no longer bothering to hide the sounds. "Good girl, let me hear you."

I reached around her body and pinched her clit as I fucked her into the chair.

"God, you're so deep like this, your cock is so big!"

I sat up and grabbed hold of her hips and pulled her back onto my cock with each savage thrust. "Take every fucking inch I give to you. Whose pussy is it? I want to hear you tell me whose pussy I'm fucking."

"It's yours! Oh, my god it's your pussy. You feel so good."

I bottomed out inside of her, throwing my head back and roaring into the expansive patio as I emptied myself into her scorching hot body. I came so much that it pushed out around my cock with each thrust, dripping down onto the chair beneath her.

She was gasping and moaning as I finally stilled inside of her as we caught our breath. "Your pussy is so full of my come, it's dripping out of you."

She mewed and looked over her shoulder at me, licking her lips. "I want to taste it."

"Fucking damn right you do." I snaked my hand under her body and grabbed her hand and brought it to her pussy, letting her fingers feel how wet her lips were from me. She groaned and I pulled out of her body slowly, delighting in how her pussy clenched tight when the head of my cock popped out. Come dripped down onto her waiting fingers, and she wiped it up and brought it to her mouth and sucked them into her mouth. I ran my fingers over the wetness and pushed them into her pussy, pushing my come back into her body.

"Mmh." She moaned, letting her eyes close as she sucked her fingers dry. I rolled her over, so she was on her back and adjusted her top, so it was covering her breasts and then slid her bottoms back on her legs and tied them for her, dropping kisses on her hips bones as I did.

"Did I hurt you?" I asked, trying to remind myself that she had only had sex twice now and once again I took her roughly, overcome with need.

"Only exactly how I wanted you to."

"Hmm." I hummed. "I came out here to tell you I was leaving for a while, and then you distracted me."

"Hmm." She hummed back, pursing her lips innocently. "Where are you going?"

"To send a message."

"What's that supposed to mean?" Her eyes squinted as she leaned back into the chair again, but played with the buttons of my shirt.

"I need to remind the world that I'm not to be fucked with. I'm bringing the dark and scary into the streets tonight to remind everyone just how good their lives are when I keep it all hidden in the shadows."

"Will you be safe?"

"Yes. And Jed will be here, along with others. Anything you need at all, you go to him, understood?"

"Okay." She paused and then leaned up to kiss my lips, gently and sweetly. "Come back home to me in one piece."

"Sexier words have never been spoken."

She smiled against my lips. "I love you, Ryker."

"Scratch that, those are the sexiest words." She laughed and laid back down again. "Relax, eat a good dinner, take a bubble bath, and then get to sleep. I'll be home as soon as I can."

"Yes, sir." She winked at me and blew me an air kiss.

"I love you, Doll." I stood up and turned her back around to face the sun and forced myself to walk away from her, even though since laying my hands on her my nerves were eased and my muscles relaxed, making my need to destroy someone less pressing. But I needed to remind the world that Ryker Lawson wasn't to be fucked with. And that included what was mine.

And Elora Dax was mine.

Tonight, the world would quake with my wrath.

CHaPTer 17 – ELOra

I walked back inside the house and paused as eyes met mine from around the kitchen. Ryker's men sat at the island and table, eating dinner as Margaret served them with a happy smile.

"Are you hungry, Ms. Dax?" Margaret asked as I stood awkwardly in my bikini with my towel wrapped around my hips.

"Starved. I'll go change and then be back down."

"Yes, Ma'am." She said with a nod, probably relieved I wasn't going to cause trouble in her kitchen.

I ran up the stairs and into my room and changed into an oversized sweater and yoga pants and then went back down in search of the delicious scent of garlic bread.

When I got back down, the awkwardness was still there as I walked up to the counter to get the plate Margaret had made for me. The men at the counter stood to give me one of their seats, but I once again held my hand up and stood at the end of the Island to eat. Jed sat a few seats down and eyed me with respect as I stood so his men could sit.

"I'll need a ride to my doctor's office tomorrow, Jed, if you're free."

"Yes, Ma'am, but boss has a doctor that comes to the house here if you'd prefer."

"A woman's doctor?" I asked, raising my eyebrow at him in question.

He smirked at me and shook his head, "She's a surgeon and family doctor. Does everything for us that we need of her, I'm sure she can take care of you as well."

"Okay. How do I get in contact with her?"

"I'll set it up."

"Hmm." I hummed as I ate a bite of pasta. He got up and poured me a glass of red wine and handed it to me. "Well, thank you."

He nodded and sat back down to finish off his own plate.

Ryker had left a few hours ago, and I was on edge the longer he was gone.

"Have you um," I paused and tried to ignore all of the other eyes on me as I talked to Jed. "Has Ryker checked in or anything?"

"No ma'am. Were you expecting him too?"

"I don't know. I just hate sitting around while he's out there," I chewed and swallowed, "how did he put it—sending a message."

He chuckled at me good heartedly and a few others smiled at my discomfort.

"I assure you, he's plenty protected and fully capable of taking care of himself."

I nodded and went back to my meal. "Do you all usually eat your meals here?"

"No ma'am, Mr. Lawson upped security on you and his home with the new threat, so there will be a larger presence around for now. We can eat in the offices or the security room if you'd prefer."

"Oh, stop it." I scoffed at him. "I don't care; I'm more of a visitor here than you all. Don't let me get in your way."

We chatted some more, small talk nonsense stuff, and then he looked at his watch and back to me. "I don't mean to sound pushy, but Mr. Lawson wanted me to make sure you did all the things he told you to do this evening."

It took me a minute to remember exactly what Ryker had said before he left, thanks to the orgasms he gave me and then my jaw fell lax a bit as Jed actually looked uncomfortable. A few of the men near him looked between us, unsure of what would make the large man uncomfortable. Instead of melting into the embarrassment, I decided to play along with his predicament.

"Are you instructing me to go take a bubble bath, Jed?" I asked with a straight face as I drank the rest of my wine.

He choked on his own and coughed as the others laughed. "I was only told to make sure you did what he said, I didn't know–"

I waved him off and picked up my plate, taking it to the sink and rinsing it out. "Fine, whatever you say, *boss*." I winked at him. "But I'm taking this with me." I said, lifting the almost full bottle of wine that had just gotten opened, and took my glass with me as I walked from the kitchen. The roaring laughter followed me as I got to the stairs, and I shook my head, laughing to myself.

I went upstairs and straight into Ryker's room with my bottle and glass and headed into his bathroom like he'd instructed.

I filled the tub with steaming hot water and nearly an entire bottle of expensive bubble bath on the shelf and then filled my glass with the delicious wine.

I had just leaned back into the water when my phone started ringing.

Swiping it open, Carly popped up onto the screen in a video call.

"Hey." I said, turning the jets off so I could hear properly.

"Are you in the bath?" she asked, leaning forward to see better. She was on her couch and had her hair up in a messy bun.

"A bath the size of a swimming pool, actually, but yes. Are you off tonight?"

"Yeah, I worked at a private party last night after you left and I needed the rest to recover tonight."

"That bad, huh?" I asked, grimacing. She'd told me about some of the private parties she worked, and the 'extra' things she did at them.

"Eh, it wasn't terrible. I actually had fun, but I didn't get home until almost ten am this morning, so I was dragging. But enough about me. Where's Mr. Dark and Dangerous?"

"Ryker? He's out doing something work-related."

"So, you're home alone in his castle?"

"Hardly alone. I think there are no less than twenty bodyguards downstairs currently."

"Seriously?" she asked, shock on her face.

"Yeah, ever since–" I didn't know what she knew, and I didn't know what I wanted to get into with her about it all.

"What happened after you went to his office?" She dropped her voice as if she were afraid someone would overhear.

"Is someone there?"

"Frankie's in the shower, but other than that, no." Ah. That explains so much.

"Nothing happened, he took care of those guys, and then we came home and went to bed."

She sat up; her interest peaked. "Okay, let's start at the club and we'll circle back to the bed comment."

"Oh, Lord."

"How did he 'take care' of them? Did he go all dark and dangerous on them?"

I laughed and shook my head, leaning back into the headrest on the edge of the tub. "I don't know about the others, but the guy that hit me—" I paused as mental images flashed through my head of him on the floor, and then the deafening crack of Ryker's gun. "He went all dark and dangerous on him."

"Holy fuck, that's hot." She gasped and fanned herself.

"It's overwhelming, that's what it is."

"I wish you could see it from the outside looking in, though babe. That man is such an untouchable enigma, he controls the world, but no one gets close to him. And then here comes little Ellie, the girl that works her life away and doesn't ever want to go out and have fun, and all of a sudden she's his Queen and he's completely enamored with her. It's so sexy!"

"Sexy?" I asked, curling my lip up. "I didn't just come along; I've known him my whole life."

"Which just adds to the sexy aspect!" She gushed.

"How?"

"Uh hello! He's like twenty years older than you and totally obsessed. Like literally going dark and dangerous on anyone who dares to wrong you! Doesn't that make you just wild with lust for him? Feeling so protected?"

"Well, I guess when you put it that way."

"And what about the sex?"

"Oh, my god!" I groaned.

"Oh, don't even start trying to tell me that you're still a virgin, there is no way after that lap dance!"

"Carly! Hush!" I blushed wildly.

"Ooh!" She squealed. "You totally let him fuck you! Oh please, you have to tell me how good he is in bed. Please, please, please!"

"You are pathetic." I groaned and tried to hide the stupid smile that covered my face from even thinking of my time with Ryker.

She gasped as she watched my face. "That good, huh?"

I smiled wildly and then gave in. "So, fucking good."

"Ah!" She screamed and rolled around on the couch in glee. "He's possessive, isn't he? Total alpha in the sack?"

"Yes. As if he could be anything else."

"Right! Oh my God, I can't believe you're in a relationship with Ryker Lawson. Jay is completely beside himself, you know! He has fucked anything with legs the last couple of days, trying to drown you out of his system."

"Ew, that's a visual I didn't need."

"I had no idea you guys had messed around until he told me the other night. He said you guys had been fooling around for like, the last year!"

"He embellishes the truth; we've messed around a couple of times over the last year. Not the whole time. But it doesn't matter, I always told him I wasn't interested in anything more and I never asked him for anything when we did hook up."

"I know, but obviously he got hooked, and now he has to walk away without fighting for you because you're with his boss. Who is all dark and dangerous and no way is he going to challenge him for you. That would literally be suicide."

"Oh, my god stop. It was not anywhere near that serious with Jay."

"Hmm, so you say!" She sang with glee and fell into a fit of giggles. We chatted for a while longer until Frankie came out into the living room and made it weird. I could feel his dislike of me through the phone and even Carly was put off by it. So, we hung up, and I told her I'd call her some other time.

I wasn't sure why Frankie had taken so negatively to me since all of this happened, perhaps it was just because of the position it had put him in originally. But I wasn't sure, and I wasn't going to dwell on it. He could get over it or he could harbor it to his grave. It didn't matter to me; it wasn't like we were all going to be hanging out all of the time now anymore.

I relaxed back into the water again, a glass and a half deeper into the wine when my phone rang again. It was a Shadeport number that I didn't recognize and didn't have stored in my phone, so I pressed decline and laid it down on the lip of the tub.

It was almost ten pm, I wasn't going to answer a creepy wrong number.

But a moment later, it rang again with the same number.

I held my phone for a moment and then decided to answer it. I swiped it open and held it to my ear for a moment before saying hello.

"Well, well, well, if it isn't the little princess of Shadeport, alive and well after all." The voice was a man's, and it was deep and gravely, as if he was older, but I didn't recognize it.

"Who is this?"

He laughed, the sound grating and pained. "I'm no one."

"Then I'm hanging up." I said, trying to keep my voice firm and calm.

"That would be a mistake."

My body ran cold, even though the water in the bath was still hot. "Why?"

"Because I may be the only one in the world that can save you from those who want you dead."

I took a deep breath and tried to think like my dad would, but the alcohol in my system was making it hard. "Who is it today that wants me dead?" I asked, trying to feign indifference.

The man laughed again and sighed almost sadly.

"You have his sense of humor, you know, your father. I always admired his sense of humor. I also think you have his smarts."

"Who are you?"

"Who I am is not important. What I can do for you, however, is."

"Why don't you stop talking in riddles and get to the point before I hang up." Anger laced my voice, and I rubbed my forehead with my fingers as a headache tried to erupt.

"Ah, and there is your mother's temperament. A much less admirable characteristic."

I didn't respond, I was done parroting his riddles, asking for answers. He called me, he wanted something so he could get to the point or not.

"Nicolas Wellington, does that name ring a bell?" He asked finally, his voice losing the humor in it.

"Should it?"

"Very good." He said, sounding proud almost. "How about Monica Wellington, his daughter?"

"Perhaps."

"They killed your father." This man was affected by those words, like he usually avoided saying them.

"I know." My heart ached as I answered him. I'd gone so long not allowing myself to think of my dad's death, and now it was thrown in my face left and right.

"They wanted you dead as well."

"Yet I'm alive and well."

"Indeed, which makes me quite happy, to be honest with you."

"Why? Who are you to care what happens to me?"

"I'm no one. But I do care what happens to you, so I'm going to let you in on a secret."

"And what are you expecting in return for this secret?" I knew how this world worked, and information was rarely free.

"I want you to live." He paused and then took a deep breath and continued. "They're expecting a large shipment of something at the yard in Hallstead tomorrow night at eleven pm. The money they plan to make from moving that shipment will be placed on the hit for your death. Interrupt that shipment, interrupt the hit, and buy your new King some time to find his way inside their ring."

"How do you know this?"

He laughed again. "Because I'm a nobody, and nobodies tend to hear things when no one else is looking."

"I know you won't tell me the truth even if I ask, but why should I trust you?"

"Because they took something from me once, Elora. And as a wise man once said, my enemies' enemy, is my friend."

All the air in my lungs whooshed out as my father's words rang in my ears in a voice that almost sounded familiar, yet I couldn't place where from.

"Eleven pm tomorrow, Hallstead shipping yard Elora. Got it?"

"Yeah, I got it." I said.

"Good girl."

"Wait—" I said quickly, but I heard the distinctive click in my ear of him hanging up.

I sat there for a moment as disbelief and fear raced through my body, followed by adrenaline.

I got out of the bath and dried off. There was a robe hanging on the back of the bathroom door and the instant I grabbed it; I smelled

Ryker like he was in the room. It was thick and black and impossibly warm, and I greedily wrapped it around my naked body, letting the scent and fabric embrace me and calm my nerves.

I hitched it up in the front so I wouldn't trip and then I quickly ran from the bedroom and downstairs, in search of someone to help me.

At the bottom of the stairs, I heard voices coming from the wing where Ryker and Zeke's offices were as well as from the kitchen and den.

My nerves were so shot I couldn't fathom running from one to the other in search of help so instead I just yelled out, "Jed!"

Within moments, heavy feet ran to me from all directions. Jed and a handful of other crew members ran to me with worry on their faces.

"What's wrong?" He asked.

"Someone just called me—" I swallowed and tried to calm my nerves so I could talk clearly. "He knew things about the Wellingtons and had information."

"Who was it?"

"I don't know, he wouldn't tell me. But he knew my dad and my mom. He said all he wanted in return for the information was for me to live."

"Okay." He said nodding and placed his big hand on my shoulder as he looked deep into my eyes. "Okay. Hold on." He took his phone out and dialed a number and put his phone to his ear as he led me to Ryker's office and made me sit down in a chair at the desk.

"Boss." He barked out. "You need to get home, it's Elora." I tried following his conversation with Ryker, but I was replaying the one in my head over and over, trying desperately to remember it all so I could relay it without forgetting something important.

When he hung up, a cup of coffee materialized in front of me as Margaret kneeled in front of me. "Drink this dear, you look as white as a ghost."

"Thank you, Margaret." I said and took the coffee, it was fixed exactly how I liked it, and I smiled at her in thanks. She patted my knee and then walked out. Jed didn't leave my side, and crew members came and went as they talked in hushed tones. A while later, the door to the office slammed into the wall as it flew open, and Ryker burst in like a monster coming for his prey.

"Ellie." He said and kneeled in front of me, running his hands through my hair and pulling my forehead to his. "Tell me what happened, word for word."

Zeke stood behind him, flanked by Jed and Dante as I gave him my phone, "I didn't recognize the number, so I declined it, but they called back, so I answered. It was a man; he had a really deep voice, and I thought—I've heard it before; I just can't remember where from."

I stood up and started pacing as I worked through it all. "He was surprised that it was me that answered; that I was alive and well, were his words. He kept saying he was no one, a nobody, but that he was the only one in the world that could save me from those that wanted me dead. I played it off, like I wasn't aware that someone wanted me dead, and he said that I had my dad's humor and that he always admired that and that I had his smarts as well. And then when I got angry with him later, he said he recognized my mother's temperament, which he called a far less admirable characteristic."

Ryker's eyes followed me as I paced his office, but he stayed put and let me get it all out without interrupting and I appreciated it because I was rambling like a madman, but I had a direction I was trying to stay in.

"He asked me if Nicolas Wellington sounded familiar, or Monica Wellington. I told him perhaps, and he said that they killed my dad, and that they had wanted me dead too."

"Fucking hell." Ryker said, running his hand over his face.

"He said that me being alive made him *quite happy*. And that he had information to help us and, in return for it, he simply wanted me to live."

"Did he tell you the information?"

"Yes." I pinched my nose as I tried to remember it word for word. "He said they were expecting a large shipment of something tomorrow night at eleven pm at the Hallstead shipping yard and that they were using the money they made from offloading that shipment to put in for the hit on my head. He said if we interrupt the shipment, we interrupt the hit and buy my *new king* time to find his way into their ring."

Ryker stared at me with the same question I had from all of this.

"How did he know everything we'd only just discovered and planned?"

"He just said again that he was a nobody, and that nobody's tended to hear things when no one else was looking."

"No way. There's no fucking way." Ryker said, as he started pacing the space too.

"There's more." I said quietly, Zeke scowled as he looked at me, waiting for what possibly could be left.

"What is it, Ellie?" He asked when Ryker was too high strung to ask.

"I asked him why I should trust him, and he said that they had taken something from him once and then he said that a wise man once told him that my enemy's enemy is my friend. Like a fucking record from my dad or from our own conversation just this morning."

"Do you think we have a rat?" Zeke asked, looking at Ryker, who finally stood still.

"No, if we had a rat, we'd be getting the opposite of information, we'd be getting fucked by Nicolas. This has to be just some—fluke or something."

"How did he know my dad so well, though? I don't get it." I said as my voice broke from the nerves coursing through my system. "If other people know about their desire to kill me, that means they're getting close to doing it."

"It means we have a shipment to interrupt." Zeke said.

"What if it's a trap?" I asked, "How do we know we can trust him!" I was getting hysterical as I wracked my brain for any bit more information that would make some of the blanks fill in.

"Shh Ellie." Ryker said, stepping into me and wrapping his arms around my body. He kissed my forehead, and it was then that I noticed the blood splattered onto his neck and shirt.

I shivered as I stepped back out of his arms. His eye squinted questioningly as I put more space between us to look at him completely. "You're covered in blood." I finally said and shivered again.

His jaw clenched, and he looked down at his shirt. "It's a part of the job, Doll." He stepped forward again, but I stepped away, once again leaving space between us as my fear got the better of me.

"Stop backing away from me." The order was clear, but I couldn't stop my feet from moving me away from him each time he tried to get near me. I put my hand up between us, holding him off, and hated the way it shook. I was so on edge from the phone call, and the wild look in his eye from the brutality he had inflicted earlier was sending my mind haywire.

"Elora!" He barked again, and I froze. He looked at me with such hurt and anger in his eyes from a step away. I turned and put the desk between us and gripped the top to steady myself.

He turned to Zeke and the others, "I want eyes on the shipping yard now, watch for anything that might indicate a trap. And form a team to go in tomorrow night and take that shipment. And I want a trace on this number." He walked over to the bar and grabbed a bottle of liquor and drank directly from the top of the crystal bottle.

"On it boss." Zeke said, pushing Jed and Dante from the room and down the hall to his own office, shutting the door behind them.

"Who's blood is it?" I asked as soon as the door was shut.

Ryker turned on me and stared at me with pure anger. "It doesn't matter."

"It matters to me, Ryker."

"No, it doesn't Ellie. This is a part of my life, of this life." He raised his voice with each word, swinging his arms out to his sides to showcase the world we lived in, and walked back towards me with slow, calculated steps. He was on edge, and so was I.

I'd recognized his temper the second he walked in the door, and it wasn't just because of what had happened to me. "You're on a high from it, aren't you?" I asked, standing my ground as he got closer to me. "From hurting someone, your pupils are dilated, and you're coiled tight."

"I'm coiled tight because someone is fucking with you on the phone, spinning webs and riddles, and it pisses me the fuck off Elora. I'm coiled tight because I only got to kill four people tonight before I came running back to deal with that fucking riddle master. I'm coiled tight because there is someone out there, actively trying to take you from me, at every fucking turn of my head whether it be by taking your life or taking your body! I'm coiled fucking tight because it's been hours since I've fucked you and you're looking at me with repulsion in your eyes because I'm wearing the blood of those I killed, while sending a message to everyone in a thousand-mile radius, that I am not to be fucked with!" He yelled out the last words with menace in his voice and I backed up into the desk, unable to hold my own anymore.

My ass hit the wood of his desk, but he continued his stalk towards me. I swallowed and held my head high as the man in front of me transformed from someone I recognized, to someone I'd only heard whispers and rumors about in the dark of night.

This was Ryker Lawson, King of the Darkness.

And I was about to be consumed by him.

He stopped when his stomach brushed the fabric of the robe I was wearing and quickly wrapped his fingers around my throat and tilted my head back to look up at him completely. "I'm coiled fucking tight because I'm insane with my need for you, it consumes me and commands me and I've never, not once, been affected by a woman like I am you." He dropped his lips to my ear and hissed. "And it drives me crazy."

"Do you think I'm unaffected by it myself?" I asked, forcing my fear down. "Do you think I'm not crazed by you as well?"

"You could be covered in sewage, and I'd never look at you with disgust, Doll. That look in your eye, you cowering from me, running away from me, it only makes me want to chase you down and force you."

"Force me?"

"Force you to take me, regardless if you want to or not. You turn me into a fucking animal."

This was the side of him my dad had always shielded me from. The side of him that even Ryker had never let me see.

I felt the heat between my legs and the way my nipples hardened against the thick fabric of the robe as he stared down at me with such hunger.

"Show me." I said, surprising myself, and rejoiced in the way his eyes glowed, and his nostrils flared. "Show me this side of you. Show me your animal."

"You want me to force you?" He bit out, his fingers tightening around my throat until I felt a restriction on my ability to get air in.

"Yes. I want you to come unhinged and show me how crazy I make you. Hurt me Ryker."

"Remember, you asked for it, Doll."

His lips crashed against mine, and his other hand pulled my head back by my hair, pressing my throat into his hand more and cutting off more airflow. I wrapped my hands around his arm in fear and desire as euphoria spread over my body laced with panic.

His large hand tore at the sash around my hips and ripped the robe open, revealing my body to his hungry eyes and desperate hands.

"No one will ever have what is mine." He promised as he pushed the robe off my body completely and left me standing naked in the dimly lit office.

Ryker pushed me backwards until I fell over the surface of his desk and lay on my back. He lifted my legs and forced his way in between them and against my aching pussy.

"Your pussy is mine. Say it."

"It's yours." I whispered and panted as his expert fingers pushed deep into me. I could feel his come from the last two times he fucked me, making the invasion smooth and silky.

"Good girl." His breath was hot against my ear where he held himself while he worked my pussy, pushing me towards a frenzy before pulling out and dropping his hands from my body all together. He stepped back a few feet and stared down at me with his chest heaving.

I whined and grabbed for him as he pulled away. "What did I do?" I asked, sitting up and closing my legs.

"Get on your knees." He pushed his jacket off and ripped his shirt open, sending buttons flying all over the room and stripping it off.

I slid off the desk and down onto my knees like he'd instructed and looked up at him through my lashes. He took the bottle of liquor and lifted it, swallowing a large amount, and then stepped back towards me. After sliding his fingers under my chin, he ran his thumb over my bottom lip before pulling down and pushing it into my mouth. He tipped the opening of the bottle against my lips and poured the amber liquid into my mouth. I drank, greedily letting the liquor slide down my throat, and coughed as it burned, but he didn't pull the bottle away, letting it spill down my neck and tits until I was covered with the expensive bourbon.

I coughed and sputtered as he finally pulled it away and slammed it down on the desk. "Take my cock out."

My eyes burned from choking on the liquid fire, but I sat up on my knees and reached for his pants, pulling them open and then down his legs, baring his magnificent cock and muscled thighs.

I bit my lip and pressed my thighs together, looking at the Greek God in front of me, aching to take him into my body.

"Spread your fucking legs. Don't you dare rub that clit." His words made me jump, and I quickly pushed my knees apart, my wet pussy hovering over the floor, empty and aching.

"Ryker." I tried.

"Suck my cock."

"Yes, sir." I moaned, fisting him, and licking the head of him. I tasted his salty pre-cum and groaned, aching for more.

"Good girl. Fuck, you're such a good girl for me." His eyes were less crazed with anger and more with lust as I sucked him off, taking him all the way down my throat. I pulled him out of my mouth and stroked him quickly as I dropped my mouth to his smooth balls and sucked one into my mouth and used my tongue to massage the skin behind his balls. "Fuck." He grunted and his hips jerked as I popped his sack from my mouth and licked his taint, reveling in the noises escaping his mouth.

I kept my palm sliding up and down his massive length with a tight grip, and his hips jerked madly as he groaned. "Good girl, baby, just like that." I moaned at his praise and ached to play with myself, but I kept my hands on his body and my knees wide as I pleased him. "Put my cock back in your fucking mouth, Doll. Suck me down to the back of your throat."

I gasped and eagerly took him again, he flexed his hips and buried it all the way into my throat until my lips touched his balls. He groaned, and I hummed, dropping my fingers to rub my saliva over the smooth skin of his taint, rubbing on the spot that drove him nuts.

"I'm going to come so fucking hard." He grunted and started fucking my mouth savagely, bruising my lips with each thrust. I felt the first rope of come slide down my throat as his cock twitched in my mouth. His balls were so tight, and I scraped my nails over them as he came, making him roar my name loudly into his office as he filled my belly.

When he was finally done, I slowly licked my way up his cock, cleaning it as I went while his head hung with his eyes closed, overcome by his orgasm. I kissed my way over each of his hips and up his stomach as far as I could reach from my knees, but didn't stand, since he didn't tell me I could.

He finally opened his eyes and pulled me up to stand and then further, wrapping my legs around his waist until my face was level with his and he kissed me. He buried his fingers in my hair and held me exactly how he wanted me and took from my mouth what he needed, and I gave it to him freely.

"Put your robe on." He said suddenly and dropped my feet back down to the ground as he pulled his pants back up.

I grabbed the cloth and covered my body with it, and a second later, he lifted me off my feet and over his shoulder and tore from the room. "What are you doing?" I was desperate and aching to be filled with him to ease my own nerves from the evening.

"Sir." One of his men stepped out of the kitchen when we walked through, but Ryker held his hand up to him, silencing him.

"Tell Zeke."

"But sir."

"Fuck off!"

He carried me to the stairs and took them two at a time, and then locked us in his room. He walked us into the master bathroom and turned the shower on before setting me down on the marble floor and pulling his robe from my body once again.

"Ry—"

"Silence."

He was still coiled tight as he ripped the rest of his clothes off and then pulled me into the massive stone and glass shower. Steam billowed around us as he backed us under the large rain showerhead, and he finally took a deep breath as he lowered his forehead to mine.

I didn't know what he needed in this moment, so I kept quiet like he had commanded me to, but wrapped my arms around his stomach and held onto him as he breathed me in. After a while, I stepped back and grabbed his sponge and soap and lathered it up in my hands and softly pressed it to his chest.

The blood that had soaked into his shirt had stained his skin, and I washed every inch, ridding him of the crimson tarnish. He watched me closely with intense eyes as I washed his arms and chest, down his stomach, and then stepped around behind him and washed his back, letting the water wash the suds down the drain with the blood. I pressed soft kisses to his muscled back as I rubbed the sponge lower, washing his ass and thighs, before dropping to my knees and washing his lower legs and feet. He turned in the water and looked down at me with wonderment as I leaned up on my knees and washed his cock and balls and then down the front of his legs.

When I was done I sat back down on my feet and looked up at him, waiting to see what he needed from me next.

"Come here, Doll." He held his hand out and helped me stand and then took the sponge from me and re-lathered it up. He started rubbing it over my skin, washing my chest and stomach and back and then dropped to his own knees in front of me and washed my legs and feet. He leaned in and pressed soft and gentle kisses to my stomach and then dropped the sponge and wrapped his large arms around my waist and buried his face in my skin and held onto me, breathing me in for a long time. I ran my fingers down his scalp and leaned down to kiss the top of his head.

"I'm sorry, Ryker." He looked up at me, "I'm sorry I ran from you, I was just so—raw in the moment I didn't know what to do but putting space between us was never what I wanted or needed and I'm sorry I did it."

He stood up and smoothed his lips against mine and kissed me so softly I could have missed it had I not felt his whiskers against my own skin. "I should have been more mindful of my appearance in front of you. I just ached to be near you after getting that call from Jed." He took a deep breath and shook his head. "Did I hurt you? In my office?"

I chuckled and shook my head and kissed his sternum, letting my tongue trace over a swirl of ink that ran from his heart out over his left peck. "No baby, you didn't give me anything I couldn't handle."

"But I also didn't give you what you wanted most." He said with a slight smirk on his face.

"And what was that?"

"Orgasms."

I mewed at him and leaned further into him, "You did that on purpose didn't you?"

"Yes."

"To punish me for rejecting you."

"Yes."

"Hmm." I hummed as I processed it. "I don't like you using sex against me, I don't want you to punish me with something we both have turned into something so much more than just sex."

"I know, Doll. Now that I'm calmer, I can see that wasn't right. But at the moment I couldn't stop myself." He smirked at me, and his perfect white teeth glinted in the light like fangs. "I want to make it up to you."

"As you should." I purred and leaned into him.

"Come here." He walked over to the large bench and sat down, spreading his thighs wide and patting them for me to sit down on him. I turned my back to him and sat my ass directly on top of his glorious cock and squirmed, feeling it press directly between my cheeks. "Lean back." He pulled me back, so I was pressed flush to his large chest with my head laid back on his shoulder. He lifted my legs over each of his legs, spreading them further and opening me up more. "Close your eyes." He whispered against my ear, and I shivered.

I closed my eyes and swallowed down my apprehension as I felt him move behind me. His hand slid up my leg, over the sensitive nerves in my clit and then up the center of my chest before wrapping around my neck, holding me still. I heard a change in the water noise and then there was a direct stream of water over my toes that slowly moved up my inner leg.

"Oh, my god." I moaned and wiggled, digging my nails into his thighs as he held the handheld shower head over my legs, dragging the stream up my thigh until it hit directly onto my clit. The pressure was perfect, and spread open like I was, it felt exquisite. "Yes, baby."

"You did this the very first day you were here and didn't invite me to watch."

"Fuck." His hand tightened on my throat as he flicked the water back and forth over my clit. "Just like that." I purred.

"You told me you imagined my hands on your body while you played with yourself and that you had the biggest orgasm of your life up until that point."

"I fell to the floor, it felt so good." I panted.

"No falling this time, love. I've got you."

"I only fall for you anymore."

He moaned in my ear and then bit the shell of it as he dropped his hand from my throat to play with my nipples. "Your nipples are so fucking pretty with these rings in them."

"I love it when you play with them. You drive me crazy."

He slid his fingers up to my mouth and I opened instinctively, and he pushed two fingers in and slid them against my tongue. "Suck on them, get them slick."

I worked them over in my mouth, coating them like he instructed. He hummed and pulled them from my lips. "You listen to me perfectly, Doll."

He dropped his slick fingers to my pussy and pushed them inside of me swiftly. I arched my back and squirmed as the dual sensation pushed me headfirst into my orgasm that I'd been on the cusp of for an hour.

"Good girl, come on my fingers like such a pretty girl."

My nails drew blood on his thighs as I shattered in his lap, but he never lessened the pressure on my body, and he worked me over and over until I came again. I pushed his hand and the wand away from my body and closed my legs, pulling them to my chest as I fought to catch my breath. He held me as I did, but his cock twitched beneath me, and I ached to be filled with him deep inside of me. "Take me to bed, I want you to teach me how to ride your cock."

He growled and stood up, carrying me out of the shower and then wrapped me in a fluffy white towel and straight into the bedroom like I'd wanted.

He laid on the bed and held his hands out to me, letting me climb up and straddle him and his rock-hard cock. "I haven't used a condom with you yet, I've told myself over and over to protect you, but I can't bring myself to cover up when I'm with you. I've never fucked without condoms before Elora. What do you do to me?"

"I'm seeing your doctor tomorrow to get on birth control; Jed is setting it up. I just got over my period a few days ago, so we're safe from pregnancy. I don't want anything between us Ryker, it feels so good to feel your skin bare inside of me."

"Fucking hell." He growled and lifted my hips, so they hovered over the top of his erection. He reached between our bodies and fisted his cock, holding it upright for me, and I looked to him for direction. "Slowly, very slowly, slide down on it. Keep your hips tilted forward."

I lowered my hips and tilted them forward, and took the head of his cock into my body. I was soaking wet, and he rolled his hips to help, and I glided down on him further.

"Good girl." He hissed as he watched his cock disappear into my body. I put both of my hands flat on his chest, on each of his pecks and rose back up until his cock came out completely and then dropped again, taking about half of him this time. He twitched inside of me and rubbed my g-spot, and I moaned. "Do you feel how hard you make me? My cock is as hard as stone because of how good you feel wrapped around it."

"Yes." I rose back up, keeping my hips tilted towards him and, on the next decline, pushed myself down, forcing my body to take all of him until my pussy lips sat on top of his fist. He moved his hand and slid his fingers over my clit as he lifted and pushed the rest of him inside of me. "Oh my God, you're so deep. Holy fuck."

"Every fucking inch of me is buried deep inside of your tight pussy. You were made to take me; my cock was created to be forced into your fucking body."

"Ryker, please. I need you–I need you to fuck me."

"No, Doll. You wanted to ride me baby, so do it. Rise up and down, that's it. Grind your clit on me, back and forth. Fuck, that's my good girl." His praise and directions were driving me wild as I started rocking my hips, pressing my clit onto him just like he told me to. He brought both hands up to my breasts and started pinching and pulling on my nipples and rings, and I threw my head back and started riding him as my orgasm crested and broke over my body.

He dropped his hands to my hips and fucked up into my body as I clenched down on him.

"Look at those sexy fucking tits bouncing while you take my cock." I looked down and saw my body swaying and bouncing as he started to really fuck me. His face was tight and the veins in his temple and neck were bulging as he gave me everything he had.

"You're so sexy." I said, watching him intently as he pleased us both. "I love your muscles and your tattoos," Rolling my hips, I grabbed one of his hands and brought it to my throat, needing the pressure on it as he lost his control. "I love how you make me feel."

"Fuck yeah." He grunted, "You need me to own you, don't you? You need me to control you and command your body, almost as badly as I need it."

"Yes. I've never felt so right until I felt your body against mine. Until I felt your body inside of mine."

His large hand spanked my ass, eliciting a gasp and a scream from me before he cracked my ass again and again.

"I'm coming, oh my god, you're making me come again!"

"Good girl. Take my cock, fuck you're so tight, you're pulling my come straight out of me. Take every last drop deep inside of you." He started coming, his hips jerked madly as he fucked me into the air, he grabbed a handful of my hair and pulled my head back as he delivered his last few punishing thrusts and I screamed in brilliant sexual agony as he gave me everything I ever asked for.

When he finally stopped fucking me and let go of my throat and my hair, I collapsed on his chest, burying my face into his neck, and peppering his skin with open mouthed kisses as he kneaded my sore muscles in my thighs and back.

"You are the epitome of perfection, Elora Louise Dax."

I groaned, hating my middle name, but smiled into his neck when he lightly spanked my ass. He lifted me, letting his cock slowly slide out of me, and then rolled me over so I was lying face to face with him on my side.

"I got you a present."

"Hmm?" I asked, struggling to keep my eyes open, but he had a very childlike excited gleam to his eyes as he got out of bed and took a medium-sized velvet box from his pants in the bathroom and crawled back into bed. "What is it?"

"Open it, love."

He leaned on the pillow next to me and watched as I slowly opened the hinged lid, and I couldn't help the megawatt smile that pulled my lips back.

Nestled on the black cushion were two emerald tear drop earrings encrusted with diamonds. "Oh, my god Ryker! They're so beautiful."

"Not nearly as beautiful as you are. I'd had big plans of coming home to you and giving them to you to wear while I fucked you senseless. But I got distracted."

"A hell of a distraction indeed." I cooed.

"Flip the cushion over and see your other present."

I looked up at him in question and he just nodded to the box in my hands; I lifted the cushion and flipped it over and laughed out loud at the two diamond nipple rings that lay opposite of the emerald earrings. They were full circles with the bar through the center. When I wore them, they would circle my entire nipple, and they would be visible under any shirt ever because of how many diamonds were on them.

"Those are so sexy, Ryker."

"They're going to be so sexy when you wear them for me."

"Mmh." I moaned and sat up quickly. "Help me put them in."

His eyes flared and his tongue shot out to lick his lips. "Fuck yes."

I quickly undid the bar of the two rings I was currently wearing, and he took them from me, but not before leaning in and biting on each nipple, sucking them into his mouth without the rings in. "Believe it or not, I've never been much of a tits man, until yours."

"Blasphemy, I can't imagine you not grabbing every pair of tits ever put in your face."

He chuckled and then handed me each of the new rings as I put them in.

"Perfect fit." I said and then dropped my hands to my lap. "How do they look?"

"Like I want to fuck your tits while you wear them and nothing else."

"Hmm, why does that sound so sexy coming from your mouth?" I asked, leaning down to kiss him and then trying and failing to hide a yawn.

He laughed and kissed my nose and then set the jewelry box down on his end table and pulled me down into the pillows next to him and wrapped his body around mine.

His hand went directly to my breast and absently played with my nipple as I kissed his chest. "I love you, doll."

"I love you, my King."

CHAPTER 18 – RYKER

"I don't like this one fucking bit." Razz said, from where he sat next to me in the front seat of my Escalade.

I hummed my agreement but didn't offer him anything else. He was one of my longest friends other than Zeke and a dark, brooding son of a bitch on a good day, but today, his negativity was warranted. We were at the shipping yard, waiting for the supposed shipment that was going to be the pinnacle point in Wellington's plan to assassinate my Queen. And there was no movement; no whisper of a car or a person to be found.

I looked at the clock on the dash, ten fifty-seven.

Zeke talked through the radio, "What do you think, Boss? We're all in position but we don't see anything."

"We wait until eleven at least." Just then my phone rang with Elora's face lighting up the screen. "Hold on El is calling me." I said through the radio and answered my phone.

"Ellie?"

"He called again, he said the shipment is right on time, coming to the yard by semi-truck with three armed trucks as support, and that the Wellington crew is arriving by boat from the North. Six boats, manned by thirteen men. The delivering crew has eight men." She rattled off quickly, high-strung and I could imagine her pacing my office as she relayed it.

"Okay, did he say anything else?"

"He said your best bet would be to take over the boats first and to take the shipment out that way because the delivering crew has men posted along the highway that they're picking back up on the way, if they don't show you'll be intercepted."

"Did he say how he knew this?"

"Just more riddles."

The clock on the dash turned to ten fifty-nine.

"Okay, I got to go. I love you."

"I love you, come home to me, even if you let them have the ship-ment, we'll find another way. Just come home to me."

"I will."

I hung up and picked up the radio. "The riddle master called El again. Wellingtons are coming in by boat from the north, with thirteen men on six boats. The delivering crew is coming in by semi with three armed cars as support, total of eight men. They have men on the highway waiting for their return, our best bet is to take over the boats first, and then we'll attack the semi. We'll take the cargo back out on the boats to the Southport marina. Let's move!"

My men all moved with trained precision, and I fought alongside of them. It was messy and chaotic, but it happened exactly as Ellie's informant had said. Bullets ripped through the air around us as I took out the driver of the semi-truck and then two of the guards.

Zeke was running point on the Wellington crew, and I listened through the radio as he gave commands to his team.

Two more men ran out from their trucks to get in the semi, and they died where they landed from my gun. Two others jumped in their car and tore off back out of the shipping yard. Jed was waiting for them though and his grenade launcher landed his shot on mark and the car blew up. The two men jumped out, engulfed in flames, and my men quickly dropped them, taking them out of their misery.

"Wellington Crew neutralized, no survivors. We're rounding the boats up to the dock now. What's the ETA on the shipment?" Zeke asked.

"One man left, he's hiding somewhere, then we'll drive the semi over to you."

"Roger that."

"I've got him." Jed blasted through the radio and shots rang out from behind the semi-trailer. Myself and my team ran towards the truck from behind shipping containers that we'd used for cover, and I jumped in the front seat of the truck. Jed jumped in the passenger seat, and I eyed him and the blood oozing from his shoulder.

"You straight?" I asked, throwing the truck in gear and roaring through the yard towards the dock.

"Just a pass through, no biggie."

I nodded at him as he radioed to Zeke that we were coming over the hill to them, so they didn't shoot.

"They're Russians."

"Yeah, I saw that." I said, "Means we've got to offload whatever is in the truck to the Cartel. It's the only way to ensure that we don't get hit with fallback."

"My thoughts exactly."

When I parked the truck, we ran around to the trailer doors and opened them wide, revealing the shipping containers that held the cargo the Wellington's had wanted.

I jumped up with Zeke and Jed and cracked the lid off of the first one and found it to be filled with guns and other weapons.

"Holy fuck." Zeke said, taking inventory in his mind of the money sitting in the crate.

I looked at the others, seven in total, and added rough numbers in my head. "Millions of dollars if they're all filled like this one."

"Let's get them loaded!" Jed said, barking orders to men and jumping behind a crate to push it to the edge of the trailer.

We worked quickly, removing the seven crates and loading them into the boats. Zeke led the boats to the marina as the rest of us took our cars back out of the yard.

We took the back way home, avoiding the highway at all costs and within two hours we were pulling up to the warehouse I'd instructed my men to take the crates to once they picked them up from the marina.

"I want these weapons off loaded ASAP, Zeke, get me a meeting with Quintero."

"Yes, boss."

"I want a ten-man team on these until we get them gone, get me an inventory of what exactly is here."

My men nodded and went to work, and I went the fuck home. Dragging a still bleeding Jed with me.

When I opened the front door, Elora threw herself at me, kissing me deeply. I wrapped my arms around her body and groaned when I felt the silk nightgown under my arms. "Why are you wearing so little in front of my men?"

"I have a robe on." She scoffed, sliding down my body, but the robe did nothing to hide the new diamonds I'd bought for her that she wore underneath it.

"Elora." I groaned.

"Oh my god, Jed!" She gasped, pulling herself from my arms and turning to her bodyguard.

"I'm fine, just a simple pass through. The doctor is on her way here to patch me up."

"Come to the kitchen and have a seat." she said, pulling him along with his good hand.

"Fuck." I muttered under my breath. "Elora, he's a big boy, he can take care of himself." I called after her. Jed shot me a look over his shoulder.

"He got shot because of me, the least I can do is see to his care."

My kitchen was filling with men as our mission ended and I hated how sexy Elora looked in a long silk emerald, green gown with her fucking sexy as sin nipples poking through the fabric as she helped Jed get his shirt off and over his head. She had her hair pinned on top of her head in an elegant bun and she looked so damn sexy.

Razz stood next to me, and I saw him watch Elora hungrily and then nudge me as she put her hands on Jed to press the gauze to his shoulder.

He chuckled at me when I scowled at him quickly before turning my attention back to my Queen. My men were enamored with her, hanging on her every fucking word as she fluttered around the kitchen like a butterfly, taking care of everyone's bumps and bruises from tonight's fight.

I saw more than a few men milking their scrapes for all they were worth as she paid them the slightest bit of attention.

While part of me was happy that they had accepted her so easily, I was jealous of the attention she was giving them and the fact that she was practically naked while she did it.

"Okay enough!" I bellowed out, making everyone in the room pause and fall silent. Just then, the doctor walked in with a large medical bag and a huff when she saw how many patients she had to attend to. "Elora, with me now!"

"But–" She started.

"Now." I said, lowering my voice to a menacing tone, and walked from the room. I didn't stop to make sure she followed me, I knew she would and by the time I hit the stairs, I heard her bare feet running across the marble behind me.

"Slow down, Ryker." She said, I looked over my shoulder as she grabbed her gown and robe and pulled it aside so she could climb the stairs quickly to catch me and then grimaced when she tripped and fell on the steps.

"Fuck." I ran back down the stairs to pick her up. She had a mark on her shin, and I felt like the biggest douche bag in the entire world. "I'm sorry Doll, are you okay?"

"I am now." She said, wrapping her arms around my neck and letting me carry her the rest of the way up the stairs and into our bedroom.

When I walked in, I headed straight into the closet to strip out of my clothes and set her down on the large table in the center of the room that was full of small drawers for items like cuff links and tie clips.

I leaned my face into hers and kissed her gently. "Are you okay?"

"Yes Ryker, I'm fine."

It was then that I noticed her clothes hanging in the empty side of the closet and raised my eyebrow at her.

"I thought it would be okay for me to move my few clothes in here since I sleep in here every night." She paused, waiting for my reaction, and I saw the fear in her eyes as I stayed silent. "But if you don't want me to–"

"Stop." I ordered and pulled my suit jacket off my shoulders. She instantly dropped her hands to my chest and started pulling the buttons of my shirt apart and then pulled it from my pants for me. "I'm going to fill this closet with clothes and baubles for you, Doll. It's just the first time in my life that I've shared space with a woman."

"Does it bother you?"

"Not in the least, actually."

"Good, because I like sharing space with you."

I smiled at her and ran my hands down to her ankles, grabbing the fabric of her gown and pushing it up her legs until my hands rested on her upper thighs.

"Did everything go okay tonight?" She asked, chewing on her lip, "Besides Jed getting shot, and your men getting hurt."

I chuckled and backed up, undoing my belt and pants. "Jed was fine and none of my men were nearly as hurt as they let you think they were, so you'd fawn over them."

Her mouth fell open as she fought me on it, but I silenced her with my lips on hers, pushing her thighs wide and stepping between them. She groaned and slid her palms flat over my abs and down into my briefs.

It was now my turn to groan.

"Do you have any idea how sexy you look right now in this gown? In front of all of my men with your nipples on display. I have no doubt every single one of them is going to jack off their pathetic cocks tonight to mental images of you."

"Oh, stop it! I just wanted to help."

"I know you did, love. But next time, do it fully clothed, please. I can't kick all of my best men from the crew for lusting after you every time you come downstairs wearing silk and lace."

She chuckled and slid off the table, kneeling in front of me as she pulled my pants and briefs down and helped me step out of my shoes and socks before pushing them down and off, leaving me standing naked and hard in front of her.

"Off your knees, love. Not tonight." Lifting her to her feet, I pulled her robe open and pushed it off her arms before leaning down to kiss her neck and over her shoulder. I scraped my teeth over the tiny strap of her gown and let it fall down her arm. I moved and repeated the process on the other side until her gown dropped down her body and pooled on the floor at her feet.

"You don't want me to suck your cock?" She asked, leaning in to kiss my chest.

"I'd love to feel your lips wrapped around my cock, baby girl, but not on your knees. Not like last night."

"Then how do you want me?"

"On your back, with your legs spread and your pussy swallowing it while I fill you up."

"Hmm." She hummed and leaned up on her toes to kiss my neck. "I think that can be arranged, but I want to try something first."

I raised my eyebrow at her and waited for her to tell me, but she just pursed her lips in challenge and took my hand. "Go sit on the bench at the end of the bed."

She pushed me into the bedroom, and I dutifully walked away from her, though it was the last thing in the world I wanted to do, before sitting on the bench with my elbows on the bed behind me.

She walked out of the closet a moment later and leaned over, placing both hands on my thighs and whispered in my ear. "I want you to fuck my tits." Her tongue licked the lobe of my ear as she pulled it into her mouth and scraped her teeth across it, and I fought to keep my composure.

She pulled back and sank to her knees in front of me and raised her eyebrow at me. "Don't tell me no, this is different. It isn't you using sex against me, I want to serve you."

Ellie bit her lip as she slid her hands up my cock, fisting it and squeezing tightly before leaning down to spit on I, rubbing it in. She sucked it deep into her mouth and let her saliva coat it before pulling back. She put one hand on each of her breasts and leaned up, so my cock pushed into the space between them.

I watched in rapture as she pressed her lush tits together and squeezed my cock between them and then rose up and down, letting it pass through the warm flesh and peak through the top where she licked the head and then stroked it down into her cleavage again.

Her tiny hands worked hard to contain her chest I took pity on her and put my large hands over hers and held her lushness tight around my cock.

"God, that feels good, and you look so sexy."

She shook her hair back off her shoulders and it was then I realized she had put in the emerald earrings I'd given her yesterday.

"Scratch that, you look divine in my jewels, Doll. I want to drape you in diamonds and fuck you wearing nothing else."

She moaned and bit her lip as she worked me over. Her nipples were hard and the diamonds encircling them twinkled in the bedside lamp light as I fucked her tits.

She was panting and moaning, and I couldn't take it any longer. I pulled her up to straddle my lap and then rolled, flipping her onto her back and threw her up the bed before stalking up after her.

She was laughing and panting as her legs fell open, spreading wide for me as I slid between them. I grabbed both of her ankles and pushed them over my shoulders as I dropped my lips to her wet pussy. I rolled my tongue over her clit as she clawed at my shoulders and begged me to fuck her.

"All in good time, Elora. I'm going to fuck you so good, and you're going to lie there like a good girl and take it the whole time."

"You're driving me wild."

I pumped two fingers into her pussy as I continued to suck and flick her clit with my tongue, and a couple of moments later, she shattered in my mouth. Her cream tasted divine as she rode my face, screaming and begging for mercy as my whiskers bit into her sensitive flesh.

I pulled my tongue out of her body and pushed her legs up into her chest as I slid up and kissed her, pushing her own taste into her mouth. She sucked my tongue wildly and held my head still as she kissed me back.

"Did you see the doctor today?"

"Yes, she gave me the birth control shot and said we're safe instantly. So please don't make me wait any longer, fuck me. Please Ry."

"Yes, love, whatever you need."

She smiled, and I pulled back to line my cock up with her and plowed into her body in one savage thrust. She screamed and clenched around me, throwing her head back as her body fought the invasion.

I was unable to take her slowly, I was too wired from the delicious game she played with my jewels and chest. And seeing her spread out in the center of my bed, wearing only my emeralds and diamonds, made me feel like I wouldn't be able to take a deep breath until I was buried inside of her.

I slid my fingers around her throat and tilted her head how I wanted it as I used her neck for leverage and started fucking her roughly.

"Yes." She hissed, clawing her nails up my back as I bottomed out inside of her over and over again.

"You're mine Ellie. God, this pussy is so fucking mine." Growling, I pulled out, flipping her over and bringing her up to her knees. She sat up in my lap, pressing her back to my chest as my hand went around to that heavenly spot between her thighs, rolling her clit as I fucked her.

She begged and pleaded frantically as she took me deep, "Ry! Oh my god, you feel so good. You're hitting it just right!"

I kept doing exactly what she liked, and she came, shaking as her orgasm wracked her entire body. Her pussy was so tight, and I was so close, but I didn't want it to end. I pushed her body forward until her tits fell to the mattress and pulled her hips high into the air and bent down.

I licked her pussy from front to back and buried my face between her large ass cheeks.

"Fuck!" She screamed and arched her back, giving me more access. I licked her ass again, and she gasped and pushed back on my face.

"Good girl." With a growl, I delivered a hard slap to her ass, relishing how she swiftly moved away from the impact, yet I pulled her back towards me and repeated the action on the opposite cheek. I pushed my tongue into her ass, and she buried her face in the blankets and moaned loud and long as I started playing with her.

Flicking her clit, I thrust two fingers deep into her pussy as I worked her ass over until I couldn't take it any longer.

"You like my tongue in your ass, don't you, Doll?"

"Oh my god, yes!"

I bit her ripe ass cheek and rose to my knees behind her, shoving my cock back deep into her.

"I'm going to fuck this sexy ass someday, and I'll be claiming another one of your firsts when I do." I thrust harder before spitting on her ass and pushing my thumb against the tight muscles there, massaging it. "Your virgin ass is going to feel so good wrapped around my cock."

She became manic as I pushed my thumb through the tight ring of muscles and into her ass. "Fuck me! Fuck me! Fuck me!" She screamed and pushed back on my thumb and my cock, and I gave her exactly what she asked for. I leaned forward and grabbed her hair and pulled her head back, arching her back and plowed into her. Ellie screamed and swore and begged and moaned, exploding wildly on my cock and my thumb as I pushed it in all the way.

She felt so fucking good; tight and hot wrapped around me, I couldn't hold off any longer and I started filling her pussy up as I came.

"Give it to me, Ryker, come deep inside of me, please!" She begged, and I threw my head back, roaring into the quiet room and stilled as my cock twitched painfully inside of her.

I pulled out both my cock and my thumb and collapsed next to her on the bed on my back and threw my arm over my head as I fought the heart attack like palpitations in my chest.

She laid flat on her stomach and smiled wildly at me. When I could finally breathe enough to talk I groaned at her, "You're going to kill me, I'm too old to fuck like that."

She giggled and slid over to snuggle against my arm. "Nonsense, only one of your balls is saggy and wrinkly, you've still got a few good years left in you."

I brought my hand through the air quickly and smacked her ass hard for the jab and then laughed as she shrieked and moaned.

"What I meant to say was, I love you, Ryker."

"I love you too, doll." I replied.

"And I love your wrinkly old man ball too."

Smack!

She eventually got up and out of bed and used the restroom, but I was still a useless heap on the bed.

When she came back out, she carried my discarded clothes I'd stripped out of and took them to the hamper. She flipped my pants around and something fell out of the pocket, and she stopped to pick it up.

I watched her intently, knowing what fell out without even seeing it, and waited to see what she said.

She ran her fingers over it, turning it in her hand to read it and then looked over at me. Her brows furrowed and her head tilted as she looked at me, holding my trinket up.

"Is this mine?" She asked, dropping my clothes, as she walked back over to the bed.

"Yes."

She shook her head and crinkled her nose as she held it up. "Why do you have it?"

I held my hand out to her and she put the metal bauble into my palm. I ran my fingers over it and fisted it, relaxing with it back in my possession. "I found it at the spot your dad died, when I went back the next day."

"And you kept it?" She sat on the edge of the bed facing me, trying to figure it out. "Why would you keep a button off my school uniform?"

The gold metal button had fallen off her blazer that night in the street, and I'd found it the next day.

"Because I kept it as a reminder of what could happen if I ever let my guard down again. I kept it because it was all I had left of you once your mom took you from me."

"Ryker."

"I carry it in my pocket, every single day. And I run my thumb over the edge, every single time I'm anxious, stressed, or more often lately, missing you. And it calms me."

She crawled up the bed and kissed me, letting her swollen lips melt against mine as her tongue licked at mine. "Why is that so sexy to me?"

"Because it shows you that my feelings for you, even before they were sexual, were deep and meaningful, even if neither of us understood them. You've been special to me since the day you were born, and I never understood just how special until you were ripped away from me. So, I kept this to remind me."

"I love you so much." She whispered against my lips and swung her leg over my lap and settled her pussy over my cock where it rested on my stomach.

I snorted at her in amusement, but wrapped my hands around her waist and rocked her on me. I was surprised that my cock stirred at all, given how hard I'd come just a few minutes ago.

"I want to worship you. I want to show you just how important you are to me." She said and kissed me. She kissed my neck and down my chest and stomach and then looked up at me under her thick dark lashes as she ran her tongue up my cock from base to tip. "I'm going to suck your cock." She said, laying an open-mouthed kiss on the head of my cock. "And lick your balls." She dropped her lips onto my sack and kissed each of them, before running her tongue over them. "And rub your taint." She covered her fingers with saliva and pushed my legs further apart to rub her fingers on the sensitive skin behind my balls next to my ass. My hips jerked wildly, as my cock hardened to steel. "And cover my tits with your come to show you how much I love you."

Fucking hell.

This girl is going to kill me.

chapter 19 – elora

I was lying on the couch in the den with a book on my chest, dangerously close to dropping it on my face as I fought to stay awake. The late afternoon sun shone in the windows, and I was in desperate need of a nap. Ryker had been keeping me up late every single night, pushing my body to ecstasy and back until morning.

I had no idea how he got up early every morning and went to run his businesses when I could hardly crack an eye before nine am after a night of mattress Olympics with the Greek God.

"Ma'am." Jed said from the doorway, startling me and my book fell directly onto my face.

"Oof." I gasped.

He cringed and shot me a look of remorse. "Sorry Ma'am. I just wanted to let you know that Mr. Lawson said you were going to dinner at the Ritz this evening. He'll be here at seven to pick you up."

"Jed, are you fucking my boyfriend?" I asked, throwing my legs over the couch and onto the floor.

His eyes flashed, and his eyebrows dropped over them yet he remained quiet in question.

I laughed and stood up, stretching my fatigued muscles. "He calls you more than me."

A smile pulled at his dark face, and he shook his head, "To be completely honest with you, Zeke called me with the message from Mr. Lawson to give to you."

"Damn, a dinner invitation, twice removed. How romantic." I drawled and then smiled at him. Placing the book on the shelf I walked past him. "I suppose I shall go get dressed. It is the Ritz after all." I said with mock adoration.

I went upstairs and into the closet to look at the dresses and gowns he had bought for me to wear for evenings such as this. But I was lacking confidence in picking, not having any context to what we were going to dinner for, so I took my phone out to text him.

> Me: Excuse me, Mr. Lawson, Ms. Dax is in need of some guidance as to which direction to take her evening attire in for tonight's dinner at the luxurious Ritz Carlton.

His response came instantly.

> **Ryker: Someone is being cheeky**.

> Me: Someone hasn't answered the question though. Are we dining alone or with others?

> **Ryker: Others.**

> Me: Grr! Must you make me pull each detail out with such resistance?

Ryker: Wear the red lace dress with the asymmetrical hem.

I looked over at the rack of dresses and pulled the red dress down and hung it on a hook to look at it.

Me: It's short.

Ryker: It's perfect. Wear the open toe black Jimmy Choo's with it.

Me: You pick out shoes now? Freak.

Ryker: Turns out your dainty sexy feet make my cock hard. And your feet in a sexy pair of sky-high heels that make your legs look miles long and your ass even bigger than it already fucking is, makes my cock even harder.

*Me: *Swooning* My very own romantic poet.*

Ryker: Watch your sass, or I'll make your ass ache the entire night.

Me: Promise?

Ryker: I promise that and so much more Doll. Try me.

Me: Hold on a second, I have to go find Jed to help me get the dress up over my hips. It's far too tight on my lush ass. I'm sure he wouldn't need to send a message through two different people to help me.

Minutes passed with no response, and I was afraid I pushed him too far.

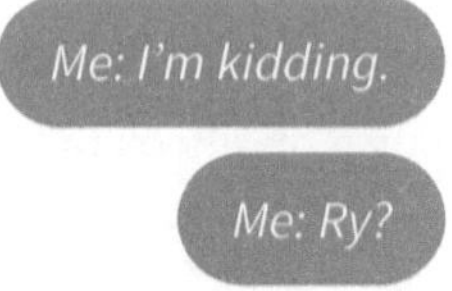

I was sitting on the floor of the closet chewing on my lip when he responded.

Ryker: I'll be home in twelve minutes. I want your face and hair done perfectly and your perfect body in that red dress. I want you bent over my desk, with it pulled up over your hips and your panties down around your ankles with your bare and wet pussy spread open and facing the door when I walk in. Understood?

Me: What if someone else walks in?

Ryker: You have eleven minutes.

Fuck.

Excitement rushed through my veins as I ran to the bathroom and quickly added a fresh face of makeup, luckily I'd already done the basics earlier in the day. I twisted my hair into a sexy bun low on my neck and ran back to the closet.

Looking at my phone I groaned; Three minutes left.

I had to fucking hurry. I grabbed a plunging lace push-up bra that matched the color of the dress and put it on and slid a red lace thong on to pair with it before shimmying my way into the offensive dress.

"Oh, come on!" I groaned as I got hung up on my tits that were pushed way the fuck up and out thanks to the expensive bra.

I finally got everything tucked away and managed to zip it up myself and then looked in the mirror.

I looked like a high paid escort.

Like sexy as hell. The fuck me, please me, breed me kind.

The dress was slightly low-cut but with the push up bra it made my tits look like a million bucks. The dress hugged my body like a second skin, and the asymmetrical hem brought the short side up to mid-thigh if I stood as still as possible, but if I moved or heaven forbid, sit down, it would ride up indecently.

"This man is going to be the death of me." I cursed.

One minute. I grabbed the black shoes he ordered me to wear and ran from the room, and down the stairs.

Jed was walking down the hallway to the offices and turned to watch me with amusement on his face as I sprinted past him, barefoot and panting.

"Are you okay?" He asked, as he plastered himself to the wall to stay out of my way. I got to Ryker's office and went to push the door open, but it was locked.

"Fuck!" I hissed, jiggling the handle. "Why is it locked?" I cried, looking over at him. I heard the alarm signal the front gate opening and groaned. "Do you have the key?"

"Yes." He stepped forward and slid the key in place, and then opened the door. I was hopping from foot to foot as I tried not to plow him over and do it faster myself when I heard the front door open.

"Thanks!" I all but screamed, running in the dimly lit office, and turning, "No one comes in but Ryker!" I ordered and then slammed it shut and ran to his desk.

I stepped into the shoes and lifted the hem of my dress and shoved the panties down around my ankles, afraid I'd tear something but I didn't have time to care. I spread my legs as far as my panties would allow, and pushed my chest to the cold polished top, hissing at the way it chilled the heated skin of my breasts that fell over the top of my dress.

I took a few deep breaths, trying to calm myself down when I heard the click of the door and then the room was bathed in bright light from the hallway.

I fought the urge to look over my shoulder as the door shut quietly.

God, I hoped it was Ryker and not one of his men.

I listened to the soft pad of shoes across the carpet towards me and bit down on my bottom lip to keep from whimpering.

"Doll." His deep husky voice laid over me like a blanket. "You listened perfectly."

His fingers touched the back of my knee and dragged up the back of my bare thigh towards my waiting pussy.

I mewled at him as he got closer to my aching center, but at the last second he withdrew his fingers and brought the flat of his hand down on my upturned ass.

"Mmh." I moaned as the delicious sting of his hand sank into my nerves.

"Is my little plaything feeling neglected?" he asked, letting his fingers touch the back of my other knee and then follow the same path up the back of my other thigh.

"No, but your girlfriend is." I bit back. When his fingers almost touched my clit, he slapped my other ass cheek harder than the first slap, and I bucked into the desk.

"Wrong." He said, flattening his palm against my wet pussy and grinding it back and forth, rubbing my clit expertly, making wet sounds carry out into the room. "My girlfriend knows exactly what I'm doing and why I'm busy doing it. So, it must be my little sex doll that's bored and lonely. My girlfriend would never be so selfish and needy."

"Fuck you." I hissed but moaned when he slid his thick fingers deep into my pussy.

"You wish I would, don't you?" He mused. I could hear the edge to his voice and bit my lip to keep from pushing him even further. "Perhaps I should call Jed in here and order him to fuck your pretty upturned pussy." He dragged his fingers out of my pussy and ran the wetness up to my ass. "Or maybe I'll have him fuck your ass while I fuck your pussy."

"Ryker." I groaned as he pushed one finger deep into my ass.

"Tell me you want his cock." He demanded. I could feel his anger through his hand. His body was vibrating with it.

"What if I do?" I asked. Stupidly.

Crack.

His hand hit my ass in the same spot, lighting the inferno in my aching pussy.

"What would you do if I told you that I'm so lonely I'd fuck anyone that would give me a cock to ride?" I asked, panting with need.

Crack.

"I'm going to fuck this ass tonight, Elora. And I don't care if you're ready for me or not. I'm going to force my cock deep into this perfect little asshole in punishment for every single stupid thing you've said so far tonight."

"Then perhaps I should keep going."

I needed to come. I was on the edge of an orgasm, and I needed it so fucking badly. I was hoping he'd be so overcome with anger that he wouldn't be paying attention to me, and I'd be able to come from his spankings and his fingers.

But I should have known better than to think he was ever unaware of anything regarding my body.

He leaned forward and pushed another finger into my ass as he brought his hand up to rest next to my face. Something clinked against the desk under his hand, and I watched closely as he took his hand away and left the gift sitting a few inches from my face.

"Ryker." I gasped.

He chuckled sinfully as he kissed my spine above the zipper of my dress. "You're going to look so sexy wearing that *all* night."

On the table was a metal butt plug.

"All night? You don't mean to dinner?" I whispered.

"That's right baby. You've talked a big game, it's time you put your money where your mouth is." He pushed his erection into my hipbone. "But wait. There's more."

He brought his hand up again to rest on the desk next to the butt plug and when he took it away a bright pink silicone toy sat there.

"What is that?" I asked, unable to tell from the shape of it what it was exactly.

"That's the toy you're going to wear inside of your pussy, next to the plug."

"Fuck." I groaned and turned my head to rest my forehead against the cold top.

"Precisely." He said, biting the back of my arm and then sucking on the sensitive skin. "Now be a good little sex doll and reach back to spread your cheeks for me."

He stood up and backed up from my body, leaving my heated skin pebbled to the cool air.

I knew I didn't have a choice. And my body ached for release, so I slid both of my hands over my flaming hot ass cheeks and pulled them apart, opening myself up further for him.

"Good girl. Fuck you're such a good girl for me."

I forced myself to take a few deep breaths as I heard him open a bottle of lube and then waited for the invasion. I jumped when the icy cold lube and metal of the toy pressed against my puckered ass. He rubbed it over the skin, coating it fully and hummed as he pushed it against me. "Take a deep breath and relax, Doll." He said. There was a tenderness to his voice, but I didn't trust it. But I did what he said, and when I relaxed, he pushed it into me.

"Oof, fuck that burns." I hissed and tensed up.

"Let me in. Be a good little slut and let me into your ass." He said between clenched teeth.

"Go to hell." I bit back but relaxed and he pushed it the rest of the way in, forcing it faster at the end in silent retribution for my sass.

I sighed when the narrow neck of it let my ass finally relax and sighed as I tried to get used to it.

"Do you have any fucking idea how sexy that is?" He said as he pulled and twisted the plug. "Damn, your ass is going to be so ready for me later."

"I need to come." I begged, near tears.

"Hmm. You think you deserve an orgasm after sassing me and threatening to fuck my men like a spoiled little brat?"

"Yes." I snapped.

"Beg for it."

"Please baby. Please give me what I need to come. I need you so bad." I begged prettily, just how I knew he loved because I was desperate, even if his degradation was grating on my nerves. But it was also making my pussy drip at the same time, and I couldn't wrap my head around why.

Other than because it was Ryker. And I fucking loved everything about him.

I heard the lube again and then he ran the end of the other toy through my lips and pushed it in. It went in far easier than the plug, but I felt the resistance from the foreign object in my ass at the same time.

I moaned and rocked my hips back and forth as he kneeled behind me and kissed each of my cheeks, spreading me further with his hands on top of mine.

"Ryker please!" I begged. Near tears.

His fingers trailed down my legs and grabbed my panties and started to slide them up my legs.

"What are you doing?" I gasped and sat up, but he ignored me and pulled them up all the way to my hips and then pulled my dress down. "Ryker!"

"I'm giving you exactly what you deserve."

"What I deserve?" I asked in anger as I stood up and turned to face him. I gasped at the full feeling and teetered on my heels, leaning on the desk for support.

"Yes, what you deserve. You're going to wear those toys tonight and not come until I tell you that you can."

"Fuck you!" I snapped. "What's to stop me from taking them out or making myself come? You act like you're the only one who can make me orgasm."

Anger flashed in his eyes as he wrapped his fingers around my neck quickly. "You're not going to do that, or the consequences will be far worse than these. You're going to be a good and dutiful Doll tonight, sitting at my side, and smiling prettily and making polite conversation when prompted and you're going to do it with a fucking smile on your face because you fucked around and pissed me off."

"That's not fair!" I nearly screamed in frustration.

"That's the point!" He snapped back. "Now let's go. Or we'll be late."

"Please!" I begged, but he slid his hand down the back of my dress and escorted me from the room. "I hate you." I hissed under my breath as we met Jed and Zeke in the hallway.

He chuckled at me openly in front of them and then slapped my ass directly against the plug and I gasped and swayed into him. He happily caught me and bit my ear as I buried my face embarrassingly into his chest. "I'm going to enjoy this. And that should make you happy." He said.

He pulled me from the house and into the waiting car for us and watched me with mirth in his eyes as I awkwardly tried to climb in without flashing anyone, or indicating to anyone I was stuffed full of sex toys mere inches above the indecent hem of my dress. Why had I bothered asking him what to wear?

I glared at him but bit my tongue to keep from saying anything that would only embarrass me more as we drove through the night. His warm hand was resting on my thigh, with his fingers pressed between my legs, only inches from my pussy.

Zeke kept looking at us in the rearview mirror, keyed into the tension in the car, but I couldn't even try to use my usual witty banter with him and Jed to alleviate it tonight.

I was a hair trigger away from either orgasming, screaming, or crying. And I wasn't interested in doing any of those things in front of them.

"The Constantine's will be there tonight sir." Zeke said, breaking the silence.

"Good." Ryker said in response. "I can show off my new toy." He patted my thigh condescendingly, and I ground my teeth together to keep from biting back angrily.

"I love you." I said sweetly to him, letting hearts and flowers radiate from my eyes towards him.

He narrowed his at me and squeezed my leg almost painfully. I decided then and there to kill him with kindness all night. Be the dutiful trophy on his arm and refuse to take the bait that I knew he'd throw my way to get a rise out of me.

I could do this. I'd have *him* begging *me* by the end of the night.

"Elora, Margaret asked me earlier if you'd had a chance to approve the menu for next week before she ordered the groceries." Zeke again tried to draw us into conversation.

I smiled at him, "Yes, I did. I loved everything she picked out. Especially the marsala. I think pairing it with–" I gasped and choked on my tongue as intense vibrations started deep inside of me.

"Ma'am?" Zeke said, sitting up in his seat to look at me in the mirror, Jed turned in his seat as well, alarm marring both of their faces.

"I—" I swallowed and squeezed my legs together. I looked at Ryker, but he never turned towards me from where he looked out the window, without a care in the world. I was about to say something to him when I looked down and saw a tiny remote in his hand on his lap. I watched in horror as his thumb ran back and forth over the raised button on it and then when he pushed it, the tempo of vibrations inside of me changed.

Son of a bitch.

I refused to curse and lash out at him like I wanted to. And boy did I want to because of the smug look on his face. He finally turned to me and raised an eyebrow at me in mockery, "Did you gag on something, darling?"

I clenched my jaw and let my eyes flutter closed briefly as I fought the urge to spread my legs and moan wildly in pleasure. Instead, I sat taller in my seat and looked back at Jed and Zeke, letting a cool composed face slide over my features. "Sorry, I got distracted. Um –" I fought to regain my thoughts. "Yes the menu looked great. Please let her know for me." I finished. Gasping and fighting to think straight.

"Yes, ma'am." Zeke said curiously, and Jed turned back around in his seat.

Ryker leaned over and bit my ear, "Do. Not. Orgasm." He warned quietly.

"You've made a critical error tonight, baby." I purred back at him as he left his face so close to mine, I could taste his minty breath.

"I never make errors."

"Usually you don't, but where I'm concerned you almost *always* do. You picked out a dress that will do nothing to hide my diamond dripping nipples when they harden from my arousal, and to keep from coming like you insist I do, I'll have to keep my legs spread wide all evening to alleviate the pressure. And in this short dress—" I tsked my tongue at him and shook my head. "Every single person in the room will get a free show of my soaked panties."

His jaw locked tight, and his nostrils flared. "You wouldn't dare."

We pulled up outside the timeless hotel, and Jed and Zeke got out and opened our doors. Zeke held his hand out for me to take, and I shot one last glare at Ryker. "Game on baby." I blew him a kiss and then slid from the car with grace and elegance I didn't know I possessed, especially not with a butt plug the size of a seltzer vodka in my ass and a vibrator dancing around in my pussy.

Game on indeed.

Ryker's mask was back in place as he took my hand from Zeke and put it on his arm and led me into the hotel.

I kept my spine straight and a sensual smile on my face as we walked through the restaurant towards our table. Thankfully, Ryker had turned off the vibration for the walk. If not, I think I probably would have fallen over along the way.

When we made it to the table, there were four other people there already waiting for us.

"My apologies for our late arrival," Ryker said as the men stood up when we got close, "My date likes to fuss and muss over her appearance for far too long sometimes."

I grinned like a brainless bimbo that he was trying to paint me as and endured the condescending glances they all passed my way.

And then I sat perfectly still and quiet the entire meal, just like he wanted me to. I tried to tell myself that not goading him on was a win for me. But the longer I sat there being ignored and only engaged in conversation when the topics fell to something mundane and brainless, the more it ate away at me.

And not just at my temper, which was rising the ruder the men got to me.

But it ate away at my heart. Ryker was purposely treating me like I was beneath him. And the entire time he was doing it; he was playing with his fucking toys like a puppet master. He was pulling my strings and controlling my reactions with threats and punishments, and nothing felt right about that.

As the plates were cleared away with my mostly untouched dinner on it still, I felt tears burning the back of my eyes and my nose burning as I fought to keep them at bay.

Ryker ordered another scotch and relaxed in his seat next to me, and I fought the urge to scream at him. I wanted to go home. I was done with the whole show.

Taking my napkin from my lap, I placed it on the table and pushed my chair back, finally drawing his attention to me.

"Where are you going?" He asked.

"To the restroom." I answered back, smiling at the table as though I were the picture of blissful happiness.

I didn't look at Ryker as I quickly walked away to the restroom. I felt Jed fall into step beside me, but couldn't look up at him.

"Ma'am?" he asked as I dashed quickly at the tears that fell from my lashes. My chest ached as I simply shook my head, answering him the only way I could. When I finally made it into the restroom I ran straight into the large stall on the end and covered my mouth as I paced the space.

I hated this. I hated every second of this.

The door to the bathroom opened, and I bit down on my knuckles to keep quiet as I stood still.

"El."

I groaned silently when Ryker's voice rang out through the empty room. Thankfully there was no one else around and I heard him turn the lock on the door.

"You're not breaking the rules, are you?" He asked challenging from the other side of my stall.

I shook my head and covered my face with my hands, refusing to speak because if I did, he'd hear my emotions. And I desperately wanted to keep him from knowing how much he hurt me. I didn't want him to know he held that kind of power over me.

"Elora, answer me."

I took a deep breath and fought to keep my voice level, "No Ryker, I wouldn't dream of breaking your cruel rules. I'll be out in a moment."

"Open the door."

"No."

"Open the fucking door, or I'll break it down."

"Ryker! Just give me a minute alone, okay!" I snapped back and tried but failed to stop a sob as it escaped my lips.

The handle on the door twisted and cracked and then Ryker ripped it open and stepped into the stall. Worry etched every line on his face as I cried in front of him.

I turned my back on him and covered my face. His hands slid around my waist, and he took a deep breath with his nose in the crook of my neck. "Talk to me."

"You're punishing me like I'm a child and I hate it!" I gasped and hiccupped. "You've treated me no better than a whore all night long and I told myself I was going to love you through it anyway, but I can't! It's too much! And you're playing with my body like I'm a fucking toy instead of the woman you love! I feel so cheap and dirty, and this dress feels a hell of a lot like a collar I didn't give you permission to put onto me."

He turned me in his arms and held each side of my face as his eyes darted back and forth from mine, and he swallowed aggressively.

"I'm sorry Ellie, I never should have done this tonight. Not while I was angry." He leaned his forehead against mine and forced me to take a deep breath with him. "I was planning on using the toys with you tonight at dinner beforehand and then you riled me up, talking about other men and I just—" He shook his head, "I let it get out of hand. I never should have taken something fun and new and exciting and turned it into a punishment. I'm so sorry baby."

"I need to come." Pulling him closer, I whined embarrassingly, grabbing the front of his dress shirt. "I need to take these toys out and come and go home!" I leaned up and pressed my lips to his hungrily and moaned when he wrapped his hands around my ass and ground his hips against mine. "Fuck me, Ryker."

"I'm going to make you come so hard these tears are going to dry right up, and then I'm going to take you home and worship your tight little body all night long." He promised as his hand slid under the hem of my dress and in one quick move, he ripped my panties off of my body.

I moaned and clung to him as he brought them up and looked at the wet spot in the fabric. He ran his thumb back and forth on it and groaned before slipping it into his pocket. "Another pair for my collection." He brought his fingers to my mouth and pushed two past my lips. "Suck them, get them nice and wet."

I eagerly sucked them into my mouth and loved the taste of his skin on my tongue. He pulled them from my lips and started rubbing them around in tight circles on my clit. He took the remote from his pocket and turned the vibrator on high and then backed me into the wall of the stall and pushed his thigh between my knees. I sagged onto his thigh, and he pushed up, putting pressure on the butt plug and the vibrator.

"Yes!" I moaned, slumping against the wall as he kissed my lips passionately.

"I want you to come, and when you do, I want to hear every single syllable of it. Do not hold back on me, be loud."

I gasped and rocked my hips, "It will echo, everyone will hear."

"Exactly. I want everyone to know that I'm giving you orgasms here in the middle of the lavish elite because you're my good girl and you deserve them. You've earned them."

"Please." I hummed.

He wrapped his other hand around the base of the butt plug in my ass and started spinning it and pushing and pulling on it as he pinched my clit.

"Ryker!" I screamed, leaning forward, and biting his peck as I crashed through a series of orgasms that wracked my body as they erupted one after the other thanks to the toys and my lover's unrelenting hands on my body. He pulled the orgasms from my body expertly and praised me the entire time.

"There she is. That's my good girl. Always so eager to please me. Let the world hear who you belong to, baby."

My legs gave out completely, and he held me up, kissing my damp forehead as I fought to remain conscious after such a tumultuous series of events over the last hour.

He took his phone out, pressed a button and held it to his ear. "We're leaving, give my regards to the table and meet us out back."

He hung the phone up and tucked a strand of hair behind my ear. "Let's go home, love. I have many more orgasms to rip from your body."

I moaned and smiled at him, feeling calmer and closer to him now that he was treating me appropriately. But I wasn't ready to let him off the hook completely. We both fucked up.

As he led me from the ladies' room, we passed a long line of women in the hallway who were waiting for the locked door to be opened. They stared in shock as we walked out hand in hand. I'm sure they all knew exactly what we'd been doing in there, given the volume of my orgasms and there wasn't a woman in this world who would have Ryker Lawson locked in a restroom and not ride him like a pony given the chance.

I smiled knowingly at them all as he dipped his head and apologized for the long wait and then dragged me towards a secondary exit.

Zeke and Jed were waiting with our car when we walked out, and before I got in, he turned me and pressed my back into the cold shiny surface of the car side.

He kissed me passionately, letting his hands roam over my body and bit my ear. "I want you straddling my lap the entire way home. I'm going to make your pussy come so hard, and as many times as possible, before we get there."

"Ry–" I gasped, but he silenced me with another kiss. He took his suit jacket off and then pushed me into the car ahead of him. When he slid in, I sat next to him, waiting to see what he did. As Zeke pulled away from the curb, Ryker addressed both him and Jed.

"It would be in both of your best interests to turn the music up as loud as possible and keep your eyes out the windshield."

Zeke raised an eyebrow at him in the mirror, but then turned the music onto some death metal and cranked it. Ry slid his hands around my waist and lifted me onto his lap with one leg over each of his. My dress instantly rode up to my waist and I tried to pull it back down, but with my legs spread wide around his, there just wasn't enough fabric to cover me.

He slung his jacket over my shoulders, and I smiled as it fell over my back like an oversized cape.

I leaned down to his ear and said, "Maybe next time you should rent us a limo so we can close the partition."

"I'll buy one and take you around in it all the time if you're going to spread your legs for me in the back seat."

"I'll always spread my legs for you, baby." I purred, looking down at my exposed pussy spread wide over his hips.

He turned on the vibrator again and I moaned, throwing my head back and rocking my hips forward as I tried desperately to get contact on my clit. I slid my hand down the front of my body and rubbed at my clit while he watched me hungrily. "Play with that pussy, baby."

I reached down with my other hand and rubbed his hard cock where it strained against his suit pants. He groaned and thrust his hips. "I need you to fuck me, Ryker. Right here. Just like this."

His eyes glowed as he looked over my shoulder at his men only a few feet from us. The music was loud, but I was sure they could hear bits and pieces, and that was turning me on, and I knew he was on the edge of giving in to me.

"Fuck me in front of them and show them how you own me. Show them how there's no chance I'd ever want anyone else when you can make my body melt in your hands." I played on the possessive part of him and knew it was a gamble; I didn't want him to go over the edge like he had earlier tonight and turn mean. But I did want him to fuck me in front of two men I trusted not to exploit it.

He reached up under the jacket I wore over my shoulders, and he pulled the zipper of my dress down and then pulled it off my arms and hungrily stared at me in the sexy lace bra. "You were made for me, Doll."

"Yes." I agreed. He undid the front clasp of the bra and let my tits free as Zeke drove us through the city, cars idled next to us at stoplights, and I wanted to roll the window down and give them a show. "You've kept me so horny all evening and now I'm crazed with need. I want to do dirty and naughty things because of you."

"Then my plan is working. Though you taking my cock in front of my men was never on my agenda."

"It turns me on so much." I moaned as he pinched and pulled on my nipples. He leaned forward and sucked one into his mouth and bit it, making me scream and moan. He pulled the vibrator from my pussy and tossed it on the seat next to him as he undid his zipper and fisted his magnificent cock.

"Ride my cock like a good girl. Bounce on it hard."

He lifted me up and then lowered me down onto him. I moaned and wiggled my hips back and forth, easing him into me. He wasn't having that though and his hands gripped my hips tight, and he fucked his cock up into me. I closed my eyes and dropped my head again.

"Open those pretty hazel eyes and watch my face while I fuck you, love." He commanded. Doing what he said, I opened my eyes and watched him intently as I rode him. I bounced hard on his lap, just like he'd told me to, and loved the way his eyes were torn between looking at my face and watching my tits sway in his face.

"Your pussy is strangling my cock with that plug in your ass. How does it feel to you?"

"Intense. You feel even deeper than usual, and I can feel every ridge of your cock."

"Lean back and let me fuck you. Spread your legs and open that pussy up for me and take everything I give you."

"Oh, my god." I moaned and leaned back until my shoulders pressed against the seat in front of me. Ryker lifted his hips and pounded his cock into my body relentlessly, pushing me into the seat.

I knew in the back of my head that Jed could hear me perfectly clear now and was being rocked by Ryker's thrusts, and it pushed me over the edge into a blinding orgasm. I tried to bite down on my knuckles, but Ryker pulled them out of my mouth and held my hands behind my back as I screamed through it. The jacket I'd been wearing slid to the floor, leaving me exposed in the moment, but neither of us could care. We were chasing bliss and blind to everything else.

"Fucking take it." He groaned and then started coming, pumping his come deep inside of me as I hung on and let him have his way. "Such a good girl. Fuck, you're such a good girl, Doll." He praised, pulling me back to rest against his chest as we caught our breaths. I turned my head and kissed along his neck and nibbled my way up to his ear and sighed when his cock twitched inside of me. The car slowed and then turned, and I looked out the window to see the gates to the front of Ryker's mansion opening for us.

"Honey, we're home." He purred into my ear. I started to slide off of him, but he held me firmly in his lap. "Leave your tits out and your dress pulled up around your waist when we walk in. My jacket will cover the necessities." He pulled his suit jacket back up my body, and I slid my arms into it. He buttoned the two buttons and I groaned when I saw that my tits were still openly exposed like a deep v neck dress. My nipples were covered but barely.

"You'd better hurry upstairs before someone sees you. I want you naked and bent over in the middle of the bed when I get up there."

"Yes, sir." I purred back to him as the car came to a stop. He held me on his lap as Zeke and Jed got out of the car and walked away towards the entrance of the house, leaving us some privacy. Thank God.

I slid from his lap and onto the seat, fighting the urge to pull my dress down. Ryker pocketed the vibrator and helped me from the car. He made sure his jacket was set on my body before leading me towards the front door and past a silent duo of guards as they waited for Ryker.

I didn't look either of them in the eye as I ran up the stairs and into the safety of our bedroom with my own blush rushing up my neck.

Ryker addressed them about normal things and envied his ability to be so comfortable with them after such an experience. I stripped out of my disheveled clothes and heels and crawled up the bed to the center of it and assumed the position I had been instructed to get into.

Ryker's come coated my inner thighs as I spread them wide and was still humming from my orgasms, but I wanted more. I wanted his cock deep in my ass for the first time, like he promised me.

The door opened, and I fought the urge to look over my shoulder at him as he stalked towards me.

"How can you look even sexier right now than you did ten minutes ago when I was filling you with my come?" He asked, running his warm palms over both of my ass cheeks and spreading them. "Tell me you want me to fuck your ass."

I swayed my hips and purred back at him, "I want your cock deep in my ass, Ryker. I want to feel you claiming me there."

"That's my girl."

I looked over my shoulder at him and watched him strip away his clothes and licked my lips as he stood at the end of the bed, naked and hard.

"I'm going to go slow and make sure you love every second of me inside of you, love. Okay?" he asked gently.

"I don't need slow, Ryker. I need you." I begged, and he chuckled.

"Arch your ass higher and spread your legs wider. I'm going to take this plug out and then put my cock in before you close back up."

"Yes." I moaned, dropping my forehead back to the bed and closed my eyes, forcing myself to just feel the sensations and not over stimulate.

He twisted the plug and then started pulling on it. It burned as it widened again, and I hissed.

"Relax, doll, let me have it."

He got to the widest part and then it tapered small again and I groaned as it felt good as it slid from my body.

"Fuck, that's so sexy." He praised. I heard him lubing up his cock and stroking himself and swayed my hips again, desperate to be filled.

"Please Ry, I need you inside of me. Don't wait."

"I've got you." He said, and then the head of his cock was pressing into the stretched hole of my ass. It burned, he was bigger than the toy, but it didn't hurt as bad as the first time he'd put the toy in. "Good girl.

Push back on my cock." He said, and I could hear the restraint in his tight voice as he commanded me.

I pushed back on him but didn't stop or slow down and took all of him in one swift thrust.

"Fuck!" I hissed and mewed as his hand came down on my cheek in a crisp slap.

"Ellie–fuck. Shit, I'm going to blow in your ass if you do that again. Fuck–"

He grunted and grabbed my hips in an iron grip and pulled back out of me until only the head of his cock remained. He slowly pushed back in and groaned the entire way.

"Does that feel good for you?" I asked, between gasps and groans myself.

"You have no fucking idea. How about you? Do you like my cock in your ass?"

"Yes!" I pulled forward and pulled off of him and then pushed back again. "But I need you to fuck me now, Ry. No gentle, slow thrusts. I want you to fuck me in the way that only you can. I want you to make it fucking hurt so good."

He leaned forward and grabbed a fistful of my hair and slammed forward into me with a jerky thrust. "I'm barely hanging on by a thread here doll, don't ask for something you aren't ready to take."

"I want it. Fuck me like you own me or get the fuck off of me and I'll do it myself with a toy." I snapped. My entire body was coiled tight and covered in a thin layer of sweat from the burn in my ass of him stretching me.

"That's my greedy little slut." He growled and started thrusting roughly into my body. The slap of his thighs against mine lulled me into a daze as I rode out the wave of pleasure and pain. "You look so sexy spread open with my cock buried in your ass, baby."

"I need more." I panted, dropping my hand under my body and rubbing my clit as he fucked me into the mattress. He grabbed my arms and pinned them behind my back, and I cursed at him in frustration.

"I give you your pleasures." He growled as his own fingers started rubbing my clit as he slammed into me again and again.

"Yes!" I screamed. "More, please give me more!"

His hand cracked down on my ass and he plunged two fingers into my pussy, hooking them and rubbing on my g spot and grunted dirty indecent things into my ear.

"Such a cock slut."

"So greedy to be filled with my come."

"You're my little whore."

I shot off, moaning, and begging for more as I tightened impossibly tight on his cock. "Just like that, Ryker. Don't stop." I could sense his orgasm moments before he started filling me up. His hips jerked madly, with uncoordinated rhythm, and I reveled in the feeling of him branding the inside of my ass with his come.

"Lay down." He grunted, panting wildly.

I slid forward, and he followed me and rolled us, so we were on our sides, with him still buried inside of me. We both lay there panting in the darkness as wonder filled my soul.

I just gave Ryker another one of my firsts, and it cemented another brick in the mortar of our relationship for me. We were building an impenetrable fortress for our love, and it gave me peace for the first time in years.

CHAPTER 20 – RYKER

"Elora!" I bellowed out of the office door in search of my infuriating Queen.

"What do you want, Neanderthal?" She snapped back as she walked in, looking drop-dead gorgeous. Which only added to my fury with her.

A devilish smile played on her lips as she cocked her hip to the side and leaned against the door frame with her arms crossed over her sexy chest.

She wore a short black dress that was simple but hugged every curve from her tits to her hips and ass and made me fucking hard.

"Did you ask Jed to take you to Lux tonight?" I snapped from where I sat at my desk.

"No." She answered plainly. That made me pause, because he had told me she did no less than five minutes ago.

"So, he lied to me?"

"No, you said did I ask him to take me; I didn't ask him. I told him we were going." She said with a shrug of her shoulders.

"You infuriating–" I started and then clenched my teeth to keep from finishing that statement.

She cocked an eyebrow at me and challenged, "You were about to say–"

"I was about to *say* you aren't going."

"Well, good thing I didn't ask you for permission." She said and turned to walk away.

"Get back here!" I bellowed, and she turned on me and stormed back into the office.

"Why can't I go?" She put her hands on her hips, and I was torn between being angry with her and wanting to bend her over my desk.

"Do you not remember what happened the last time you were there?" I stood up and placed my fists on the top of my desk and leveled her with a challenging stare. She walked forward and put her own hands flat on the desk opposite of me and cocked her hip seductively.

"Do you mean the part where I got a sexy as hell lap dance? Or do you mean the part where I gave you one?"

"I mean the part where a man back handed you and got a bullet between his eyes for it!"

She scowled at me and stood back up. "I'm bored, Ryker."

"Then get a hobby."

"Kind of impossible to do while being a hostage in a gilded cage."

"As any intelligent person knows, a gilded cage is used to keep the pet safe."

"A cage is still a cage. And tell me this Ryker—" She leaned forward again, "When has a caged animal ever not escaped when given the opportunity." She tsked her tongue and started to stand up, but snapped her eyes back down to my desk.

Like she said in the car the other night on the way to dinner, I only ever made errors where she was concerned. And I'd just made a giant error.

"What is that?" she asked, grabbing the file off my desk before I could move it out of her reach.

"Give it back here." I ordered, but she stepped back and opened it. Pain and confusion crossed her face as she looked at the pictures inside.

"What the fuck is this?" She whispered, finally looking up at me, shaking the file in her hands.

I held her gaze and stood up to my full height and moved around the desk towards her, slow like a predator. "Did you think I wouldn't look into her?"

"What does that mean? Look into her? She's being tortured in these pictures!"

"Hardly anything she doesn't deserve." I said, snapping my hand out and grabbing the file from her and throwing it back on my desk. "Have you suddenly started caring about the woman that let men pay her to rape you? Or the one that starved, beat, and drugged you?" I wrapped my hand around the back of her head and pulled her into me, and she wrapped her arms around my waist. "Tell me you care about the woman that took you from me, and I'll release her. No questions asked."

"I–" She licked her lips and shook her head. Her eyes were wide with confusion and anger. I watched her features as she went down memory lane to everything her mother had done to her and watched as she built up the strong spine she needed again. "I wish you had told me."

"I didn't want you to carry that burden on your soul. It's not meant to know these types of things. Your father protected you growing up, and now I'm doing it."

Her tired sigh cut through me, "You're not my Dad, Ryker. You're my partner. You have to treat me as your equal." She hesitated and then asked what she was desperate to know, "How long have you had her?"

I took a deep breath, and kissed her forehead, pulling her around my desk and into my lap as I sat down in my chair. "A week."

"And what happened?"

"She was hard to find at first in LA, but once I did, my men went in and brought her up here."

"And you've been torturing her?"

"Yes, and no. Some days I don't touch her. Other days, I make her beg for death." I heard the coldness in my voice, and she shivered as she tried to wrap her head around it.

"What do you plan on doing to her?"

"I have considered a few options but haven't decided yet."

"What are they?"

"I'm not telling you that, Doll. It will darken your sunshine too much. Just know that she's regretting every single thing she has done to you over the course of your life. I'm getting justice for you."

"Justice?" she asked, laying her head on my shoulder and taking a deep breath at my neck. "I don't know how I feel about this."

"I know. That's why I didn't tell you."

She lay in my arms for a long time and pondered everything over in her head silently. I had a million things to do right now, but the most important thing I could do was hold her while she needed me, so I did just that.

"Would you judge me poorly if I told you I wanted her to suffer for a long time?" She whispered.

I tightened my arms around her. "Never."

"Doesn't that make me as bad as her?"

"No, it makes you a product of her actions, though. And it's reasonable for you to want to inflict pain on the person that hurt you most." She was quiet again for a while and then her lips pressed into the side of my neck and again at the base of my ear before her teeth bit it. A rush of warm breath covered my skin and I groaned. "What are you doing?"

"Would you judge me poorly if I told you that I'm soaking wet thinking about you going all dark and dangerous on her for me?"

I groaned and kissed her deeply, holding the side of her face with my hand and devouring her.

"Why does that make you wet?"

"I feel like you're honoring me. Making her pay for everything she's done wrong to me in the most primal way it just–turns me on." She slid off my lap and stood without breaking contact with my lips. She leaned forward and whispered in my ear. "I want to deep-throat you so badly right now, baby."

"You could just ride my cock instead." I challenged, it was stupid to turn down a blow job from her perfect lips, but I was desperate for more than just her throat.

"I can do that after I gag on you for a while." She bit my lip and sucked on my tongue as I fought to remain in control. I'd dreaded this conversation for a week now; afraid she'd get mad at me for keeping it from her. But knowing it was making her horny, did something to me. It showed me how alike we were in yet another way.

She dropped to her knees and pulled my belt from my pants and pulled down my slacks roughly until my cock bobbed in front of her face as she licked her lips. "I want you to hold my head and fuck your cock deep into my throat, Ryker. I want you to make me cry and gag and beg to breathe. I know that's what you like."

She fisted my cock and licked the head of it. "If that's what you want, Doll, who am I to tell you no?" My office door was open, but I didn't fucking care, I needed this as badly as she needed to give it to me.

She sucked my cock deep into her mouth over and over again, coating it with saliva and then looked up at me expectantly and bared her teeth over the taut skin. "Use me."

I threaded my fingers through her hair on both sides of her face and stood up. "Hands behind your back, open your mouth and keep your eyes open and on me." I commanded.

She spread her thighs wide and stuck her tongue out flat for me to press my cock against. I pushed it into her throat in one rough thrust, and she gagged and then groaned when I pulled back out. She smiled sinisterly up at me as she licked her lips and then opened wide with her tongue out again. "Fuck yes." I groaned and bottomed out again. "Take it."

She kept her hands behind her back as she gagged and cried and gasped while I picked up a fast rhythm and slid my cock all the way down her throat. It was tight and hot and the way it tightened around me as she gagged felt incredible.

"No one sucks my cock like you do, Doll. You're so fucking good at taking me deep." She moaned and hummed around me, and I tightened my grip on her hair and pulled her head back and forth roughly as I fucked her, chasing my orgasm. "Such a pretty mess."

I pushed deep into her throat and held still, watching her eyes water and her body convulse as she gagged at the invasion, and I started coming. I pulled out of her mouth and held her by the hair in one hand and stroked my cock with my other and covered her face and tits with my come. She stuck her tongue out and caught everything I gave her before sucking it into her mouth and swallowing.

"Such a fucking good girl."

She looked down at her messy tits and smiled up at me. I grabbed a towel and wiped it over her face and tits, cleaning up as much as I could, and then pulled her up to straddle me in the chair.

"Did I do good for you, Sir?" She mewled, licking her lips.

"You were a very good girl."

"Good enough for a reward?" She bit her bottom lip and hid her eyes, and I recognized it as something she did when she was uncomfortable.

"Depends on what you want, Doll." I said, pulling her dress up over her hips and rubbing her ass.

She looked back into my eyes and whispered, "Make her hurt for me."

My cock jumped where it laid under her silk panties, but I treaded carefully. She was toeing a line she couldn't cross back over once she stepped on it. "Make her hurt how?"

"I don't know. But I want to watch you hurt her."

"You want me to video it?"

"No, I want to watch it in person. I want to hear it and smell it. I need to feel it."

"Ellie." I groaned. "You'll carry that darkness around in you forever."

"I already carry the darkness around in me, Ryker. You put it there every single time you fill me with your come. You've branded my insides with it. Now I'm asking you to brand my soul with it. I need to watch her die, to know that it's over for real."

I held her stare for a moment, trying to recognize any hesitation or uncertainty, but there wasn't any. Fear, yes. Confusion, yes. But no doubt.

"Go change your dress. And clean your face. Wear something sexy."

"Yes, sir." She purred and jumped from my lap and ran from my office to do my bidding.

I put my cock away and scrubbed a hand over my face as I fought to lower my libido and strengthen my resolve and smarts.

A couple minutes later, she came back to my office, wearing a sexy gold tank top that was cropped right below her tits and a tight black skirt. She didn't have a bra on, and her tits were begging to be sucked on where her hard nipples and rings pressed against the tight fabric.

"God, you look sinful." I said, walking towards her.

"You told me sexy."

"And you delivered." I growled, leaning down to lift her top, and I sucked one of her nipples into my mouth, eliciting a loud moan from her lips. "You'll be rewarded for that too."

"Hmm. I don't know if I like misbehaving and being punished or behaving and being rewarded more."

I pinched her nipple and slapped her ass.

"Misbehaving." She gasped. "Definitely misbehaving."

"Good, because I like punishing you."

I'd learned after my mistake at dinner the other night that she loved being controlled and punished, but she needed words of affirmation and praise at the same time. And I'd been doing more of that lately and she flourished like a blooming flower under my care.

"Let's go." I said, pulling her top down and grabbing her hand. Exiting my house through the back door, I smirked as Elora's brow knitted in confusion about our destination. I walked across the garden path towards the large shop at the back of my property as it started to click to her.

"She's been here the whole time?" She gasped, tightening her hand in mine.

"Yes. I wanted her close so I could monitor her treatments."

"What kind of treatments?" She asked as we got to the large double doors.

I turned and looked down on her, "Waterboarding, electrocution, sleep deprivation, on top of physical beating and starving."

"Hmm." She mused, looking away from me and towards the door with longing in her eyes. She was so much like me, deep down.

"Anytime you want, just say the word and we leave."

"Got it." She said, and I opened the door and walked in.

Four heavily armed men guarded Paula Granger, stationed outside the interior shop door. Zeke and I controlled her torture, and we kept a constant rotation of guards on her, helping to make her miserable.

When we walked into the bright shop, Elora's hand tightened in mine again as we walked towards the chair that Paula was shackled to. Her head flopped forward against her chest, and she looked like death. Smelled like it too. I dropped Elora's hand and grabbed the bucket of water lying next to the tools table and poured it onto my future mother-in-law.

She coughed and sputtered as she fought against the shackles around her wrists and ankles. She shook her head to clear her vision and then locked her bloodshot and swollen eyes on me and sneered. Only then did her gaze flick past me to where my Queen stood with her head held high and an unamused look on her face.

"Ellie?" Paula gasped and started crying, "Baby! Oh, my god. You're alive!"

"No, thanks to you." Ellie snapped back, effectively shutting Paula up. Her fake crying dried up instantly and her face took on a menacing edge that made my hands ache to wrap around her throat.

"Did you expect her to beg me for your release?" I asked Paula as I walked over to the table at the edge of the room that held various tools of torture. Paula's eyes followed me with jumpy edginess and then snapped back to Ellie.

"Please Ellie, I know I did you wrong. I know I wasn't a good mom to you; I was just a kid when I got pregnant!" She pleaded as I grabbed a heavy mallet and turned towards her. "If you want me dead, just do it, Ellie. Please, just end it!" She sobbed, "Please don't let them hurt me anymore!"

"Who said I wasn't here to hurt you myself?" Ellie asked, stepping forward and holding her hand out for the mallet I'd picked up. I eyed her for a moment and then placed it in her waiting palm. The door to the shop opened and Zeke walked in, if he was surprised to see Ellie inside, he didn't show it. He walked over to the computer room and opened the door, kicking out the guard that had been sitting in there monitoring the security cameras around the property and then stood guard himself at the doorway. "What were you going to do with this?" Elora asked me as her mom continued to beg and plead.

"Fingers, toes, ribs, collarbones. Those are all good places for low amounts of pressure to create the most pain."

"Got it." She said, turning towards her mother and stepping forward.

Paula changed the tactic, letting her eyes travel down her daughter's adult body and sneered. "He turned you into his whore, didn't he?" She snapped.

"He turned me into his Queen. I thank him generously for it with my body."

"What would your daddy say if he knew you were spreading your legs for his best friend?" Paula bit out and the mallet swung so fast, I didn't even see it coming myself, and neither did she. It landed with a crunch against her fist on the arm of the chair. She screamed and thrashed in the chair.

Ellie dropped down to look into her mom's eyes and calmly said. "You do not speak of my father."

Paula gasped as she looked in her daughter's eyes closely, "What has he done to you?"

"He saved me."

"He ruined you! He turned you into a monster!"

Ellie swung the mallet again and broke Paula's collarbone. "You turned me into a monster. He just gave me the power to embrace it."

"You're not worthy of the title of Queen!" Paula sneered when she stopped screaming. "You're a worthless whore who will never keep him. He'll get bored of you when the fantasy plays out, and he'll cast you out on the streets, and then you'll spread your legs to survive, just like I did!"

"Wrong!" Ellie yelled back. "You spread your legs because you're a drug addicted loser who couldn't even survive on the thousands of dollars Ryker and Dad gave you weekly over the years. You pissed it away on drugs and booze and pimps who used you like the fucking idiot you are. We are nothing alike."

"Maybe you're right, because I at least knew when I was being used. You obviously can't see you're just a couple of wet holes for him to stick his dick into. He'll probably knock you up like your daddy did to me because we both know these alpha men can't stand to wear a condom. Only when he puts a spawn inside of you, he'll start running around on you and destroying you one little bit at a time until you're nothing, but a drug addicted loser like me."

I swung my fist and punched Paula in the face, knocking her out, and grabbed the mallet from Ellie's hands. I'd heard enough.

I knew Ellie would play every word over in her head for days as it was, and I refused to allow Paula to give her anything else to analyze. Pulling Ellie's icy hand back into mine, I dragged her toward the control room, addressing Zeke on the way.

"End it. But make it hurt."

He nodded his head and winked at Ellie before shedding his suit jacket and calling in a couple of guards to assist him.

I shut the door behind us and turned off the lights. Leaving the room in darkness, the guards and Paula out in the room couldn't see in through the tinted glass, but we could see out.

"What are we doing?" She asked as her chest heaved and her eyes flitted back and forth from me to her mother.

"We're watching Zeke end her life."

She held my stare and then turned towards the room and rested her hands on the long control panel to watch. I stepped behind her and grabbed her hips, pulling her back against me and grinding my cock into her ass.

She gasped and looked at me over her shoulder. "Hurting her got you hard?"

"No." I said, sliding my hand up the front of her skirt to her wet pussy. "But it got you wet." I pulled her panties aside and pushed two fingers into her. "Watching you wield your power, that is what got me hard."

She moaned and stood up, giving me better access to her pussy, and I lifted her leg, setting her foot on the desktop and opening her to me completely.

"Watch them while I finger you." I whispered into her ear.

Zeke hooked the chair up to the electricity and poured another bucket of water over her head before flipping the switch on the wall.

The hum of electricity carried through the room, and it made Ellie's body start to sing with it. Paula started screaming and thrashing around in the chair as enough electricity to hurt her but not kill her tortured her body.

"Yes, Ryker." Ellie moaned and lifted her shirt to bare her tight full breasts as she started playing with them while I finger-fucked her. "Just like that. I'm going to come so hard."

"Come on my hand and then I'm going to fuck you while they kill her for everything, she's ever done to you."

She shot off like a rocket, screaming and begging for more, as I pinched her nipples and clit in sync.

When she sagged against the control panel, I freed my cock and pulled her skirt up. I pulled her panties to the side and impaled her dripping pussy so hard she fell forward and put both hands on the glass window to support herself.

I hit the button on the two-way radio to the room and commanded my men. "Turn it higher."

Zeke adjusted the electricity to a higher level and my cock got even harder knowing Paula was suffering for every single thing she put the love of my life through over the years. The animal in me roared as I felt vengeance being obtained for the wrongs.

"Your pussy feels so good on my cock."

"You feel so good inside of me." Ellie mewed back, rolling her hips and thrusting back onto me as she took what she needed.

I wrapped my hand around her neck and pulled her up until her back pressed against my chest. She arched her spine hard, pressing her ass against me to maintain leverage and avoid choking.

"Please Ryker. I need to come again, and I want you to come at the same time. I need to milk your cock and take it all."

I pressed the button again, "End it."

I lifted Ellie's knee onto the counter, opening her up for me, and slammed into her so hard she screamed as she held on. Zeke turned the electricity off on the chair and took his pistol out of his pocket, casting a glance towards us before turning back and firing one shot into Paula's head, ending everything.

"Yes!" Ellie screamed again as she started coming. Her orgasm rolled from her toes up to her head and she gasped and shook with it, tightening even more around my cock and igniting my own orgasm. I pushed her flat against the desktop and fucked her so hard that her head lolled back and forth with each punishing thrust until my balls emptied themselves painfully.

Pulling out, I threw myself into the desk chair behind me and covered my eyes with my arm as I caught my breath.

"Is it really done?" She whispered, and I moved my arm to see her standing in the same spot but looking through the glass where her mother sat with her head lolled to the side with a dead look in her eyes.

"It's done." I confirmed. She turned and looked at me, letting her eyes drop to my semi erect cock and licked her lips. "Don't look at me like that, Doll."

"I can't help it." She said with a small smile on her lips and then turned to look back out the glass. "I feel bad that I don't feel bad."

"She never felt bad for torturing you, don't let yourself feel bad for anything she got in return for it."

She crawled onto my lap and laid her head on my shoulder and just sat there for a long time, absorbing it. "Thank you." she finally whispered.

"For what?" I asked, I knew it, but I wanted to hear it. I was a selfish man.

"For getting me the revenge I didn't know I wanted."

"Anything for you, Doll."

I didn't want her around the dead body of her mother any longer, so I forced us both to get dressed and walk back to the house. She leaned against my side, under my arm, the entire way.

When we stepped back inside, she paused a moment and looked up at me with a cheeky grin on her face. "Does this mean I still can't go to Lux tonight?"

I groaned and walked away from her.

"Hey!" She yelled.

I turned and smiled at her as she started getting mad at me. "I will take you myself."

"Really?" She asked, eyeing me speculatively.

"Yes really. And you aren't leaving my side the entire night. Take it or leave it." I said, turning away and walking back towards my office.

"Take it!" She yelled back as I walked around the corner. "And I plan on taking you while we're there too!"

Minx.

CHAPTER 21 – ELORA

A few weeks passed since Ryker came back into my life. I'd been living with him, spending every single night wrapped up in his arms with him buried deep inside of my body as he brought me to ecstasy and back over and over again. But other than that, I'd hardly seen him.

He was working hard to secure my safety, but he kept me on the sidelines, locked away in his castle where I was *safe*.

He had been working with the cartel to offload the weapons they'd seized from Monica's crew while not giving away any information to link them to it.

The night I had gotten the first call from the mysterious man, or the riddle master as Ryker called him, Ryker had killed four men from an opposing crew in the middle of the street in a crowded market district to send a message that he wasn't going to let anyone get the better of him. And from what I'd heard from the chatter of his men around the house, it had worked.

Rivals that were pushing in on any of his territory, backed off. And allies had come calling; asking to do more business or offering their support in upcoming wars. He was the most wanted, and the most feared man, which was apparently how he liked it.

Carly had come over a couple of times and hung out by the pool with me, sipping margaritas and enjoying the eye candy patrolling the perimeter. And today, was one of her visiting days.

We laid out on the loungers and enjoyed the hot sunshine. Carly lay next to me completely topless, wearing only a tiny thong bikini bottom, and I shook my head at her comfort while being naked.

Ryker wasn't home, so I wasn't worried about him seeing her tits, and I didn't care if anyone else did if she didn't.

The patio door opened, and I cracked my eye open to see Jed walk out with two fresh margaritas in his hands. "My Margaret, how you've changed in the last half hour." I mused at him, and he shot me a wink and a one-sided grin.

"Margaret is busy, so I figured I'd keep you two ladies refreshed."

"Hmm, convenient." I challenged.

Carly nudged me and eagerly took a glass from Jed's hand before he handed me one.

"Thank you, Jed, it's so hot out today, these drinks are yummy." She purred at him, and I thought for a second I saw a flush on his neck. She just sat there topless, without a worry in the world. God, I wish I had her confidence. My own black bikini wasn't modest, but it wasn't anything special either. I made a mental note to go get some new sexy bikinis and lingerie sometime when people weren't trying to kill me.

"Why don't you join us, Jed?" I asked, looking from Carly to him and back.

"Yes, please. Why don't you!" She added and moved her feet, so he had somewhere to sit, even though there were no less than twenty other seats around the pool.

"If you insist." He joked and sat at the end of her lounger.

"So tell me Jed, how does a man like you end up as my bestie's personal bodyguard? And where do I get one like you?" Carly asked, leaning in to stage whisper the second part.

He laughed, showing off perfect white teeth as he rubbed his hands back and forth between his knees. He was wearing black dress pants and a black t shirt that hugged every single muscle in his chest and back. Both arms had intricate colorful tattoos and I found myself trying to study them as they chatted back and forth.

"Are you okay, Ma'am?" He asked after a moment, and I let my eyes leave his forearm and land on his gaze locked on me.

"I'm fine." I answered and laid my head back on my lounger, sipping my margarita, chastising myself for letting the alcohol cloud my mind.

My phone rang and I looked at the screen and then sat up all the way, pushing my sunglass onto my head.

"What is it?" Carly asked, seeing my change in demeanor.

"It's him." I said, looking up at Jed.

He nodded and pulled his phone out, "Answer it, and put it on speaker."

I took a deep breath and put the phone on speaker as Jed held his own phone up to the speaker, recording the call.

"Hello?"

"Long time no speak, my Queen."

"I was hoping by your silence, that it meant I was in the clear."

He chuckled almost sadly into the phone, "No, I'm sorry dear. That isn't the case. I've just been busy keeping my ears to the ground."

"And I'm guessing you've heard something." Dread filled my heart, and I sourly finished my entire drink. I wanted that cloudiness back after all.

"I hear all sorts of things. Like how your King is no closer to infiltrating the Wellington house than he was weeks ago."

"He's been working tirelessly at it."

"Has he? Or has he been occupying his time doing something else?" he asked, with a slight bite to his tone.

"What do you mean?"

"The Wellington's have secured the funds for the assassination. They bought the hit this morning."

Carly gasped next to me and covered her mouth quickly. Jed placed his palm flat on her calf.

"So that's it then." I said, hating how defeated my voice sounded. I was a dead woman.

"My dear, your father would be ashamed of how soft your backbone has gotten."

"Don't speak of my father's disappointment in me. Apparently, I'll see him soon enough and I'll deal with that then." I was angry, defeated, and sad and I was lashing out.

The man tsked at me. "Perhaps it's time we switched tactics."

"I wasn't aware that you and I had tactics."

"Then perhaps it's time we started, Elora."

"What do you propose?"

"I think it's time you reenter society, if you will. As the Queen of your people."

"But you just said the assassination order has been called. Wouldn't that be suicide?"

"Perhaps. But chatter says that Shadeport's Allies are all lining up for the chance to earn it's King's favor. Perhaps now would be the appropriate time to call upon them. And you haven't been seen in public besides at Ryker's clubs, and one unsavory dinner at the Ritz."

Ignoring the awful failure that dinner had been, I pushed for more information. "How do we do that without tipping our hand to the Wellington's and letting them know we know of their deception?"

"The hit isn't easily traced to them. Tip your hand that you know of the hit, but not of its origin. Ask the allies to help you decimate the shot caller of it and send them out into the world with the task of discovering who it is. Also ask the Wellington's for their help, as they are your ally as well. That will make them worry about being discovered and will either force them to call it off, or to act on it quickly. Either way, this business shall be over sooner rather than later."

"With me in peril one way or another."

"Have I let you down yet?"

I didn't answer him as I looked to Jed for direction. His lips were pressed in a thin line and his eyes were blazing. I'm sure he wanted to yell at this man, but he was controlling himself to keep from losing this lead.

"I suppose not."

"And I won't either. Go out on the town, my Queen. Take your throne, and wear your crown high, for I have no doubt your loyal subjects will rally behind you and their King."

"You say my Queen and their King, does that mean Ryker is not your King as well?" I asked, trying to decipher his riddles.

He chuckled and sighed, "There she is. There's Gavin's daughter with her smarts and whit." He didn't answer me directly, but that was answer enough. "Until next time, my Queen."

And with that he hung up.

I collapsed back onto my lounger as Jed saved the audio.

"I'm sending this to Mr. Lawson." He said and pushed a few buttons on his phone before pocketing it. "You okay?"

I shook my head, and Carly took my hand in hers, offering silent support. "What do you think I should do?" I asked Jed.

He shrugged his shoulders and took a deep breath. "Whatever Mr. Lawson tells you to do. He'll know best."

"Ugh." I groaned and threw my hand over my eyes. "That's the worst answer you could have given me, Jed!"

He scoffed and then looked me straight in the eye. I sat up and faced him head on. "I think you should do what the riddle master said to do. I think there's merit to what he said."

"What about the part of him doubting Ryker's efforts to uncover the information we need? He asked if he was occupying his time with something else. What do you think he meant by that?"

"I don't know, maybe nothing?"

"No." I answered quickly, shaking my head. "That man has never uttered a single word to me that he didn't plan ahead of time to say. It's all part of the riddle."

"Then I guess you need to ask Mr. Lawson what that means."

"I suppose I will."

Ryker called Jed and they conversed about the call amongst themselves. Ryker had originally asked to talk to me, but I was too rattled, and I told Jed to tell him I had a migraine. He frowned at me but followed along, and I made a mental note to keep that in mind because I owed him one for lying to his boss.

Carly had to leave soon after the call to get ready for work, and I was left alone with my thoughts and doubts.

I was sitting in the sitting area of Ryker's bedroom, or our bedroom I guess, when there was a knock on the door. "Come in."

Jed poked his head in and stood in the doorway. "Mr. Lawson called, you two are attending an event tonight. We will leave here at seven and meet him and Zeke at the venue."

"So, I guess that's the direction we are going." I said, taking a deep breath and turned to look back out the window. "It was nice knowing you, Jed."

He stood there for a moment longer, "None of us will let anything happen to you, Ma'am."

I nodded and looked over my shoulder at him. "I appreciate your dedication, Jed. More than you know." He didn't reply, there wasn't anything for him to say. Nothing he could say would change anything. I was just spiraling and he was just standing around, ordered to watch.

Noting the time on the clock, it was already half past five already. "I suppose I shall don my crown."

I worked carefully, showering, shaving, exfoliating, moisturizing, drying, styling, and war painting my body.

Looking in the mirror I admired my long dark hair, its beachy waves catching the light, a diamond clip securing it behind one ear. I wore dark black eyeliner and thick false lashes, with shimmering gold eye shadow paired and a glossed nude lip.

When I stepped out of the bathroom and heard a light knock on the bedroom door again. I tightened the sash at my waist, holding my silk robe closed and answered it.

"Sorry to interrupt you," Jed said, "But Mr. Lawson just had this delivered for you."

He held up a garment bag and passed it to me with a sweet smile, and then handed me a smaller wrapped box in gold paper.

"Thank you, Jed." I took the bag and box and looked at him. "I'll be down shortly."

"Would you like a glass of wine before we leave?"

I smiled at him and leaned into the door a bit, "Sometimes Jed, I worry you know me better than Ryker does." He smiled broadly but I heard the sadness in my voice, even if we both tried to pretend we didn't. "That would be fantastic, a white please."

"Got it. I'll have it ready for you when you're dressed."

"Thank you."

I walked back into the bedroom and opened the bag and pulled the dress out.

"Oh my goodness." I gasped as I held the beautiful floor length gown out in front of me. "Oh Ryker."

I slid the dress on and walked into the closet to look in the floor length tri-angled mirror and melted on the inside a bit.

It was gold and it looked like a million diamonds adorned the long fabric as it cascaded to the floor around a thigh high slit. The neckline was a deep V with thin straps and the back was completely open down to the very top of my tail bone. I paired a strappy pair of gold high heels that matched perfectly and lifted me six inches. Gorgeous and elegant didn't even begin to describe it and I felt both of those things and more when I wore it.

Next, I opened the box and gasped when I looked at the gold and diamond hoops nestled in the cushion and shook my head, "God, I love this man." I whispered to myself.

I put the earrings in and felt complete and regal.

Going downstairs and into the kitchen where Jed, Dante, Razz, and a few others stood around shooting the shit, my step faltered subtlety when I noticed my three long lost friends standing amongst the other men. Jay, Frankie, and Mason were wearing dress slacks and black suit jackets to match the other men and it surprised me because I wasn't told that they had been moved up from errand runners to personal guards.

They all turned when my clicky heels announced me and they looked at me as awe and shock lined their faces.

I kept my spine straight and my head high as I walked in and passed Mason where he stood by the counter with his jaw lax. As I passed him, I gently placed my fingers under his chin and lifted to close his mouth, and he snorted at me and turned as I stepped around him.

"Dang El."

"Good Evening."

Jed stepped forward, eyeing Mason and handed me a glass of crisp white wine. "Thank you, Jed."

"My pleasure Ma'am. We're leaving in ten minutes."

"Sounds good."

Mason leaned forward on the counter as I sat down on a stool and crossed my legs. My dress's slit opened and bared both of my legs from my upper thigh to feet and his eyes dropped to the exposed tan skin thanks to the obscene amount of time I spent at the pool lately.

"Eyes back in your head boy, or I'll remove them for you." Razz bit out in his direction and I looked over at him as he nodded to me and I smiled at him, nudging Mason who just shook his head and whistled.

"How have you been Ellie?"

"Living the dream." I said sarcastically. "Are you three guards now?"

He looked over his shoulder where both Jay and Frankie stood watching from the window seat, they stood up and walked over as I motioned for them to help themselves to wine as they stood around the counter.

"Yeah, we got promoted after the shipping yard job."

"You were there?"

"Yeah, we rode with Zeke's crew."

"Hmm." I said, noticing the way Jed and Razz stood near, with their arms crossed over their chests and unreadable looks on their faces. "I hadn't heard that."

"Are you surprised?" Jay asked, letting his gaze travel down my face to my lips where they stayed for a moment.

"No. Nothing surprises me anymore."

"So, someone wants you dead huh?" Frankie asked with a bit of mirth in his tone, and I raised my eyebrow at him, trying to read him.

"It would seem so."

"And we're here to keep that from happening." Mason said, sending a pointed look to Frankie and then to Jay.

Frankie's attitude was still rubbing me wrong, given that I did nothing intentionally to him, but it shouldn't surprise me because he was always a bit standoffish with me. I turned on my stool to face Jed, smirking at him.

"Did Carly give you her number before she left earlier? She asked for yours, but I told her I didn't have it."

He eyed me for a moment and then Frankie must have made some sort of face or mannerism because something lit in his eyes, and he nodded to me. "She gave me her number; we're making plans for some time soon."

"Good, she could use a strong powerful man like you in her life."

Jed kept playing along and I secretly loved him for it. "She said something very similar to me too out by the pool while she was sunbathing."

"Hmm." I mused. Razz laughed out loud and shook his head and then looked at his watch.

"It's go time, Ms. Dax."

I nodded to him, drinking down the last of my wine and taking Mason's arm that he held out for me, letting him walk me to the front door.

"You always were my favorite, you know." I whispered to him, leaning close.

"I'm pretty hard not to love." He whispered back.

I tilted my head back and shook it, laughing.

"I'll take it from here." Jed said at the bottom of the stairs on the driveway.

I let go of Mason's arm and Jed took my hand, helping me in the back of the black Audi SUV Ryker had bought for me and then he climbed in beside me. Razz and Dante took the front seat and then our convoy of three cars was in motion.

A while down the road, I turned to Jed. "I don't trust Frankie and Jay."

He raised his eyebrows at me, and I watched a look pass between him and Razz in the rearview mirror. "I thought they were your friends." He said.

"They were friends with Carly. Frankie and her hook up, and Jay and I messed around a few times. Frankie took it personal when Ryker got territorial with me in the start, and Jay tried to get me to check out on Ry and go live with him. And I'm not getting warm and fuzzy vibes from them."

"You picked up on those vibes too, huh?" He asked. "What about Mason?"

I shrugged my shoulders, "Mason was only ever strictly a friend, and I don't think there's a true evil bone in his body, he's always so happy and go with the flow, probably from all the pot he smokes. But I don't know. I could be wrong." I looked away from his deep eyes and stared back out my window.

Jed interrupted my thoughts, "Trust your gut, ma'am. I've seen it ring true too many times already to let you doubt it." I looked back at him. "I'll make sure they aren't on your personal detail and that we watch them closely for the time being. They're good soldiers, but they're definitely sporting a slapped pee-pee right now if you catch my drift."

I snorted at him and shook my head. "Oh, the mental images."

He laughed and I listened as he spoke through the radio in his ear about our location as we neared downtown. The swanky part of Shadeport never ceased to amaze me.

Millionaires walked around like it was Beverly Hills except every single millionaire here was in the pocket of someone dark.

When we pulled up outside of the venue, camera flashes lit off and I looked out the window in horror. "A red carpet? I can't walk down that Jed, I'll be a sitting duck."

Just then the door opened up and I turned back towards it and found Ryker standing in the doorway looking down at me appraising my body as he blocked the flashes with his back.

"Ryker." I whispered in awe. He wore an all-black tux and looked divine. His lapels were glossy but the rest of his tux, shirt, vest, and tie were matte, and he looked like a million bucks. His dark hair was freshly faded on the sides and styled on top, and he had a bit more than a five o'clock shadow on his jaw. My lips itched to feel it on them.

"My Queen." He said with a soft smile on his lips as he held out his hand for me. Jed and the others got out of the car and lined the red carpet behind him.

"I don't think I can do this, Ry."

"I'll never leave your side, Doll. I'm right here."

I looked at his warm eyes and took a deep breath before forcing myself to slide my hand over his and let his warmth and strength pull me from the car. I readied myself when my feet were firmly on the ground, and he let his eyes travel down my entire body and I felt it like a caress.

"You look divine, I love you Elora." Ryker said before stepping aside to face the cameras. I looked up at him and couldn't help the giant smile that pulled my lips back.

"I love you, Ryker." His chiseled face turned back to me as he leaned down, kissing my lips hungrily. I was aware of the flashes of cameras as we kissed but tried to ignore them.

"Let's go." He slid his hand down to settle on the very top of my ass, letting his fingers play with the bare skin above the top of my dress as we walked down the red carpet. Paparazzi stood behind a velvet rope and screamed things at us.

"Mr. Lawson! Mr. Lawson!" They screamed, fanatically trying to get his attention. He nodded to a few of them and then pulled me along with him to pose against the backdrop for the event we were at. I hadn't even bothered to ask where we were coming tonight but when I saw the logo for the homeless charity that my dad always donated to, my pride in Ryker swelled.

Ryker caught my eye on the logo and smiled down at me. "I donate millions to them every year in your father's name."

My heart melted and, I leaned into his chest as he pulled me around his front. "You're incredible."

"The Dax's have made me into the man I am today."

I shook my head and tried to focus as he turned back to the cameras. I schooled my face as I looked back at the blinding flashes, standing in Ryker's embrace and gave a slight smile as I looked from one section to another.

"Who's your date tonight?" A cameraman yelled.

Another one screamed back. "Elora Dax! Smile for the camera!" Multiple gasps sounded out from the row of cameras as well as from other guests and staff walking the carpet. Soon, every single eye in the area was on me.

I looked away but, another man caught my attention when he yelled out louder, "What would daddy say if he knew you were sleeping with his best friend?"

Taking a breath in, I tried to keep the pain from my face at his dig. I caught a glance from Ryker, and he leaned down to kiss my forehead, pulling me along the carpet towards the entrance to the venue. Right before we walked inside the venue, I briefly saw Jed standing behind the man that heckled me, with nothing short of pure menace in his eyes as he put his hands on the man's shoulders and pulled him backwards away from the rope.

And then they were gone. I tried turning around to see better but Ryker's grip on my back tightened and he leaned down towards my ear, "Eyes forward, don't draw attention to it."

"But—" I started but bit my tongue as we stepped into the elaborate venue with Zeke following closely behind. The room was decorated to the nines, and men and women attending were all in elegant black-tie attire weaving in and out between tables, mingling.

"I need a drink; would you like one?" Ryker asked, leading me towards the bar.

"Yes, please." I answered. I rolled my shoulders and took a deep breath as Ry slid my body between his and the bar, caging me in with his arms on each side of me. He dropped his nose to my neck and took a deep breath.

"You smell heavenly, darling. And you look breathtaking." He kissed up and down the curve of my neck, sending shivers over my skin and making my eyes drop closed.

The bartender saw us standing there and came over, ignoring her other customers, "What can I get for you, Mr. Lawson?" she asked, with a deep purr in her voice. I opened my eyes and looked over my shoulder at her, but she ignored my presence altogether.

Typical.

I looked up at Ry as he blatantly ignored her other than to say, "Blue label scotch, and your best Cab."

"Yes, Sir." She answered, scurrying away to do his bidding.

A man walked up to Ryker's side and interrupted our silent moment, drawing his attention away. Ryker's jaw clenched, but he placed a relaxed look on his face as he acknowledged him with a curt nod in greeting to him and his wife. The wife was probably in her fifties, and she hung on her husband's arm, but her eyes were fucking Ryker in open admiration the whole time they chatted, even after he introduced me as his girlfriend.

We'd been here five minutes and the first two women to come within ten feet of my boyfriend couldn't focus on anything else but his looks and power.

And logically I understood it, but it still brought out the catty bitch in me.

We luckily had arrived right before the event started and soon Ryker was pulling me towards our table near the front of the venue.

"Ah Lawson, how do you do this evening?" A man asked, clapping Ryker on the back as we found our seats.

"Dom, I'm well, you?" Ryker answered, pulling my chair out for me and helping me arrange my skirt before sitting down next to me.

"Well, very well. I've been trying to get connected with you the last few days, seems you've been quite busy." The man said, eyeing me up.

"Busiest I've ever been. Allow me to introduce you to my Queen, Elora Dax." Ryker said, sliding his hand over my shoulders to rest on the back of my neck.

All of the eyes at our table turned to look at me in wonder. They all seemed to size me up, giving me cautious smiles, but I just politely nodded to them all and turned my attention to the stage as the emcee took his place and started the evening.

The woman sitting next to me was young, probably late twenties and actually seemed unphased by Ryker's power emanating off of him unlike everyone else was.

"If I fall asleep, nudge me before my nose hits my pudding, would you?" She asked, leaning over, and nudging my shoulder with a small smile pulling her bright red lips.

I smiled and nodded, "I will, if you will."

"Deal." She said, laughing quietly. "I'm Aimee Scott." She held her hand out and I shook it.

"Elora Dax." I replied.

"Oh, I've heard your name more times in the last few weeks than any other name ever. Even more than Ryker's, and that's unheard of considering we're in *his* city."

I raised my eyebrows at her and looked back at the emcee, pretending to pay attention.

"My husband does quite a lot of business with Ryker, Tate Scott." She said, nodding her head to her other side where a good-looking middle-aged man sat, resting his large hand on her dainty knee under the table.

Ryker's fingers were drawing lazy lines over my neck as he looked at the stage, but I didn't for one moment think he wasn't listening to every single thing said between us.

I noticed Zeke standing along the edge of the room about twenty yards away, looking out over all of the tables, watching out for us.

"Do you often come to these?" I asked, trying to make some polite conversation.

"Not if I can help it." She chuckled. "How about you?"

"Hmm." I hummed, "First time actually."

Her eyes widened as she looked between me and Ryker. "Well, you wouldn't know it to look at you. You look like you belong here."

"Well, thank you." The events rolled on and dinner courses were served as we conversed lightly with our table guests. More than once, someone would approach Ryker and he'd get up from the table and walk away talking with them in hushed tones.

I watched him move about the room and noticed how he never got far from me, keeping his eyes facing me and the table at all times.

And every time he walked away, Jed or Zeke would step closer. It was fascinating to watch them work in sync with each other without any words being spoken.

Ryker was talking with a man who looked like he more often frequented a jail cell, than a charity event. And I was utterly bored.

"Here." Amy nudged me again and passed me a glass of champagne that matched hers. I watched as the waiter walked away with his empty tray and took the glass.

"Do I look like I need it that bad?" I asked with a small smile, pulling my lips.

"I was afraid if I didn't give you something to focus on, that your eyes would start falling closed."

"It's just been a long day." I replied, letting the cold bubbly tingle on my tongue before swallowing it.

"Can I be frank with you about something for a moment?" She asked, setting her glass down and leaning forward on her elbows and looking at me from under her lashes.

I raised my eyebrows at her and let her continue.

"I run in the same social circle that Monica Wellington does." She said, letting it hang in the air between us.

I tried not to let the name raise my hackles visibly, but it was probably a wasted effort. She laughed awkwardly and smoothed her hands over the tablecloth. "I know. Don't hold it against me too hard, would you?" She joked. She turned her attention to me from the tablecloth and then her face got a serious sort of gleam to it. "Be careful." Her voice was low and intense.

"What do you mean?"

She held my stare for a long moment without saying anything and then took a deep breath. "She's dangerous when she's threatened. And judging by the looks of it," She looked past me to where Ryker stood chatting still. "You've not only stolen the attention of the man she wanted most, but you've stolen the attention of everyone else in the world. And she's bitter as hell over it."

"I've never stolen anything from Monica Wellington." I said with a brisk tone. "She never had any of those things to begin with. I can't steal what wasn't hers."

A sly smile pulled Amy's lips back, and her eyes widened. "I have underestimated you, Elora. And I think most of the world has. And I know for a fact that Monica has."

I grinned back at her knowingly. I was counting on that.

A while later, I was listening to a rather boring story about a business acquisition by a man at our table when warm hands dropped to my shoulders and stubble tickled my neck. "Dance with me, Doll."

I looked over my shoulder as Ryker stood over me and held his hand out. A few couples were dancing, but not many people had stepped foot on the shiny surface, even though the live band was magnificent.

I smiled up at him and slid my hand into his waiting one and let him lead me away from the terribly boring table.

All eyes watched us as we walked across the room and to the center of the dance floor, where Ryker turned and pulled me into his arms gracefully, plastering me flush to his body before dropping his lips to my temple. "I've missed you terribly." He said.

"I've been right here." I tried to keep the snappiness from my tone but failed, so I tried to soften it by turning my head and kissing his neck.

"I know. I apologize. I've just been so consumed with riddles, but I've been neglecting you and that's not fair either."

"I can't really hold it against you, but I did have a moment today where I felt like I was closer to Jed than you."

He groaned and his jaw clenched in time with his hand holding mine. "I hate that."

"The call today–" I started, waiting for him to look down at me. "He sounded doubtful when I said you were working tirelessly to keep me safe. He said he thought you were occupying your time with other things. What did he mean?"

"How am I supposed to know Elora?" He asked, but I could feel the aggravation in his voice.

"What did you do today? What consumed your time?" I asked. I didn't know why I asked, but it just felt like the direction this conversation needed to go.

Ryker looked away from me and rested his chin against my forehead and took a deep breath, and to the prying eyes watching us dance, we looked like the picture of happiness and closeness. But I saw it for what it was, a diversion from my question.

The physical space he put between us was one thing, but now to put the mental space there too, was too much.

"Tell me." I demanded.

He looked down at me, but then looked away and shook his head. "No."

"Why?"

"Because that's now how this works."

"Excuse me?" I asked, my feet stopped moving to the music and I stared up at him. "How what works?"

He growled deep in his chest and wrapped my body tighter in his arms and lifted me from my feet, moving us around the dancefloor again.

"Ryker!" I hissed.

"Not now Elora. We'll talk about it later."

I stepped back from his arms and folded my hands in front of me as I glared at him. "That's not how this works," I threw his words back in his face, "I need to use the restroom."

"Elora—" He started, reaching for me, but I walked away quickly from him and headed to the restroom.

Jed met me a few yards away and walked in step with me as I rounded tables towards the restrooms on the other side of the room, but I stayed silent.

"Are you okay?" He asked quietly.

"Fine." I answered but we both knew I was anything else.

When I got to the hallway that held the female restroom, he stopped as I went on, but I heard his words carry down the corridor after me. "Keep your head high, Elora, or your crown will slip."

My fucking crown was going to slide down around my throat and strangle me.

I was glad to see the restroom was large and mostly empty as I stepped into a stall and rested my forehead against the cool metal door. "Fuck." I hissed.

How did Ryker and his men expect me to go on and act as if I wasn't a sitting duck, the red dot of a rifle burning a hole into my head? I hated feeling so needy and emotional, but I was on edge given that at any moment I could end up dead.

I didn't want to be here, paraded around on his arm as he introduced me so sweetly and doted on me. I wanted to be home, in his arms, alone in peace where I could forget everything else going on and just love him.

But that fucking riddle master had put doubt in my head and now I couldn't get it out.

I took a few more deep breaths and then forced myself to leave the stall and walk to the sink.

I ran cold water on the insides of my wrists for a moment before turning it to warm and started washing my hands.

I heard heels clicking across the marble floor towards me and I slid my armored mask back over my face just in time as a flash of blond hair caught my eye in the mirror, forcing my eyes to rise and look at the woman when she stopped behind me.

There were twenty empty sinks, yet the newcomer stood directly next to me. Red flag.

"Well, hello Elora."

Ice ran through my veins as I stared into the eyes of the woman that had paid millions of dollars for someone to kill my father and me. And the woman who had warmed Ryker's bed before me.

"Melissa right?" I asked, squinting my eyes at her in the mirror before looking down and shaking my hands off and wiping them with towels.

She pursed her lips at me, and her forehead wrinkled, "It's Monica."

"Oh, my apologies." I said, tossing my towels away before turning to walk out of the room.

"You'll never be able to keep him. You know that right?" Her voice cut out through the quiet room, and I stopped and looked back at her.

Sliding my clutch under my arm, I faced her and quickly assessed her body to see if she was a physical threat to me in that moment.

"And you think you could? You've already proven inadequate in that category, Monique."

Her nostrils flared and, she took a step towards me before quickly sliding a sickly-sweet fake smile on her face and physically brushing off my name blunder.

I wanted to rattle her, so I pressed on, "Just like you came up short when you went after my dad all those years ago too, and you were even in your prime then." I let my eyes drop over her body wrapped in white tule and curled my lip up a bit at it.

Her smile slipped as anger covered her features. "You think you're so much better than me, but we're both the same. Both of our fathers-built empires that we were groomed to run someday. We are both princesses. You're no better than me."

"That's where you're wrong." I said coolly, locking her in my intense gaze as I pointed at her quickly before dropping my hands to my side. "You are a princess of a small town, a blip on a map if you will. Your father runs small operations and has never been able to overcome his gambling addiction and therefor has left you with nothing more than a barnyard of misfit animals to run when he finally croaks." I stepped towards her, looking down my nose at her. "My father built a kingdom, and Ryker has turned it into a dynasty since then. And I'm no longer just a princess, who sits by and watches from the sidelines. I'm a motherfucking Queen. I run the shit I was born to. You've tried and failed repeatedly to fuck your way into a throne, while I've earned every fucking step up into mine. We are nothing alike."

My chest heaved as I looked down on her until I could no longer bear to be near her ugly soul, so I turned to walk away.

"I didn't fail to fuck Ryker though. In fact—" she said, letting her words hang between us as I paused with my hand on the door handle. "I fucked him just this afternoon." She said as I glared at her, she rolled her lips together and then licked them like she could taste him. "I can still feel his come deep inside of me. There's even a chance he's done what he wanted all along and left a baby inside of me to carry on his name." Blinding rage burned every nerve in my body. "I love the new artwork he's added to his abs, right above his cock. Mmh." She moaned and rubbed her hands together, "So sexy."

I didn't say anything, because I couldn't force my lips to form words as my heart shattered. Ryker had gotten a new tattoo the other day of a set of King and Queen crowns, right at his belt line. And if she'd seen them, then that meant that she'd seen him naked, just like she said.

She laughed and cocked her hip against the sink as she leveled me with an evil stare. "I won't lie, I'm not a fan of being summoned to his office for him to fuck me, since you have mooched your way into his home. God, I miss his bed. But if he needs me so badly that he has to bend me over his desk, and then have me ride him in his chair, and then fuck me into his couch because he's so overcome with unsatisfied needs, I'll gladly give him every single thing you can't." She laughed at me as I still remained silent.

Still she went on. "Aw. Poor little Elora finally realizes she'll never be enough." She stepped towards me until she was standing a few feet from me. "Not enough to keep dear old dad alive, and not to keep Ryker out of other women's beds. You're so pathetic, a nobody." She spit out, letting her eyes drop over my body. "You matter to no one. Why don't you just go back to being homeless on the streets of South LA?"

She laughed sinisterly at me, but I tightened my grip on my clutch and turned on her quickly, relishing in the way fear filled her eyes as she hastily stepped back away from me. I gave chase until I was chest to chest with her back pressed flat against the wall.

"You'd do well to remember exactly what I've survived if you want to throw it in my face like it makes me weak. Because you're wrong. Everything I've survived has taught me invaluable lessons that will come in handy against you. I haven't lived the posh privileged life you have, Monica, and we both know I have you and your father to thank for that." I lifted my hand until I pointed my finger directly in her face as she tried to shrivel away from me into the wall. Later, I'd probably regret it, but I couldn't help myself from making my move and tipping my hand to her. The bathroom door banged against the wall as Ryker and Jed rushed in, looking for me and freezing when they saw me toe to toe with Monica. "If you want war with the Queen of Shadeport, you've got it. But you should have spent Daddy's money on an army, instead of a hitman."

Her eyes widened and her lips fell open in shock. I backed up and walked away, shooting a glare over my shoulder at her where she shriveled into the cold wall in relief.

I shoved past both men and into the hallway, forcing a deep breath into my lungs for the first time since she cornered me.

Ryker caught up with me and wrapped his hand around my arm and pulled me to a stop, but I ripped my arm away from him and leveled him with a glare that spoke volumes. "I'm leaving."

"Ellie." He tried again as I neared the entrance into the ballroom.

"Fuck you, Ryker!" I seethed. It hurt to even look at him as he stood there silent with his own anger radiating off of him. "She's what you were consumed with today, wasn't she?" I asked, hurt lacing every word, but I didn't wait for his response, I didn't need too, "Well, I hope it was as good as she made it sound." I turned from him again and opened the door to the ballroom. "We're done."

Zeke stood outside and looked past me to Ryker and then turned and followed me as I walked quickly across the space towards the side door. "How do I get the fuck out of here without cameras?"

"This way." He took my arm and led me to the door I'd been aimed at and pushed it open for me. He talked into his radio on the way and by time we got to the end of the sidewalk, Razz pulled up, skidding the car to a stop and Zeke ripped the door open and I jumped in.

Jed followed after me, having caught up and Zeke stood at the door for a moment, looking at me and then back to the venue, torn.

He finally looked at Razz and then at Jed, "Take her home."

"Yes Sir." Jed said, and Zeke slammed the door shut.

Razz tore off through the darkness towards Ryker's castle and every mile we got closer to it, more pain and dread filled me.

"I told her we knew." I whispered and Razz looked at me in the mirror as I held his stare. "Do with that information what you need to, to protect Ryker. But leave me out of it. I'm done. I'm done with all of this. If they want me dead, so be it. I can't live like this, anymore."

Jed spoke with sincerity. "I never saw her go in, she must have come in from the hallway, or I would have come in after you earlier. What happened?"

I laid my head against the headrest and closed my eyes. "She fucked Ryker today in his office."

It hurt so fucking much to even say those words out loud.

"Bullshit. He wouldn't do that." Jed said, angrily.

"Then how did she know he had new ink below his belt?" I asked, staring at him straight in the eye, nearly begging and pleading for him to tell me something that I could use to dispel her claim.

"I don't know. But he didn't fuck her." He said, shaking his head.

"I agree." Razz said, "For what it's worth, Ellie, there's no way he slept with her today."

I shrugged as stupid, traitorous tears burned behind my eyes, leaving me unable to even respond.

In the darkness of a car worth more than I would have made in a year, I cried. Silently, because I learned too young that someone would always use your weaknesses against you, but still I cried.

Only for a few moments, after those, I wiped my face and forced the walls back around my heart and the iron rod back into my spine as we drove through the dark city I once loved.

Suddenly, Razz slammed on the gas, throwing me back into my seat as Jed looked over his shoulder out the back window, and something passed between them silently.

"What is it?" I asked.

"Slide down onto the floor." Jed said, undoing my seatbelt and pulling my hand until I crouched between Razz's seat and my own.

"What is it, Jed?" I demanded again.

"We're being followed." He barked out into his radio that we had a tail. All of a sudden the car lurched forward as the car behind us rammed into us and I screamed before I covered my mouth to silence my fear. Jed slid over on the seat and put one leg on each side of my body, still sitting on the seat, encasing me between his knees and left his hand on my back, pushing me low.

Painful memories rushed through my brain to the last time I was crouching in a car, running for my life. Mental images of my dead father lying in the middle of the rain covered street assaulted me next.

Jed was radioing our location to their men and coordinating things as I barely clung onto my sanity.

Noise filled the cabin of the car that sounded like rocks hitting the windows over and over again. "Are they shooting at us?" I gasped, looking up at Jed.

"The car is bulletproof but keep your head down Ellie." He barked out.

My phone started ringing loudly in my clutch on the floor next to me, but I ignored it and held on as Razz started driving erratically. Seconds later, our car was hit from behind again and we fishtailed before Razz regained control moments before we lost control completely.

My phone started ringing again and I swore as I grabbed it from my clutch.

"It's the Riddle Master!" I screamed as our car lurched again.

I answered it putting it on speaker.

"Turn left onto the highway!" His voice yelled through the phone in place of greeting.

I looked at Jed and he nodded to Razz who swerved the car violently I'm assuming onto the ramp, though I couldn't see anything.

"Get into the carpool lane and hammer it. You've got way more horsepower than they do." He ordered.

Razz did just that.

Jed relayed the information through his radio, "He called her again, he's giving us instructions."

"Are you okay Elora?" The man asked me through my phone.

I nodded my head at first and then forced myself to speak after a moment. "Yes."

"Good. Just stay calm and stay down. I'll get you out of there."

"How?" I demanded. "How do you fucking know everything?" I was close to panic.

My leg ached and I put my hand over the spider web scar on my thigh from the bullet wound I'd gotten the last time I'd been in a car chase, and I forced myself to take a deep breath as I felt an anxiety attack clawing at my heart.

"Pass the truck on the inside." He barked out, ignoring my questions.

Razz swerved again, and I watched out the window as we passed a semi-truck with only inches between us and it.

"Three cars are tailing you."

"Fuck!" Jed growled and relayed the information.

"Your men are close to catching up to them. Just keep it straight, Razz." The man said.

I looked up at Jed questioningly as I tried to figure out how the riddle master knew Razz's name or that he was the driver. Were the men he was talking about Ryker and Zeke? I was so angry at Ry, but a part of my heart hoped it was him. He'd move heaven and hell to save me.

Or at least I would have thought so before tonight.

Our car was hit again, this time on the side and we got sandwiched between them and the guardrail, sparks and chucks of metal tore off the outside of our car as Razz fought to keep from crashing.

I bit down on my lip to keep from screaming, trying again not to distract anyone. More bullets peppered the sides of the car and the window above my head spider-webbed from so many bullets hitting it. Jed looked worried

"We're running out of time." He said on the radio and into my phone.

The Riddle Master kept going, "When I tell you, brake hard and go to lane one and get off on the Jefferson exit. Understood?"

"Got it." Razz barked back.

"Wait for it—" My caller said, pausing. "Wait for it–" I closed my eyes and took a deep breath as Jed put one hand on my shoulder and the other on my back to hold me in place, given that I wasn't wearing a seatbelt. "Now!"

Razz slammed on the brakes, and I flew into the center console and then against the door as he swerved violently and crossed five lanes of traffic and shot off the ramp. Jed looked out the windows as we drove into the dark downtown district, which was where most of Ryker's crew worked and lived and where most of our resources were.

"You've lost them." The man said something similar to relief passed through the speaker and into my ears. "Go to Ardoran Tower, you'll be protected there." He said and sighed again. "Elora, you need to be smarter than you were tonight, I don't know what she said to rattle you, but you leaving early left Ryker's defenses divided, and you were vulnerable. Don't do it again." He barked and hung up.

I wilted on the floor as my adrenaline started fading from my system. Razz kept driving and then drove into a parking garage or something and slammed on the brakes.

The doors were ripped open, and I looked up from my spot on the floor between Jed's feet and saw an infuriated Ryker standing in front of me.

"Come here." He demanded and grabbed my arms, pulling me up and into his arms where he crushed me to his chest. "I just died a million fucking deaths, all over again." He growled into my ear and squeezed me tight.

I held onto him but fought my emotions because of my anger and hurt I'd felt before all of this. I looked around and men stood all around us on every side as we stood in the underground parking garage, watching our interaction in fascination.

Frankie, Jay, and Mason stood amongst them, and I thought perhaps there was concern in Jay's eyes, but I couldn't be sure.

Turning my attention back to Ryker, he slid his hands over my arms and face, checking for injuries. When he got to my sides, I winced and pulled away from his hand. Worry etched his face as he turned me and pulled my dress away from my rib cage, thankfully the open back allowed him the slack in the fabric so he didn't rip it.

"You have a busted rib or two, they may be broken." He bit out as his eyes went nearly manic.

"I hit the center console, but I'm fine."

"Elora, I'm so sorry." Razz said, as he shook his head in defeat.

"Don't you dare!" I snapped at him, surprising me and everyone around me. "You did exactly what you needed to do to get us out of that alive. I'm sorry you were put in that position because of me."

I turned to Jed and put my hand on his arm. "Thank you for protecting me."

He nodded quickly and then looked to Ryker who looked less than pleased at my gentleness with my guard.

Yeah, well screw you.

I shivered as I looked at the car where it sat, torn to pieces. Ryker took his tux jacket off and slid it over my shoulders.

"Let's get you inside, doll." He said and kissed my hair.

Letting him lead me inside; he barked out orders about patrols and protections and pursuits, but I just closed my eyes and walked in a trance as we stepped into an elevator, and I sagged against his side when the doors closed.

"I was so scared." I whispered.

"I should have been there with you. I never should have let you leave without me." His tense body spoke volumes; the tremor in his hands, the set of his jaw, and the barely controlled anger in his eyes all screamed of his contained rage.

The elevator stopped on the top floor, and we walked out into a hallway with a single door. He pressed his finger to a scanner, and it opened, and we walked into a dimly lit penthouse apartment.

"Wow." I said, looking around at the stark metal and glass over-looking the city. "Is this yours?"

"Yes, though I hardly use it anymore."

"Why did you use it before?" I asked, walking forward towards the windows to look down over the city. We were at least fifty floors up and I got woozy from looking down and stepped backwards, tripping on my gown.

Ryker was there though, catching me and holding me tight to his chest. "I used to stay here when I was too tired to go all the way home for the night, or if I had company."

"Women, you mean?" I asked, turning in his arms.

"Yes, on the rare occasion I would bring a woman to my place instead of going to hers, I'd bring them here."

"Gross." I said, turning up my nose and looking around. Suddenly, the stark and modern space had less appeal.

He chuckled slightly and then sobered. "We need to talk about what Monica said to you in the bathroom. And what you said to me in the hallway as you fucking ran away from me again."

Everything she said flooded back into my brain and I stepped back out of his arms and took his jacket off, tossing it on a chair before I sank down into it. "Are we staying here tonight?"

"Yes." He said, eyeing me.

I nodded and then slid my foot from under my gown and leaned over, trying to work the straps of my heels open but struggled from the tenderness in my side.

Ryker walked forward and dropped to his knees at my feet, letting his eyes hold mine as he pulled one foot into his lap and gently slid the strap free and removed my foot from the shoe and set it down next to him. He held my foot in his hand and pressed his thumbs into the arch of it and I groaned in a trance from the ache that had settled in the muscles from wearing the heels for hours.

He leaned forward as I relaxed back in the chair, and he kissed the inner arch of my foot, watching me closely.

He rubbed my foot for a while longer and kissed it again and then set it down and grabbed the other foot, taking my shoe off and giving it the same treatment.

"You told me you were done." He said, I wasn't sure, but it felt like hurt laced his voice.

"No, I said we're done." I corrected him.

"And then you fucking ran away from me. We agreed you wouldn't do that again."

Anger built inside of me, pushing hurt out of the way to use the energy as effectively as possible. "The alternative was stay and make a scene in front of the entire room. I chose to walk away to save your reputation."

"Do you think I give a fuck about my reputation?"

"Don't you?" I screamed at him, "That's what you've been working so hard to solidify hasn't it?"

"What did she say to you?" He asked.

I looked him straight in the eye and lifted my chin defiantly. "That you fucked her ten ways to hell and back in your office today, and that you probably got her pregnant."

"Fucking cunt." He swore, and I watched him closely as his body wound up tight with uninhibited rage boiling under the surface. "She's lying." His eyes were the color of death and pain, and I shivered at the intensity.

"Then how did she see your new ink?" I asked, lifting my eyebrow at him in challenge.

"She came to my office today; I'd just gotten back upstairs from the gym and was shirtless. Zeke was there for the entire conversation Ellie, I swear I never even got within ten feet of her."

"Why the fuck was she there to begin with? Why even humor her with a fucking conversation, Ryker?"

I couldn't help the anger that bubbled up in my own body when I thought about her being near him at all, let alone when he was shirtless and without me.

I believed him when he said he didn't go near her or fuck her, but it still made me angry.

"I didn't. She showed up and I entertained her conversation for no more than five minutes before I told her she needed to go. I wanted to know if she was going to give me any information I could use against her. But she just wanted to talk about the gala tonight."

"So you knew she would be there? That's why you chose that event to take me to? Why didn't you give me a heads-up?" I yelled, placing my foot on his chest, and kicking him backwards so I could stand up and walk away. He landed with his hands behind him and stood up quickly, giving chase.

"Because you were already upset about being paraded around to begin with, I didn't want to add to your stress."

"So instead she was able to catch me off guard in the restroom and spit her lies and I was unprepared for them! That's not any better!"

"I'm sorry!" He snapped, his chest heaving, and his fists clenched. I looked at him for a long time, unable to say anything as I fought for control of my emotions. I wrapped my arms around my waist and held myself as my head ached almost as bad as my heart did.

"The things she said to me Ryker, my god." I said. "My guard was down, and I took her bait, and I told her I knew about the hit man, and that they were responsible for my dad's death. I played right into her fucking hand, and then I left because she got to me, and I put not only myself but Razz and Jed in danger too!"

"They accepted the risk when they signed onto the crew baby, don't you worry about them." He said, putting both hands on my face and holding me still as he leaned his forehead against mine.

"I am worried about them Ry, they're your men, which makes them your responsibility, which makes them my responsibility."

He took a deep breath and kissed me, letting his warm lips coax mine open and pushed his tongue into my mouth to glide against mine. When he pulled back, he breathed me in deeply, "Only incredible leaders worry for the wellbeing of their men, Doll. And you my dear, are an incredible leader."

I shook my head, "I'm not. Not yet. You haven't taught me everything I need to know yet."

He smiled and then kissed me again. "I promise you, I will. But for now, you need rest."

He took his phone from his pocket and held me close as he spoke with Zeke. "Call a meeting with the heads of each family that has offered their support lately. I want to meet with them all in an hour here at Ardoran. We're declaring war on the Wellingtons tonight, but I think we'll be able to do it without killing them all if we play our cards right."

He hung the phone up and slid it into his pocket before dropping his arm under my knees and picked me up, cradling me to his chest as he carried me through the dark apartment.

He walked into the master bedroom and over to the giant bed against the wall of windows. "When was the last time you brought a woman here?" I asked, eyeing the bed suspiciously.

"Three or four months ago." He said and sat me down on my feet next to it.

I groaned and turned my lip up to the bed and rolled my eyes at him when he chuckled at me.

"It's not funny. How would you feel if I took you to my apartment and expected you to lay naked in the bed I got railed in by hundreds of other men?"

His face darkened and his smile faded quickly. He tangled his fingers in my hair and pulled my head back sharply, forcing me to look up at him.

"Don't you dare ever use that combination of words together to describe your body and past ever again, do you understand me? I swear to God I'll lose my fucking shit and kill every single man that's ever even fantasized about you!"

I held his stare for a while before dropping my eyes in submission. I wrapped my arms around his waist, and he loosened the hold on my hair and let me lean into him. "I'm sorry."

He held onto me as his muscles relaxed.

"I want to be there when you meet with the others." I said, pulling back to look up at him.

"You've had a rough night already Ellie. You're weary on your feet as it is."

"Your day has been twice as long as mine has, I just laid topless around the pool all day with Carly."

"Elora Louise!" He snapped, and I quickly covered his mouth with my hand and gave him a don't you dare glare.

"I'm kidding. I was completely covered, though Carly sure wasn't."

He shook his head and sat down on the bed and pulled me forward until he rested his head against my chest and wrapped his arms around me. "You're fucking killing me; you know that don't you?"

"Hmm. Am I in your will yet?" I asked, letting my fingers play with his hair as I tried not to get distracted by his warm breath on my exposed breasts through the neckline of my dress.

"No, and I'll never put you in it if you're going to play roulette with my anger." He dropped his hands to my ass and massaged my cheeks through my dress as he turned his face and kissed my cleavage.

"How much time do we have before this meeting?" I asked, my voice husky with arousal.

He looked up at me and squinted his eyes like he was adding in his brain. "Long enough for you to have four orgasms at least."

"Four?" I asked as I pretended to mull it over in my head. "You are at least two loads of come away from being calm enough to conduct yourself in a respectable manner."

"Oh am I?" He asked with a boyish grin on his face.

"At least. I suppose I should get busy if I'm to take both loads into my body to keep you from ruining my dress with them."

He groaned, and I put his hand to my zipper under my arm and turned. He dutifully slid it down and then pushed both straps off my shoulders, letting the gown slide down my body, leaving me standing in a nude lace thong and diamonds.

"I never got the chance to thank you for my dress and earrings."

"Did you like them?" He asked and he leaned in to kiss each of my nipples where I wore his other diamonds.

"Yes, I love them so much. You have exquisite taste."

"I think of you when I pick things out and it makes it easy."

He kissed down my stomach and pushed my panties down my legs and helped me kick them off.

I helped him slide his tux from his body, loving in the man beneath each layer that I removed until he stood bare and iron hard in front of me.

"I need to taste you, love." He said, turning me and laying me down on the bed.

Ryker blew on my clit, and I groaned, arching my back, and pushed my pussy higher in the air towards his face. He wrapped his hands around my waist and held me down as he buried his face in my wetness and sucked hard on my clit, pushing his tongue into my pussy.

He rubbed his face back and forth over my sensitive skin, letting his whiskers scrape and stimulate every single nerve ending and before long I was begging for mercy as I came loudly on his face.

Drinking me up like I was his favorite taste, then he crawled up my body and pushed his cock deep into me. "Take my cock like a good girl." He said, pulling out and slamming back in. Dragging his lips up my neck and ear he bit down hard on my shoulder as he started pounding into me. He reached above me and gripped the headboard in his fist and used it as leverage to push and pull, and I was mesmerized with his physique and appearance. His arms were ripped with muscles as he held himself over me and his chest and abs clenched and rippled with each thrust of his hips. I ran my nails down his back until they dug into his ass cheeks, and he threw his head back roaring like a crazed animal and exploded inside of me.

His cock twitched and jerked inside of me and the sensation of his hot come coating my insides pushed me over the edge of my own orgasm. Ry slowed his thrusts and slowly fucked his cock from root to tip in and out of me, letting every ridge and every bump stimulate my body.

"Hmm, two of four down." He said as he palmed my breast and flicked my nipple.

"One of two down for you, big guy."

"Good thing I can go again without ever stopping with you. You drive me that insane, my cock is always hard when I'm near you."

"Good thing indeed." I mused.

"Roll over and push that glorious ass into the air for me to lick."

He pulled out of me quickly and I felt his come coating my lips and groaned at how good it felt being claimed by him.

I rolled over onto my stomach, feeling the slight twinge in my side from my bruised ribs and he wrapped his hands around my hips and lifted them into the air, pushing my knees wide. He laid his hand on my spine and pushed down until I arched it and laid as much of my chest flat on the bed as I could, so I was presented to him just how he liked.

He leaned down and blew warm breath on my clenched hole and then licked it with the flat of his tongue as his large hands held my cheeks wide.

He pushed his tongue into my ass and toyed with my clit as I moaned and begged to be fucked.

"Play with your pretty nipples while I tongue fuck your ass Doll. Pinch and pull them, but do it so it fucking hurts, almost too much for you to handle."

I slid my hands under me and did as he commanded. I played with them rougher than I normally would and groaned with the pain mixed with the pleasure of his tongue in my ass and his fingers in my pussy.

"I'm so close." I gasped as I swung my hips from side to side over his face.

He pulled away from me and I shrieked in dismay and was rewarded for it with a quick slap to my upturned ass.

"Ryker!" I screamed and he spanked me again and again all over both of my cheeks.

"Better be quiet, Doll, or my men will hear you begging to be fucked like a naughty slut.I smiled and moaned even louder. "Fuck me, Ryker, that's your pussy, please fuck it."

He groaned and then forced his cock into my pussy in one deep thrust. "Your pussy is so sexy spread open around my cock."

"Yes!" I screamed and I exploded violently, my spine bent to an unimaginable angle, and I pushed backwards with each thrust, fucking Ryker as hard as he fucked me. "Put your thumb in my ass, please." I begged.

"Jesus fuck." He cursed, but did exactly what I begged for. He spat on my ass and pushed his thumb in deep, all the way up to his hand and then thrust it in time with his cock as he went balls deep.

I shot off again and in the mix of my orgasm, he alternated from spanking me loudly to pulling my hair until I was a blubbering mess of begging for more and for mercy at the same time.

"Again. I need to feel that pussy come on my cock again."

"No!" I begged. "It's too much. I need you to come, baby."

He pulled out of me again, leaving my ass and pussy empty and aching and then rolled me onto my back. He grabbed both of my legs and pushed them over his shoulders and then used them for leverage as he impaled me again.

"This pussy is going to come again, and it's going to milk my cock and take every fucking drop of come I have left in my balls. Do you understand?"

"Yes, Sir." I panted.

"Good girl."

He fucked me towards another orgasm but when I got close he put his hand flat on my stomach, right above my pussy and pushed. Intense pressure on my bladder made me gasp and I started clawing at him to get out from under him. "No!"

"Yes." He growled.

"I can't, you're going to make me pee."

He jerked his hips harder and rolled his palm harder into my stomach, "That's not pee baby, I'm going to make you squirt."

"Oh, my god." I groaned as his eyes took on a wild animalistic gleam and he pushed my body past limits I didn't know I had until I was passing them.

"That's it, baby, just like that. Let loose and let go. Let me make you come and let it all out." He ordered, and my body snapped around his.

Hot electric jolts shot down my spine to my toes and my pussy clamped down hard on his cock before intense pressure pushed out of my pussy and hot liquid coated my thighs around his cock.

It. Felt. Incredible.

Stars danced in my vision and my hearing came and went as he cursed every word in the book and bellowed out my name over and over and shot his come deep into my pussy, mixing with my own orgasms and his other one until I was filled and dripping.

He collapsed on top of me, pushing my legs wide and down to lay on the bed around him as he kissed every single inch of skin that he could reach.

"You are incredible, Elora. I can't believe you gave me another first like that."

I snorted in a very un-ladylike way and pushed him off of me so I could take a deep breath. "I didn't give you anything, Ryker. You forced that from my body, just like you said you were going to."

"Well, I suppose you're right."

I laughed loudly and walked to the bathroom with jelly legs and a deeply satisfying ache in my core. At least I'd be calm when facing the leaders of every family and crew he had in his pocket.

CHAPTER 22 – RYKER

I stood in the center of my penthouse living room as men from every corner of society sat around me, waiting to see why I called this urgent meeting. We were the six most powerful men on the West Coast, our reach was vast.

Elora sat in a leather armchair to my side, and she looked like a goddess. She wore her gold gown and diamonds and the only thing missing was an actual crown atop her head.

Men that I'd worked for, then worked with and then surpassed and now commanded looked to me for answers. These men were invited tonight because they had all reached out since my public take down of the Seven's gang in the middle of the street and offered their increased support in future endeavors.

"It has recently come to my attention, that Nicolas and Monica Wellington were the ones to order the hit on Gavin Dax."

Shocked expressions and questioning glances fell around the room as the men murmured.

"They also paid for the death of his daughter, Elora Dax." I said, motioning to the beautiful woman behind me. "They thought they were successful because after Gavin's death, Elora was taken from Shadeport by her mother. Upon her return, I've anointed her to her rightful place as Queen at my side. However, the Wellingtons have ordered another hit on her. Just this evening they've tried and failed to take her from me, once again. And they will pay for it with blood."

Curses and angry faces filled the room.

"I am at war with the Wellingtons as of this moment. I had hoped to avoid wiping their entire crew off the map like I did with the Southside gang that carried out the hit on Gavin, because I didn't want to deal with the empty seat in power that Nicolas will leave when I kill him. But they have solidified their own future by renewing this call for Elora's death."

"What do you need from us?" Thomas McCrae asked, he was one of the founding fathers of the Scottish gang in the Northern part of California. His family was ruthless and nearly as large as mine, and he was a good friend to me and Gavin over the years.

"I want any of my allies that agree, to declare war on the Wellington's with me, in unity. If we publicly sign his death warrant, my hope is that he will surrender, and the transition of power will be smoother."

"So you plan on giving him an easy out?" Diesel Ames asked. He was the president of the Reaper MC, and he was always thirsty for blood. I knew it was a gamble to invite him to the talk, not because he wouldn't support me, but I knew he would want his pound of flesh. Nicolas and he had history and it wasn't pretty.

"Do not insult me. What I have planned for Nicolas and Monica will easily satisfy even your need for bloodshed, I assure you." I said with a sinister smile. "I'm just hoping to avoid taking out his entire line of power as I've worked closely with his men in the past and know that most of them are honorable and trustworthy. They will make good soldiers for me in the future.""Why did they want to wipe out Gavin and his kid, but let you take the throne and pretend to be friendly with you for so long?" He asked.

I turned and looked at Elora, giving her the floor. She straightened her spine and addressed the men. "Monica's thirst for power is to blame. She tried obtaining the power that the Shadeport Kingdom could give her by sleeping with my father years ago, but when he was unwilling to commit to her, they killed him. That left Ryker in power, and he's been more—" She paused, and her top lip curled back with disdain, "amicable to her desires, and entertained her power for hunger while using her for his own gains, unaware of her deceit from years ago. When I returned to Shadeport, Ryker dropped her and committed himself to me, and thus renewed their desire to eliminate the obstacle in their way."

Blood coursed through my body at her elegance. She was so incredibly brave and intelligent. Pride swelled in my heart as I watched the men hang on her every word.

"You have the support of the McCrae family, dear Elora." Thomas said, standing up and walking forward to shake my hand before tipping his head to her in acknowledgment.

The three others that had been mostly quiet through this conversation agreed, standing to shake my hand and acknowledge my Queen. That left only one, and really the only other one I needed.

Diesel.

"I have one condition."

Elora raised her eyebrow at me but stayed silent, leaving me in charge.

"What is it?" I asked, taking a sip of the bourbon I'd been carrying around with me this whole time.

"When it's all said and done, I get Monica."

"Get her?" I asked.

"No one hurts her, but me." There was a sinister gleam in his eye. "And she comes with me."

I wasn't a good man, and I'd done my share of sick and twisted things to prisoners, including women, but Diesel was an entirely different game.

"What is your intent with her?"

He chuckled and stood up, slowly walking towards me and extended his hand. "Take the deal or leave it."

I paused, for the simple fact that if I shook his hand and let him in on the plans, he was no doubt going to take Monica as his slave. He'd torture her, rape her, keep her captive and force her to do god knows what else. And perhaps being with Elora as of late had started to soften me a tad, but I had envisioned giving her a swift death for her part in all of this.

"You have a deal." Elora said, walking up next to me and placing her hand in Diesel's with an unmistakable steel to her voice.

Diesel raised his lips into a gnarled smirk as he looked down at my woman and shook her hand before letting his eyes drop down her body as he dipped his head in a bow. "Pleasure doing business with you, your Majesty." He said and then looked up at me. "You have my full support." He looked down at Elora again as she pulled her hand from his. "Something tells me we'll be doing much more business together with your new ruthless Queen at your side Ryker."

"Hmm." I said in response. Unable to say anything else about it in the moment as anger coursed through my veins. I turned to the other men in the room. "We will formulate a plan and be in contact. I appreciate your support and it will be rewarded in the future."

Zeke led the men out of Ardoran Tower, and I turned my gaze on the woman that both stared in and haunted every single thought and fantasy of mine.

"We'll be staying here tonight. Everyone else can leave." I said to Jed and Razz.

They eyed me suspiciously for a moment, given the heightened threat to Elora. Razz turned and walked towards the front door, but Jed stayed where he was.

"Was I not clear about something?" I asked, snapping at him. Elora had told me earlier she felt close to him, and I'd seen her gentleness with him the last few days and it grated my every last nerve.

He eyed me and then looked at Elora where she stood beside us. "Do not look to her for direction!" I yelled.

"Ryker!" She snapped at me and stepped forward, but I put my hand out, stopping her.

"Don't fucking take one more step towards him." The menace in my voice was unmistakable and I was on fucking edge.

She'd stepped out of line and made a deal with a man she had no business trusting and now she was getting between my men and me again.

"Jed. If you value your fucking life, you'll turn around and leave with Razz while you still have fucking legs to walk out on."

He was a big man, and I have no doubt he'd give me a run for my money in a physical fight, but he didn't have the intense out of control burning power inside of him that I did from being near Elora.

Or perhaps he did.

Razz called out to him. "Let it go kid."

"I'm fine Jed. He's all bark and no bite." Elora said, but her eyes bore into the side of my face from where she stood, no longer moving towards him.

"Yes, Ma'am." Jed finally said and turned to walk out of the apartment, but not before holding my gaze way longer than any other man but Zeke would dare to do.

When the front door closed and locked behind him I turned on Elora and she glared daggers at me. "What the fuck was that about?" She snapped, putting her hands on her hips.

I growled at her but didn't trust myself to be in her presence when I was so unhinged, so I turned away and walked towards the bedroom, putting space between us for her safety.

"Don't you dare walk away from me!" She screamed at me, and I heard her heels run across the room.

I stopped in the bedroom and tore my shirt from my pants and ripped the buttons apart as my hands ached to wrap around something else.

"What is your problem?" She snapped, poking her finger into my chest.

"You!"

"You can't seriously be mad that I agreed to his terms." She deadpanned.

"They weren't your terms to agree too." I pulled the belt from my pants and twisted it in my hands, looking at it longingly before tossing it to the floor. The further it was from me right now, the safer she was.

"You tell me to be your Queen and lead your men, but you draw the line at punishing your girlfriend?"

I shook my head, locking my jaw shut.

"You have feelings for her." She said, a lethal calm laced her voice.

"The fuck I do." I spit back at her.

"Then why do you care?" She swung her arms wildly.

"Because you don't know what that man is capable of!" I screamed back. My ferociousness surprised us both and she wilted a bit. "You have no idea what you've just sentenced her to."

Her chest heaved and her eyes expelled her hurt, letting it flow across the room and into my chest.

Fuck.

"What about what she sentenced me to? She took away the only man to ever love me and cast me out into the world, vulnerable and ripe for the taking. And that's exactly what the world keeps doing. It keeps fucking taking from me, and the one time I try to take something back from it, you suddenly grow a fucking heart?"

I was on her in an instant. She clawed at me as I grabbed her hair and pinned her body between me and the wall, but I grabbed her wrists and trapped them above her body. "Don't you dare insult me like that, Elora. You're the only fucking person in this world that has ever made my heart beat in my chest. I know you loved your father, but he was not the only man to ever love you and you fucking know it."

"Bullshit Ryker! You don't love me. You just want the power of controlling me. I can't believe I ever mistook that for love."

"I already have power and control over you, Doll. You're already mine, you gave yourself to me the same day you opened your body and let me into it. I gave you my heart in return."

"Fuck you!" She hissed. "I hate you, and I hate that I let you touch me after she found us that day in the kitchen. I wish I'd never let you near me ever again."

"Tough shit baby. Because you did, and you can't take it back. I claimed you and your body as my own and I told you what that meant. And you're stuck now, so get over yourself!"

"My dad would have burned this fucking city to the ground to protect me from those who want to hurt me because of him, and instead you protect her!" She thrashed wildly under me. "Let me go!" She screamed when she couldn't get away.

"Never!"

"I don't want you. I can't stand to look at you, let alone have you touch me."

I laughed in her face at her bold-faced lie.

"You don't want me, huh?" I asked, suddenly calm and quiet.

Her eyes rounded and her body sagged into the wall momentarily. "No."

"So, if I pushed your legs apart, your pussy wouldn't be soaking wet for me?" I raised my eyebrow to her in challenge.

She blinked as she bit her lip.

"Why don't we place a wager on it doll? If your pussy is dry, then I'll let you go and let you walk out of my life forever if that's what you actually want. I'll give you money and protection and anything else you ever desire, except me, if that's what you think is best for you."

Her breath hitched like the thought of that was painful. Even saying the words caused my chest to tighten painfully.

"But when I push your legs apart and find your pussy weeping with arousal for me, I'm going to teach you a lesson you won't be quick to forget and it's going to hurt. Understood?"

Her lower lip trembled before she clamped it between her teeth. Her throat tensed and bobbed as she swallowed quickly, and my palm ached to squeeze the column in it.

"Do. We. Have. A. Deal?" I asked in emphasis as she remained quiet instead of screaming at me like she had been doing.

Her cheeks turned pink, and she dropped my gaze, looking over my shoulder and I knew I had her. I chuckled and then leaned down to press my lips against her ear and licked her skin, watching goose bumps rise on the supple flesh of her cleavage as she gasped.

I shifted my weight and pressed my knee between hers and she fought against the intrusion. But I was so much bigger than her though, and it took no power at all on my end to force my way in. I kept her wrists bound above her head and dropped my other hand over her neck and traced a line down the center of her breasts and over her stomach with the backs of my fingers.

She was panting and so was I as I grabbed the fabric of her gown at the slit on her thigh and quickly ripped it away from her body. She gasped and fought against my grip on her arms as I bared her to me from the hip bone down to her toes with her golden gown ripped to shreds around her legs. She wore no panties and I looked down her body to the silky-smooth skin of her pussy and licked my lips.

"Want to place a bet on who wins?" I asked as I put my hand flat on her stomach, enjoying the way her heated flesh branded the palm of my hand.

"Fuck you." She whispered, pulling her lips back to bare her teeth.

I chuckled at her and thrust my hips forward and rubbed my hard on against her side. "No, but I am going to *fuck you*, doll. I just haven't decided in which hole yet."

I kicked her feet apart, making her step wide in her beautiful fuck me heels and held her there so her legs were spread for me. Dropping my hand I pushed my fingers down until they slid through her soaking wet lips and plunged two deep into her tight pussy.

I chuckled and rested my lips on her ear again. "That's my good girl, always making sure my pussy is nice and wet for me to fuck."

"I hate you." She whispered as her eyes fluttered shut. When she opened them again her pupils were dilated, and she licked her lips as she looked at mine.

"I know you think you do right now. And that's why I'm going to give you the hate fuck you didn't know you needed. I'm going to hurt you so good, that you'll beg for more Doll. And when I'm done, you'll never doubt my feelings for you or your position in my world ever again."

"No." She said, biting back a moan as I pulled my fingers out and rubbed her clit roughly. "I don't want you. If you fuck me right now, you'll be raping me."

I laughed again at her and pulled my fingers up to my mouth and sucked them into my mouth, drinking her taste into my soul. "What makes you think I care?"

Her mouth fell open and fear burned in her eyes. But beneath it, burned arousal, and I could taste it on my tongue.

I pulled off of the wall and dragged her with me into the closet by her wrists. She cursed and fought it every step of the way. When I stood between her and the exit of the large room, I let go of her wrists and she used that moment to strike. Her palm cracked against the side of my face, burning a path down my cheek and into my cock as I barred my teeth at her.

"God I'm going to enjoy this." I growled at her.

The closet was full of clothes because I used to stay so often so I reached to the side of me and grabbed four silk ties from the drawer and shoved them into my pocket.

"What are you doing?" She asked, backing up a step.

I took a step forward and she took another back, trying to keep space between us. Her back quickly bumped into the island that sat in the middle of the room like the closet at home and she squeaked before trying to cut to the right and take off.

I quickly grabbed her and turned her, forcing her stomach against the marble countertop, and pinning my body behind her. She kicked at me wildly with her dagger heels, but I barely felt it. All of the blood in my body was in my cock and that was what I was thinking with.

I tore the remaining scraps of her gown off of her body until she stood there in nothing but diamonds and heels. "You look so tasty right now, Doll." I moaned into her hair as I squatted lower and thrust my cock against her ass. With her heels on, she was at the perfect height for me to act on my impulse to penetrate her.

She lunged for the lamp on the countertop and managed to swing it at me, but I deflected it with my arm before ripping it from her hands and throwing it across the room at the wall where it shattered. I pinned her hands together in front of her and expertly tied them, so she was unable to get them out, no matter how hard she struggled.

"Come now darling, it's time for the hate part." I whispered into her ear before pulling her backwards and out the door by her bound wrists. I grabbed the square chest of drawers that sat along the wall and placed it a couple of feet from the end of the bed. It was tall enough to come up to her stomach and fucking perfect.

"What are you doing?" She snapped.

I chuckled at her but didn't answer her.

Fear was just as important of a lesson here as obedience was.

I grabbed her hands and pulled them down to the bottom of the footboard and used one of the other ties to bind her wrists down low to the floor. She bit my shoulder as she fought against me, but I was too quick, and soon she was crouched down on the floor with her hands bound to the bed like a rabid animal looking up at me.

"Now be a good girl and bend over with that sexy fucking ass in the air for me."

Her eyes flared before she squinted them and glared at me. "Go to hell."

I tsked at her and grabbed her waist, lifting her over the chest until her stomach laid flat against it with her head hanging off the other side.

I grabbed one of her ankles and quickly tied it off to the leg of the chest and then pulled her other ankle wide and tied it off to the other one. She thrashed around, fighting the binds but it was useless. I was too good at this.

I was crouched behind her and turned my face to rub my stubble on the back of her thigh, inches from her bare pussy and she stilled and whimpered. I kissed the sensitive skin under her ass cheek atop her thigh and then used my thumbs to spread her flesh apart and spit on her pussy.

"You smell divine darling." I cooed and smirked at the obscenities that fell from her lips lacing her threats. "You look breathtaking all tied down and spread open for me. Perhaps this will be a regular position I put you into."

"As soon as I'm free, you're dead. You'll never touch me again once your cold fucking body is buried in the ground you son of a bitch."

I pressed my face in her exposed pussy and scraped my whiskers over every inch of her, covering my entire lower face in her wetness. She moaned and pulled at the binds, pushing back into me.

"Your mouth says one thing and yet your body screams another." I said when I pulled back.

She didn't retort, and I loved the way she bit her lip to stay quiet as she looked at me over her shoulder, straining her neck to do so.

"Now it's time for the hurt part." I mused and stood up behind her, letting my hands fall to her upturned ass. "God, these heels put your ass at the perfect angle to take my cock."

"Don't you fucking dare." She seethed. "I mean it Ryker, let me fucking go!" She screamed in frustration.

"You don't mean that doll. And we both know it."

I walked away from her and felt her eyes on me as I bent down and picked up the leather belt I'd stripped off earlier and folded it in my hands, enjoying the way the stiffness felt.

"You wouldn't." Her voice dropped low, and gravel mixed into it as she eyed me walking back towards her.

"How many lashes do you think you deserve baby?" I asked and then I rushed on to cut her retort off, "If you say none, I'll automatically double the number I've already planned in my head. So be wise."

Sweat glistened along her spine from her fear and my cock hardened even more from it.

"Time's running out darling. I'll let you choose, if you're smart about it. You've been naughty and you're deserve this as much as you need it. So tell me, how many lashes with my belt do you think you deserve?" I laid my hand on her ass cheek and rocked it back and forth, making her ass ripple and groaned. "Fuck, that's going to look so good with each strike."

"Five." She bit out between clenched teeth.

"You want five lashes?" I asked.

"Fuck no, I don't want them you psycho!" She screamed.

"Ah, I'm sorry I thought you said, five but apparently you said ten."

"What!" She thrashed around again.

"Hold still and count each one out loud and if you're good about it I'll reward you."

She was silent and her body was tense.

I stepped backwards and looked down her spine as I snapped my wrist and let my belt kiss her soft skin for the first time.

"Fuck!" She screamed and bowed her back, trying to get away from the pain.

"Count."

"One!"

"Good girl." I groaned. Her ass had a bright red strap mark across it, and I was losing all practical thought as I looked down at it.

Her pussy was pink, her legs and back were tanned, and her ass was red.

I snapped my wrist again, dropping a mark on the other cheek, and she screamed again before counting, "Two."

I dropped a third and a fourth and she moaned with the fifth.

I rubbed my fingers against her core and pushed four of my fingers deep inside of her, stretching her out.

"Please!" She begged, pushing back on me.

"Good girl." I cooed and rubbed her clit vigorously.

She was so close to an orgasm, her hips swung madly, and she begged for it with two more lashes.

But I had upped her punishment to ten and I was going to see it through.

I dropped my hands from her body and dropped two quick lashes to her upper thighs on each leg.

"Nine!" She moaned. "Please Ryker, fuck that feels so good." She slurred her words, and I knew she was in the haze of pain and pleasure.

"Last one love. Where do you want it?" I asked, rubbing my hand over the blooming red skin of her ass. I knew where she wanted it, and I knew where I wanted to put it, but I didn't know if she was brave enough to tell me.

"On my pussy, please for the love of god, hit my pussy. I need to come baby."

Crack.

Her inhumane scream split through the air, and I dropped the belt to the floor and impaled her with my waiting cock.

"Yes!" She moaned over and over and over as I fucked her pussy with punishing thrusts. She came like a fucking damn breaking, shattering around me into tiny pieces.

I fucked her through it, using her tied hands and ankles as leverage to fuck her like a fervent animal. I was aware of her pleas and moans, but of nothing more. The world could have been burning down around us, and I wouldn't have had a clue.

"You're such a good girl when you want to be, aren't you?" I asked, spitting on her ass crack, and pushing my thumb into her body. "But when you step out of line, this is the kind of treatment you'll be getting from now on."

"Hate fucking the naughty out of me, huh?" She asked, mewling, and rocking her hips as I filled her ass with my finger.

"Exactly."

"I think I'll misbehave more often; you're finally showing me what it's like to be with a real man."

Crack.

I slapped her ass hard, watching it ripple, and took my thumb from her ass and traded it for two of my fingers.

"Holy fuck." She arched her back as best as she could with her hands tied and looked over her shoulder at me, locking her eyes on mine as I hate fucked her.

"And here I thought that if I fucked you like a grown woman should be fucked, you might start acting like one."

"Asshole."

"Yes Doll, I'm finger fucking your pretty little asshole." I added a third finger and she groaned. "I can't wait to fuck your pretty little ass again. I'm going to video it so I can watch it over and over again. I'm going to listen to the soundtrack of your moans as you beg me to fuck your ass like the dirty little slut you are." Slapping her cheeks, I hooked my fingers in her ass, stretching her. "My little slut."

She turned forward again, and I recognized the signs of her impending orgasm and focused on pleasing her, doing every single thing that I knew she loved and as her orgasm tipped over her body, so did mine.

We both called out and rode our orgasms until nothing else mattered. I filled her pussy and roared when I felt the pumps of come against my fingers in her ass. I pulled out of her body and laid down directly on the floor as blood flow returned to my limbs. Her head sagged between her arms.

"Please untie me." Her soft voice was muffled from where it hung, and I forced my exhausted body to reach over to her. I gently untied one ankle, undoing the strap of her heel at the same time and kissed the back of her legs as she sagged into the chest of drawers and then did the other.

I got up and undid her hands and then scooped her up in my arms and laid her on her stomach in the center of the bed. Kissing her, I drank her soul through her lips and she kissed me back with just as much passion.

I gently massaged salve into the welted skin on her ass and thighs and then pulled the blankets up our bodies and planned to pass the fuck out.

Right before I slid under completely, she kissed my chest and whispered, "Thank you for hate fucking me into a grown woman."

I laughed gently and kissed her forehead, "Thank you for being naughty so I could."

"Hmm."

Maybe now she'd be calm and levelheaded for a while.

CHAPTER 23 – ELORA

"**Y**ou can't be fucking serious." I snapped, chasing after Ryker as he tore from the bedroom.

"I am." He barked at me as he descended the stairs.

I ran after him as he walked into the kitchen. Men filled every single room of our home as they geared up for the assault on the Wellington Estate in less than an hour, but I paid them no attention as I rushed across the floor.

"I have a right to be there!" I demanded but Ryker ignored me and grabbed a coffee cup off the counter to fill with coffee. Running forward, I pushed the carafe into the sink as he reached for it, pouring the coffee down the drain. "Don't ignore me!"

He spun on me quickly and wrapped his hand around my neck, slamming me back into the fridge and pinning me with his giant body.

Men rose from their seats, alarmed for my safety, but I couldn't conjure the fear I knew I should feel when I was so filled with anger. I felt Jed's presence right behind Ryker, knowing he would lash out if

Ry took it too far, but at what cost? Zeke was standing along the side of the kitchen scowling at me like I was an errant child.

"Don't think for one second I won't put you in your place here in front of my men." Ryker seethed.

"Don't think for one second I'm actually afraid of you!" I shoved at him and when he wouldn't budge, I kneed him in the groin. He grunted and folded slightly, but his hand tightened around my throat and his jaw clenched.

"Sir!" Jed put his hand on his shoulder, but Razz pulled him backwards.

"You can't stop me from going!" I hissed through the blockage against my windpipe.

Ry's eyes were deep infernos. "I'll tie you to my fucking bed if that's what it takes to keep you here where you are safe!"

"I don't care about being safe! I need to see this through, I need to be there when you destroy them."

"No."

"I didn't ask your permission, Ryker! For fuck's sake they killed my dad! They're the reason I was kept from you for seven years, doesn't that mean anything?"

His voice dropped dangerously low, "Of course it means *everything* to me, and you fucking know it. But you aren't going into a dangerous situation just to see the end. I will tell you all about it when I get home." He leaned down and kissed me roughly, and then dropped his hand from my neck. "Let's roll out." He commanded his men and turned to leave the room.

"Don't expect me to be here when you return."

He whipped his head around to look at me, his fists clenched at his sides, and he lifted his chin, looking down his nose at me.

"Zeke." He bellowed out and his second stepped forward with a dark look in his eyes. He too, stared at me with authority, and I hated that he thought he had something to say over me as well. Ryker held his hand out to his second, and Zeke reached behind him to the small of his back and then handed something back to Ryker.

The glint of metal caught my eye as Ryker turned and stepped towards me.

No!

I cut to the side and tried to escape his grasp when I realized what Zeke had handed him, but it was too late. Ryker caught my hair and pulled me back to his body.

"Don't you fucking dare!" I screamed. He lifted me in his arms and carried me from the room as I kicked and screamed. He walked us into his office and threw me down in his chair and then quickly snapped the cold metal of the handcuff around my wrist and then attached the other one to the leg of his massive desk. "Ryker! This isn't funny!"

"I wasn't trying to be funny, Elora!" He snapped at me as his lips twisted in rage. "You won't fucking just do as you're told and you've left me no choice."

"I. Need. To. Be. There." I said, with malice in my voice.

"I wouldn't be able to think straight if you were with me, near the very people that want you dead while I demand their lives in payment for taking Gavin's. You are my biggest weakness, and I cannot be weak! Not today." He kissed me again, and I bit his lip, drawing blood, and a laugh from him. "I can't wait to fill this mouth with my cock tonight when I get home. You'd better think of ways to show me how much you appreciate me after I destroy them."

"I'll bite off anything you put near me if you don't let me go!" I shook my arm, desperately trying to get free as the metal cuff cut into my wrist.

He stood up and adjusted his suit jacket and then let his eyes wander down my body. "I love you Elora. I'll be back soon."

"Ryker!"

He shut the door behind him, and I listened as dozens of feet walked by the office and out the front door, loading into vehicles to take them to the Wellington house.

I screamed into the rafters and fought against the handcuff holding me hostage, accomplishing nothing but injuring my wrist even in the process. None of the drawers would open when I went searching for something to pick the lock with, so I resorted to trying to drag the desk across the room with me. But the fucking thing was massive and bolted to the damn floor.

I fell back into the chair and plotted my revenge on him for close to an hour, dreaming up all of the ways to inflict physical pain on Ryker when he returned. And then the worry started to seep into my heart.

What if something happened to him while he was there? And the last words I'd said to him were in anger. I laid my head back against the headrest of the chair and fought to keep a clear head when I heard something off in the distance.

I sat up and tilted my head, trying to decipher what it was that I heard, when it finally clicked.

Gunfire.

Chaos erupted on the property as gunfire broke out all around the house. I knew that Ryker had left guards with me, but I also knew he didn't leave many, given that his home was in the center of his own turf, and anyone would have to be crazy to attack here. Nearly pulling my arm out of its socket, I tried to get to the window to see out of it, but it was too far. I had nothing near me to help defend myself, and I was handcuffed to the fucking desk anyway, I couldn't get away.

The door to the office slammed open and Dante ran in. "Ma'am, we have to get you out of here."

"What's going on?" I asked as he ran to my side with a machine gun slung across his chest.

"We're under attack—" Gunfire blasted into the room, and Dante fell to the ground as bullets ripped through his body.

I screamed and covered my mouth in shock as I fell back into the chair; he didn't move and blood quickly pooled under his body, soaking into the carpet. Masked men walked into the room in full black tactical gear and with an array of weapons strapped to their bodies, their eyes landing on me.

"What do you want?" I asked, trying to sound calm and authoritative.

"We want you." One man said, his voice was nasally and weak, but his body was anything but. "Come with us willingly, and we won't slaughter any more of your men." He ordered.

I held my hand up where it was still cuffed to the desk and raised my eyebrows at him, "As if I have a choice one way or another."

His eyes rounded, and he looked at his cohort and back. "Aren't you Elora Dax?" He asked, confused.

"Who wants to know?" I asked, knowing he was shocked to find the Queen of Shadeport shackled to a desk.

"That's her." The other man said with a smile on his lips. "Must be even her man can't stand her and had to handcuff her to keep her put."

My body nearly shook with fear, but I forced my face to remain indifferent and sat still in the chair as they looked at me with menace in their eyes. The first man walked around the desk and pulled a tool from his hip and quickly undid the cuff. I'd been calm and docile until that moment, making myself appear as no threat to them, but that had been my plan. When he released my wrist from the cuff I used my other one to grab the long knife on his hip and swung it wildly at him, plunging it into his neck and tried to fight the nausea that rolled through my stomach as his warm thick blood quickly covered my hand. His eyes went wide under his mask, and I grabbed it, ripping it off his head to see his face.

I knew Ryker had cameras in this room and if I could reveal him to the cameras, perhaps he'd have a trail to follow when they took me.

I pulled the knife out of his neck and grabbed his pistol on his leg, but he punched me in the face as he gurgled and staggered. By then, his partner grabbed me by the hair and threw me to the floor face down and jumped on my back. Pain exploded in my spine from his knees, and my face burned from the punch I took, but I didn't stop fighting.

I couldn't.

"I'll kill you, you fucking bitch." The man said that kneeled on my back.

The man I stabbed fell to the ground next to me and laid still with wide eyes as he bled to death between me and Dante's dead body.

"Get off me!" I screamed, but the man grabbed both of my hands roughly behind my back and zip-tied them together. My heart raced so fast I thought it would explode as I tried to calm my mind to make a plan. It was all happening so damn fast though.

He rolled me over onto my back and stared down at me before glancing over at his dead partner. "You'll pay for that." He spoke.

"What are you going to do?" I asked, sneering at him.

"That's up to the boss, though if I had it my way—" He paused and let his eyes drop over my body where I lay under him. I was wearing distressed jeans and a tank top, but I felt naked when he stared at me like he was. "I'd fuck you like a blow-up doll until I had nothing left and then I'd give you to my men. And then, and only then, would I start killing you. But it would be a very, very slow process."

I swallowed and tried to remain levelheaded. "Yeah well, who's it up to if not you?"

He chuckled at me and then stood up off of me and lifted me to my feet by my hair. "You'll find out soon enough."

He dragged me from the room, as I fought and kicked at him as best as I could with my hands tied behind my back.

Ryker's men laid on the ground in various states of injury and death as we walked through the house. I prayed that someone would find them soon and help them.

More men of his congregated in the foyer and walked out the front door with us towards waiting cars, and they threw me in the back of one and slammed me against the other door. I screamed in agony as he grabbed me by my hair and forced me onto the floor of the SUV and kicked and punched me when I fought back.

One extra painful punch hit the back of my neck and then darkness surrounded me.

When I came back to, I was being dragged from the car into a warehouse. I looked around quickly, trying to figure out where I was, but I didn't recognize any other buildings and had no idea how long I'd been out. When we got inside, there were men waiting in the center of the warehouse and I tried to drag my heels when I saw the medical exam table next to them with an array of tools on the tables.

The man that had handcuffed me pushed me ahead of him and laughed when my fear was obvious.

"Not so brave now, are you?" He sneered.

When we got to the circle of men, I looked from one to the next, trying to figure out who they were, but I recognized none of them. I did, however, recognize who was in charge. An older man stood in the middle of the circle, he was probably in his fifties or sixties and wore a suit of expensive quality. I was pushed down onto my knees in front of him, and he smirked at me with genuine mirth in his eyes.

"Hello Elora." He said, looking down at me.

I didn't bother responding to him and instead turned my lips up at him in disgust.

He laughed and looked around the group of men, and then a few of them joined in his laughing.

"Our introduction is long overdue dear, I once thought perhaps I'd be your pseudo grandfather, but alas, here we are instead."

"Nicolas." I said, eyeing him up.

"Ah, so you've heard of me." He smiled and tilted his head.

"Only of the terrible things that are coming your way." I said, jutting my chin out.

His eyes fell to small slits, and I saw the evil in him for the first time.

"My Monica told me you knew of our plans, but fear not, dear. I'll be able to smooth things over with Ryker still. Not all is lost."

I laughed grandly at him, shaking my head in pure mockery. "You are as dumb as she is."

Crack.

I was kicked in the side, blindsided, and pain erupted through my lungs and chest as I crumpled to the floor.

I forced myself to rise back up onto my knees, unwilling to cower or lower myself anymore for this man.

"Do you really think Ryker is willing to go to war, over someone like you dear?" He asked, trying to seem haughty and aloof, but I saw the anger ticked into his jaw, just under the surface.

"The war has already been declared, the allies recruited, and the wheels put into motion. Your death warrant has already been signed. The Angel of Death is knocking on your door, old man."

Fear and anger flared in his eyes as he took another step towards me. He grabbed me by my hair and lifted me onto my feet, holding my hair in a tight grip, yanking my head back to look at him. "You're lying. I've been an ally of Ryker's for decades."

I rolled my eyes at him and then laughed. "Like I said, as dumb as your cunt daughter is."

"I'll fucking kill you; you bitch. You have to know that you don't leave here alive at the end of it all." His bad breath was hot on my face where he spoke.

"Do you think I care?" I asked, raising my eyebrows at him in ridicule. "I've known since I was fourteen that I wasn't going to be blessed with a long life. This is nothing shocking to me. But I do know that you've only made things worse for yourself."

"How?"

"Because you've taken your death from a quick and humane death to something far, far worse. He was going to be charitable to you and give you the option to go out respectfully. But now," I chuckled, "Now you've sealed your fate to be worse than even the one Monica has earned."

His eyes squinted as he tried to figure out what I meant. I had to tread carefully here, given that I wasn't sure if Ryker had attacked yet or not and didn't want to give him away.

"Did you know that Diesel Ames has a hard on for making Monica his slave?"

Nicolas' eyes flared and his mouth hung open.

"He has all sorts of sick and twisted plans for her; he pledged his allegiance to Ryker in exchange for the pleasure of hurting your precious pride and joy." I tsked my tongue at him. "And you think you're gaining anything by doing this to me?" I asked, nodding over to the exam table, and then laughed in his face. "You're just deciding how much worse it gets for the both of you."

He gave himself away when he looked away from me and at a man that stood next to me.

"Oh, come on," I said, "I thought you were the big man here? Why ask someone else what they think you should do?"

Crack.

The old man punched me in the face, nearly in the same exact spot the masked man in the house had, and stars danced in front of my eyes, but I laughed through the pain and the fear.

Blood pooled in my mouth from my tooth cutting through my cheek, and I spit it back into his face, covering him with the red stain.

Rage boiled into his eyes, and he was about to punch me again when phones started going off all around him.

His men looked at them and then cursed.

"Sir, the house has been attacked. Monica has been taken. All of our men killed."

"What!" Nicolas screamed, letting go of me and turning on his men. I sagged to the floor as pain and fatigue filled my bones, making my limbs heavy.

This meant one of two things would happen to me now. They'd either use me as leverage to get Monica back, or they'd inflict incredible pain and suffering on me in retaliation for the attack.

I looked around me for a weapon or anything I could use, but with my hands bound behind my back still, I was short on options.

Nicolas strategized with his men and then turned an evil glare on me.

Shit.

I guess he was going with option two.

I took a deep breath and squared my shoulders, and refused to cower as his lips turned up in a sinister smile.

"Strap her down. It's time we send a message to Ryker."

Hands grabbed my arms and lifted me, but I fought back the entire time. I noticed one of his men held up a phone, recording my fight, and hated the idea that Ryker was going to see whatever they did to me next.

They cut my hands free, only to strap them down out at my sides like I was on a cross and then strapped my legs down as well. My chest heaved as I bit and thrashed, trying to get free.

Nicolas stepped forward and stood between me and the camera, facing it and started making his video.

"Ryker, it appears that you have something that belongs to me. Which I guess is fitting because I also have something that belongs to you."

He moved out of the way, and the camera focused on me. Just then, a fist shot out and punched me in the face again.

I screamed and fought against my binds.

"As you can see, I am prepared to torture your bitch for as long as she can survive if you do not return Monica at once."

He nodded to the man standing next to me and I watched in horror as he turned and grabbed a scalpel from the table next to him and turned back to me.

I fought anew, thrashing around as he brought the surgical blade down to my arm and slid it down from my shoulder to my elbow.

Burning agony seared into my arm and I screamed a horrific scream as he cut a foot long slice into my skin.

It wasn't deep enough to get any artery, but it bled badly, quickly covering my entire arm in blood.

"You have five minutes to decide and call. At minute six, I start letting my men rape her as I take chunks of flesh from her sexy little body."

The man videoing stopped recording and then sent off the video. Nicolas turned to me and looked down at me.

"You'd better hope for your sake that you're a good enough lay for him to negotiate."

I fought to calm my breathing as I looked at my arm and then up at the ceiling. I tried counting in my head, begging that Ryker called but also praying that he wouldn't.

He couldn't let her go. She deserved every single thing she got, and perhaps so did I.

I tried to convince myself that I could endure this and then it would finally be over for me. Every pain and struggle I'd survived for years, would no longer matter if I was dead.

I could fade into nothing, and maybe I'd get to see my dad again.

I could almost envision his face in my head, could almost hear his voice telling me he loved me. Maybe death wouldn't be so bad if I could see him again.

Five minutes passed quickly, and Nicolas was irate that Ryker hadn't made any attempt to contact him.

I tried not to let that burn in my heart like it wanted to, and instead I tried to focus on anything else, like how much pain I was about to be in.

Nicolas walked back over to me, wringing his hands together. "I guess it's time to spread those pretty little legs, darling."

His men moved quickly, and they unstrapped my legs. I kicked violently and used every single muscle in my body to fight them off, but there were so many more of them than me. One forced the button and zipper open on my jeans and started pulling them down my legs.

"He'll kill every single one of you!" I sneered at them. "He'll eliminate your entire family line for this. Your mothers, your sisters, and daughters. He'll do far worse to you and them than anything you could ever dream of doing to me."

The man pulling my jeans down paused for a moment and looked at his cohorts.

"Ignore her!" Nicolas screamed from where he stood off to the side, holding the phone in his hands, recording my assault. "Rape her!"

Another man ripped my shirt open and grabbed my breasts with hunger in his eyes. I spit on him and was rewarded with multiple punches to my face and stomach from the men.

I was fighting to stay conscious. The pain in my head and stomach was blinding and darkness tried to pull me under. I wanted to go with it, I figured if I was unconscious, at least I wouldn't have to be awake when they raped me. My eyes rolled as I embraced the darkness coming for me when glass exploded above us.

The windows at the roof line all blew out, and I tried to cower away from the shards as they rained down on me but it was impossible. My skin burned as it was sliced by the falling daggers, and I screamed again. The men that had been preparing to attack me scattered as gunfire erupted through the building.

Without the men holding me down, I was able to wiggle my hand enough to free one arm, and I used it to free my other and then I rolled off the table, using it for cover as I pulled my jeans back up and wrapped my tattered shirt around my bleeding arm. My bra was soaked through, and I shivered from cold and fear.

I watched in awe as men descended from the roof on ropes and shot Nicolas' men as they ran for their own weapons.

Hands wrapped around my hair, dragging me from under the table, and I clawed and fought back as Nicolas pulled me in front of his body and pressed the scalpel to my neck. The men from the roof landed and aimed their guns at us.

I looked for Ryker, or Jed or Zeke, or *anyone* I recognized, but I saw no familiar faces.

These were not Ryker's men. Fear coursed through my body anew as I swallowed hard and felt the scalpel slice into the skin above my jugular.

"Don't take another step closer or I'll slit her fucking throat!" Nicolas screamed.

His body shook behind mine as I gripped his arm. Blood dripped from my neck and still fell from my bicep, coating my lower arm through my shirt bandage.

One man stepped forward of the others, he was dressed much like the original masked men that attacked Ryker's house. He wore tactical gear and a heavy machine gun. There was something about his eyes that were familiar to me where they stared deep into my own, but I couldn't place it. He was older, about Nicolas' age, but so much fitter and more muscular, his face and body were intimidating as authority oozed from him.

"Let her go, Nicolas and I may put a bullet in your head before I give you to Lawson." He said, and my heart fell into my stomach as I listened to his gravelly voice.

The Riddle Master.

"You think I'd fall for that?" Nicolas screamed, pressing the scalpel into my neck further. I grimaced and groaned as I tried to move away from the blade, but I had nowhere to go. He held my hair in his iron fist, and my head was pressed against his shoulder as he cowered behind me.

"You don't have much choice." The riddle man said back.

"I could slice her head clear off her shoulders and go out with a bang either way."

My eyes fluttered closed as more pain erupted in the side of my neck.

He was going to kill me whether he meant to or not by just slowly cutting my throat open.

My dad's face flashed in front of my face again as I listened to the two men argue back and forth. I could see his face as clear as day in my mind, his kind eyes and hulking form, and I heard his voice in my head.

"The death I imagine for you is far worse than anything Ryker could do to you, Nicolas, but I imagine between the two of us, the one we deliver to Monica could be awe-inspiring."

"You son of a bitch!" Nicolas screamed. "What do you want? I'll give you whatever you want. I'm a man of means I can give you the world if you let me go."

The mystery man bared his teeth, "You've already taken everything I've ever wanted from me, and now you've tried taking what I didn't know I even had anymore."

"What do you mean?" Nicolas yelled, fear and frustration were making him manic.

"You took my son from me. And I thought you took my granddaughter at the same time, but I was wrong. But I won't let you be successful this time, either."

He looked at me, and it was then that I realized how I knew his eyes.

They were my father's eyes.

The Riddle Master was my grandfather.

Holy fuck.

"You're Dawson Dax." Nicolas whispered in awe.

My grandfather's eyes flared with incredible menace, and a smile pulled his lips back. "My reputation precedes me."

Nicolas ripped my head to the side further, and the blade pressed deeper. The blood from my arm was still pouring, and I was starting to feel faint, almost like I was floating out of my body.

"I don't have long here." I said to Dawson, trying to put pressure on my arm as my head started getting fuzzier.

"Let her go." Dawson said, lifting his gun to Nicolas's head as he took another step forward.

"Fuck you." Nicolas sneered, and then his entire body tensed.

It was the only warning I had that he was about to end it all as the scalpel started sliding towards the center of my throat.

I gasped and screamed, but it was outdone by the single gunshot from Dawson's gun.

Warm, wet blood splattered the side of my face as Nicolas' body went limp and fell to the floor behind me, taking the scalpel with him.

I crumbled, falling forward and into Dawson's waiting arms.

He barked out orders to his men as he lifted me, tucking me against his massive chest and carried me out of the building, into a waiting vehicle.

Things happened quickly as they laid me down on a stretcher and started dressing my wounds, putting pressure on them, and pricking me with needles as they started IV's.

"Elora, stay with me. Focus." Dawson said, looking down into my face.

"You look just like him." I whispered with a smile gracing my lips as my eyes closed. "I can see him now." Darkness once again fought to pull me under.

"Elora!" He yelled, but I gave in and faded into nothing.

CHAPTER 24 – RYKER

Nicolas wasn't here.

"Fuck!" I roared as I tore out the front door and towards the waiting cars out front.

"I still get my prize, Lawson." Diesel called to me from where he sat on his motorcycle, smoking a cigarette.

Monica was currently handcuffed, gagged, and thrown in the back of my Tahoe, awaiting my decision on what to do with her. Part of me wanted to just put a bullet in her fucking infuriating head, but the other part of me wanted to turn her over to Diesel and ask for fucking videos of every single thing he did to her.

I tried to think of Elora and honor her with what I decided.

"Go ahead—" I started.

"Sir!" Jed yelled, running up to the car. I turned to face him, and my heart seized in my chest at the look on his face. "The house was attacked, all of our men there are dead, and they took Elora."

"How?" I roared. He thrust his phone to me, and I looked at the video footage of my office.

Men walked towards Elora, and she sat in the chair, unable to get away because I'd handcuffed her to the fucking desk. I watched in horror as she plunged a knife into one of the men's neck and tried to get his pistol before he slammed his fist in her face and the other man attacked her.

"No." I whispered. My skin felt like it was tightening around my muscles and suffocating me.

Zeke ran up to my side and watched alongside me as Jed paced back and forth. Diesel walked nearer too and threw his cigarette to the curb.

Their cars tore off through my mangled front gates and my frigid shriveled heart that had begun growing again since having Elora back in my life burst into flames and exploded into a million pieces as they drove away with her.

"Who are they?" I asked.

Jed took the phone and zoomed in on the face of the man that Elora had unmasked before she looked at the camera directly over the door to my office. She was trying to give us a direction to follow. "Do you recognize him?" I asked, thrusting the phone at Zeke. His face was solemn as he shook his head no.

Diesel took the phone and then swore. "Wellington."

"How do you know?" I asked.

"That's Flame, he was a member of the reapers years ago before he jumped ship and took up with the Wellington crew. He's been the bane of my existence since, but I guess I'll have to thank your Queen for finally killing him for me."

I was a man possessed as I tore the door to the Tahoe open and dragged a blindfolded and gagged Monica out and threw her onto the ground.

I grabbed her by the hair and slammed her body into the side of the car as I ripped her blindfold off. Her hands were tied behind her back, and she screamed in terror as she saw me. I wrapped my hand around her throat and squeezed so hard her face turned a molten purple color instantly and she gurgled; drool and snot fell from her mouth and nose.

I leaned in until I was inches from her face. "I'm going to ask you a question, and I'm only going to ask you one fucking time. You tell me every single thing you know, and I might let you live long enough to see your dad again. You fuck around with me, and I'll give you to Diesel here and let him make you his new slave. Nod if you understand."

She quickly nodded her head with wild eyes. Blood vessels already burst in her eyes and along her neck and I squeezed her throat tighter even after she answered me.

I dropped her to the ground where she sputtered and coughed before I picked her back up by her hair and slammed her back into the car again, and pulled her gag down.

"Where is Elora?" I asked. As she started to talk, I cut her off again, slamming her head off the car. "Remember what I said. Do not fuck with me right now."

"My father's men were to take her once you left your house, I—" She coughed and cried, "I heard them talking about the old cigarette warehouse, but I don't know for sure if that's where they took her."

"Where is the warehouse?"

She coughed again and fought to catch her breath; her raspy voice cut out on her "—Off State Avenue. Next to his sawmill."

My phone vibrated in my pocket, and I fished around for it and opened the message from an unknown number. I dropped her in a heap on the ground again.

"Oh, my god." I said, as the video started playing.

"Ryker, it appears to me that you have something that belongs to me. Which I guess is fitting because I also have something that belongs to you."

Nicolas Wellington stood in the center of the screen, but behind him I could see men fighting with someone as they strapped them down to a torture table.

"Ellie." I said in disbelief. She screamed and fought back against the men.

One of the men at her side punched her in the face, and Nicolas turned back to the camera.

"As you can see, I am prepared to torture your bitch for as long as she can survive if you do not return Monica at once."

My eyes frantically followed the men on the screen as one took a scalpel and cut Elora's arm open from her shoulder to her elbow. Her scream echoed through my ears and straight into my heart. It was like someone shoved a hot branding iron down my spine as her agony resonated into my soul.

"You have five minutes to decide and call. At minute six, I start letting my men rape her as I take chunks of flesh from her sexy little body."

"Put her back in the car. Razz, take your team to the house and aid any survivors. Zeke and Jed, our teams are going to the warehouse.

Diesel looked at me and I waited to hear what he had to say, unwilling to ask him for help.

"Are you going to trade her for your Queen?" he asked, eyeing me strongly.

"No. I'm going to make her watch me slaughter her father and then I'm going to pay you a large amount of money to make sure she suffers for an unimaginable amount of time."

My body felt like I was exploding from the inside out as adrenaline and testosterone fought for control of me, I walked away from him and headed to the front seat of the Tahoe.

"The Reapers will ride with you." He called out. I nodded my head and slammed the door shut behind me as Zeke got into the driver's seat and we tore off towards the manufacturing district.

Zeke's body was nearly as tight as mine as we burned blacktop through the city. I called every man in my employ and aimed them at the warehouse, prepared for a fight.

"Are you calling them?" Zeke asked me.

"We'll be there shortly after the six-minute mark. We'll let him think I'm not interested in trading and then we'll attack."

"And if they rape her before we get there? Or mutilate her?" he asked, before he slammed his fist down on the steering wheel.

"You'd better just focus on driving." I said.

Jed was in the back seat with a sniveling Monica, who cursed me and then begged me in the next moment. He was as keyed up as we were and I looked over my shoulder at him, "Shut her the fuck up." I said to him, and I watched as the corner of his lip turned up in a gleeful smile.

"With fucking pleasure."

He pulled back and slammed his fist into Monica's face, knocking her out cold, and then threw her body over the seat into the cargo area of the back before cracking his knuckles and taking a deep breath.

"We're getting her back." He said, and I turned back to look at him again and held his stare. "She's the light in the darkness of this life. If we don't get her back, none of us stand a chance of ever standing in the sunlight again, the darkness will pull us all under for good."

I said nothing back to him, and instead turned back in my seat, mulling it over. He was right, though. If they managed to kill her, there wasn't a corner of this planet that I'd be able to escape her haunting memory.

With a lethal menace, I replied. "If we don't get her back alive, Zeke is the new King of Shadeport, and you can bury me next to her and her father."

Zeke looked over at me with an evil glare, and I could feel his anger at that statement from my seat, but he didn't say anything else, and neither did I.

When we got a few blocks from the building, I took a deep breath and looked to the sky in silent question.

Gav, if you're there-

I didn't know what I was doing. Or how any of this worked. I had no clue if I believed in God anymore, or if he even cared to listen to a man like me, if he did exist. So, I spoke to the only man who would ever hold any holy standing in my eyes.

You have to help her; she can't suffer twice because of us and the life we built. She's survived too much to let this be the end of her life. I love her too fucking much to lose her like we lost you. Please, man, please help her. Send her an angel or a helping hand.

Please.

When we turned the corner and barreled into the parking lot, military style Humvees and tactical trucks sat circling the building.

"What the fuck is going on?" I asked.

"Those aren't Wellington's men, they had SUVs like ours on the cameras." Zeke said.

"Then who are they?" Jed asked, leaning forward in the seat.

"I don't know, but we're about to find out." The doors to the warehouse tore open and men ran out running to one of the Humvees with a man in the back carrying something.

"Elora."

We were speeding towards the group and the man carrying a limp Elora in his arms looked at us barreling towards them and he barked out orders to his men. They set up a perimeter around the vehicle as he climbed into the back, but they didn't aim their weapons at us.

Zeke skidded to a stop, and a dozen more of my cars flanked mine as I tore out of the front seat.

"Give her to me!" I roared.

A man stepped forward with his hands raised, his weapon laying across his chest.

"Ryker Lawson?" He asked as he eyed all of my armed men and Diesel's crew roaring up behind us on their bikes.

"Who are you?" I demanded, stepping forward, but he blocked my way.

"My name is Pete. We're getting her medical care for her injuries, that's the best thing for her right now, we're not here to hurt her. We've killed everyone in that building and extricated her."

"Get out of my fucking way." I said and stepped around him. He grabbed my arm to stop me, and I twisted, turning, and ripping his arm out of socket and dropping him to his knees. I pressed my knee into his back and pulled on his dislocated arm harder, drawing a curse from his lips as his men raised their guns at me.

"Lower your weapons! All of you!" A demanding voice called out, and I snapped my gaze to the Humvee that Elora was in as the man that carried her out of the building jumped down and walked forward, between his men and me.

I looked at him and felt my body stiffen as I recognized certain things about his face.

"Dawson?" I asked, my voice deep and disbelieving as I looked at my dead best friend's dead father standing before me.

"Ryker." He said, nodding his head in my direction before looking to his man whose arm I still held pinned behind his back. I dropped the man and stood tall as I let my eyes travel his wide frame.

"Let me see her." I demanded. Stepping forward towards him.

He stepped to the side, but as I went to pass him to get to Elora, he grabbed my arm and stopped me, leveling his gaze on mine. His voice was low, for my ears only. "I don't know what all happened before we got to her, but she was strapped down and undressed." His gaze dropped as pain crossed his face. "He slit her throat before I could get a shot at him, but it didn't get her artery. She's unconscious now."

I tore from his grip and hurled myself into the back of the Humvee and ached as I looked at the love of my life laying there, pale and bleeding as medics worked on her.

"Sir." One of them said addressing me, "She's unconscious from the blood loss. We need to get her to the hospital now or she will continue to bleed out and we won't be able to save her."

I nodded, taking her hand in mine, and bringing it to my face. I kissed her palm and then the inside of her wrist. "Don't you dare die on me, Elora, I only just got you back." I closed my eyes and took a deep breath before looking back to the medic. "Take her to Memorial Grace. I have a private wing there." I said before I yelled out the open door to Zeke. "Call Dr. Boyd, get her team to Memorial Grace now! We're going there."

He nodded and took his phone out and dialed our private surgeon and her team.

Men moved around me, and the vehicle started moving, but I couldn't focus on anything else other than Elora's unmoving frame.

Her neck and arm were wrapped with blood-stained gauze and her face was swollen and turning black and blue. Her hair was a matted mess and dirt covered her stomach and sides under the blood.

She was in only her bra and her jeans, and I cursed, forcing images from my mind of those men assaulting her because I needed to stay calm for her and if I thought of that, then I'd explode like a cannon.

"Ryker."

I looked at Dawson where he sat in the seat opposite of me with a forlorn look on his face.

"It was you all along, wasn't it?" I said, shaking my head as the pieces clicked into place. "The riddle master."

He looked down at Elora and smoothed his hand over her hair, pushing it out of her face. "Yes."

"Why didn't you just fucking tell me? We could have worked together to protect her and maybe this wouldn't have happened!" Seething and yelling, I desperately tried to keep my head on straight, fearing it might rip off my shoulders at any second. I leaned down and held Ellie's hand to my cheek and closed my eyes, trying to keep from losing it completely. "I failed her."

"We both did, all three of us did, actually." He said, never taking his eyes off of his granddaughter.

"How is this possible?" I asked, "I was at your funeral. Gavin and I were barely legal, and we fucking buried you with full military honors."

He shook his head and then wiped his hand over his face, rubbing it down over his stubbled beard. "I was left for dead, and then the government lied to my family and killed me off, never expecting me to make it back out alive."

"How long have you been back? How long have you been watching from afar?"

"I got back stateside three years ago. Returning home, I learned my only child and granddaughter had been buried. I essentially went apocalyptic." He sighed and looked up at me. "I threw myself into finding out everything I could about their deaths and avenging them and was close to making my move on the Wellington's when chatter started about Elora being back and being with you."

His lip curled up a bit when he said the last part.

"I won't apologize or feel bad for being in love with her, and I won't explain it to you either." I said firmly, challenging his alpha with my own.

Growing up, Dawson had been absent from Gavin's life because he'd always been deployed and serving the military while Gav and I got into all sorts of trouble. When he'd heard that Gavin had a daughter while he was away serving overseas, Dawson had come home and went full rage freakout on him. Only when he laid eyes on his breathtakingly beautiful granddaughter did he finally stop raging and soften.

I remembered being so in awe of how a man that I'd grown up being scared shitless of, could soften, and go gaga over a little babe, even if I did the same thing every single time I was near her.

But his life was not an easy one, and his duties had taken him away from Gavin and Elora more and more over the years until toddler Elora didn't know him at all. When Gavin got the military notification that his father had been killed in action, it had taken a large fucking toll on him.

Dawson held my stare, wanting to tear me to shreds for being with Elora sexually, no doubt he thought I was a predator. His gaze was challenging, like he was considering fighting me for her, and taking her away from me to protect her.

"Ry."

I snapped my eyes away from Dawson and down to Elora where she laid, her eyelids fluttered open and closed as her hand tightened around mine.

"El? Oh my god." I said, leaning down and kissing her face over and over. "I'm here. I'm so fucking sorry, but I'm here. You're safe."

She cried as I kissed her over and over again. She turned her face into mine and sobbed, trying to cling to me.

"I'm so sorry. I'd been so mad at you and then—" She said weakly as her eyes rolled and then opened again as she tried to stay awake.

"Shh, you're okay. We're going to have plenty of time to talk when you're healed. Just rest now, Doll."

"I love you." She whispered.

"I love you so much more, you're the very reason my heart beats at all."

She faded back asleep again as we pulled up outside the Emergency room at the trauma hospital in Shadeport.

A trauma team led by Dr. Boyd met us with a gurney as we came to a stop and Dawson, and I picked her up and transported her onto the gurney and then ran alongside the doctors as they took her straight into the ER and started working her.

They kicked us out after a moment, and we both fought them like hell to stay with her, but in the end, we stood in the hallway outside of her room as we waited for word on her.

I paced the hallway with Jed and Dawson. Zeke stayed at the warehouse to clean up the mess with Dawson's team. But he checked in almost every five minutes, asking for an update on Elora.

My heart swelled knowing that we all cared deeply for her. We were an army of men who cared for nothing else other than her wellbeing, but today, it still had almost been too little.

"What happened with Nicolas?" I asked, stopping to face Dawson with my hands on my hips. I'd taken off my suit jacket and rolled up my sleeves, walking around with my holster visible without a care in the fucking world. We were in my city, and I'd do whatever I wanted.

Dawson raised one eyebrow at me, "He had her by the hair with a scalpel at her neck and I tried reasoning with him, so he wouldn't hurt her, but she was bleeding out and running out of time. He made his move and started to slit her throat, so I took my shot and took him down. I'm guessing the arm was cut beforehand. But he's dead."

I worked my jaw back and forth, "He cut her arm on video and sent it to me, to convince me to exchange Monica for Elora."

"You have Monica?" he asked in a quiet voice.

"Yes, and No. We went to their home this morning to decimate them for Gavin and for last night's attempt. When we got there, Nicolas was already gone, and so were a large number of his men. We took out who we needed to and took Monica, she's the one who told us where he was holding Ellie."

"So where is she now?"

"Diesel Ames has her. She's his problem now."

"Diesel Ames, the Motorcycle club president?" Dawson asked with a scowl. I nodded. He shook his head and then nodded his shoulders, "Can't say she doesn't deserve every single thing she gets."

"Does Elora know who you are?"

"I think so. She knows my name is Dawson Dax and I know she recognized my voice, but I don't know how well she was paying attention when everything was falling to shit around her."

"Do you plan on being in her life now? Sticking around for more than just some creepy phone calls that freak her out?" I tried to bite back my annoyance with him, but I failed. I took a deep breath and then leaned my back on the wall next to him, pressing my head into the wall and tried to relax.

"I want to know her, she's all I have left of Gavin and—" He paused, choking down the emotion that tried to bubble up. "Maybe I'll still be alive when she gives you kids, and I can get a do-over at the grandparent thing."

"I only want you to be a part of her life if you're going to stick around. You can't pop in and out like you did with Gavin. She has never been able to rely on anyone but Gavin, not even me until recently, and I won't let people continue to do that to her."

"I won't." He turned and looked me straight in the eye. "My biggest regret in life is taking for granted how much time I had left with my son and losing out on the opportunity to know him better. He was the best man in the world, and he didn't even know me."

"Mr. Lawson." Dr. Boyd stepped out of the room Elora was in and addressed me, ripping off bloody gloves and a surgical gown, and throwing them in the trash.

"How is she?" I stood up off the wall with Dawson and Jed at my side.

"She's okay, she's resting, but she's going to be fine. We've stitched up both of her lacerations and did x rays of her entire body. She has a facial fracture in her cheek and two fractured ribs. Most everything else is just bruising and contusions." She spoke. Her eyes flicked to the men standing next to me and then back to me, like she had something else to say but didn't want to in front of them.

"He's her grandfather, and he's her bodyguard, just say it." I barked out, my fists clenched at my sides, and I crossed them over my chest.

"She was in and out of consciousness, but she said they tried to assault her, but they were interrupted by her rescuers. I thought you should know though, because an attempted rape is still catastrophic on a person's mental health, even if the physical assault was stopped."

My jaw clenched so tight I thought my teeth were going to crack. "Thank you." I said, fighting the urge to break everything in the hallway at the thought of any man touching her at all. "I need to see her."

"She's being transported upstairs to a private room in your wing right now, you can meet her up there if you'd like."

"Okay. Thank you for taking care of her."

"You're welcome Mr. Lawson." She said and then walked down the hallway.

I went upstairs with Dawson and Jed in tow in a daze. It was late already; the day had flown by from one catastrophe to another and I was worn out.

When Elora was settled in her room I walked in alone, needing time with her before others joined.

The room was dark, with only a light on over the window. Elora laid in a white hospital gown in the center of the oversized luxury hospital bed. She looked so tiny and fragile, her skin was pale, and her chest hardly rose and fell with each breath.

I kicked my shoes off and gently climbed into the bed next to her, pressing my body against hers and taking a deep breath at her temple, letting her floral scent calm me like a rush of nicotine.

"El." I said softly, not wanting to disturb her, but I wanted her to know she wasn't alone.

She turned her head without opening her eyes and nuzzled her nose into my neck. "Ryker." She sighed.

"I'm here baby. I'm never leaving your side again."

She turned onto her hip, gently avoiding any sore spots as she curled against me. "I think I met my grandpa today. But it may just be the pain medications."

I felt my lips smile in her hair, even though my body was broken from her own pain. "You met an incredible man today indeed."

"He looks like my dad." She said, and her breath shuddered in her lungs. She pulled back and opened one eye to look at me, the other one was swollen shut and her cheek held together with bandages. "I saw dad today, like he was floating over me, watching out for me, but I couldn't get to him." A tear slid from her eye. "I miss him so much, and today he came to me and made me feel safe for a brief moment." She shook her head and burrowed deeper into my neck. I slid my arms around her, holding her to me. "You probably think I'm talking nonsense."

"Not in the least, right before I pulled up at the warehouse, I prayed to your dad." I whispered. She looked at me with such wonder in her eyes. "I begged him to protect you. I told him I couldn't lose you like we lost him, and I begged him to watch over you or send you an angel. I guess he listened."

She cried harder for all she had lost and all she had endured from it, and I held her, whispering sweet words of affirmation and love to her, trying to soothe her in a way I didn't understand. I'd never been gentle with any woman in my life but Elora Dax, and I'd never intended to do it or understood what I was doing in the moment. I just knew how to soften for her. So I allowed myself to soften and be comforting and gentle with her instead of my usual brute and asshole self while she clung to me.

I'd forever be gentler with her; I'd be exactly what she needed for the rest of my life.

I owed her that much.

And so much more.

EPILOGUE – ELORA

I stood admiring my reflection in the long mirror in my closet. The gown Ryker had bought me was breathtaking and the jewels he had adorned me with, made me feel worthy of it all.

All he provided for me, all he gave to me willingly without question was more than I ever dreamed of having, yet he gave me all of that and more.

My kidnapping had changed him and me both. He was a gentler man with me since then. When I walked into a room, he'd stop whatever he was doing and address me with affection and delicate caresses that made me swoon. It had been what I needed to heal physically and emotionally from my injuries, and I'd melted into him each time he adored me that way.

"There's one last gift from him." Carly said as she stepped behind me, holding a large square box wrapped in black paper with gold ribbon.

"I don't have a spot left on my body for any more jewels." I said with a girly smile on my face.

She just raised her eyebrows at me and pushed the box into my hands. She wore a champagne-colored gown that made her look like she was glowing with her hair done elegantly on the back of her head. Ryker had bought her a beautiful set of rubies for her ears and a magnificent gold and ruby choker necklace to wear today, and I'd thanked him eagerly with my mouth for it.

I loved how he took care of her simply because she was important to me, and I was important to him. But it also warmed me to know she didn't need me to take care of her as much anymore since she had stolen the attention of Jed.

He was positively smitten with her, which was a sight to see for sure considering he looked like a menacing giant to the rest of the world. But he smiled like a fool and even blushed from time to time when Carly was near.

She told me that he had asked her out on a date next week and I couldn't be happier for her. He was a man that would protect her and treat her like his very own queen. And I had it on good authority that being treated like a queen was positively enchanting.

I laid the box down on the island in the center of the closet and pulled at the ribbon, and then lifted the lid off.

"Oh, my goodness." I gasped and covered my mouth with my hand.

"Ellie!" Carly squealed from next to me as she looked down at the box with me.

Seated atop a black satin cushion was a golden crown. It had large, white and light pink diamonds upon its points and hundreds, if not thousands, of smaller diamonds encrusted around the rest of it. It was dainty and elegant and so incredibly regal.

"I'm so jealous right now." Carly whispered next to me, but I was unable to form any response as I stared down at the beautiful piece of jewelry. "Put it on!" she said excitedly.

Carly reached down into the box and gently lifted the crown into her hands and nodded towards the mirror for me to turn and face it.

I crouched down so she could reach the top of my head and watched in astonishment as she laid it atop my head, nestled perfectly in my hair.

"Oh Elora." She sighed, looking at me in the mirror as I stood up and squared my shoulders.

The crown sat atop my head with my dark brown hair styled in a romantic textured updo on the back of my head with wisps of hair curled at my temple and neck. My makeup was flawless with a soft shimmery pink eyeshadow and dark eyeliner and lashes. My soft pink matte lip stain matched perfectly with the pink diamonds on the crown and the ones in my ears that Ryker had gifted me with this morning.

The white fitted gown I wore was low in the front and adorned with beads that made it look like it was alive when I moved. The skirt was long and satin with the beads embellishing the timeless rounded train.

My wrists each were dripping with diamond bracelets that Ryker had surprised me with last night at dinner and all together, they completed the look.

Well, almost completed the look.

The giant clear bright diamond on the ring finger of my left hand was the real MVP of the show, though.

Ryker had proposed before I was even released from the hospital. He wooed me with lovely words about how he'd never imagined getting married and how he'd never wanted for a wife or someone to share his life with until the first time he kissed me.

Life had been a whirlwind since then.

"Let's go show Ryker just how lucky he is." Carly said, smiling at me as she swiped at a tear on her cheek.

"Lets." I said back and picked up my gown and walked downstairs. At the bottom of the stairs, my grandfather turned and watched me descend towards him. He looked so sharp in a timeless black tux. His graying dark hair was styled perfectly, and his tanned face was the picture of awe as I came to a stop in front of him on the bottom step.

"My dear, you look breathtaking."

"Thank you." I was still getting to know him, but I loved having a piece of my father with me in life. I took a deep breath and looked towards the back patio where I knew Ryker was waiting for me.

"Are you sure this is what you want to do? Just say the word and I'll whisk you away from here to a place he'd never find you again."

I laughed nervously and then leaned up to kiss his cheek. He stilled and sighed as I pulled back. "I'm sure. Are you ready to walk me down the aisle to him?"

He smiled sweetly and then placed my hand on his arm and led me towards the back of the house. "I'm ready, darling. What an honor it is."

Carly arranged my train and then handed me my bouquet of white and gold flowers and squeezed my hand before walking out the door and down the steps towards the silk aisle laid out in the grass.

Music started playing as she walked towards the altar and I took a deep breath again.

My grandfather patted my hand, "Let's go, it's time to marry your King."

I let him lead me down the steps and around the corner to the start of the aisle. I smiled at a few people before Ryker came into view and everyone else faded to the nothingness.

My dark handsome King stood at the end of the aisle in a black tux with his dark hair faded short on the sides and messily styled on top. His dark stubble made my fingertips itch to touch it and I bit my lip to keep from moaning from just looking at him.

His eyes were locked on me, burning my skin with an intensity only he could master. He smiled at me and then pinched his nose as tears threatened to spill from his dark eyes as he watched me walk towards him.

Zeke stood to his side and placed his hand affectionately on his shoulder and squeezed as he smiled warmly at me.

I was such a blessed woman.

I had an army of men behind me who adored me and protected me with their lives. With their King as my number one.

Dawson passed my hand to Ryker's and then leaned down and kissed my cheek before taking a seat in the front row. I handed my bouquet to Carly and turned to face the man of my dreams.

Ryker's hand was warm where he held on to mine and he stared down into my soul. I heard the minister saying the things he needed to say, but I was hardly aware of what any of it was. I was mesmerized by Ryker's loving gaze and only barely managed to recite my vows and say I do when prompted.

Ry laughed at my distractedness and affectionately said his vows to me, and when the minister announced it was time to kiss me, he eagerly stepped into my space and drank from my lips.

His hand cupped the back of my head, and he tilted it and kissed me so deeply I could hardly tell where his body started and mine ended.

Cheers and celebrations rang out from the crowd and after a while, he finally pulled back far enough to look down into my eyes.

"Well, how was that for romance, Mrs. Lawson?"

I giggled like a schoolgirl and leaned into him in glee. "I'd say that was top-notch where romance is concerned, Mr. Lawson."

"Good, because I think I'm done being romantic for the rest of the day."

"Oh, are you?"

"Yes, I have a much more pressing emotion running through my body, taking over as it goes."

"And what is that, exactly?"

"Carnal need."

I mashed my lips together and pressed my thighs tight as his words took me by surprise and ignited a fire in my belly. "And what do you plan to do about that need?"

He smiled down at me with a sinister flare as he stood up to his full height and adjusted his tux jacket. "Well, Mrs. Lawson, I'm going to make sure you wear nothing but that crown and my come for the next week at least."

My lips parted and my eyes widened as he said those words loud enough for Zeke and Carly to hear, who both laughed and snorted at us in jest.

"Oh."

Yes, please.

The End.

OTHER BOOKS

Did you know Ally writes across so many other types of tropes and themes?

Check out some of her other books here.

Looking for Series and Duets?

The Line Walkers Series:
https://a.co/d/bx376wq
Beauty In the Ink Series:
https://a.co/d/6tc8M7M
Bailey Dunn & Co Duet:

https://a.co/d/i9gwqL2
<u>Shadeport Crew Series:</u>
https://a.co/d/dVzGcyo
<u>Kings of Hawthorn Series:</u>
https://a.co/d/h1AITKM

How about some spicy standalones?

<u>Sinister Vows:</u>
<u>https://a.co/d/gbe35fF</u>
<u>Guilty For You:</u>
<u>https://a.co/d/1ef3UPU</u>
<u>Secrets Within Us:</u>
https://a.co/d/cTZ04XQ

STaLK Me!

Want to stay up to date with all of my shenanigans and upcoming news? Pretty Please?

Check out my website: www.ammccoybooks.com

How about TikTok, are you there? https://www.tiktok.com/@amm ccoy_author?is_from_webapp=1&sender_device=pc

Facebook? I've got a readers group there! Twisted After Dark: A.M. McCoy's Reader Group is mostly unhinged and full of exclusive news! https://www.facebook.com/share/g/b41rkBMkSurWz43i/

IG? https://www.instagram.com/ammccoy_author/

Amazon? https://www.amazon.com/stores/A.-M.-McCoy/author/B07QNRJ

MLB?ref=ap_rdr&isDramIntegrated=true&shoppingPortalEnabled
=true

I think that's all for now!